Beyond FAMOUS

FAMOUS NOVEL-THREE

Kahlen Aymes

This book is a work of fiction. Names, characters, places and incidences are either a product of the author's imagination or used fictitiously. Any resemblance to actual persons, living or dead, or to actual events or locales is purely coincidental.

Beyond FAMOUS: The Famous Novels, Book Three
Copyright © 2015 Kahlen Aymes.
All rights reserved, including the right to reproduce this book, or portions thereof, in any form. No part of this text may be reproduced, transmitted, downloaded, decompiled, reverse-engineered, or stored in or introduced into any information storage and retrieval system, in any form or by any means, whether electronic or mechanical without the express written permission of the author. The scanning, uploading, and distribution of this book, via the Internet or via any other means without the permission of the publisher is prohibited, illegal and punishable by law. Please purchase only authorized electronic editions and do not participate or encourage electronic piracy of copyrighted materials.

Cover designed by Sarah Hansen, Okay Creations

Cover photography: © ASJack

Interior Formatting by Cassy Roop of Pink Ink Designs

Published by Kahlen Aymes Books, Inc.

Visit the author's website: http://www.KahlenAymes.com

ISBN ebook: 9781311241122
ISBN Paperback: 9780996734417

Version: Sample: 2015.12.14

Special Thanks

Thank you to my readers for your loyalty and unending encouragement and support. Without you, I am nothing. You are the reason I write. I love you.

To my street team, review team, & beta readers; I adore you all, and I couldn't do this without you.

The many bloggers who offer your incredible support of my work, reviews, posts, release blasts, tour organization, take-overs, etc... thank you from the bottom of my heart.

Thank you, Cassy Roop of Pink Ink Design for your friendship and formatting expertise.

Thank you, Sarah Hansen of Okay Creations, for your amazing design skills on the FAMOUS covers. I love them! They are truly amazing.

The many authors whom I admire and am honored to consider friends... your support means the world to me. The romance community is like no other.

Olivia... Thank you for understanding when I'm "in the zone." I promise to look up when you yell. <3 I love you. <3

My editors on this series: Kathryn Voskuil, Donna Cooksley Sanderson, & Stacy Hahn; thank you for your hard work, dedication and fast turn around time. Without you, I'd be a compound word, and comma challenged, mess. I sincerely appreciate you and every hour you spend pouring over my words. I love you all.

Thank you to my wonderful P.A., Jennifer Singh, for her work day in and day out. Love and hugs.

Thank you to Shira Hoffman and Liz Winick Rubinstein of McIntosh & Otis Literary Agency for your work on foreign rights! Looking forward to world domination. ☺

Finally, to Matt; Thank you for inspiring the emotions that allow me to create characters that live & breathe. The deepest pain is only felt when preceded by truest love. Always & forever. <3

Beyond
FAMOUS
Famous Novel–Three

Chapter 1
Three Thousand Miles Before I Sleep

Caden

A LOUD POUNDING REGISTERED somewhere in the back of the dream I was having. Brook's body, alive and responsive under mine, the smell of her skin all around me, and her voice moaning my name as her muscles started to convulse around me.

"Cade... babe don't stop," she whispered against my mouth. There was nothing sexier or more beautiful to me than Brook when she was in the throes of orgasm, and it was like a high-powered aphrodisiac that made my dick harder and my orgasm inevitable. I was close, so close...

Boom! Boom! Boom! The crashing noise got louder and more insistent.

I tried to ignore it and stay where I was inside my bed... inside Brook, but the whole thing dissolved in a puff of frustration as Ethan's voice intruded with the beating on the door.

"Dude! I can hear you breathing heavy in there. Open up, you douche! I'm aging out here, and it is a fucking waste for humanity. All the girls who won't get to adore me are going to blame you, shithead!" I could hear Ethan chuckling on the other side of the door to the suite.

I dragged myself out of bed and placed both fists over my eyes, rubbing the sleep away on my way out of the bedroom. The raging hard-on in my shorts would be difficult to hide. I stared down at the obvious bulge before I shrugged and closed the distance between me, and the door.

Fuck! What a waste of a good wet dream. Or at least, almost wet dream.

"Dude!!! Get your ass out of bed and let us in!!"

My hand closed around the knob. "Shut up, Ethan! Bloody hell! You're going to wake the entire floor."

I opened the door slightly so he would be able to push it open before I turned and walked back into the suite. I hurried to the bar, so I could hide the evidence of my dream behind it until I calmed down. I ran my hand through my hair as I went.

"Jesus, Cade, it's almost two in the afternoon. No one is sleeping except *you*. You look like hell, by-the-way." Ethan grinned, his white teeth flashing. Dawson followed Ethan through the door.

"Yeah, you just interrupted a sweet dream, you wanker." I rolled my eyes at him as I leaned on the bar.

"Wait. You didn't just jizz in your pants, did you?" He laughed, and Dawson gave one of his shoulders a shove.

"No, you interrupted me. That's the problem!" I groaned as I started to make some coffee. Ethan mocked me by sticking his lower lip out in a pout. "It was bloody hot, too."

He shook his head. "By the look of you, you're humping constantly. Isn't that why you're asleep at two in the afternoon? I raised you right!"

He smirked again.

I ignored his comment and turned my attention to my other friend. Dawson rolled his eyes.

"Hey, Dawson. What are you doing hanging with this asshole?" I nodded toward Ethan, who snorted. "Slumming?"

"Yeah. I was hoping you'd join us and make things more bearable," Dawson said as he flopped down on the sofa.

"Hey, you fuckers! Out of all of us, I'm the one that knows how to have *fun*. You two would rather moon around with your dicks in your hand. I say we get the hell out of here and terrorize some fan girls."

"Seriously, that's fun? In *what* universe? It literally makes me crazy. Why don't we just jump off a building instead? That sounds safer. Want coffee?" I asked both of them as I poured a cup for myself. "Better yet, I could go back to my dream," I said as my face split into a wide grin.

Brook was filming with the girls, and I had the day off, so it was nice to see the guys.

Ethan raised his eyebrows and scoffed. "Pfffftt. Fuck the coffee. Got beer?" he said in disgust. "So, are you gonna share the dream details, or what?"

I laughed and reached into the refrigerator and threw him a Heineken. "Dawson? You want one?"

"Sure, Cade. Thanks." Dawson nodded and reached for the bottle I offered.

"*The dream?*" Ethan persisted and then took a long pull on his beer. He wagged his eyebrows at me over the top of the bottle. "Was it starring a certain hot little somebody?"

"Leave him alone, Ethan, for Christ's sake," Dawson tried to come to my rescue.

"What? She's smoking. I want to know."

"Yes, it was about Brook, but that's all you get, you horny bastard." My tone sounded irritated, but I was enjoying the banter. "Are you guys in town for the party tonight?" I moved into the sitting room, my stomach grumbling loudly.

"Yeah, and to take your ass out for your birthday." Dawson grabbed the remote and turned on the TV. "We won't be here next week, unfortunately."

"I'm not planning much anyway. I just thought I'd take Brook to dinner."

"What's the deal with the studio? Are they letting you off the leash these days?" Ethan asked me before turning his attention to the TV and Dawson. "Dude, put on some sports." Ethan wrestled the remote away from him. "Cade's probably got the Discovery Channel on lockdown." He smiled at me as he flipped to ESPN.

"Yeah, I exercise my brain." I retorted. "Try it sometime."

"Yeah, sure! All you've, uh, been *exercising* is your jock!"

His comment made me laugh out loud. If he only knew how right he was.

"Ethan only thinks of two things, Cade. You know that. Sports, and chicks." Dawson leaned forward on the sofa to place his beer on the coffee table.

"And proud of it. When I can combine the two, that's even better." Ethan glanced at me. "Cade, get your ass dressed. Aren't you sick of staying in? Don't worry, *gorgeous*. I'll protect you from the *big, bad, girls*," he mocked.

The look on his face was priceless as he gave me rations of shit. I was laughing, and Dawson shook his head at Ethan. "Okay, I'm starving, anyway. Brook wears me out even in my dreams." A happy smile split my face wide open.

"Man, your ass is *so* whipped. Fuck, it's pathetic," Ethan admonished.

Their laughter followed me down the hall into the bedroom when I went to shower and dress. I smiled. He could make fun of me about Brook forever, and I would smile right through it.

Brooklyn

IT WAS ALMOST TIME to go. Thank God. Cade and I retreated to the patio for cigarettes as often as possible, but the night went so slow that I thought it would never end. Maybe it was because I was tired, but we couldn't get out of there fast enough to suit me.

The new cast members were finally all in town. The actress they chose for Jane was one I'd heard of and recognized because I'd seen her in the news a couple of times. She was a child star and while younger than Cade, she was older than me. She seemed so worldly which probably came with being in the business for so long. Most actors who started out as children had a better chance of a successful transition into an adult career if they had strong managers and Leah St. Clare had a shark. The hair on the back of my neck stood up the first time I saw her in person, and I wondered if it were just more of my character manifesting in real life or this was a woman I should keep my eye on. I couldn't help glancing at her numerous times over dinner and the cast party afterward. Martin was big on the cast bonding, and while the second movie wasn't quite wrapped, he brought some of the actors from the third film to the set early to meet us and acclimate with the crew.

It was 3 AM, and we were walking out to the curb when some fans grabbed us for pictures. We paused briefly, letting them shoot us before I dove into the open door of a waiting limousine. Cade followed and sat directly across from me. The cameras flashed, and we both turned to see what was going on. Paparazzi were shoving their way in front of fans and taking picture after picture. I wondered if it would ever ease up. We would probably get in trouble for leaving in the same car and alone together.

Cade's brow raised before he reached out and slammed shut the door.

"So, I guess the others aren't coming with us?"

He leaned back in his seat and stared at me as the driver got in and asked us where we wanted to go. Cade mentioned my hotel, then moved to sit next to me and threaded his hand through mine. Suddenly I was calm. His touch was something I'd been craving for the past six hours when the most I could do was lean on him a little on the patio while we were away from the others.

"I've had enough togetherness for one night, haven't you? With anyone other than you, love."

"Did you like Lloyd?" I asked. He was one of the new production managers. "He seemed nice but kinda stiff."

"Yeah, and much more structured than Kathryn." She'd been on the first two films but had some family issue that demanded she spend some time at home. "But he's brilliant. I think he'll be cool," he said as his thumb rubbed over the top of my hand. I found myself wanting to kiss him. I knew I couldn't.

"You didn't talk to Curtis Walker. Why not? He's a big part of the next film."

"Uh, you were talking to him enough, and besides, our characters don't get on and so I didn't think it in the best interest of the film to get too cozy with him at this point." His tone was flat, but his eyes were mischievous as he watched me.

I laughed.

"I did see he cozied up to you quite a bit." Cade's lips quirked in the start of a grin, and my heart did a flip-flop in my chest. He was wearing a red and black plaid flannel shirt over a white T-Shirt and black jeans. I noticed some faint stubble on his face. I sat there and took him in. He was beautiful without even trying.

"I was?" I smiled at him.

"Yeah, sure, Brook. I saw you talking to him, and he certainly had his eyes on you." He nudged me with his shoulder.

"Oh, did he? I didn't notice, was he cute?" I smirked at him as the limo pulled up to the hotel. His little show of jealousy did something to me. It was sweet the way he was teasing me with it.

"I'm not into guys, so you'll have to ask Jennifer," he said before he climbed out of the limo and waited for me to get out.

Despite the lateness of the hour, there were at least one-hundred paparazzi and fans waiting for us outside the main doors.

The limo driver came around and asked us for a photo for his granddaughter, and it was only then that I realized we'd gotten into the wrong car. Jeanne and Denise were going to have our asses. I could hear it already. I glanced at Cade and saw the same realization in his eyes.

"Sure, we'll take a photo. Right, Cade?"

"Yes, it would be our pleasure."

"My granddaughter is going to die. She loves you both, but especially you, Cade. Personally, I think you're the cuter of the two, sweetheart." He smiled from underneath his cowboy hat.

"Thank you. That's sweet of you."

One of the other fans agreed to take the photo of the three of us, and after we'd signed some autographs and posed a few more times, we moved into the hotel. Not touching, but side by side as the cameras continued to flash around us. I was sure the photos would be online in thirty seconds.

"I agreed we'd keep things discreet, and I'm sure Pinnacle isn't going to think this fits that description. How in the fuck did I not notice that wasn't Peter's limo?" He was agitated and was running his hands through his hair repeatedly.

In the elevator, I placed my hand on his chest to calm him. "Hey, babe, it's not a big deal. I'm already over it, and the suits will get over it, too. It was an honest mistake."

The doors opened on my floor, and he wrapped his arm around me in the empty hallway. I felt his lips as he kissed my temple and I slid my arm around his slim waist.

"It was great to see the gang tonight, huh? Did you have fun with Ethan and Dawson today? You all seemed very happy when I got there." My voice was low as I snuggled in underneath his arm.

"Yeah, but I'm tired. We started drinking twelve hours ago, and Ethan ragged on me all day... about your hot little ass."

"Wow." I handed him my key and wound my other arm around his waist to hug him while he opened the door.

"God, you feel good, love. I missed you today."

"Yeah? I missed you too. Noah was in a snit, and I didn't think the day would ever end."

"Why?"

"Um, he thinks Mike should kiss Julia in the photo shoot scene, but I argued that it wasn't part of the script. He's just getting a little big for his britches."

Cade tensed slightly but didn't say anything.

We walked into the suite. Cade was already kicking off his shoes and taking off his plaid shirt, seconds after we hit the bedroom.

"Why was Ethan teasing you today, hmmm?" I walked into the bathroom and looked at myself in the mirror. My mascara was smeared, and my hair was a mess. I groaned.

God, I look fucking terrible.

I washed the makeup off and brushed my teeth before running a brush loosely through my hair.

"You don't really need to know everything, do you, Brook?" Cade was laughing as he turned on the shower and pulled his T-Shirt over his head. I stared at his chest as he undid his jeans and stepped out of them.

"Oh, I think I do," I gave him a throaty laugh as I watched him. I loved his body, looking at it, touching it, lying underneath it. Mmmmm. Heat rushed through me at the thought.

"He thinks I'm whipped, and, uh..." he hesitated as he stepped under the spray.

He piqued my interest, "And, uh, what?" I pulled my shirt off and then stripped out of my jeans.

"When he and Dawson woke me up, I was in the middle of a great dream. I answered the door with a raging hard-on."

An incredulous laugh burst out. "Uh uh! You did not! Really?"

"Yeah, laugh it up. You weren't the one with blue balls and Ethan's incessant teasing all day!" He tried to sound aggravated, but I knew he was smiling.

"Which was worse, I wonder?" I was still laughing; I couldn't help it. It *was* really funny. "Were you going to tell me about the dream?"

"I would have gotten around to it…but I'd prefer to show you. Why don't you get in here?"

I guess we thought alike because I was already naked and stepping in behind him. I wrapped my arms around his waist and up his chest, raking my nails across his wet skin as I brought my hands back down lower. Cade gasped softly, as I ran some open mouth kisses across his back.

"Was it anything like this?" I said so softly I wondered if he could even hear me over the sound of the water running. My hands went lower to grasp around his already enormous erection, "Or, this?"

He threw his head back, and his body tensed. "God, Brook, I love you."

I wanted to taste his skin, so I licked his back then kissed it. He trembled under my ministrations, as I reached out with one hand for the soap and lathered up the front of his body so my hands slid more easily around him. He groaned as I brought both of my hands around him and pushed and pulled his hot flesh. He leaned back against me and the movement pushed me against the tile. He was plastered against me; I felt his body go limp as he gave himself over to the sensations.

"Uhhh, babe. Stop or you're gonna make me come. I'm wound so tight. Wait, Brook. Uhhn…God." He was panting hard, but not protesting what I was doing to him.

I continued to move my hands up and down the shaft and then around the head of his dick. I squeezed as I pulled up toward the top and I knew he was close.

"Shhh, Cade. Just let it happen." I ran my open mouth across his back, placing kisses and sucking on his skin as his body tensed. I could feel his muscles constrict, and he groaned my name when he burst in my hand.

"Bloody hell, Brook...oh, Brook..."

I kept pulling as he surged and pulsed in my hand, my grip lightening a little as he relaxed against me.

"I don't deserve you..." he said as he turned in my arms and lifted me, so my mouth was level with his. One arm wound around his neck, my hand sliding into his wet hair and I brought the other up to touch the side of his face. His eyes were languid, and he had a soft, satisfied smile on his lips. He was the sexiest thing I'd ever seen.

"I love you, Brook," he whispered against my mouth before he bent to kiss me, his tongue delving into my mouth. We kissed again and again, our mouths and tongues mating as our bodies would. He was the most delicious thing I'd ever tasted. His mouth finally lifted from mine, but I pulled his lower lip back into my mouth, not wanting it to end. "You taste so incredible. I love kissing you." His words echoed my thoughts.

I kissed his shoulder and turned my face into his neck. "Was that as good as your dream? Did I make it all better? I don't like it when my boy is suffering." I smiled into his skin.

"Mmmm.... I like the sound of that. You're so beautiful." He placed another small kiss on my lips and then turned to trade me places and set me down. He took down the shampoo and squeezed some into his hand before running his fingers through my hair and working up a lather.

His fingers on my scalp felt so good. "The hotel will kick us out for using so much water," Cade teased.

"Don't care. Uh, that feels so great," I said as I leaned back into his body.

The suds ran down my body, and his hands followed over my

shoulders and down to my breasts where he stopped to cup them and play with the nipples. Tugging and tweaking them between his thumb and index finger. "Cade, its 4 in the morning. We have to be on set at 9. We should go to bed."

"I agree. Bed sounds good," he said the words, but I could tell he wasn't thinking about sleep. His tone was full of sex.

He turned me in his arms again to finish washing out the shampoo and then put conditioner through my hair. I just stared up into his face while his hands wound in my hair. "Do you know how hot you are? How fucking beautiful? I could stare at you forever."

"Hmmph. No." His response was curt, and I was astonished.

"Why don't you see yourself? Not just how you look, but everything about you."

He shut the water off and pulled me from the shower, wrapping a towel around me as I kissed his chest.

"Brook, you're crazy. Sleep deprivation is clouding your judgment. Let's get you into bed, minx." He touched the tip of my nose with his finger.

He put a towel around his waist; we both brushed our teeth, and went into the bedroom.

He brought our clothes out of the bathroom and pulled the towel away from me and then discarded his own before pulling back the sheets and shutting off the lamp.

I crawled under the covers and to the far side of the bed as I waited for him to join me, but he knelt beside the bed and reached for my knees. His hands closed around them, and he pulled me toward him.

"Cade?"

"Shhh. One good deed deserves another."

"But baby, it's so late," I said softly.

"Just give me two minutes, Brook. You know how good I can make you feel. I want to give you this. Just lay back and relax. Tasting you is so fucking hot, my love."

He parted my legs and hoisted them over his shoulders as he bent to ghost kisses over my stomach. He pressed his tongue against the skin over my pelvic bone like he would place a French kiss on my mouth, sucking as he lifted away from my skin. A few of those kisses had me breathing hard and arching toward him.

He blew on my skin and continued kissing lower as I lay back on the bed.

Two minutes, huh? Wow. We'll see.

One of his hands moved up my stomach and over my rib cage to close around my breast, his head moving lower toward the burning flesh that was crying out for his touch.

He nuzzled and kissed around the place I wanted him most, teasing and taunting until I was gasping.

"Uh, Cade..."

"Okay, honey," he breathed against me, then in one motion he slid two fingers inside me and his mouth closed around the sensitive little bundle of nerves to suck gently on it.

"God, uh...Cade... that's amazing." My head fell further back, but my whole body tensed, instantly the orgasm started to build as his fingers thrust in and out of me and his mouth kept the sucking constant.

He was going to literally kill me. My breath hitched, and my hips moved against his mouth, which only drove him on even more.

"Mmmmm, baby, that's it, Brook," he murmured against my body.

My muscles trembled, and my body began to convulse around his fingers and spasm against his tongue. "Cade, oh Cade...mmmmm..." I moaned his name as I came hard, my back arching, hands going into his hair as I jerked with the strength of my response.

His touch lightened and finally stopped and then he moved up and kissed me deeply on the mouth. Sliding his arms around me and under my legs, he moved me up onto the pillows and crawled in next to me.

I snuggled into his body and wrapped my arms around him at the same time as his folded around me to pull me close. The warmth from his body was seeping into mine as I tilted my head up and ran a series of soft kisses along his jaw. It was stubbly and rough, but I loved it.

"How do you do that? You're so unreal."

"Do what, exactly?" he teased and turned to kiss my temple, leaving his lips to linger there.

"Know how to touch me, what to do to make me melt, and how to stop just at the right moment?"

"Are you serious?" His breath washed over my hair at the top of my head as he spoke softly. His velvet voice was so gentle in the dark, a slight smile behind his words.

"Yes. I mean, it's just so..."

"Love, I *know you.* I literally know every inch of your body. I know the way you respond to my touch, my kiss, my tongue. I can tell by the little tremors, the way you moan my name, how you get tight, where you're at, how close you are. I told you before; I replay every moment we're together over in my mind. I love that I can bring you to that, I love that *you* can bring *me* to that, and I love that I can choose."

My brow dropped over my forehead. "What? Choose?"

"Yes. I can choose how fast to make you come, based on what we're doing or if I want to make it last longer. If I want I can do that, and I want to, often. I love the sounds you make, the way you smell and taste, the way you move and respond. It's so hot. Bloody hell, just talking about it makes me rock hard."

I closed my eyes at the reverence in his words. He took my breath away.

"Unbelievable," I breathed into the skin of his neck.

"Why is that? Can't you tell yet, how much I fucking love you? How much you make me want you?" He turned more toward me and took my leg over his hip as he pressed into me. "Jesus, I can't think about anything else. It consumes me day and night."

I surged against him, desire at his words and arousal was making it impossible for me to do anything else. "I love you, so much. You make my heart ache with how much."

"God, Brook, we're going to die if we don't start getting some sleep, but damn if I care. I'll sleep in bloody New York."

My heart tightened at the reminder of our pending separation. He was right, this time wasn't to be squandered on something as meaningless as sleep.

He rolled me over and sank slowly into my body as his mouth found mine, and I met his hungry demands. Each long, slow thrust of his body into mine, each sucking motion of his mouth, both of us clinging and pulling each other closer; we made love like it was the last time.

Emotion welled in my chest and I knew Cade felt it too. Just like he knew me, I knew him as well, and the longing we felt now was only a fraction of what we'd have to deal with in the coming months.

I wouldn't think about that now, as I lost myself in him.

Chapter 2

I'm All Yours

Brooklyn

I MOVED OFF TO THE side as I waited for Martin to get the lighting checks right. Jennifer, Wendy and I were filming retakes of a scene in the Matthews boys' apartment, just after Julia comes home from the hospital. Cade was running rehearsals first and then filming the scene where Ethan's character, Aaron, tells Ryan of Julia's accident.

Even though it was just a scene, it was unsettling. Cade and I were about to have a long separation. Not as long as the characters in the film, but anything could happen. Cade was going to New York and my lack of experience with it had me worried. He would have his entourage of bodyguards, but who knew what could happen.

There were only a couple of hospital room scenes left and we were scheduled to film them early tomorrow morning; when everyone gathers at Julia's bedside and the major one where Ryan begs God not to let her die. That would be emotional and I could feel Cade gearing up for it the night before because even though he made love to me, we didn't talk about the next day's shoot. He shushed me, saying he had to do it in his head and we probably shouldn't spend the night together. The thought of being without him made me sad. Silently, I began to move away from him but his arms tightened, and I settled back into his arms, but this morning he was gone before I woke up.

My phone buzzed in my pocket. Only *one person* texted me in the middle of the day, now that David was history and Wendy and I were barely on speaking terms. I hadn't expected to hear from Cade before the shoot but, my heart beat a little faster as I opened his message.

Hi, love. Miss you. Denise just chewed me a new bum. Have you heard from Jeanne yet?

Getting into the wrong limo last night was already coming back to haunt us. Both managers had already been contacted by the bitch brigade at the studio, and the pictures of us were apparently all over the Internet, and Twitter accounts worldwide.

Jesus, so yeah, we took a ride in the same limo. So what? How did that translate into fucking? We sat across from each other, but apparently our feet touched for a second. *Big fucking deal.*

I didn't get it. Cade just laughed it off. For some reason, he thought it was hilarious.

Yeah, Mickey asked if I could get you to let him lick your, um... shoes. LOL

My fingers flew over the keys as I sent him a message.

What did you tell him? Haha!

That he has great taste in shoes.

I smiled seeing Cade's face in my mind as he read my words. His laughter would go all the way into his eyes. Beautiful.

Earlier that morning, I'd spoken to Lillian and made the final arrangements with her for her and Carter's trip into Vancouver for Cade's birthday two days later. The time was going so fast and next week, Cade would be jetting off to France for the Cannes Film Festival and I'd be left in Canada to film any retakes of scenes that didn't include Cade's character.

Stupid Pinnacle, they planned on moving me into Cade's hotel while he was gone, because it was one of Cade's demands at their meeting, but news flash: he was flying directly to Italy because by then, filming would be over.

Finished with *Don't Forget to Remember Me.* My heart dropped at the thought.

The time had flown and I was doing a pretty good job of not letting myself be sad around Cade. It was obvious he was struggling as well and both of us were doing what we needed to do to keep each other happy.

Four nights ago, we snuck out at 2 AM because Cade wanted cereal and junk food when I didn't have any in my room. It had been fun to run around the store with no one watching us and we joked and teased each other about the stupid rag mag headlines we saw in the checkout line. There was a risk of getting seen, but Cade had an "I don't give a fuck" attitude and I went along with it.

Cade's picture was on almost every one of them, and most were speculating about our relationship or my relationship with David. We felt almost normal until one of the cashiers caught us laughing and glared at us. Cade threw a wad of money at the woman and we bolted out of the store giggling.

It was another reason for the managers to get on our case, but we just wanted to have some fun. I never asked for the instant fame and constant stalking, or all the bullshit that came with it. It bothered Cade more than it did me. He was used to it for himself, but he was worried what would happen to me when I was in L.A. without him, and I hoped there would be decent security for him while he was in New York.

So much of *Only Us* would be shot on the streets of the city or in public places. What he put up with was unreal; screaming fans would undoubtedly be clamoring to see him or touch him.

Missing him was only part of what was bothering me. I was worried about him. Cade was so sensitive to things going on around him, more than most people and he would be uptight about it. Even though he was used to it, he'd confided how much he hated all of the attention.

My phone brought me out of my reverie as it vibrated in my hand.

Leah wants to get together with us tonight.

Ugh! My head fell back in exasperation. Cade!

Really? With US?

Well, she said me, but I told her that she should get to know you, too.

I rolled my eyes as I typed.

I'm sure that thrilled the shit out of her.

I would probably order pizza to be delivered to my suite, so we wouldn't give the paparazzi another photo op.

"Places, Brook, Jennifer!" Martin yelled from the main set. Jennifer moved toward me and smiled as she scratched at her temple.

"Damn wig. Hating it." She rolled her eyes as she said the words.

"Are you happy we're almost done? Will you be going back to L.A. next week?" I asked as we walked together onto the living room set.

"Yes. It will be a nice break, but I'm really looking forward to Italy, but I wish it were just a vacation. Are any of the others coming with us?"

"Not sure, why?" It seemed to me that she had something she wanted to tell me, but she hesitated to do so. I could only imagine. That bitch, Wendy, would probably show up uninvited.

She shrugged. "Nothing, just wondered. Ethan told me he might come over and I wondered if there was anyone else, that's all."

"Oh. Nope. Pinnacle won't pay for more than four of us, so I think it's just us, Cade and Gavin. Ethan mentioned it to Cade, but that's because he figures Cade will stay with me so he can use Cade's room. Isn't it silly? We're in this huge movie and we worry about paying for hotel rooms."

"Crazy," she said as she took her place on the couch in the house and the makeup people descended and began their touch ups.

Mickey's smiling eyes were soon peering into mine.

"Hey, girl."

He was dressed in a flamboyant magenta shirt and tight skinny jeans.

"Hey," I laughed. "Those jeans make your ass look good." I grinned. "Maybe I can borrow them."

Mickey laughed out loud and he brushed blush over my

cheekbones. "The day my ass is the same size as yours is the day your man becomes my boy toy."

My brow shot up. "My man?"

Mickey's mouth pursed and his expression twisted in amusement. "Bitch, please."

I smiled, because I couldn't help myself.

Caden

DINNER WITH LEAH ST. CLARE. I winced. Call me crazy, but I couldn't get enthused. She was cool, and I understood we needed to get to know her for the next movie, but there would be plenty of time in pre-production.

I guess it won't kill me to be gracious. For an hour or two.

I didn't want the evening to drag. The time I had left with Brook was dwindling, and I didn't want to squander even one moment. I'd be back to sending her those text messages with the countdowns until we could see each other again.

I tried to shake it off. That was still almost three weeks away, and I wanted to enjoy every minute. I wished the studio wasn't sending me to France alone.

In our earlier phone conversation, Denise told me that they'd probably be placing me in situations where there would be women around because they were trying to downplay any of the public appearances with Brook.

"I thought we were beyond all of this rubbish, Denise. I'm bloody over it," I spat at her.

"Yeah, well, that was *before* you and Brook made your little run about town getting groceries and hopped in the wrong limo after the party. Are you trying to piss the suits at Pinnacle off? We just worked out the Italian Film Festival as a cover for your little vacation and for the shoot of *A Love Like This* to be more like you wanted, so what were you thinking? Are you trying to make my job harder, Cade?" she was pissed.

I sighed and struggled for a response. She'd always been good to me, and she was right, in a way.

"No! I just want to be *normal* and more; I want to be with Brook. Didn't I make that bloody plain enough in L.A.?" I sighed, "Besides, the limo fiasco was a mistake. We didn't do that on purpose."

"No, but you need to be more careful. The two of you could have been kidnapped for God's sake. Jesus, Cade!"

"We didn't even realize it until afterward! Nothing happened anyway." I tried to dismiss her concern, but she was right.

"No, nothing except there was suddenly documented proof that you and Brook were spending time together. *Alone.*"

"We shared a bloody limo. We weren't having sex in the back of it! Though, that sounds like a good idea."

"Sure, make jokes. You're not the one that has to deal with those assholes, Cade," she said, her voice full of exasperation.

I ran my hand through my hair and expelled my breath. "Look, it wasn't a deliberate plan to derail the bloody production company's promotional plan. We were hungry, so we went to the market, and the other time, it was late, we were dodging all of the cameras and we accidentally jumped in the wrong limo. There were five of them sitting there. Anyone could have made that mistake. Bloody hell!"

She paused for a minute, and I was tired of arguing about meaningless bullshit.

"What about the other thing?" she finally asked in a more quiet tone.

"What other thing?"

"You walking into her hotel and going up to her room in front of everyone?

I sighed and dropped my head, rubbing the back of my neck wearily. I was so tired of having my life dissected like I was a lab rat.

"That was unfortunate, but I was already photographed with her, and she is where I want to be. For Christ's sake! I'll be away from her for almost three months, soon enough. I don't even want to do that stupid movie," I said more softly into the phone.

"I know. I'm sorry you guys have to go through this, Cade, but it's all part of it."

"This isn't what I signed up for."

"I know. It would probably be easier if you weren't with Brook. You didn't think you'd be with her either, did you?" she said.

"I *hoped* I would be with her. And fuck it all... I wouldn't change it. Even to end this madness."

No, I wouldn't change a minute of my time with her.

I glanced at my phone to check the time. My rehearsals were done, and as soon as Martin came to this set from working with Brook and the others, we could begin. The assistant director was here getting things ready, but this was a pivotal scene and Martin had to be here. We were also waiting for Brook to arrive.

My phone rang as I waited; I cringed when I saw who it was.

"Yeah?" Why did I even answer the damn thing?

"Hi, baby. What are you doing?"

"Wendy, I told you to stop calling me. I'm about to go to work," the impatience I felt seeping into every syllable.

"I'm only calling to ask what you want for your birthday. We said we're going to be friends, so..."

The ache in my gut that occurred whenever something had the potential to screw up my relationship with Brook started to burn. "I don't want any gifts, and I don't want to be friends. Look, I thought your friendship with Brook was so important to you, but you are seriously screwing with it, and you're putting me in a position where I don't want to be. I *will* tell her about this call." I hung up on her before she could respond.

I hoped she wasn't going to just show up on my birthday the way she had last week when Ethan and Dawson were in town. I wasn't sure if she was just persistent or just incredibly stupid.

Brooklyn

I WAS EXHAUSTED. The scenes of Ryan crying at Julia's bedside were killers. Cade was even more spent. I could see it in his expression and the way his movements were slower than usual.

"What kind of pizza do you guys want?" I asked as Jennifer laid down on one of the sofas and Noah flopped down in one of the upholstered chairs and commandeered the remote to the television. We were winding down and having Leah here without a buffer might make it too easy for Cade and I to act like, well, Cade and I. We didn't know the new actress and were not sure we could trust her.

"Everything!" Noah said enthusiastically, hanging one muscled leg over the arm and leaned back in his chair.

"Brook, are you ordering a vegetable pizza? If so, I'll just grab a slice of that," Jennifer answered and then yawned. "It's been a hellaciously long day. I'm lucky I don't have any retakes tomorrow."

"At least you get to go to Italy," Noah said absently, as he settled on a reality TV show channel. "When is Cade gonna get here, Jules?"

I rolled my eyes. Noah called me by my character's nickname often, and while I supposed it was sweet in a weird sort of way, it sometimes grated on my nerves.

"I think soon. That new actress, Leah St. Clare is also stopping by. Do you know her Jen?"

The other girl huffed. "No, but I've heard of her."

"Wow, that doesn't sound good."

"She makes Wendy look like cotton candy."

My heart dropped. "Awesome. I'm going to order the pizza and then hop in the shower so I can go to bed early. Are you guys going to be okay out here until I'm finished? I'll be quick."

I walked into the bedroom and dialed the pizza place, ordered two large pizzas, then peeled off my clothes and got in the shower. It was 6:30 and I hoped that Cade would be done by now and on his way back to the hotel. I'd left him on set to go over some things with Martin. Peter would have to drop him in the garage, and he would have to run up the stairs once again. It didn't matter that other cast members were here for the paparazzi's benefit; Cade would want to avoid the mobs of fans.

The water felt wonderful as I let my muscles relax and my eyes close. I was so tired all I really wanted to do was crawl into bed. As I towel dried my hair and threw on some cut off sweats and a small white T-Shirt, hoping I'd see Cade in the living room with Noah and Jennifer, but he wasn't there yet.

I went to the bar and got a Diet Coke. "Do you guys want something to drink?" I offered. When neither answered, I grabbed a Coke for each of them and plopped down on the other chair to wait for the pizza. Jennifer was asleep, and Noah was engrossed in the TV.

My eyes were drooping and I was feeling sleep starting to seep into my muscles and brain when a knock at the door startled me awake.

I ran my hands through my hair and I went to find my purse. Noah looked up from the TV.

"Is it Cade?" he asked anxiously.

"I think it's just the pizza," I said. "Cade has a key." I stopped and glanced at Noah underneath my lashes. His mouth tightened and he nodded. We had become good friends in the time we'd spent filming together, but I was aware of the crush he'd developed. He was aware of my relationship with Cade. It wasn't like it was a secret on set anymore, plus, we'd talked about it, so his reaction made me a little uncomfortable. Also, I knew he wanted the professional connections Cade represented.

I paid for the pizza and found some plates, silverware, and napkins in the cabinet behind the bar.

"Help yourselves." I started to pull a piece of the vegetable pizza onto a plate when I heard the door open and I knew it would be Cade. I turned toward him and a big smile split my face as he came toward me. He was dressed in a red button-down shirt and a gray jacket over his jeans.

"Hey Jennifer, Noah," he said as his eyes met mine and he strode straight toward me. "Will you both excuse us for just a moment?"

"Hey!" I began to greet him. "Ooof," I grunted as the air left my lungs. He bent and hoisted me over his shoulder and walked away from them. Jennifer laughed and Noah just watched without speaking.

"Cade, what are you doing? You're acting like a caveman." He chuckled and continued to haul me away.

"Thank you, I feel like one," he said in a low tone as he kicked the bedroom door shut behind us.

"You're giving Noah a very nice view of my ass," I teased him. "Was that your intention?"

"Not at all," he murmured, as he moved me off of his shoulder and slid me down his body. His arms went around my waist and his hands fisted in my shirt as he pulled me close. "This is my intention."

My hands moved up his chest and around his neck as his mouth swooped down to devour mine. Our tongues laved each other and it felt so incredible my knees went weak. Kissing, licking, and tasting; we continued until finally I dragged my mouth from his, gasping for breath.

"Cade. Noah and Jennifer..."

He bent to slide his hands lower over my butt to my thighs as he lifted me against him. My legs parted and wound around his waist as he pressed me to him.

"Who cares? Oh, God. You feel so good," his velvet voice was so seductive that I doubted I'd have the strength to stop if I let it continue for one more minute. But I wanted it and wanted it bad.

"Cade. I don't want to stop, but we have to." I rested my head against his as we both stroked each other's face. Since I'd denied him my mouth, his lips made a hot trail across my cheek and down my neck where he sucked and licked making me tremble.

"Stop, now, honey." His mouth stilled and he slowly set me on my feet. I gave him a sad smile and let my hand trace down his chest.

"Aren't you hungry?"

"Starving. But you won't *feed* me." He grinned at me and kicked off his Nikes as he moved to the bathroom.

"I'd love to *feed* you. You know that, but with Noah and Jen..."

"Ah yes, Noah. So what are you doing parading around all soft and wet from your shower in front of him, hmmm?" I leaned on the door as he threw some water on his face and dried it.

"I'm not all soft and wet..."

"Yes, you are." He picked me up again; placing another kiss on my mouth as he moved to the door. "Let's get this bloody evening over with, shall we?" His arms tightened in a hug before he opened the door and walked me out with his arm still around me.

Noah was already eating, but his eyes rose to take notice of us coming into the room. Jennifer was at the bar getting a piece of pizza.

"Hey, Cade," she smiled at him, "how was it today?"

"It was good. It was all very focused. I'm tired." Cade let go of me to pick up a plate. "I'm not looking forward to the couple of days we have left on the cover sets."

Noah glanced between the two of us and continued eating.

"Are we rehearsing something, tonight?" Cade teased Jennifer. "Is that why you're here?"

"Thanks a lot, dickhead," she shoved him as she made her way back to the couch but she was laughing.

My eyes widened, and I laughed out loud. Jennifer wasn't one to swear or call anyone names; she was so sweet, and it took me by surprise.

"That's me. Ethan must be wearing off on me." Cade took his pizza and sat down on the chair opposite Noah. "Seriously, I knew you'd be here. Brook told me when we spoke on the phone earlier." He laughed, and she smiled back at him.

After I'd gotten Cade a beer from the refrigerator, I took a piece of pizza and my script for the next film and sat down on the couch next to Jennifer.

Caden

I SAT BACK ON THE couch and watched Noah's eyes follow Brook as she took my plate and hers to the sink behind the bar. I could tell he really liked her, more than liked her. I felt my body tense in involuntary reaction. Who could blame him? She was amazing in many ways.

I tried to be objective and concentrate on the task at hand.

"Jen, can you read the narration in the places we can't act it out?" I asked and handed her my copy of the script.

"Oh sure, don't you need the script?" she took the copy from my hand and I shook my head.

Noah had followed Brook to the bar and when he came up beside her to set his plate down his hand came up to touch the back of her waist. My eyes narrowed as I watched. He was saying something to her and she was smiling, and despite my determination to blow it off, it didn't sit well with me.

Why am I so bloody jealous? I know she loves me.

I was still watching them as they came back to the main sitting area and Brook's eyes met mine. I wondered if she could tell I was irritated. Her eyebrow rose in question and I averted my eyes.

"So, how are we going to do this?" Noah wanted to know. "Am I reading the Spencer part?"

"Just read all the guy parts that aren't Ryan," I said. "Since Ethan isn't here yet."

Jennifer sat in one of the chairs at the end of the two sofas and when Brook came to sit on one, Noah followed and plopped down next to her, and scooted closer to her. She raised her eyes to mine and I realized she knew what I was thinking.

This would never do.

"Okay, no scripts. Jennifer can prompt if we need it," Brook murmured as she inched slightly away from Noah as I looked on. I got up and went to the bar to pull another beer from the refrigerator.

I stopped by where she was sitting and held my hand out to her. She looked up at my face and I pulled her up and over to the other couch with me. I moved in closer, flung my arm around her shoulders and kissed her temple before glancing at Noah.

It was just a subtle message to get my point across. There will be no life imitating the art of the film... I won't have you pissing on my territory, dog.

My lips quirked into a grin as I huffed, "Hmmpft," and I could sense Brook's uneasiness as she stiffened beside me.

"Let's get started. Cade, you have the first line," she said.

The only reason we were rehearsing a scene that wouldn't be filmed for months was because Martin had confided he wasn't sure about Curtis and he might recast him if he didn't like the screen test we were doing the next day. I didn't like the guy enough to invite him in to rehearse. Sink or swim, it would all be on his acting chops. I wouldn't stack the deck in his favor. We proceeded with the scene and it went well, even with Noah reading Ethan's part.

"You guys are really great. You're nailing it," Jennifer interjected.

Brook shook her head. I could tell that she hated the interruption when she was in her zone, but we were at the part where Ryan takes Julia away to the dance floor and that wouldn't be part of the test.

"Okay," Noah broke in. "That's it. It was great."

Jennifer threw her script on the coffee table. "I thought that Leah chick was supposed to come over. Where is she?"

I shook my head and inhaled deeply. "No clue. I'm relieved if you must know." I leaned back into the deep cushions of the couch and reached for Brook's hand.

"I'm beat, and you don't really need me, do you? You guys did a great job!" She gave Noah and I a hug before Brook walked her to the door.

Noah turned enthusiastic eyes on me. "That was incredible, dude. Should we run it again?"

Bloody hell! I thought. I wanted to be alone with Brook. I had to tell her about Wendy's call and how she crashed lunch last week.

"How do you improve on perfection?" There was always room for improvement, but I wanted him to leave.

Brook wandered back from the hall and plopped down on the couch. I could see how tired she was.

"It's great working with you guys, but if you're tired, I guess I should go. Cade, should we share a cab or do you have your limo?" Noah asked me.

"Well, I wasn't going to leave just yet, Noah. Sorry," I responded quietly, my eyes steady on his.

"Oh, yeah. Okay. Well, thanks for the pizza, Brook. You did a good job. I don't know how you turn on the tears like that, but it's amazing." He grabbed her arm and pulled her into a tight hug. Her eyes met mine over his shoulder and I smiled at her.

"No problem. See you tomorrow."

As soon as the door closed I scooped Brook up over my shoulder and ran into the bedroom.

"Not this again, Cade!"

"Okay," I unceremoniously dumped her in the middle of the bed and laughed when she squealed. "I'm gonna hop in the shower, but there is something I want to talk to you about. Will you come in, and talk to me?"

"Are you asking me to come in there and stare at your naked body? You have a lot of nerve…" Her face split into a grin as she crawled off of the bed. "But, okay."

I turned on the shower and peeled off my clothes, while Brook sat down on the rug and leaned against the wall. "Nice view," she ran her hand up my calf as she looked up at me, and I knew if I didn't get in the shower instantly, I'd have a huge hard-on. Her eyes were lidded; so sexy, and I could see her nipples harden through her T-Shirt. *Holy Hell.*

"Stop flirting with me, honey. We have to sleep tonight," I groaned as I stepped under the hot spray.

"We do? Dang." I couldn't see her because the steam was covering the glass of the shower door.

"Okay, so…."

"Yeah? That doesn't sound good…. You've got that tone…"

"What tone?" I hedged.

"The *Brook, you're not gonna like this*, tone. *That* tone."

I closed my eyes as I lathered up my hair. She knew me too well. I decided just to dive in and say it.

"Wendy called today because she wanted to know what I wanted for my birthday."

Silence.

"Brook?"

"Yeah. I knew she wouldn't give up so easily. But, I trust you, Cade. What did you do?"

"Basically, told her I didn't want a gift and hung up on her."

"Well, that was hardly worthy of *the tone*," she admonished.

Now it was my turn to be quiet. "Cade?"

"There's obviously more, so just tell me."

"I should have told you this last week, but I didn't want to upset you, but the day of the cast party, she crashed my lunch with Ethan and Dawson." I grimaced as I waited for her response.

"The day you drank for twelve hours?" I could hear the tension in her voice.

"She wasn't with us the whole time. She showed up at lunch, and I barely spoke to her. She was asking all kinds of questions about Italy, and hinting around that she wanted to be there, but I told her to piss off. It wasn't worth upsetting you, love. She's insignificant."

Brook didn't say anything for a moment, but when she did it wasn't good.

"If she were so fucking insignificant, you would have told me about this when it happened," her voice had an acid edge to it. "Why didn't she come to the cast party if she was in Vancouver?"

"Because I asked her *not* to. I told her I didn't want her there, and that I didn't want anything to do with her. I was so anxious to see you that I completely forgot about her being there. Then when we were finally alone, I got lost in you and I didn't think about it."

More silence. *Fuck.*

I rinsed my hair and shut the water off as I opened the shower door.

She was still sitting on the floor, absently plucking at the fibers in the carpet as I dried off.

"Besides, shit happens, doesn't it?"

She finally raised her eyes to mine and then got up off of the floor. "What do you mean?"

"Well, you've been spending a lot of time with Noah, and I see how he watches you. I know he wants you, and I struggle with it, too." I threw off my towel and put my arms around her and forced her to walk backwards into the bedroom.

She looked into my face, bit her lip and nodded. "Yeah, but you know…"

"Yeah, I do know. And you should know, too. That's all I'm getting at."

I lifted her off her feet and kissed her mouth before pulling back the sheets and putting her in bed.

"You're wasting your time, you know," her lips turned up at the corners.

"What? Wasting my time, how?"

"You know."

"Doesn't matter. I've still got to brush my teeth."

I let her up and followed Brook reluctantly back into the bathroom, then filled my own brush with toothpaste. She grabbed the tube from my hand.

"Whatever you say…" she said, following suit.

We both finished and I grabbed her hand and I walked out of the bathroom pulling her behind me. She was so sexy, soft and warm and I was chastising myself for what I was about to do. I turned the light off in the bathroom and then the one beside the bed.

"Whatever I say, hmmm?" I whispered as my hands cupped her breasts and I moaned against her neck as the nipples hardened in my hands. "I love the sound of that, Brook, because what *I say is I want you*."

My mouth hovered over hers as I lowered her to the bed.

"I'm all yours…" she said. "Always yours."

Chapter 3

Cade's Surprise

Brooklyn

I PACED AROUND MY room, waiting impatiently for Jeanne to answer her phone. It was Cade's birthday and I was fidgeting. I wanted everything to be perfect. He was in wardrobe and I was going to the makeup trailer before we filmed with Jennifer, Leah, Gavin, Sarah and the rest of the cast. I didn't have many moments without him lately, and it made getting the arrangements made more difficult, so I was making the most of this one. I had to rely on Jeanne and Ethan to help me with the big stuff.

"Hello?" Jeanne finally answered and my hand tightened around the phone.

"Oh, Jeanne! You had me worried. I haven't gotten the bracelet yet. Are you sure it's been shipped?"

"Jesus, Brook, I'm running my ass off trying to get hotels and rides done for Cade's parents, and you're concerned about the bracelet?"

I let out an exaggerated sigh. "I ordered the damn thing a month ago, so yeah, I'm frustrated!"

"I'm sure it will be fine. Denise is helping with that. She's calling FedEx as we speak to check on the tracking, and Cade's driver is on his way to the airport to get Lillian and Carter. Did you want me to get them checked in and then bring them to the set?"

"Yes. I thought they might enjoy watching us work for a while, and then Cade can go back to their hotel with them. I'll go to the dinner with Jennifer, and meet them back at the hotel later. It's really important to me to get that bracelet in time, so will you text and let me know if you and Denise track it down, please?" I bit my lower lip and chewed on it as I walked toward my trailer. My hand closed around the knob to yank it open before I stepped in to find Mickey smiling in my direction and pointing with a waving hand at the chair in front of him.

"Brook, you know Cade won't care if it's a day or two late." Jeanne's voice took on the calming tone she always used when she wanted me to relax. "All he cares about is being with you."

I was sure she was right, but I was still anxious. Cade had made two of my birthdays amazing and it was my turn to surprise him.

"It's important to me, Jeanne. So, just please find it if you can, okay? I'm running late, so I'll talk to you later." I hung up my phone and flung myself down in the makeup chair in front of the mirrors. Mickey was milling around organizing his station. He cocked his eyebrow at me, and I braced myself for the grilling that was to come, no matter how hilarious it would be.

"Hey, Mickey. What's up?" I offered up a coy smile.

"Oh, honey, that depends! Where's *my boyfriend*? Didn't you bring him with you?" He started to run his hands through my hair and grinned at me in the mirror.

"Hmmm. Well, I think he's in wardrobe," I laughed. "He'll be here soon."

"Girl, mmmm, mmm, mmmm! He is one yummy man. He does all sorts of things to my insides!"

"Yeah, I know the feeling."

Mickey stopped messing with my hair and reached for a brush from the drawers in front of him and to my right, stopping dead in his tracks at my comment. Both eyebrows shot up.

"Was that an admission, missy?" He smirked slyly.

I just rolled my eyes and grinned back. "If you really want to drool, check out those photos online from the GQ shoot he did for last month's issue." My mind flashed to the pictures of him in those tight jeans and the black leather jacket. Jesus, he was gorgeous. "He looks amazing." I pursed my lips derisively. "They make him look all messy and he's still so hot. It's not fair. If they did that to me, I'd look like a drowned rat."

"Have I *seen* them? You must be kidding! I saw them before that mag even hit the stands. And when doesn't Caden Carlisle look amazing?" He paused, dramatically fanning himself and then looked at me as something dawned on him. He pointed a finger in my direction. "Wait. You didn't just turn into a fan girl, did you?"

"Hmmph!" I expelled my breath and shook my head in self-admonishment.

Shit. I hated being lumped in with the fans that screamed and fainted whenever he was within a hundred yards or went to see his movies twenty-five times each.

"Um... Well, Mick, *you have*, that's for sure!"

"You have to tell me everything. What's he taste like? He looks so flippin' delish. I want all the details! Oh my God, I'm so jealous that you get to be so close to him, kiss him, touch him!" He started to brush my hair as my eyes widened, when I saw the trailer door open and Cade walk in. I bit my lip to hide my smile and dropped my head to shield my expression from the object of our discussion as he came to me. "It gives me the goosies just thinking about it!"

"Uh... Now isn't a good time to tell you, Sorry," I said as I lost the fight with the laughter as it burst from my chest.

Cade took the chair beside me and looked over in my direction, up at Mickey and then back at me again. Clearly, there was a question in his dark blue eyes. "What?" he asked, his brows rose as he spoke.

I shrugged and shook my head, trying to wipe the smile from my face and failing miserably. He kept looking at me like he wasn't buying it. Heat rose underneath my skin and a blush flooded my face. Cade's mouth twitched in amusement, but he just stared forward into the mirror.

Sally, the head hair stylist, came in and stood behind me. It took me ten seconds to realize she'd be working on me and Mickey was going to work on Cade.

Oh boy. This should be good.

A huge ass smile split across Mickey's face and he winked at me. I could see Cade visibly tense in his seat. He sat up a little taller, and brought his hands to grasp around the arms of his chair when it dawned on him who'd be working on him today.

"In honor of your birthday, *I* get a present, Mr. Hottie," Mickey said and started laying paper towels on Cade's lap to keep makeup from soiling his costume. "I get to do you today."

Cade's horrified expression was priceless, as he quickly took the towels from Mickey's hands and laid them over his pants himself.

"Uh... thanks," he murmured stiffly, "I'll do that."

We all knew that *doing Cade* was, as in makeup and hair, but that Mickey *wished* it were something else entirely.

I thought I was going to die laughing and brought a hand to my mouth to contain it, but my shoulders started shaking with the force of my amusement. Cade shot me a dirty look that said he didn't find the situation in the least bit amusing. He was straighter than straight, and the attention of a gay man was bound to make him squirm.

His costume was standard aquamarine scrubs, but it was a V-neck so he would need some body makeup down his neck and onto his chest. Mickey was going to have a hay day.

Cade glared at me in the mirror, eyes wide, and mouthed the words "Help me," which only made it harder for me to keep a straight face. I just cocked my head to one side and jutted out my lower lip in a sympathetic pout to tease him even more.

"So, Cade-ilicious; what are you doing for your birthday?" Mickey began to put the makeup on his chest, clearly reveling in the ability to finally get his hands on the object of his obsession.

Cade's mouth just dropped open as he searched for words. He sat up straighter in his chair again to move as far back as possible. I felt so bad for him, but it was fucking hilarious and I couldn't help egging him on further.

"Yeah, *Cade-ilicious...*" I echoed Mickey's words devilishly. "What ya got going on tonight?" I smirked at him and unable to curb it a second longer, finally burst out laughing.

"You are *so* going to get it later, Halloway," he growled under his breath. "You're having way too much fun with this."

Mickey stopped what he was doing and stared at me to emphasize his words, shaking his head.

"You are one lucky, lucky, bitch," Mickey stated emphatically and smiled; winking at me in the mirror as he continued his work.

I smiled as I glanced mischievously at Cade and wagged my

eyebrows at him wildly in exaggeration.

"Yeah, I know. You have no idea, Mickey. The boy has *skills*," I said dryly. Even Cade laughed in surprise. His eyes shot to mine and his face flushed as his head snapped around. I met his gaze steadily and licked my lips. "Serious skills."

"Oh fuck, don't tease me," Mickey begged. "I can't stand it!"

Cade put the heels of his hands over his eyes, but his shoulders were shaking as he finally laughed out loud.

"You guys are killing me," Sally dissolved into laughter with us as she started working on my hair. "Mick, concentrate on what you're doing and leave the poor guy alone. If we don't have them on set in twenty minutes, they'll have my ass."

"Spoilsport," Mickey retorted.

I glanced at Cade in the mirror and he was smiling back at me. "Love you," I mouthed to his reflection.

"I know," he said out loud. "Miracles do happen."

Sally had my makeup finished before Mickey was done with Cade, so I excused myself and went to find Martin. He was working on the lighting with the production manager on a cover set of the hospital room.

I talked to him a few days previously to let him know I was inviting Cade's parents to the set today and he'd been great about it.

"Hey Brook, when will Cade's parents get here? I want to make sure to have some filming left so I'll stall a little if needed."

"Thanks. You've been so nice about this. We sent Cade's driver to get them about two hours ago, so I expect them any minute. They're great people and they'll love you, Martin. I hope you'll come to dinner tonight. Ethan couldn't come, but he arranged it at the Glowball Grill at 8:30."

"Wouldn't miss it." He smiled as he went back to work.

Jeff Jackson, who would play Spencer Black, was there and overheard our conversation. He looked so different in his costume and makeup. He was so boyish in real life, but he looked completely stiff all made up as the boorish psychologist. From what I'd seen so far of his acting, he was going to deliver a great performance.

He smiled and walked up closer to me, his dark eyes flirting with me. "So it's Caden's birthday, eh?"

"Er... yes. Ethan planned a surprise for him tonight at the Glowball Grill. You're welcome to join us if you'd like. The others, too. We should make sure to invite everyone." I looked at my feet nervously as I saw Cade walking toward us out of the corner of my eye.

"Yeah, I'll spread the word," he said softly. "See you in there." He moved off toward the other actors to let them know about the party.

Cade's eyes narrowed a little as he came to stand next to me. He was calm, but his eyes were sharper and threw daggers at the other man's retreating back.

"What was that all about?" he asked.

I crossed my arms and looked up at him; a smile dancing around my mouth.

"Don't go getting your panties all in a bunch, Ryan. He just wanted to know some good places to get dinner tonight. Just small talk. Nothing really." I punched him in the arm playfully.

"Well, you'd better be careful or your panties might end up in a bunch," he said with a grin. "You're being very saucy today, and then leaving me at Mickey's mercy like that was unforgivable. What's gotten into you?" His eyes were warm as his hand moved to my lower back and his fingers ran up to my shoulders and back down. My skin tingled through my shirt at his touch.

"Well, maybe I'm really happy today and it's fun teasing you. Happy Birthday, babe," I said softly so no one else could hear.

"Mmmm... I'm really looking forward to my, um, *presents*. What did you get me?" His eyes were alive with devilish teasing, the blue depths gleaming.

"I thought you didn't want me to buy you presents."

His brows went up and he let his breath out. "Hmmph! Who said anything about *buying* me anything?"

I wanted to reach up, wind my hand around the back of his neck and pull that beautiful mouth down to mine, but all I could do was stare at it and then look into his eyes. I could tell by his expression that he knew what I was thinking as his gaze fell to my mouth as well.

"Hmmph!" He let out his breath again.

There was a movement at the side stage door and I saw Carter and Lillian coming toward us, being led by Mark, the production assistant that had gotten me roses for my birthday, two months before. Cade was facing me and didn't see them. I waited until they were just about to us and then I put my hand on his arm to get him to look into my face.

"Here comes one of them now." I nodded in the direction I wanted him to glance. "Thanks, Mark," I said as they reached us.

He turned around and his mother opened her arms to him.

"Bloody Hell!" he said, stunned, as his mother enfolded him in an embrace and his dad patted him on the shoulder.

"There's my baby," Lillian said. "I'm so glad to see you, darling."

"Happy Birthday, son," Carter said warmly, a smile spreading out on his gentle face.

"Mum, Dad... how?" Cade's face was incredulous as his mother gathered him close again. Even shocked, he was so beautiful he took my breath away.

"Hello, Brook," Carter said, then scooped me up into huge hug that left my feet dangled off of the floor. The familiarity of the contact didn't go unnoticed by the rest of the cast and crew, but I didn't care.

My arms automatically wrapped around his shoulders as I hugged him back. "I'm so glad you came." Tears welled in my eyes. "Look at me getting all sappy. The makeup people will be all over me if I ruin their hard work."

"You're gorgeous!" He set me down and turned to Cade. "Son, it's so good to see you. You're looking a little pale, though," he laughed as the two men embraced.

"I think he's too thin," his mother put in.

"Hello, Lillian, you look beautiful," I said, and she hugged me before placing a soft kiss on my cheek. She always smelled of lilacs and French perfume.

"Thank you for inviting us dear. We're so happy to be here. Have you been taking good care of my boy? He looks so wonderfully happy, even if he's skipping a few meals."

I nodded in answer. "I think so."

""Mum, I'm not!" Cade protested. "We just work hard, and I get sick of hotel food. We don't get out much. What are you doing here? I mean..." He shook his head in wonder.

His mother lowered her voice. "Brook invited us. Layla and Oliver as well, but they couldn't get away. They've sent gifts with their regrets that they couldn't attend."

Cade reached out to take my hand. "Thank you, love. This was extremely thoughtful. You're perfect."

I blushed and gave his hand a little squeeze before pulling back as the rest of the cast and Martin came over. Lillian and Carter exchanged a look, and I could only interpret it as pride and happiness for the two of us.

"Are you going to watch us film, then?" Cade's eyes lit up at the prospect. He'd told me in one of our overnight talks that he rarely let his family visit the set. I'd been having issues with my mother's impromptu visits to set on the first film. Mostly, I just didn't want my time with Cade interrupted, and I knew she'd be able to tell I was in love with him just by looking at my face, and I didn't want to deal with it. Like now, I couldn't stop smiling. It was so bad, my face hurt.

"Yes, Brook arranged it with your director. You don't mind do you, my boy?" Carter asked.

"Not at all. I'm so happy to have you both here!"

Cade's strong arm slid around my waist, and he pulled me close to his side. Glancing up into his face; I could see the love radiating from his eyes. "You're amazing."

"Awww, shucks," I teased him. "I just love you; that's all."

His arms went around my shoulders and he pulled me close into a full-on hug. "Cade, the crew..."

"I don't care. I love you. You're so good to me."

My arms slid around his waist, and I hugged him back. Closing my eyes, I inhaled his scent and wished I could kiss him as my hands splayed out on his back pressed him closer.

"They know, anyway," he whispered into the hair above my ear.

After introductions were made to the rest of the crew, his parents were settled into their chairs off to the side while we ran a quick rehearsal to get the blocking and camera angles down. After the technical stuff was completed we ran through the scene once without film and then finally, we began shooting.

They watched the filming of the first part of the scene where Aaron and Jenna, Ellie and Harris have dinner with Ryan and Julia the first night she comes home from the hospital, and they were questioning why Ryan couldn't just tell Julia about the past. Things were filmed out of sequence so most of the others could leave, and then I sat with Cade's parents as he filmed a scene with Jeff. It was easy to get completely lost in the scene, letting myself feel the possibility of forgetting Cade.

We didn't get all of the apartment scenes finished and would be filming them over the next few days before they would strike the set. They were more involved and had several segments to them which all had to be set up and filmed separately, then edited together later in post-production. There were a lot of emotional scenes and the love scenes would be filmed on a closed set, at Cade's request.

When we finished for the day, I said goodbye to Cade and his parents. "So, we'll meet at the restaurant at 8:30, okay?" I would only be away from him for a few hours, but my heart still fell a little.

His hand ran down my arm. "Okay, love. See you later, then. I'll miss you," he bent down to whisper so no one could hear him but me.

"It's only a little while. Enjoy the time with your parents." I leaned into him and gave him a little shove with my shoulder as Jennifer ran up to us.

"Hey," she said, slightly out of breath. "I was afraid I'd miss you! I'm Jennifer Wade," she said warmly, extending her hand to both of them in turn. "It's so nice to meet you!"

Cade finished introducing his parents to Jen and they were completely taken with her. She was gracious as always, flashing them a beautiful smile and asking them about their trip over from London.

"Happy Birthday, handsome. We'll see you all tonight," she said as she hugged Cade goodbye. Then we all got in the cars that took us back to the different hotels.

Caden

"BROOK IS REMARKABLE, son. The two of you together were wonderful," my dad said as we rode back to my hotel in the back of David's limo. "Your mum cried. All of you that we got to see today... just incredible work," he beamed.

"The scene was amazing!" Mum said, as she took my hand. "The two of you are beautiful together, Caden. I'm so proud of everything you've accomplished. Layla does her own thing, but your brother is a bit green."

I rolled my eyes. "Mum, it's not that big of a deal. I feel lucky to be on this series."

"Caden," my father admonished, "let the woman be proud of you. It's her right and you have done very well for yourself. And, you've gotten a wonderful girl in the process." He winked at me.

I smiled, "Yeah, I know what a lucky sod I am. So... it's great you've come to visit. I wish we were in L.A. or New York, though. I'll give you back the money for the airline, or I'll buy you another trip."

"Brook arranged everything, honey. She said it was part of her birthday gift to you."

I took a deep breath. *What?*

"What is it?" Mum asked.

"Oh, nothing. Just... leaving, going to New York has been weighing on me quite a bit. I know *Only Us* is a great opportunity because of the director, and I'm probably a complete moron for not being excited about it, but I couldn't care less. I'm really going to miss her. I've never dealt with this type of feeling before, and I worry about her."

My dad nodded. "Yes, I can see how much the two of you adore each other. It won't be easy, but you'll get through it and be even better for it," he said reassuringly. "You'll see. Brook told your mum on the phone that she has a movie to film as well. You'll both be busy and the time apart will pass quickly, son."

"The saving grace is that Brook is filming in L.A. and can stay at her parent's home."

"That should make you more at ease." Mum leaned her head on my shoulder and squeezed my hand. "Can we do anything to make it easier for you, my darling?"

"You being here today is amazing, but when I'm in New York, it would be great if you could encourage Layla and Oliver to visit me there. I'd especially love it if Layla could hop the pond. It's a much shorter flight than L.A."

I was close to both of my siblings, but Layla was a lot of fun and had a way of getting me out of any funks. Brook would be busy and we wouldn't be able to see each other very often, so I'd definitely have a few of those.

"I'm sure she'd love that, Caden," my mother said as she patted my hand. "Let's just concentrate on celebrating your birthday, now, shall we?

"Is your suite near mine?" I asked, trying to change the subject. The less time spent thinking about being away from Brook, the better.

"Yes. Brook's manager told us that we were just across the hall from you, so that'll make it easier to see you. I can't believe all of the mobs of people," Mum said as we pulled up to the hotel and the volume of the screams rose several decibels. "This is all for you? Is it always like this?"

"Sadly, yes. It's overwhelming. Wait until the doors open, you won't believe how loud. While I appreciate it, I'm growing rather tired of it. I just want to be normal again. Making movies is fun, but the rest of this stuff is bloody maddening," I said as Peter opened the doors. "Just keep walking and don't stop or talk to anyone." I flipped the hood of my sweatshirt up, somehow gaining a little security from the fake shield it provided. It was crazy, but the clothes, the hats and sunglasses were all I had to hide behind. My world was open for observation and that wasn't going to change.

The bodyguards were there to meet us and flanked us on all sides as I followed my parents out of the car. I was immediately barraged with fans asking for photos and autographs and then there was the never-ending stream of paparazzi and the blinding flashes of light. If the public viewed celebrities in sunglasses as a symbol of arrogance, it was more for function. Even at night, it was hard to see through the constant cameras.

"Holy hell!" my dad murmured as he wrapped his arm around my mother's shoulders protectively.

"Cade! Cade! Ahhhhhh! Agghrrrr! Happy Birthday!" So many different people were screaming at me and women were thrusting flowers and gifts at me. My bodyguards put up their arms and pushed them back. Sometimes I thought it rude, but I couldn't take the risk.

My parents stepped back as they watched me, and the paparazzi kept screaming questions at me and asking me to pose for photos.

"Cade, are your parents here for your birthday or to meet Brooklyn?"

"Cade, are you seeing Brook Halloway? Are you in a relationship with her? Is she your girlfriend? Did you break her and David up?"

"We saw you go to her hotel, are you guys seeing each other or just hooking up?"

"Do you have plans with her for your birthday?"

It was usually around the time they started mentioning Brook that I wanted to punch something. I ignored all of the rude comments and signed a few more scribbled autographs before extricating myself and guiding both of my parents through the hotel doors.

"Holy Mother of God! Caden, that's unbelievable!" my father said as he walked beside me and laid his hand on my shoulder.

"Dad, really, that was nothing. You've been at the premieres. It can be so much worse than this at the events. The hotel does have a few more than usual, I suppose, due to it being my birthday, but not by much."

Three hours later I was getting ready for dinner when my phone rang. *I Will Remember You* by Ryan Cabrera; the new song I'd just assigned as Brook's ringtone filled the air. The song was so apropos of our movies, of me leaving... I was happy she was calling but filled with melancholy as I answered the phone.

"Hey, gorgeous." I forced a lighthearted tone. She was so happy and I didn't want to bring her down with thoughts of our impending separation.

"Hi! Are you ready for your birthday party? I'm so happy your parents came."

"Yeah. It was amazing of you to ask them. Very sweet. They simply adore you, Brook," I said as I ran my hands through my hair a few times, then realized there was nothing to be done with it and gave up completely. "As do I."

"Hmm, well, it's mutual. I'm just glad I was able to help make you happy today."

"You always do, love." I smiled into the phone. "Even when you're leaving me at the mercy of delusional, gay men." She laughed and the sound spoke directly to my heart.

"Did you get any, uh... *packages* today?"

I laughed. "Only from Ethan and Dawson. Those wankers!"

"Ethan mentioned he was sending you something, but wouldn't tell me what it was," her voice was anxious and lilted. "So? What was it?"

"Um..." I hesitated.

"Cade! Tell me! I'm dying to know!" She laughed into the phone.

"You won't say that after I tell you. Those jackasses," I said in exasperation. "They sent me a Julia blow up doll, or rather one they dressed up like you. They even got some of your costumes from the last film to dress the damn thing in. Happy now?" My face hurt, I was smiling so much.

She burst out laughing. "Ethan has such a twisted sense of humor. That's hilarious! At least it was dressed. Was there a note?"

I rolled my eyes as I bent to pull on my shoes. "Oh *yeah*, there was a note alright." I went to get it so I could read it to her. "It says; 'Ryan, on the lonely nights when Julia can't blow you, you can blow *her*! We wouldn't want our boy to get blue balls while in New York. She can't make lemon muffins, but you get the idea! Love, Daws and Ethan'." I said through my chuckles. "Dickheads."

Brook was giggling so hard she was gasping for breath. "Oh my God! I'm dying!"

"How in *the fuck* am I supposed to get rid of this bloody thing? If the press gets a hold of it, it will ruin me. I'll be a laughing stock! I should beat the hell out of them when I see them next." I tried to sound irritated, but in reality I was smiling. Okay, it *was* bloody hysterical, I have to admit it. "I'd suggest giving it to Mickey, but it lacks certain appendages that he might require," I added sardonically, as I threw on my black hooded sweatshirt and headed for the door.

"That's for sure. You know before you yell at Ethan, you should know that he helped make the arrangements for tonight."

"He did? He's a good guy, even if he is a fucker."

"Yes, he's great. I've got to run, babe. Meet you at Blowball... um, I mean Glowball," she teased, her eyes sparkling with glee.

"Yeah... keep it up, Brook. You're going to pay for that little stunt with Mickey earlier, too, so get ready." I knew she could hear the smile in my voice.

"Ummm... really can't wait. Love you," her voice dropped and took on that sex tone I loved.

I felt my body tighten in anticipation. "Mmmm... love you, sweets. See you in a few."

I went to collect my parents before heading downstairs to face another mob of fans, but I was so happy, nothing would ruin my mood.

***

AS I WATCHED BROOK with my parents throughout the evening, my heart swelled until I thought it would burst inside my chest. She laughed and played with my dad, and fell into easy conversation with Mum. She glanced and flirted with me as they spoke. I figured they were telling all sorts of horror stories from my childhood and she was eating it up and would certainly use it to blackmail me later.

I was talking to Martin about the possibility that he would direct *A Love Like This*. He was open to it, and I found myself hoping the suits would make him an offer to do it. He knew us all so well by now, and though he had a scheduling conflict, I would speak to Denise about getting the studio to work around all of our schedules. It was the last one and if anyone could do it justice, I knew it would be him.

The party was small. Jennifer, Jeff Jackson, and Martin were the only others from the cast there. It was very relaxing for the most part and I spent most of the night laughing with everyone. I had a beer and ordered Brook and my mum champagne cocktails, and we had some of the delicious pot stickers I adored, before ordering dinner. After we'd all eaten, the group of us moved into the lounge portion of the restaurant.

My mate, Daniel Mayfield joined us and I talked with him over a drink. He was working in Vancouver and Brook had called him to ask him to meet us out. We talked about his music and possibly working on some together in the near future. I didn't want to produce anything new during filming because I felt like I wasn't being true to the craft and that any success I would have would be more due to the films then the music. That wasn't how I wanted it to happen. It had to be about the music or it felt like cheating, somehow.

My parents gave me a new laptop with a built-in web camera, so Brook and I could use Skype to talk to each other. My dad winked at me, effectively telling me without words that the real purpose was so that I could use it with Brook while I was away from her. It was silly really. I had more money than they did and didn't need them to buy me anything, but I shut my mouth and showed the proper amount of gratitude.

Thump. My heart dropped.

Despite my determination to keep my demeanor on an even keel, my throat thickened as once again our pending separation hung over me like a storm. Brook looked over at me and what I saw in her eyes took my breath away.

She was so beautiful; happy in her talks with my parents. It gave me so much pleasure to watch her with them. Seeing how well she fit into my family meant the world to me. I loved knowing how well they got on together and I could clearly see our future having children, building a life, growing older together. Her intense blue eyes roamed over my expression and the smile fell from her lips. I tried to shake it off and smile back at her because I didn't want her to feel the pain I was feeling.

It was asking for the impossible, but I wanted to try and alleviate as much of it as I could. I got up and walked over to where she was huddled up with my dad and mum.

"You look like you're having too much fun over here, without me." I smiled down at them, and my hand reached out to brush gently against Brook's chin.

Her eyes took on a worried expression as they met mine. "Are you okay?" she asked as her hand came up to cover mine.

"Yeah. Come outside with me for a minute? Mum, Dad, do you mind?"

We didn't really wait for an answer and I barely registered the silent shakes of their heads. Brook and I went to sit behind a stone wall, sliding to the ground behind it in case there were any paparazzi lurking, so they wouldn't see us. The crowd of fans had been steadily growing outside since we'd arrived, and I knew it was due to everyone twittering our whereabouts. I hated it, but tried to push it down and block out the din of the screams. I wanted to be normal. I wanted to concentrate on Brook.

I pulled out my cigarettes and offered her one. She took it absently and held it between her fingers as I lit mine and blew out the smoke. It was a nasty habit we both needed to kick but I was anxious. She moved closer, so our legs and shoulders were touching and instantly I found myself calming down. I leaned my head back against the wall and looked over and down at her beautiful face.

Her eyes sparkled in the soft light as she studied my face. "We'll get through it, Cade. Somehow. We have to."

"How do you know me so well?" My fingers threaded through hers.

"You're a part of me. I know you inside and out. Just like you know me. That's what we have to hang on to. It's *always* going to be *us*." I could hear the trembling in her voice as she said the words.

Brook. I closed my eyes in reverence as her name ran through my mind. Finally, I opened them again so I could look into her face. I'd never get enough of looking at her; I wanted to devour every line of her face and memorize every second of this night.

Her features were softened with love and something more. The long hair, darkened for the film, fell over her shoulder as she leaned into me and the sweet scent of her shampoo engulfed me. My heart ached and beat faster at the same time, as I tried to commit it all to memory.

"It isn't that. It isn't that I'm afraid I'll lose you, but I'm going to miss you so much. I don't know how I'll get through those months without you. I'm trying hard to push it away and not think about it, but... I can't bloody help it."

She squeezed my hand and I saw the tears well in her blue eyes, as she tried to blink them back. "I'll miss you, too. Every day. Probably more than I'll be able to stand, but distance isn't going to change how I feel about you." She swallowed and her chin jutted out as she fought with the emotions. "You told me once that you'd make sure to remind me how much you loved me, remember?" I nodded, before she continued, "I'll do the same for you. I promise."

She leaned against my shoulder and I leaned my cheek on the top of her head. We sat side by side, and I traced circles on top of her hand with my thumb. I wanted to leave, to be alone with her, to lose myself in her and erase the anguish I knew we both felt. I wanted to store up memories of holding her, making love and telling her how she made me feel... I wanted to spend every minute we had left, alone with her.

"Let's go soon, okay? I know it's only eleven, but your parents are dealing with jet lag and it's 5 A.M. to them." She read my mind again.

"Yeah. Okay." I stared into her face and snubbed out my cigarette on the slate of the patio. "I love you."

She smiled softly at me. "I know. Miracles *do* happen." I felt my lips quirk despite myself, as she repeated the words I'd spoken earlier that day in the makeup trailer. Just like me, she remembered the little things that were totally and utterly *us*.

***

BROOK CUDDLED CLOSE to me in the back of the limo as it drove us to our hotel. When we arrived, my parents and I got out at the front and she huddled down so fans and paparazzi wouldn't see her, then Peter took her back in through the garage, as had become our covert habit.

My parents were beat so I said goodnight to them and went to my room to wait for my girl. I took off the button-down I had over my T-Shirt, kicked my shoes off and turned down the lights; leaving only a small one on over the TV. TV was something Brook and I rarely did. We preferred to spend our time playing music, talking, or making love.

Mmmm... The thought of her naked skin against mine made my body tighten in anticipation. I ran my hands through my hair as I went to move the gift from Dawson and Ethan into the closet. *Ugh!* I would ask Denise to bring in some scissors so I could pop the damn thing and she could take it out in her bag and dispose of it. I smiled despite myself. It was bloody funny, but for Christ's sake, I had to get rid of it, and fast.

I pulled down the sheets on the newly made bed, stripped all of my clothes off, and climbed in to wait for Brook. I sat, leaning up against the headboard and listened for her. It wasn't long before I heard the door open and her footsteps padding toward the bedroom door.

"Hey, sexy," she murmured as she moved into the room. When she got to the bed, she crawled across it to kneel beside me. Her little hand came up to grasp my chin as her lips came down in a soft, slow kiss and her tongue gently slid into my mouth. I groaned as my arms snaked around her to pull her closer. She gave in to the kiss for a minute or two before pulling her mouth away from mine.

"Wait. Cade, I've got something for you. Just give me a minute." She placed another soft, sensual kiss on my mouth that left my body clamoring for hers then moved away from me toward my iPod dock on the desk across the room. She removed mine and put hers into it before turning it on. My eyes followed her movements as the soft music filled the room.

"Are you planning on seducing me for my birthday?" I murmured quietly as I watched her lift her shirt over her head. My eyes narrowed as I took in the black lace bra she wore underneath. It was delicate and beautiful, leaving the top half of her perfect breasts bare.

"No." Her eyes were locked with mine and her voice was low as she slid out of her shoes and stood at the end of the bed as she slowly unbuttoned and opened her jeans.

"No?" I asked as my eyes roamed up and down her body. My dick thickened and hardened as I watched her. I wanted her. I was hungry to touch her and taste her. "Brook..."

"No. I want to seduce you for the *rest of your life*," she whispered as she slid her jeans down her hips and off of her shapely legs. Her translucent skin glowed in the soft light and her eyes never left mine as she stepped out of them and kicked them off, revealing a matching black lace thong underneath. My heart quickened in my chest and my breath came in more shallow rhythm.

"Mmmm... You look good enough to eat. Come here," I whispered as I reached a hand out to her.

She was stunning; her curves perfect. Even though she was small, she was so womanly; her body called to the man inside me, which created strong feelings of protectiveness, selfishness, and filled me with possessiveness like I never felt before with anyone else.

She crawled toward me from the foot of the bed and I watched every move. She was so svelte and firm; my hands ached to touch her, my mouth watered at the thought of her kisses as she came to straddle my lap just above my knees, but she wasn't close enough to suit me. I wanted her closer.

She bent to ghost her lips over mine, licking my top lip before my need overwhelmed me and my hand moved to pull her closer and take her mouth in a passionate kiss. She tasted sweet, luscious like champagne and all Brook. She was completely intoxicating and I was drowning in her. I was losing myself, but more than willing to do so.

My hands moved to her bare ass cheeks to pull her closer, pressing her heat to my hardness. Everywhere I touched her she was on fire, her skin burning mine. "Jesus, Brook, you're so beautiful," I groaned against her mouth as her arms wound around my shoulders, and then one hand fisted in my hair as she pulled my mouth closer to hers. Her breath fanned out on my face in a hot rush before my mouth crushed down on hers, demanding she open to my tongue. She moaned, giving me what I wanted. Always giving me what I wanted; what I needed.

My hands roamed her body, over the little lace strips across the top of her bum and her back as I kissed her again and again. Her hips moved against mine as she ground her softness against my length, eliciting a similar response from me. She was so hot, so wet against me; I worried I'd come before I even entered her; I was so excited. I'd been dreaming of this every second of the day, and her outrageous flirting earlier had wound me tighter than a drum.

My hand released the clasp on her bra and then slid it from her shoulders. I brought one hand up around her breast before dipping my head to take an already erect nipple into my mouth, her gasps as I laved and flicked the nipple driving me mad with desire.

Her head fell back, and she gasped. "God, Cade."

"I love it when you say my name; when I know it's me who drives you to this."

"Feel how my body reacts to yours." She moved against me again and I could feel the slippery wetness as she ground her body into mine. "That's what you do to me. I want you... so much, Cade."

My dick was throbbing, begging for release as I moved the small strip of lace between her legs aside and slid my hand inside. "Oh God, Brook... Jesus," I gasped against her neck as my fingers sank into her softness. I was so hard I felt I would burst. I searched for the little nub that I knew longed for my touch and found it, moving my thumb in gentle circles.

Her head had been buried against my neck and shoulder and suddenly it snapped up so that she could look in my eyes. I knew my eyes were hungry, burning into hers as I took in her expression, the pleasure I was bringing through my touch, her hair wild, her mouth swollen and her eyes so soft with love. It was my undoing.

"I have to have you, babe. Now."

She held my gaze as her hand slid down my chest, across my stomach, and finally her fingers closed around my erection, gently squeezing and pulling. If felt so amazing, I was so turned on, it wasn't going to take much to make me come.

"Cade, you're so gorgeous. I never want to stop looking at you," she said softly. "I never want you to stop touching me, your hands on my body, you inside me, filling me…"

I pulled my hand from her and brought my fingers to my lips as I sucked and licked her wetness from them. "Mmmmm…" I moaned, as I tasted her on my tongue. Her mouth opened and her teeth came out to bite her lip. She was so sexy, I couldn't stand it and I moved my finger to pull her lip from her teeth and then bent my mouth to hers as she moved over me, lifting up to sink around me, clenching around me, drawing me deep into her body. It was heaven on earth.

"Oh, my love… Brook, fuck, I need you." Her hips moved and rocked against me, her muscles squeezing and milking around me as I grasped the back of her head with one hand, bringing her mouth back to mine for a barrage of deep, sucking kisses. Jesus, her body was sucking on my dick at the same time our mouths were sucking on each other and I felt my body start to tighten; the building beginning and I knew I wouldn't be able to stop it.

I moved my other hand back down between us to start the rubbing again, and she gasped.

"Uh, yes, Cade… that feels amazing. You feel so good inside me." The movements of her body increased; her thrusting over me coming faster as she started to come. I held on until I was sure that she was at the point of no return before I let myself fall into my own climax, thrusting faster as I spilled into her body.

"You're mine, Brook... mine," I groaned into her mouth as the twitching of my body subsided. Brook trembled in my arms and her head fell to my shoulder. She kissed and bit at the skin and my arms tightened around her, our breathing heavy as we struggled to come down. I continued to move against her wanting to get every last sensation out of her, bring her the most pleasure I could.

"I love you so much," she whispered against the side of my neck before kissing my jaw and then my lips.

"You better. You just better," I said breathlessly without loosening my hold around her. I didn't want to let go, didn't want to pull out of her as emotion welled in my chest.

"Brook, there are no words... I can't tell you how much I love you. It could never fully explain how I feel." My arms finally moved over her body, up and down her arms, when my fingers came across something around her left forearm, just below her elbow.

I pulled back and brushed the sweat-dampened hair off of her face. I moved us both so that we were lying together side by side, and I pulled her to me. Her head settled to the curve of my shoulder and she snuggled into me, her arm coming around me as my fingers brushed up and down her body.

The soft strains of a piano introduction filled the air around us. I'd heard it before and the lyrics were powerful and fit the moment; we didn't talk as the song played; no words were needed between us as the singer spoke of deep need, separation and loss. My heart fell and swelled at the same time. I let myself get lost in Brook's body, the song and my emotions. It was overwhelming, painful and amazing. The love we felt covering over us like a blanket, the sadness at the impending months apart. I felt sated, content, yet full of loss and longing. My throat constricted as the words of the song sank into my conscious brain. Brook's arm slid up my chest and around my neck, her hands clenching against me and her face turned into my skin. Our lovemaking was slow and steady, deep and intense, but still sweat began to coat my skin in a light sheen.

Her hand reached for mine, and our fingers threaded together and tightened. I felt my chest constrict and my throat ache. It was evident that we were both dreading the coming months, the weight of it sucking the very life from both of us. I felt Brook's tears fall onto my skin and my throat tightened even more. Neither of us spoke, we just let the song speak for us, the lyrics falling around us, every word such a perfect echo of our feelings.

I could feel her shoulders shaking against me and I fought back the emotion threatening to make my own tears fall. Her free hand moved, and pulled the thing around her forearm down. When I tried to unthread my hand from hers so I could move to see what she was doing, hers tightened around mine in an unspoken request for me not to let go.

She moved the object over our entwined hands and onto my wrist, before turning into my chest and giving into her tears. My free hand moved around her small body to my wrist to investigate the thing she'd placed there. It was a metal mesh band with a solid metal cylinder that slid around on it. The metal still held the warmth from her skin. I knew there must be great meaning to it, similar to the one I'd given her on her birthday, but there would be time to see it more closely later. The fact that she'd pulled it from her arm onto my wrist over our combined hands left me breathless. It was a simple act, but it meant so much.

My hand tightened on hers and the other came to her face and I slid a finger under her chin to lift her mouth to mine, I finally found my voice. It hurt to speak, but she needed to hear the words.

"Brook... I'm always going to love you this much or more. Do you understand me? I need to know you understand. I'll never make it through this if I'm not sure you know how much you mean to me. I literally can't live without you, and I wouldn't want to," I breathed against her mouth.

"I do. I know, Cade, and you're my whole life too. I love you more than anything."

We fell into a desperate kiss that communicated everything that words couldn't come close to describing.

Chapter 4
We Cannes Do This

Brooklyn

TWO WEEKS LEFT.

Two weeks until Cade would be in New York for the summer. My whole body felt sick at the thought. Time was going much faster than I wanted it to, and it seemed the more we enjoyed it, the faster it flew. It was a cruel consequence of being happy. How ironic.

The past two days since Cade's birthday party had passed in a super-fast blur. Lillian and Carter's visit had been so good for Cade. He adored both of his parents, and they worshiped him. It made me feel great they were so warm and welcoming. Carter was funny, like Cade, and Lillian was very easy to talk with. I could see her and I becoming very close to each other as time passed.

They came to the set again while we filmed the big fight scene but were asked to leave set for one of the most intense love scenes of the entire series. Those had been some tough scenes that left me emotionally wiped out. Lillian even cried from the sidelines during the fight, which was good, because it indicated it felt real. I thanked

God again for Martin's sensitivity when filming the more intimate scenes between Cade and I. This film was going to be even better than the first one.

The remainder of our time in Vancouver would be spent with Martin; Jeff and myself working on any retakes needed and the second unit director was working on some of the scenes focusing on Cade's character.

Wendy flew back to L.A. yesterday. Jennifer and I were flying to Italy early next week and Cade, Martin, and Dawson were meeting us there for the Italian Film Festival. We were done.

Done. My heart dropped in my chest.

It hadn't been easy for me when Cade left earlier this morning. He was jetting off with his parents and Denise, the four of them taking the same plane to New York and then splitting up. Lillian and Carter would be heading to London and Cade was going with Denise to Cannes.

I let myself think back to our time alone together after Cade's birthday party. It had been so incredible. Painful in part, but incredible.

The song playing on the iPod made it the perfect moment for me to slide the bracelet onto his wrist from mine, and he knew exactly what I was trying to say with the gesture. He held me as I cried and then made slow, tender love to me again. In the morning, he'd seen the bracelet and read the engraving; it was so special. He was so beautiful, his features soft as he looked at it. I'd never get used to how incredibly beautiful he was and how utterly overwhelmed I felt by my love for him.

I had the infinity symbol engraved on the front, echoing the gift he'd given me for my birthday. I wanted to connect him to me the way he had connected to me.

"Brook... this is perfect. Thank you," he'd said softly as he moved to cup my face with his hand and bent to place a soft kiss on my mouth. "I love it."

I crawled onto his lap after the kiss and my fingers ran over the metal cylinder on his wrist. I snuggled in closer and his arm tightened around my back and the one with the bracelet on it began to rub the top of my thigh.

"I'm going to miss you so much. I'm trying to be strong and tough about this, but I'm afraid I'm not doing a very good job. I'm sorry."

He kissed the side of my temple. "Brook, there is nothing to be sorry about. I'm a bloody wreck myself."

I lifted his hand and turned the cylinder over. "There's more," I continued softly.

His blue eyes met mine before moving so he could read the words engraved underneath.

C- I can see forever when I look into your heart. I love you, -B

His arms tightened around me and he buried his face in my hair.

"Oh, babe. You *are* my forever, Brook. I love you longer than that," he whispered into my neck, kissing it and then dragging his mouth in a trail of kisses to my mouth where it ended in a deep soul wrenching kiss. His tongue and mine encircled each other and our mouths were sucking and lifting, coming back for more again and again.

"I know you won't be able to wear it very much, but maybe someday..." I said quietly after his lips finally lifted from mine.

"Do you want me to wear it anyway? I don't give a fuck about the paparazzi, you know that."

I thought about it for a minute. "No, I want it to be between us.

I don't want speculation about it right now. Maybe something else, though. Something that says *up yours* to Pinnacle for not letting me go to Cannes with you? The bracelet wouldn't be able to do that anyway, since it has nothing to do with the films." I smiled up at him, trying to lighten the mood.

His hand was holding mine, his thumb rubbing over the engagement ring I wore on my finger as Julia. I had a habit of leaving it on. It seemed easier than remembering to keep putting it on and I didn't want to risk losing my real one by taking it off and on.

"What about this?" He lifted my hand and nodded toward the ring? "Would that be ostentatious enough for you, sweet?" He flashed me the crooked grin that always made my knees go weak.

"Do you mean you'd wear it? Babe, it won't fit these huge hands of yours, not even the pinkie," I teased as I kissed one of them.

"No, I know, but maybe there's another way. I could wear it around my neck on some sort of chain or something."

"Eh... chain? That's just nasty," I teased and wrinkled my nose. "No, how about a cord of some sort?

"Yeah, whatever. We'll figure it out," he said as his fingers brushed my cheek and he brought his mouth back to mine. The morning ended with another marathon make-out session before meeting his parents for brunch.

Yesterday we ended up asking Cade's production assistant to get a few of the necklace assortment they'd brought in for props on the film, for some of the college students. We picked the most functional one that was a black rawhide cord with a shark tooth on it. I objected to it, thinking that it wasn't really his style, but Cade just shook his head and took it.

"Brook, the necklace isn't the point we're trying to make, so what does it matter?" He yanked the tooth off and tossed it unceremoniously toward the trash can under the desk in the hotel room. It hit the mark with a hollow clank, and then Cade was sliding Julia's ring onto it and tying it around his neck.

He was right. So now my ring was on its way to Cannes, with Cade, and Julia's R & J bracelet was firmly in place on my wrist; both pieces from the film and so a subtle hint to the die-hard fans we were together without setting off Pinnacle's watch dogs.

I let out a big sigh as I remembered the past few days that had become a series of work, having meals with Lillian and Carter and then making love for long hours every night. Both of us were trying to store up the closeness for the lonely months ahead. Not sleeping much left us both exhausted, but the moments in his arms were worth it.

I felt the now familiar aching in my heart begin again and tried to swallow back the pain. I was going to get my hair done and then spend the day shopping with Jennifer and Noah: something I wasn't particularly enthused about; not because I didn't want to spend time with them, but because I couldn't shake the sadness. Maybe this would help. Jennifer insisted it was better than moping around my room all day long.

I went into the bathroom and looked at myself in the mirror.

What a mess.

My face was swollen from all of the tears, and there were bags under my eyes from lack of sleep. The tears I did manage to hide from Cade, not giving into them until after he'd gone. It killed me because I could hear his voice crack and feel his pain in the way he held me as he told me goodbye. I knew my crying would make it even worse for him, and I'd shed enough tears over the past week as it was.

I turned on the shower and started to peel off the T-Shirt and sweats I was wearing when my phone vibrated on the nightstand. I ran to get it, and found a message from Cade.

Mum and Dad have just gone, and Denise and I are boarded for Frankfurt, where we make our connection to France. I'll call you when I land. You're always with me, love.

Caden

I CLOSED MY EYES and waited for Brook's response. Denise glanced at me and laid a hand on my arm.

"Aren't you excited? You'll be the biggest attraction at Cannes," she said softly.

Bloody Hell. Who said so?

"Who cares and who wants it, anyway? I hate it. It's completely ridiculous. I feel like a moron on parade." I was exhausted. Brook and I hadn't gotten much sleep lately and then the time difference, once we got to Cannes, was going to kill me.

"I know it's hard Cade, but this is the price of fame."

"The price might be too high. This level of fame was never what I wanted. I just want to make films. It's gotten way out of control," I scoffed as I settled into my seat and looked anxiously at my phone. "It all gives me a bloody headache."

"Waiting for a message from Brook?" Denise asked, knowingly.

I nodded. "She must be in the shower or something or she would have responded by now. I have to turn the phone off soon and then I won't be able to contact her for eight hours." When I said the words, I realized how pathetic I must have sounded and sighed.

Yes. Okay? I miss the fucking shit out of her and I've barely left her.

I swallowed hard at the thought of the coming madness at Cannes and then the brief time we had left together in Italy. Denise squeezed my arm where her hand rested.

"Jeanne and I are trying to work with the studios to get some of your schedule rearranged. As it stands, you two only have one weekend off together around the Fourth of July. Did you know that?" Her voice took on an edge whenever she was angry.

"Yeah. I've been trying to keep it from Brook and hoping to hell that something can be done about it before then. Damn them. I guess there's more than one way to keep us apart."

My phone pinged in my hand and I had the message open before the tone was even done playing.

I miss you every second you're not with me, but try to have fun... just not TOO MUCH! LOL

I smiled when I read the message. "Hmmph!"

Denise smiled when she saw the look on my face. "She's handling it better than you, huh?"

"Something like that, yeah. She's amazing."

OK, my love. You, too, but don't be kissing any frogs while I'm gone.

I knew she'd be laughing when she got the message.

***

AFTER WE LANDED, we attended a party on someone's yacht, and I didn't even remember who it belonged to or what the party was even for. It was an endless stream of introductions, women fawning and asking me questions about my films and too much alcohol, but what the hell? My full glass had been the most comforting part of the evening.

In the back of my mind, I was sure there would be paparazzi telling the wrong story, pushing photos and trying to make it seem like I was out and completely single. To the world I was, but in my heart, I couldn't have been less available.

It was eight hours earlier in Los Angeles, so I called Brook when I got back to my hotel suite. I was over-tired, slightly drunk, and I missed her.

"Hey." Her voice was low and sexy, at least to my alcohol infused brain. "How's Cannes?"

"Lonely. I miss you, Brook."

"Um... you sound a little..."

"Inebriated? Yeah, I am," I laughed.

"I saw some pictures online of you tonight. You looked hot, babe."

"*You're* hot. I wish you were here with me," I sighed into the phone and pictured her lying in her bed, all warm and soft. *Mmmm...*

She laughed softly into the phone and the sound did strange things to my body. "Maybe I'll have to get you drunk more often, you're awfully cute."

"What did you do today?"

"Well, it's been raining, so Martin had us do some retakes on the office set... " Her words dropped off as I pictured her working with Noah. "And, um... I had to tell Martin I lost Julia's ring. Props had a back-up, so it was fine."

"Did Noah behave himself?" I was aware he was trying to spend more time with her off set while I was away and my guard was up.

She sighed. "Yes. He's been sweet."

"That's not what I asked." I rubbed my hand over my eyes. I was lying on the bed with my head hanging off of the foot of it and my neck was starting to hurt.

"Hey, you're the one getting mobbed with legions of women. I'd relax about Noah if I were you."

"I know. I just miss you, love. And I'm a little jealous that he gets to be near you when I don't." I moved up off of the bed and over to my laptop and turned it on.

"It's only a couple more days. At least, that's what I keep telling myself. And he doesn't get to *be near* me. Not like you are." Her voice dropped and I heard the rustling of the blankets that must be wrapped around her body. "I miss your body, your hands, your mouth... ugh..."

"Oh God, Brook." My body reacted to her words and the tone in her voice. "Are you trying to kill me?" My voice ached along with my dick as it grew and strained in my pants.

"I'll make it up to you in Italy."

"You promise?" I knew I sounded like a pathetic baby, but that's how I felt.

"Like I'll be able to help myself, Cade! Come on!" I heard her breath leave her body in a rush and more rustling of the blankets. "I miss you."

I pulled up iTunes and searched for a song to send her.

"Me, too, honey. Jesus." I ran my hand through my hair as I tried to control my breathing. "It's early for you to be in bed, yeah?" I asked as I found the song I wanted. "I'm sending you something on email, sweetheart. Can you go get it?"

"Mmmm... yes, I guess, but I'd rather lay here and pretend I'm kissing you..."

My heart stopped at her words considering the song I'd just sent, but I heard her move to her computer and call up her email.

"I sent you a song. Listen to it and think of me, Brook, ok? I'm going to listen before I try to sleep, too."

"Cade, it's 4 AM there, isn't it? You need to go to bed," she admonished.

"I will, but after the song is done. Brook... is it still raining?"

"Yes. I've been listening to it pound on the windows," the dulcet tone of her voice was like music to my ears.

"I'll be thinking of you. I love you so much and I'll call you tomorrow, okay? You can tell me how you liked the song," I said softly.

"I will. I'm sure it will be perfect. Everything you do is perfect, isn't it?" Her words left me speechless and I closed my eyes. "Bye, sweet boy."

"Bye, love." I was reluctant to let go of the sound of her voice as the phone went dead.

I shed my clothes and put my earbuds in my ears and cranked the volume as I crawled into bed alone.

Brooklyn

AS I HUNG UP THE phone, I was already missing the velvet voice that had become the most important sound in my world, but I smiled as I opened my email.

B-

I wish I could kiss you right now... But since I can't, Kiss the Rain. Listen to the song and go outside and kiss the rain, Brook. It's me kissing you. I can taste you and I love you so much. Counting the minutes until we're together again.

-C

I downloaded the song of the same title to my iPod and then threw on my clothes and Vans. I looked out into the hall to see if anyone was there, before making a mad dash for the stairs. I climbed to the top floor pool deck and pushed open the doors so I could rush out into the rain. My heart was pounding as I pressed play on the song and turned up the volume.

The music pulsed in my ears, followed by single piano notes... and then the lyrics began. It fit our separation perfectly and the fact that he found a song referencing rain when it was pouring in Vancouver was so typical of him.

"Whenever you need me, Kiss the rain..." The chorus played as the rain fell softly around me, soaking through my hoodie and jeans, but I didn't care. I listened to the words of the song and smiled as I lifted my face to the wetness, and laughed happily as the drops ran down my face.

When the song ended, I played it again and again, before finally making my way back down to my suite. My heart was full and I was completely soaked to the skin, but I was smiling. I'd memorized the lyrics and the artist's name. Billie Meyers. I'd never heard of him, but now I'd be looking up every song he'd ever recorded.

Could Cade get any more fucking perfect? I sighed heavily and pushed the door to my suite open, going into the dark room alone.

I stripped off my sodden clothes and started the shower as I shivered in the bathroom. I stepped inside and the warm water replaced the cold rain. I felt content knowing that when Cade and I were separated over the summer, we'd be okay. We'd still be *us,* despite the distance.

I knew what I had to do to make sure we did. If I could just make it through the goodbye next week without completely losing it, that would be a start.

No chance in hell of that happening. I scoffed at myself.

We could make it through it, but it was still going to rip both of our hearts out. I knew it... and Cade did, too.

Caden

I MADE IT THROUGH the photo calls and the interviews the day before. It seemed like they were endless, taking literally hours. The photographers all screaming and the fans lined up to see me do, I didn't know *what*? Stand on the pier, or talking to a reporter for an interview? I didn't understand the fascination that they found in it; to me it was bloody ridiculous.

Thank God Denise was with me and I had the band of bodyguards to ward off the hoards of fans.

It was my last night in France; I was on my way to another premiere with Denise. I didn't even want to be there, but the film was getting a lot of hype and Denise said she wouldn't be doing her job as my agent if she didn't get me in front of this director, but I was preoccupied and I didn't even recall who it was. More bloody photo calls were sure to ensue, but I knew Brook would be watching for them. I smiled as

I remembered how she said I looked so gorgeous at the Academy Awards; she liked seeing me in a tux. My heart sped up a little at the mere thought of her. The world could think I was Adonis and I didn't give a rat's ass, but Brook saying I was handsome meant everything to me, and put a silly grin on my face.

She was the beautiful one; so insanely beautiful.

We were texting most of the day and Denise had to remind me that it didn't look good for me to always be looking at my phone, especially in pictures that were constantly being taken.

I didn't bloody care.

These situations drove me bonkers, and Brook's presence, even if only on my phone via text messages, helped me to get through it.

I realized that the mobs and fans weren't going away in the near or distant future. Even if I decided to stop acting, it wouldn't go away, and no amount of worrying or whining would change anything. I might as well make the best of this bloody mess.

Hundreds of fans and photographers waited for me as I stepped out of the limousine onto the red carpet, followed closely behind by Denise. She moved to the side as they all started shouting and screaming and what seemed like a million cameras never ceased their flashing. Screaming my name, various magazines, televisions shows and freelance photographers had me turn this way and that as the cameras clicking began to explode around me. I felt like a bloody puppet.

Christ, I hate this shit.

I was going blind by the lights on the cameras, and it was harder and harder not to squint in the face of it all, so again, even though the sun was down, I pushed on my sunglasses.

The movie was amusing and I tried hard to focus on the plot, so I wouldn't make an ass of myself later when Denise paraded me in front of the director. I found him to be an interesting person and I enjoyed talking to him.

They basically herded us into an after party and on the way, I checked my phone to see if Brook had called or texted. Denise nudged my arm, but I smirked at her.

"Okay, last time, I promise."

You looked amazing, my love. Remember, you're mine.

A big grin split out across my face as I quickly texted her back.

No need to remind me. You know where my heart is.

We had assigned seating for the dinner at the after party, and by some coincidence, Patrick Armstrong, his girlfriend, Brianna Denfeld, and a couple of his friends were placed with Denise and me. Patrick would be directing Brook in a new romantic comedy and he was sure to pick my brain about her.

I was seated across from Patrick and Brianna, Denise was on my right and a woman by the name of Erika something or other on my left. I ordered a Crown Royal and lit a cigarette as I assessed Patrick from across the table. He had his hair slicked back and looked completely different to how I'd seen him in the past. He had a flick he was promoting that would be coming out a month or so ahead of *Don't Forget to Remember Me*, and we spent several minutes talking about that before the conversation came around to Brook.

"So Cade, how'd you like working with Brook Halloway?" he asked over his glass of wine.

"Oh, I liked it," I said with a careful smile. "She's great."

"Yes, isn't she? I find her very intriguing. She's quite intelligent, inquisitive and very beautiful. I really enjoyed talking with her before her audition. She seems very dedicated."

My eyes narrowed involuntarily as I looked at him talk about my baby. "Um, yes, I agree. I think anyone who gets the opportunity to work with her will be extremely lucky. She and I are, uh... well, we've become very close through all of this madness." Denise kicked my leg, so apparently she thought I was about to spill more details than would be appropriate.

"You know, I recommended her to Martin Deering for this series; he's is a close personal friend of mine. I'd seen a screen test she did for a TV movie and though she didn't get cast, I could tell she was going to be very sought after. I was glad to hear he gave her the role. She should send me a diamond or something," he laughed and the women all joined him, but Denise looked at me nervously.

"I'll let her know when I see her in Italy in a few days."

I was concentrating on him, but somewhere in my subconscious, I was aware of Erika leaning in toward me to try to get my attention. I was polite and gracious to the woman, but I was more interested in what Patrick was saying about Brook.

"Oh, you're going to Italy? I love Italy," Erika interjected to get my attention. I looked at her for the first time that evening. She was blonde, pretty, but nothing to turn my head, even if I wasn't in love with Brook. "Especially Florence."

I ordered another drink and lit another cigarette as I turned my head toward her. "Yes, we're attending the Italian Film Festival. I'm meeting Brook and some of the other cast there when I leave France tomorrow."

At that moment, one of her friends asked that I lean into her so that they could get a picture. Erika scooted her chair closer and the woman with the camera asked me to put my arm around her. I put my arm around her chair and she took the photo. Right when I did it, I realized the mistake I'd made. Instantly moving my chair away and leaned in to whisper to Denise.

"Fuck, what did I just do? Can we get that photo back?"

"I don't see how, Cade. It's not a big deal. You didn't have your tongue down her throat. Pinnacle will be happy to have public attention diverted from you and Brook, and it was innocent."

I ran my hand through my hair a couple of times, leaned back in my chair and downed my drink.

"We don't even know this girl; who is she? And will she make more of it than there is? Nothing is ever bloody innocent with these damned paparazzi!"

Denise shrugged and shook her head. "Now isn't a good time to discuss it."

"Cade, do you want to go somewhere else? I'd love to talk to you some more," Erika said.

"Uh..."

Shit. How can I be nice about this? I wondered.

"Thank you for the offer, Erika, but, uh... I have an early flight tomorrow and I need to be rested. I'm going straight back to the hotel after this," I knew my tone was flat and disinterested.

"Well... I could... come with you? " The words sounded coy, but the invitation in her eyes was obvious.

I looked at Denise, my eyes widening slightly in annoyance.

"Thank you, really," I said again as I put out my hand to stop her words, "but I must be going now." Her expression hardened and she was clearly put off.

Thank God Denise had called the car minutes before. I couldn't get out of there fast enough as I felt the heat start to flush my face. I said goodbye to Patrick, who rose and shook my hand.

"I'm sorry you feel the need to run off, Cade. It was good to meet you. Tell my little Brooksy I look forward to working with her."

I stiffened at his words and glanced at his girlfriend who had a strained look on her face.

"I will. It was very nice to meet you as well, all of you. Goodnight Erika, Brianna. Enjoy the remainder of your evening."

I put my hand behind Denise's back to turn her from the table and she preceded me to the door.

In the limo back to the hotel, I worried about that damned photo, and not because the world would speculate that I was banging some nameless woman in Cannes, but because I didn't need for Brook to be put through any stress, wondering...

"She'll be fine, Cade. Wipe that goofy look off of your face. She'll handle this shit better than you will. Trust me." Denise rolled her eyes.

"I hope you're right."

"I'm right. You just tell her the truth... *before* she sees that picture. Got it?"

I sighed and stared out the window as we made our way through the streets of Antibes.

Fuck, I can't wait to get on that bloody plane tomorrow, to see my baby girl the day after... but I'd be bloody damned if I'd ever call her Brooksy.

Chapter 5
Ciao, Julia!

Brooklyn

THE WEEK WENT BY relatively fast. I missed Cade, but we kept in touch with texts and talked on the phone a couple of times a day. I kept busy with the reshoots and hanging out with Noah and Jennifer.

I still had one day of shooting left before Jennifer and I were headed to meet up with Cade in Italy. I sighed and ran my hand through my hair. These would be the last five days I'd see him every day, sleeping with him at night, holding him, touching him... breathing him in. I was acutely aware of the time ticking away like a bomb about to explode.

I was overly emotional. I knew it and made the decision I needed to get myself in control. I was excited because I was going to see Cade in twenty-four hours, yet, sad that he would leave soon. I had a long talk with my mother the night before on the phone, and she had centered me a little, insisting that Cade and I would be just fine. I knew it wouldn't be easy being away from him, but we both needed to decompress and I needed to start compiling a body of work that would set me up for success as I moved beyond this series.

I'd spent the rest of the evening packing up my things, surfing the Internet and looking at pictures of my man. I'd seen hundreds of them, but I could look at them forever. It was like an addiction; he was so damn beautiful, each and every feature perfect on its own, but when you combined them, it was enough to make women swoon and men turn green with envy.

My heart beat faster, and my body reacted when I realized how lucky I was. I got to do what every woman in the world could only dream about. A secret smile played around my lips at the thought.

Cade and I spent many an hour looking at all of the videos of us posted on YouTube. It was utterly amazing how obvious our feelings had been, even back as far as our very first interview last year. Jesus, even I could see it in the way we looked at each other. I'd still been with David but how I felt for Cade had been painted on me like a scarlet letter.

Re-watching the interview, I could see how happy Cade was, laughing and teasing me. "Yeah, no, she's awful to work with. We don't really like each other!" he'd said as he shoved me, a little too hard, in the shoulder and I'd burst out laughing and slugged him hard in return.

It was so clear how close we'd always been and when I listened to our words, we *said* it again and again; both of us and not even realizing it.

I wanted the world to know he loved me, and that I loved him. Cade wanted us *out* even more than I did, but we were both worried about the fan reaction to a degree. Fuck the studio, but the fans mattered. From what we found online, it seemed like most of them wanted us to be together and to be happy. Sure, there were some crazies and haters, but they were few and far between.

I was ready for my flight, and had everything packed except the one outfit I would wear on the plane. Jennifer said she'd have the bellman bring my bags to her, and then she'd pick me up when my last scene was done. I was shoving my last pair of shoes into the front of my carry-on when my computer jingled to alert me to an incoming email.

When I sat down to see what it was, I was shocked and surprised. It had been more than a month since I'd heard from David, but here he was, sitting in my inbox.

I hesitated to open it, worried that he was just trying to stir up another shit storm, but I sighed and clicked on it.

> *Hey Brook,*
> *Thought you'd be interested to see the picture I've enclosed. It seems that while the cat's away, he gets to play. I don't want you to get hurt. I'm here if you need me.*
> *David*

Asshole.

Before I had time to download the picture, my phone began playing Cade's ringtone.

I smiled as I ran to get it.

"Hey, babe," I breathed into the phone.

"What are you doing, love?" His British accent oozed through the phone and made me weak in the knees.

"Just checking email before I pack my laptop. Almost time to fly!"

"Yeah, I'm excited. In fact, I'm already here. It's beautiful. You're going to love it, Brook."

"I saw the pics of you at the airport online this morning. I thought you weren't scheduled to leave France until about now?" I sat down on the bed and started to shove my feet into my sneakers.

"I didn't see any need to stay, and uh…"

I stiffened at his tone, and my mind flew back to David's email attachment. "What's going on, Cade?"

"Nothing, really. Last night at dinner, your new director, Patrick Armstrong introduced me to this woman who was seated at our table, and then someone snapped a photo of us. It was casual, but I didn't want you to get the wrong idea, sweetheart. That's why I left Cannes last night. I didn't want there to be any question in your mind, and I know how the bloody press always twists everything."

As he spoke, I moved to my computer and opened David's little gift.

Sure enough, it was Cade with his arm around some blonde woman. He didn't look that enthused and it was obvious she was the one leaning into him. He did have his arm around her, but nothing different than a million other times I'd seen him pose with fans.

My heart beat faster at his gesture of leaving Cannes early to ease my mind, but I couldn't resist playing with this a little. I smiled as I typed a reply to David.

> *David,*
> *Cade told me already… it's nothing, but thanks for trying*
> *to protect me.*
> *I trust him completely.*
> *~B*

I hit send and shut down the laptop and closed it, holding my phone to my head with my shoulder, as I packed it inside the case and zipped it closed.

"Yeah, I saw the new girlfriend. She's pretty. Getting started a little early, aren't you?" I tried to keep my tone even and serious.

"No, I'm not getting started on anything, Brook! Bloody hell, I knew this was going to happen. *Fuck!*"

"Maybe we can do a threesome. She's kinda hot." I couldn't keep the smile from my voice.

I heard his big intake of breath. "It wasn't anything, really. Denise was there the entire time and I was more interested in Patrick's lengthy commentary about you, *Brooksy*," Cade said, his tone turning acid as he emphasized my name.

I gasped, my eyebrows shooting up. Jesus, is this what I could expect on set with Patrick Armstrong? The nickname reduced me to the status of a little child, and it seemed Cade didn't have much more time for it than I did.

"Oh, *really*? What did he say?" I teased.

I could picture him, running his hand through his hair, stress painted across his face.

"That you intrigued him; that you were beautiful, talented and emotional. He seemed... *somewhat* respectful, I suppose," Cade said, tiredly.

"Pfffft! Cade, lighten up, hon. I know that pic is nothing. I've even seen it, okay? Thanks for telling me, though. I love you."

"Jesus. You scared the hell out of me, Brook," he said in a rush. "Are you stalking me online now? If so, I think I bloody like it," he was chuckling now, his demeanor clearly more relaxed. "But... um... how does that sod know you're emotional, Brook?"

"Ugh! Cade, who the fuck cares about Patrick Armstrong? I have no idea why he said that shit. He barely knows me. The audition? Who cares?"

"He took credit for you getting cast in *Remembrance* and said I should tell you to send him something in *undying* gratitude."

"Well, then did you thank him for all the yummies you've been getting? I mean, if the jackass thinks he's responsible then let him be responsible for something that actually *matters*."

"I love you, you know," he said, his tone dropping a couple of decibels. He sounded so sexy; I wanted to eat him through the phone.

"I know." A huge grin split across my face. "I'm sorry about playing around about the picture. I couldn't resist busting your balls a little." I chuckled softly into the phone.

He laughed out loud. "Like they *needed* busting. Wait... does this mean the threesome's *off*, then?"

We both giggled as I packed my laptop into my bag and moved toward the door so I could make my ride on time.

"Um... I think I can handle you *all* by myself, baby."

"Absolutely, without question. I can't wait to get my hands on you, sweetheart." His tone turned serious and my expression sobered. I was in the elevator on my way down to the lobby of the hotel where I was meeting Noah for the last time. "My hands, my mouth, my..." he groaned as he let the words drop.

"Yes, me, too. I miss you." I almost whispered as the elevator doors opened and I stepped out. Inside the hotel, several people glanced at me as I walked through the lobby, but didn't bother me. "But stop turning me on. I'm meeting Noah."

"Was he overly attentive while I was gone?" I loved the lilt in his voice when he teased me.

"Nope, just a little ankle biting," I said as I played along.

"Hmmmm, guess I may have to tell him to back off, yeah?"

"Whatever you want," I replied flippantly.

"I like the sound of that. I'm missing you so much. I hear the elevator, so do you need to go?"

"Reluctantly, yes. I'll call you from the airport tonight."

"Okay, my love. Counting the minutes." His velvet voice melted all around me.

"I'm counting *seconds,* then. Bye." I heard his sharp intake of breath at the other end of the line just before I ended the call.

***

JENNIFER AND I FLEW into Venice and were met with several bodyguards to escort us to the limousine that would take us the twenty miles or so north out of Venice, where Pinnacle had rented a small villa for all of us.

They hustled us through the throng and cameras were flashing, and people were yelling at me in Italian.

"Julia! Julia! Dov'è Ryan?"

"Brook, vi state frequentando? Siete innamorati"?

"Si fermi per una foto per favore! Brook una foto!"

"Posso avere un suo autografo?"

All I recognized out of that mess was "photo", "autograph", "Ryan and Cade", "Cade", "Cade!" And, "amore", which I knew was Italian for love.

If only we could be honest!

I smiled and waved, but the bodyguards had us by the arms and wouldn't let us stop to interact with fans. I looked at them apologetically as we moved quickly through the airport.

I saw the limo on the curb and followed Jennifer inside. She was taking off her sunglasses and smiling, running her hands through her hair.

"Wow, that was intense!" I was looking at her face as I climbed through the door and was instantly pulled back into someone's arms. Cade's scent enveloped me as the door closed, and he pulled me onto his lap. I gasped as he nuzzled into my cheek and jaw and hugged me tight.

"Hey," I said, burying my face in the curve of his neck and then turning up to kiss his jaw.

He felt so good as I breathed him in.

His strong arms tightened around me and his soft lips moved against my face as he spoke. His hair felt like silk under my hands when I slid them to the back of his head and the solid muscles of his thighs beneath mine reminded me of how they'd be entwined with mine later that evening. It all felt like heaven.

"Sorry, Jenn," he murmured as his mouth closed over mine. I melted into him completely as he kissed me like he'd never be able to again. My mouth opened to him and our tongues glided together, we sucked on each other's mouths again and again.

God, he tasted so good.

Finally, he dragged his mouth to mine and across my face to my neck where he sucked the skin into his mouth softly and moaned. "God, I missed you, Brook."

I glanced at Jennifer, who was smiling and looking out the window, trying to give us as much privacy as possible during our reunion.

"Mmmm. I missed you more," I whispered, as I snuggled into his neck and he placed a kiss on my temple. "What are you doing here? I wasn't expecting to see you until we got to the hotel."

"Look at her, would you? Here two minutes and already complaining!" he teased and Jennifer laughed. His arms tightened around me again. "I couldn't wait one more minute to see you."

"She practically chewed her fingers off on the plane! She was jumping around in her seat for the entire flight."

"That's not true. I even slept a little." I had the grace to flush. "I can't help it. I was so anxious to get here. Stop teasing me, both of you."

Cade just laughed. "Did you have a good flight?" His hand was threading through the back of my hair over and over as we traveled along the highway on our way out of Venice.

The city gave way to green rolling hills and lush landscapes as Cade and Jennifer made small talk about the film and some people we met on the plane. I was tired and snuggled into Cade's arms and closed my eyes; soaking him in. His fingers brushed my cheek and ran down my arm to hold my hand; our entwined fingers rested on my thigh for the entire hour we were in the limo. We couldn't stop touching each other.

Cade sighed and leaned his head against mine as I watched the countryside fly by the racing car.

"The flight was uneventful," Jennifer answered. "How was your time in Cannes, Cade?"

"Oh, you know... *maddening*. Hmmph!" He let his breath out and I could hear the smile in his voice even though I couldn't see his face.

We spent the remainder of the ride in silence, except for the random comment about the beautiful scenes outside the car. My skin burned where he touched me and I knew he felt it too. He shifted underneath me and I could feel his body's reaction to mine.

The air felt different in Italy, energized, exciting and I knew the next few days would be a huge rush of activity and a lot of special times for Cade and me.

The city of Venice was beautiful with ancient stone architecture among the famous waterways. The sun was starting to set and the lights placed among the buildings created a very romantic vision.

I stared out the window as we left the city behind until we would return for the festival in four days. "It's just gorgeous."

Cade nodded and rubbed my back. "Yes, actually, it's a collection of islands and is slowly sinking, sadly. The architecture and art here are rich in history. We need to get some time to see some of the sites. I've spoken with Martin already and he's agreed that we can explore a little. We'll have a read through of a couple of the first scenes from the next film tomorrow morning over breakfast and then we're free for the next few days."

I looked at him in wonder. "Together?" I asked hopefully.

"The whole cast. I can't touch you like I want to, but we'll at least be able to get out together." His smile held a hint of sadness.

"Well, I'm just happy we have this time! You're amazing for arranging it."

"What's the villa like?" Jennifer asked as she joined me in looking out the window.

"It's small and private, only a dozen or so rooms. There is a quaint little courtyard attached to one of them, and they have room service. It was built around two hundred years before the town rose around it, by a future Pope, I believe, but I can't remember his name."

We both looked at him in wonder. "How do you know all this stuff?" I asked in awe.

He shook his head and shrugged. "You'd be surprised what you can learn with a little free time waiting for your favorite person to arrive." He leaned in to whisper in my ear. "As promised, the studio has us staying in the same room this time, my love; though they probably had to bribe the staff to keep quiet. No phones will be allowed; so no photos."

His fingertips traced down my bare arm and I shivered. My breath hitched and I leaned my head on his shoulder. I reached for his hand and he laced his fingers through mine.

Jennifer shook her head at us. "Well, I guess I won't bother asking you two to join me for dinner!" she scoffed.

Cade smiled and answered in a quiet, but deliberate tone. "The others will be around tonight, and we... will see you for breakfast." We headed inside and went down an opposite hall away from Jennifer.

When the door to our room closed behind us, I was instantly in Cade's arms. He was lifting me up to bring my mouth level with his and then kissed me again and again. My hands held the sides of his face and one of them slid down to wrap around the back of his neck. Our mouths were wild on each other, as the five days we'd been apart melted away.

"Jesus, Brook... I can't stand being away from you. You're so beautiful, love." He quickly pinned me up against a wall and ground into me after my legs automatically wrapped around his waist. I could feel him, hard and hot, pressing into me, and I wanted him closer still. My hips surged against his of their own volition and he groaned into my mouth.

His chest was plastered up against mine as our bodies moved and rubbed together in our frantic attempt to get closer to each other. I wanted to rip his clothes from his body. I was that hungry for him, desperate to feel his skin against mine. His hand moved up to cup my breast, his thumb brushing across the nipple again and again, and I felt my body respond, opening, seeking his, heat and wetness pooling.

"Oh God... Cade," I gasped against his mouth. "Don't be gentle, just make love to me," I begged against his mouth.

He brought me down off of the wall to set me on my feet. His hands clutched at the bottom of my T-Shirt to move up my body from the sides of my waist, lifting the shirt over my head and then flinging it across the room. Cade fell to his knees in front of me and began to place a series of open-mouthed kisses on the skin of my chest, neck and shoulders.

It felt so amazing; I could barely move. His tongue left a wet trail from one lace covered breast to the other, his lips closing around and tugging on my left nipple. My head fell back as the sensation shot through my breast and down between my legs. I needed to touch him, so my hands wound in his glorious head of hair then his hands found the clasp in the lace at my back and he released it. The offending piece of clothing fell away, fluttering in a whisper to the floor.

I felt the soft scratch of his nails dragging down my back and the goose bumps that they caused made my nipples even harder, more erect. Cade groaned, as one grew under his tongue while he continued to lick and suckle. Heat was building deep inside me as his other hand made short work of the button and zipper of my jeans, exposing my bikini panties beneath.

He rested his forehead against my body below my breasts as he suddenly slowed down, his breathing coming in heavy rasping gasps. "Bloody Hell, Brook. I want you." His hands resumed their slow task of pushing my jeans and panties down my body as he continued to run butterfly kisses over my skin. I kicked off my shoes and stepped out of the clothes, standing before him completely naked.

He reached for me, his hands closing over my hips as his eyes burned over my body, and his thumbs rubbed back and forth over both of my hip bones, as he pulled me close. I was dying, on fire as his open mouth came back to kiss my stomach and lower over the curl covered mound. His breath was hot, rushing over me and eliciting even more responses from me. I couldn't deny him, even if I'd have wanted to. I wasn't thinking, only feeling.

I took one of his hands and pulled him up to stand in front of me. My fingers lifted to the front of his button-down and worked my way down as fast as I could. I pushed his shirt open and off his shoulders as I kissed his muscled chest. Cade pushed it impatiently down his arms to let it fall to the floor. My breath left in a hot rush over his skin as his hands wound in my hair, his thumbs going under my chin to tip my face up to his.

"Make love to me, Brook," he whispered against my lips before he claimed my mouth in a deep, soul wrenching kiss, our mouths moving together in perfect union. It was so beautiful, too perfect.

Without breaking the kiss, he bent, placing one arm beneath my knees, the other around my back, he lifted me as if I weighed nothing and carried me to the bed.

He laid me down without taking down the covers and stepped back to remove his pants and boxer briefs.

"Damn it," he said when he struggled to kick his shoes off at the same time as he kicked away the pile of material at his feet.

I laughed softly, as he came back and moved over me. He spread my legs wide with his as he settled into the cradle of my body, my arms coming around his shoulders to pull him closer and I arched up toward him. I felt his hard cock, soft and urgently pressing against my thigh. It did amazing things to my insides; I was full of want and I needed him inside me.

I put my lips to his ear and tugged the lobe between my teeth, pulling away until it popped from my lips. Cade gasped as I whispered against the curve of his jaw, "Cade, don't play, don't be gentle. Just fuck me. I'm ready, and I want you."

His eyes met mine as one hand moved to guide the head of his dick to my opening, feeling the wetness waiting for him there, he rubbed it up and down my core, teasing my clit until I gasped and begged for him to enter me.

"Cade, please... *please*." I pulled his mouth to mine as I felt him fill me to the hilt.

"Jesus, Brook. Oh God, you feel so good," he moaned as he started to move within me. Hard and fast; we matched each other's rhythm and he moved his hips in circles so that his pelvic bone ground onto my clit. It felt so incredible.

We were breathing hard and moaning each other's names over and over again. My heart thumped in my chest as he continued to kiss me as hard and fast as his body was pounding into mine.

"Yes, babe," I panted against his mouth as I felt my body start to clench around him, the sensations exploding within me and leaving my hips surging hard against his as I urged him to let go. "Cade, come on..."

The muscles of his back and ass were flexing under my hands as he continued to thrust into me, until finally, he tensed against me. "God, Brook. I love you," he moaned softly into my neck as he came hard inside me.

I kissed his sweat-dampened shoulder and then his temple as he jerked against me. "Oh, babe. I missed you so much, Cade."

The minute I said the words, I felt my eyes sting and my throat ache as once again the reality of our situation came back into focus. "I'm... *going* to miss you..." I began.

His face turned toward mine and he kissed me again. "Shh... Shhh, my love. I still have five days with you and every second is going to be glorious, I promise." His blue eyes were liquid as they burned into mine. "There will be plenty of time to cry later. Just love me right now. We're together, so let's concentrate on making memories and not dwell on the summer, okay?"

I blinked back the tears and nodded.

"That's my girl."

"Always," I whispered as his mouth found mine again.

Caden

OVER THE NEXT DAYS, we didn't talk about the coming separation. We went sightseeing with Jennifer, Dawson, and Martin, and then lounged around at local restaurants for dinner and nightlife before heading back to the villa.

The nights we spent alone together, talking, playing music and making love over and over again. We were soaking as much of each other up as we could.

I'd never got enough of Brook. I wanted to memorize every line of her body, how she tasted, her scent, the sound of my name on her lips, how her hair felt on my skin as we loved each other... everything.

I told her we should try to make these last days as joyous as possible and we were happy, but the cloud that hung over us was ever present. Just because we didn't talk about it didn't make it go away, and the pain I saw in her beautiful blue eyes at times when I caught her watching me, made my heart literally stop beating.

The last two days we were in Italy would be spent at the festival, making appearances and giving interviews. Like magic, Denise and Jeanne showed up to herd us around like cattle and make sure all of our ducks were in a row.

Brook and Jennifer, along with Dawson and I, rented two Ferrari F12berlinettas to drive around when we managed to get away. We tore over the streets and country roads between Venice and the villa. The cars were sweet. We had a black one, and Dawson was driving an atrocious yellow one. I didn't understand why anyone would ruin a car like this by painting it such a hideous color.

When I told Brook I liked it; she snorted playfully. "And I thought you were too talented and deep to care about material shit."

The next day our sightseeing plans were put on hold because Martin got a call from the second director on the film and there was a problem; editing lost an entire segment of one of our most important love scenes. To keep the film on schedule, it would mean a reshoot in a short amount of time and by some miracle, Martin managed to arrange a sound stage with an Italian production company and have a part of the bedroom set reconstructed. It wasn't perfect, but the scene was dark and the camera operators were told to avoid shots that showed room proportions too well. Martin would have to keep the shots tight, very close to our bodies and faces. Instead of being annoyed I was happy to have another day of shooting with Brook, and one that kept us close and intimate, though I would have preferred a different scene being lost because we nailed it the first time.

Brook was basically bare above the waist beneath a man's white button-down, except for flesh-colored panties. I was dressed in sweats and a T-Shirt, but she'd strip those off of me during the take.

She giggled and rolled her eyes as they started working on her makeup while I grabbed a water bottle and downed the contents. I watched them work on her, brushing her hair and dusting her face with powder. She sneezed as one of the brushes tickled her nose. My heart skipped a beat at how beautiful she was.

When she was finished, Martin called us over to go over the scene.

"Okay, guys, so first we're going to get the whole piano scene. We'll be filming from a lot of angles and we're starting from where you come out of the bathroom while Cade is playing the piano, just like in the previous takes, okay? Let's roll."

"Cade, we only have three days left until you leave. That's what I'm working off of in this scene," she whispered to me as she gently touched my stomach. My eyes met hers and I saw the pain there and I felt my heart squeeze. She was so smart. She knew that if we let ourselves feel the loss and desperation that we would face, we'd smoke this shot; maybe even better than the first time.

I swallowed hard as the feelings rushed over me. "Okay. I'm with you."

Her chin jutted out and she bit her lip as she moved to her mark offset and waited for Martin to cue the sound. I took my place at the piano and ran my fingers over the keys.

Martin held his hand in the air and spoke into his headset. He dropped his hand, and motioned for the cameras to roll. "Get ready. Action!" he said.

Brook came to sit next to me, her creamy thighs straddling the piano bench so she could face me, the tails of the shirt pooling between them. I let myself forget about Martin and the camera crew, and just melt into the scene; letting the love between us show. The love between these characters echoed our own, and I was so thankful they'd brought Brook into my life.

I played the song and she leaned against me, resting her head on my shoulder, her hand ghosting down my back and making goosebumps cover my skin and then said my lines.

"Do you remember anything about that song? Other than the lyrics?" I asked in a husky whisper, my lips still up against the top of her head. She smelled so enticing and my body stirred anew, but her nearness was something I had to have; as Ryan; as myself.

"Yes. I gave you that sheet music, right?" Her words were low and sensual and my body began to react for real.

"Uh huh. We've done this before. I play, you sing." I brought my arm up and around her, pulling her closer. "Are you okay?"

"No," she began. "I don't think I am." Her voice was weak and shaking. I wasn't sure if it was from sadness or desire.

"Julia, what can I do to make this easier?"

She shrugged but didn't raise her head and her hand reached out to slide down my thigh to the inside of my knee.

"Tonight, dancing...it felt so right to be in your arms, Cade. I want more."

With the speed of light, my arms swept around her and I pulled her onto my lap as my mouth slammed into hers. We kissed as if we were starving, both of us holding each other's heads as we kissed over and over again.

This was Brook, the love of my life, and I needed her, needed to convince her that I loved her and always would. The people around us vanished, the cameras all gone, as we lost ourselves in each other.

"Cut!" Martin said after a time, but we continued to kiss. "Uh... cut!!!" he admonished as he came and touched me on the shoulder.

I pulled my mouth from Brook's and we locked eyes. I let out my breath as she pulled her arms from around me and slid off my lap, running a hand through her hair.

"Uh, that was really great guys, but Brook, you called Cade's name, not Ryan's," Martin said with a smile and rubbed his chin. "And... the kisses can't have tongue, guys." He winked at Cade.

"No, I didn't," Brook said with an embarrassed laugh. "We... uh..."

"Yes you did, honey, but that's okay. I can edit the other takes."

I threw up my hands and grinned at Martin. "What? She likes it when I tongue her. I thought you wanted it to be realistic." I laughed softly, amused when Brook gasped.

Martin shook his head. "Keep it in your pants, Cade. Let's do it again. Places."

I started to run my hand through my hair but stopped when I came in contact with the stiff hair gel they'd used to plaster it in place. I felt my skin flush as I looked at Brook. She was trying hard not to smile as she rubbed the back of her neck and made her way back to her original mark for the next take.

Later that evening, Brook was in a bathtub full of bubbles lost in thought, when I knocked on the doorframe. She'd left the door open so she could hear the music playing from the bedroom. Our room in the villa was smaller than we were used to, but very nice and painted in soft tones of sandy yellow.

She didn't hear me come in and I watched her for a moment before I sat down beside the tub and took her hand in mine. She glanced at me and her eyes focused on me while I brought her fingers to my lips.

"Are you okay?"

My hand was still holding hers and she pulled it up to her mouth, kissed the top of it then laid her velvet cheek against it.

"Yeah," she said softly, her eyes soft as she looked at me, before she closed them.

"You seem so lost in thought. What are you thinking about?" I was almost afraid to ask, but I really needed to know.

"Nothing really." Brook shrugged slightly. "And everything, I guess."

My eyes ran over her features and her blonde hair piled on top of her head. Wet tendrils had escaped and were sticking to the side of her face and neck. I reached out to brush them back and then traced the line of her chin with my fingers.

"I'm sorry I called your name today. I feel so stupid."

"Don't be, love. I bloody loved it. It was brilliant." The corners of my mouth lifted in a slight smile as I watched her eyes open again. They were clear and bright and I wanted to drown in the blue depths. "It was us, and it's very difficult not to let that show now."

You're so beautiful, I thought.

"It is."

"I'll turn down the bed and then I'll come back in and get you when you're ready, babe. Okay?"

"Okay," she sighed and leaned her head back on the tub as she sank further down into the water. My chest tightened and my eyes began to sting as I walked back into the bedroom.

Jesus Christ! Just pull it together, Cade. You can fall apart in New York.

I turned down the bed, lowered the volume on the music and lit one small votive candle before turning off the lights. I went to the ice bucket and wrapped several ice cubes in a towel and set them on the bedside stand, and then stripped off my shirt and jeans, leaving only my boxer briefs on.

I was tired, the jet lag and the shooting schedule had exhausted me and I knew Brook was wiped too. I grabbed a couple of beers from the small refrigerator near the loo, set them on the bedside table and then went to help Brook from the tub.

Her eyes were closed and her breathing was deep and even. She had fallen asleep.

"Brook, my love, wake up. I have to get a towel around you then you can go back to sleep," I said as I kissed her forehead and slid my arms around and under her to lift her from the tub.

"Why are you so good to me?" she said sleepily, her lids still closed as her head fell onto my shoulder. I carried her into the other room and laid her on the bed and proceeded to dry her off as she lay back on the pillows.

"Because I love you more than life," I said simply. It was the truth.

"No... don't dry me off. It feels good to go to bed all wet."

"What?" I was astonished at the notion.

"Pull the covers up to my neck. The evaporation relaxes me and it steams up under the blankets. It feels nice. You should try it." I sat down on the side of the bed and leaned in to kiss her softly on the mouth.

"I would have rather looked at your sexy body, but uh, your wish is my command."

She lifted her drowsy eyelids and smiled. "Will you try it with me sometime?"

"Hmmph." I shook my head in disbelief. "Sure, love, of course."

She rolled onto her side and closed her eyes again. "You'll like it, I promise," she sighed as she drifted back to sleep. I lifted the covers and propped her ankle up on a pillow before holding the ice on it for a while. When it started to melt, Brook shivered and I took it off and threw it in the sink before stripping off my underwear and sliding into bed beside her.

My arm snaked around her body as the heat coming off of her radiated toward me. I pulled her close against me and spooned her body with mine, before kissing her shoulder and neck and letting sleep overtake me.

"Cade?" Somewhere in my sleep-drugged brain, I heard Brook call my name. "Cade!"

The candle was almost out but still casting flickering shadows throughout the room. I rubbed my eyes and looked at the clock. 3:12 AM.

Brook stirred beside me, but seemed to be fast asleep. I untangled my arm from under her head and sat up, grabbing the now warm beer from the nightstand and taking a long pull from it.

I stood up and went to use the bathroom and when I was finished, I heard Brook tossing in the bed. "Cade! Where are you?"

"Shh... Brook," I murmured softly as I crawled back under the covers. "I'm right here beside you."

Her hand reached out toward me and mine closed over it so I could pull her closer, but she gasped and then her eyes opened suddenly.

"Cade?"

"I'm right here, Brook. Did you have a bad dream?"

She turned toward me and reached out to touch my face. "Just that you were gone and I couldn't find you... that's all I remember."

I propped myself up on one elbow and looked down into her face. Her eyes were searching mine and her hand came out to trace patterns on my chest.

"I'll be back in a minute," she said tightly. She kissed my mouth lightly and turned from me to get out of the bed and pad into the bathroom. She closed the door almost all the way but didn't turn the light on. I could tell by the look that she'd had on her face that she was hurting.

I rolled onto my back and sighed, covering my face with my hands and then rubbing the stubble on my chin as I waited for her to come back.

"Brook? Are you okay?" I asked after a couple of minutes.

When she didn't answer, I pushed the covers back and moved toward the door of the bathroom and leaned in so I could hear beyond the door. I could hear her crying softly and I pushed the door open with my fingertips. The candle from the other room filled the bathroom with soft light and I saw her naked body, leaning over the counter, braced by both of her arms and her head dropped.

I walked up behind her and put my hands on her shoulders. She straightened; leaning into me. I slid my arms around the front of her body as I turned my face into the curve of her neck and started placing kisses on her neck and shoulders.

"I'm sor... sorry, Cade," she whispered brokenly as her arms covered mine around the front of her body. "I'm trying so hard not to be sad..."

"Shhh... I know, my love. We'll be okay."

I let my hands roam over her as I watched her in the mirror. She was so perfect, the candle light casting soft shadows over the swells and curves of her body, and I wanted to memorize how she looked and how she felt underneath my hands. Her head fell back against my shoulder, her mouth fell open and she gasped as one of my hands slid below her waist, and the other up to cup a breast and to ghost over a nipple; echoing the scene we'd shot that day.

"I'm going to miss you so much, Cade... oh God. Make love to me."

My dick had already hardened against her, and I couldn't resist pressing into her. I groaned against her shoulder. The emotional and physical bond between us was overwhelming.

"Brook..." Her hands reached behind her to move between our bodies and close around my erection. It felt amazing to have her hands on me, moving up and down, pulling, squeezing, driving me insane. My breath left my chest in a rush.

My hand parted the flesh between her legs seeking and finding the little bundle of nerves, I began to rub soft, gentle circles until she was gasping. My mouth moved up the side of her face, from her chin to her temple and I could taste the salt of her tears.

My heart was breaking, even as she set my body on fire.

The hand teasing her breast moved around to her back and up to her shoulder as she leaned forward, silently asking me to take her. I pulled my hand down her back and she shivered. I continued to stimulate her clit with one hand while the other held her hip to steady her as I pressed into her. She was so wet, and I entered her easily.

"Uh... Cade." Her face was so amazing as I watched her in the mirror. Her mouth was open and her eyes met mine as I thrust into her, slow and long. I pulled out almost all the way before pushing in to the hilt and as I did so, she clenched around me. I repeated the motion many times as I continued to watch the emotions flood her beautiful features. The love, the sensations she was causing around me, and watching her reaction was more than I could take.

"Jesus, Brook. I don't know if I can hold it. You're so sexy... seeing you like this, so beautiful, it drives me crazy. I want to see you come, Brook," I moaned into her neck as I pushed into her.

"I love you, Cade," she said softly as her body tensed and clenched around me. She bit her lip and closed her eyes before her head fell forward. "Oh, God."

I closed my eyes as well and finally spilled into her body. I wanted to brand this woman as mine, to mark her, to scream to the world that I loved her. My breathing labored, I fell against her, my forehead resting between her shoulder blades as we both struggled to breathe.

I pulled out of her and turned her in my arms, my hands sliding to her rib cage to lift her onto the vanity. I felt emotions overwhelm me and tears flood my eyes. I crushed her to me and her arms and legs enfolded me as we embraced like we'd never be able to let go.

My hand went to the back of her head as I slammed my mouth into hers frantically. We kissed as if we were starving, both of us crying into each other's mouths. When I finally pulled my mouth from hers, she buried her face in my neck and sobbed.

My heart would stop beating when I had to leave her in three days. I knew it as sure as the sun would come up in the morning.

Chapter 6

Best Kiss

Brooklyn

THE TIME IN ITALY with Cade had been bittersweet. We'd finished filming the bedroom scene yesterday in something like twenty-one takes, made more difficult by the set being imperfect and the need to adjust the camera angles. I smiled at the memory. There were worse things than kissing Cade for twenty-one takes. I smiled as I looked at him sitting next to me in the first class cabin of our Virgin Atlantic flight back to the States. He was asleep, finally. It was unusual that I ever had a chance to observe him sleeping. He looked like a little boy, his face so relaxed... but beautiful.

Always so beautiful.

We'd stayed up all night making love, and my body and heart warmed at the memory. These past few nights had been desperate and urgent. Both of us had been frantic to get closer, as if by doing so, we could avoid what was coming.

I sighed, and Cade stirred beside me, his hair falling over his right eye as he shifted in his seat. His hand held mine tightly underneath the blanket, and my thumb ran circles around the top of his. My eyes welled with tears and my vision blurred. So little time left...

Tonight was the MTV Awards and *The Future of Our Past* had been nominated in something like seven categories. No doubt Cade would win Best Actor since these were voted on by fans and there was no one more loved and adored than him. I was nominated for Best Actress as well, but I wasn't sure I'd win. I was sure that we'd win Best Kiss.

I turned toward Cade and pulled my legs up to curl up on the seat so I could get a better look at him. I studied his features in repose as he slept. He was so perfect he took my breath away and my gaze dropped to the mouth responsible for the best kisses of my life. I blinked back the tears and drew in a shaky breath. I would miss those kisses.

We talked about the Best Kiss moment if we won, and Cade wanted to go for it. Of course, he did. He wanted to let the world know that we were together and he didn't care what the repercussions would be. Denise and Jeanne would get angry calls if we went through with his plan, but he was willing to face the two of them as well. Pinnacle was still asking us to keep our relationship quiet because of the other two films and the fan girls who fantasized about Cade. It was a legitimate concern if I was honest with myself; even if it did annoy the shit out of me.

My biggest concern was that I didn't know if I'd be able to keep it to the chaste "on stage" kisses if I wasn't in Julia's head.

I blushed, remembering that it didn't matter two days ago when I'd called Cade's name and we French-kissed in front of God and everyone on the set. He was leaving 18 hours after the show ended, and I didn't know if I could repress those feelings, live TV or not. My throat tightened as I tried to push the pain down.

We were landing in Chicago and then had to change planes for the last leg of the trip to LAX. Jeanne hadn't been pleased that Cade and I had taken the same flight back, but the hell with it. We only had so much time together and it was too precious to waste. Jennifer came with us, so hopefully that would be enough to suppress any romance rumors. If my chest weren't aching, I would have laughed. How ridiculous it seemed.

Jeanne agreed only after insisting on sending separate cars for each of us from the airport. That suited me because I had to meet up with Nathan before going to the Beverly Hills Hotel where Cade had booked us a suite. He was feeling a little defiant in the face of the months we'd be apart and told me he had an entire evening planned for us. My heart was so full of him; I found it difficult not to scream out loud.

I'd asked Nathan to pick up a couple of new iPods so that I could create the new account that I wanted to share with Cade while he was away. I'd asked Nathan to set it up and gave him the list of the many songs that had come to mean so much to us over the past year. The one's he'd played for me, the one I sang to him in London, the one I'd sent to him before Tokyo and we'd made love to when we finally got back together after the Wendy fiasco.

It was funny. His new movie was called *Only Us*. It seemed ironic and poignant to our situation, except for the fact that it was a romance and it wouldn't be me with him in it. I brushed back a tear as the wheels touched down in Chicago, and sat up straighter in my seat.

"Cade..." I leaned over and rubbed his arm with my free hand. "Babe, we're in Chicago. Wake up." I shook him gently, he startled and his eyes opened.

"Hey. Sorry, I slept so long, love," he said quietly so no one would hear except me.

I shook my head. "Don't apologize, you needed it."

Reluctantly, I separated my hand from his and started to fold the blanket and Cade ran both hands through his hair. The flight attendant announced our arrival and went through the gate assignments for all of the connecting flights.

Jeanne had arranged for our security people to get special clearance so they could meet us and take us to our next plane without being mobbed. Sometimes it made me feel like a little kid and I hated it.

Cade hated it even more, but he was more eloquent dealing with it than I was. The fans could be intrusive to me, but they would literally chase him through the airport in mobs if not surrounded by bodyguards. There were always paparazzi lurking in some dark corner, waiting to get that *million dollar shot*. It made bile rise in my throat every time I was blinded by a camera flash that I wasn't expecting. We just wanted to be normal... like real people.

"I guess I did. You haven't had much sleep either, babe. Did you get a nap at all?" The beautiful smile that he normally wore was missing today and his eyes looked sad. I wanted to put my hand to his stubbly chin and kiss his mouth.

"A little." My smile echoed the sadness in his face as I shrugged. "It's going to be okay, Cade. You said so, remember?"

"Hmmph." He let his breath out as he unbuckled his seat belt. "If you say so, Brook."

He got up and opened the overhead compartment, taking down his mustard colored duffel and my carry-on before moving back so I could exit in front of him.

"Cade, you have to give me my bag. You can't carry it for me."

He reluctantly set the bag on his vacated seat so that I could pick it up. He waited for me to walk ahead of him and Jennifer was in front of me. We all prepared for the madness of the crowds. Cade flung the hood of his sweatshirt up and we all shoved the sunglasses in place as we walked down the ramp to the terminal.

Caden

I STAYED AWAKE during the last leg of the flight between Chicago and L.A. and spent most of it staring at Brook.

"Cade, stop," she finally said.

I reached out and took her hand between both of mine. "No," I said simply as my brow dropped over my eyes. "I won't."

"People will talk." She tried to pull her hand away from mine, but I wouldn't let her.

"I don't bloody care, Brook, okay? Let them." My stomach was in a twisted knot and I was praying for time to stop, but it just kept ticking away, second by second, each one dropping like a stone around us.

"You've been so quiet, do you want to talk?" I knew she was aching too, but she was doing her best to suck it up and make me feel better.

"I don't deserve you, Brook." The corner of my mouth lifted reluctantly.

She cocked her head to one side and leaned it back against the seat. "I think it's the other way around," she said softly. "Tell me about your plans for us tonight." She squeezed my hand, finally giving in to my wish to touch her despite who was watching.

"Nothing much. Just dinner and time alone together." My eyes rose to hers and searched her face, hoping to see something other than sadness behind the beautiful blue eyes.

"Dinner? How will that work? Are we bringing someone with us?"

"Uh... not part of the plan, baby, no."

She sighed and smiled softly.

"Thank you." My heart thumped in my chest. No matter how many times she told me, how much I felt it when she touched me, I would never understand or get used to the fact that she was finally and completely mine. "I love you."

I pulled her hand to my lips and brushed my mouth across her knuckles.

"There are no words, Brook. I can't put it into words. A year later... I'm just... bloody *speechless*." My voice dropped and thickened and finally, she reached out to touch my face and then went back to my wrist to rub over the bracelet she'd given me for my birthday.

My gaze never wavered from hers, as my thumb traced over the emerald and diamond embedded symbol on her wrist as well. I knew my necklace was hiding underneath her T-Shirt, but the ring was in her drawer in Los Angeles. She couldn't have anyone seeing it and couldn't risk losing it either, but I yearned for it to be on her finger permanently.

"I hope it will always be that way."

"It will, I promise. I can't wait to marry you, my love. I just... can't *fucking wait*. Do you think then Jeanne and Denise would let us take the same bloody car from the airport?" I asked in frustration.

"Cade, it's okay that we have to take separate cars. I have to go home and get my things and then to the hotel to get ready. You can meet me there later, or just have Peter take you straight there from the airport?" I nodded. "Is Denise making sure you have clothes for tonight?"

"I guess." I shrugged. What I was wearing was the last thing on my bloody mind.

"I bet I can make you smile." She smirked at me and then released my hand so that she could dig around in her purse for something.

"Not likely," I dismissed the possibility.

Brook pulled out her phone and scanned through some texts before handing it to me to read.

Girl, you bring that luscious ass with you for makeup or I'll have to rip all your hair out. And I don't mean YOUR luscious ass, either!

I smiled, but I groaned. "Okay, I smiled," I said reluctantly, as she laughed.

"Mickey is so in love with you and your uh... man parts."

I couldn't help but laugh with her. "Well, my uh... *man parts* are spoken for," I said in a low voice and hoped she thought it was sexy. "Doesn't he know that, yet?"

She glanced at me with sparkling eyes. "He doesn't care. He's willing to share," she said with a smirk.

"Yeah, well, I'm not. Not even close."

Brooklyn

MICKEY WAS FINISHING up on my hair when Cade finally came back to the room. Dressed in black jeans and shirt with a bright blue jacket that brought out the color of his eyes, he looked incredible and good enough to eat.

He'd gotten ready and gone down to the hotel bar when his team arrived. I knew he wanted to avoid Mickey as much as possible, and I completely understood it, but it was so damn hilarious seeing the guy drool over him.

I didn't know why I needed a whole *team* to get me ready, but Ruth insisted.

The dress she picked out was cool and edgy and I felt sort of like the futuristic chic type my next role would embody. It was short too, which worked well for my plans, but the shoes were very high and spiky. I looked at them with disdain. The first time I'd tried them on I twisted my ankle. It was still aching and I didn't think I'd be able to do those shoes.

I was still considering it, when Cade walked in and took the one I was holding and threw it on the bed. "Uh uh," he said. "Not happening. Okay, love?" He reached out and brushed his thumb against my chin.

"Okay, *honey*." Mickey was staring at Cade, who was bristling uncomfortably as his brows rose and his mouth opened in a retort, but he stopped himself and shut his mouth before rolling his eyes.

I laughed at his expression as he turned and started digging around in my open suitcase. All I had with me besides this dress and those heels was a clean pair of jeans, a T-Shirt and a pair of converse sneakers.

"Not sure how *luscious* it is, Mick, but here's my ass. So there won't be any ripping out of Brook's hair, yeah?" He threw the remark flippantly over his shoulder. He was in what he would deem a *sassy* mood and I loved it.

Mickey's face was in total shock as I burst out laughing. Cade turned back to kneel at my feet and help me into my sneakers, doing his best to keep a straight face. He looked up at me as he laced up the shoes and finally gave me that crooked grin that I adored.

"Oh no you *didn't!* Did you show him my text? Girlfriend do you share *everything* with him?" he said incredulously.

"Uh..."I stammered.

"Yes, she does. She even shares my uh... *man parts* with me," he laughed as he winked at me and held out his hand. "Or rather, *I* share them with *her*. Shall we go, Brook? We don't want to be late."

Mickey gasped but I couldn't see his face. I was laughing so hard I was crying and my vision blurred.

"Oh my God!" I gasped and put a hand to my mouth.

Mickey rushed up to me to hand me a tissue. "I would let you ruin your makeup if it wasn't my artistry, you little traitor!" He laughed and hugged me.

Cade put an arm around me as we walked to the door of the hotel suite, smiling at each other.

"Cade, can I just touch your ass? Just *one* time? I'll die a happy man!" Mickey's voice was close behind us as he followed us to the door.

"No!" Cade and I both said in unison as the door shut behind us.

I was dying and we laughed all the way down to where the limousine was waiting for us. Peter held open the door and gave us a quizzical look, noting how hard we were laughing.

My side was aching, I was laughing so hard as Cade climbed in beside me and pulled me into his arms. We both sobered immediately as our eyes met and I reached up to touch his face, my fingers closing around his chin before he lowered his mouth to mine.

Cade reached over and pushed the button that separated us from Peter as the kiss deepened. After a few minutes, I pulled my mouth from his and he reached for my face to bring it back to his.

"Hold on, baby," I whispered against his mouth before pressing the intercom button to speak to the driver. "Peter, when we get there can you let me out on the red carpet and then take Cade around to the side entrance, please?"

"No problem, Miss Brook," he replied.

"And Peter? Can you give us some extra time? Take a long way, okay?" I was climbing on top of Cade's lap to straddle his legs as I spoke. I knew I sounded out of breath but I didn't care. His blue eyes smoldered as he realized my intentions.

"Of course."

I let go of the button and wound both of my hands in Cade's hair, nuzzling his nose with mine as he lifted his face up to kiss me and his hands settled on my thighs.

"Do you care if I mess your hair up, babe?" I breathed into his open mouth that was reaching for mine.

His lips lifted in a smile before he sucked my lower lip into his mouth. "No. I'm counting on it, love. This is *so sexy*, Brook. I've thought about doing this for months."

"Then *do it*," I moaned as his hands slid up my legs under my dress and around my flesh. His mouth closed on mine and we kissed wildly, our tongues mating and filling each other's mouths.

"Oh my God!" Cade gasped as his hands rose higher on my body to my hips and he discovered I wasn't wearing panties. "You're a beautiful, naughty girl, Brook."

"For you; I'm anything you want." My hands pushed the jacket from his shoulders and went to work on the buttons of his shirt.

His hands pushed my dress up over my hips and his eyes looked at the nakedness that he'd revealed.

"Jesus, Brook. You... amaze me."

I finished with the buttons of his black button-down only to find a white T-Shirt beneath it. So many fucking layers, but I wanted to feel his bare skin beneath my hands, so I sat back and pulled it up over his head, forcing him to let go of me to raise his arms in assistance.

"No, I just love you," I said as his hands slid to the sides of my face, holding it and pushing the hair back that was hanging down as I leaned toward him to undo his pants. My hand brushed against his enormous erection and he groaned at my touch. He wanted me as much as I wanted him and I felt the rush in my body that needed to feel him inside me. I pulled back his boxers just enough for him to spring free.

His hands lifted my hips as one of mine closed around him to guide him to my entrance. My other hand closed around the back of his neck and I kissed him as he slid deep inside my body.

"Uhhh..." He gasped before his mouth began to devour mine again. My thighs trembled as I moved over him, sliding him in and out of me in rhythm with the way our tongues were working together, our mouths as far open as we could get them, dying to get closer, deeper.

"Brook... slow down, baby." His hands stilled my hips to guide me to a slower movement as he stared up in my face. "You're so gorgeous," he whispered and he brought one hand around to the front of my body to touch me in the place that only he was allowed to touch. My head fell back at the pleasure he caused and my breath left in a rush. "That's it, Brook."

His head fell forward against my breast, his breathing harsh as I felt my body start to tremble and clench around him. I couldn't help myself, so I let my hips move faster. I wanted him to explode, to not be able to hold back, to pour all of his love into me.

"Mmmm, babe—"

I stopped his words with my mouth as we moved together in

climax and his mouth sucked on mine. I wanted to be connected to him in every fucking way possible. I needed him to want me, crave me and need me when I wasn't with him over the coming months. I needed him to dream about me and ache for me because that was what I would be doing for him.

Our bodies finally slowed and his arms wrapped around me, pulling me tight against his chest and I kissed his neck and jaw while he held the back of my head and kissed the top of it.

"You surprise me, Brook. I love you."

I rested my forehead on his shoulder as I heard the screaming in the distance. My breathing was still labored as I rose off of Cade and moved to sit next to him.

"I love you more," I said as I climbed back off of his lap to begin pulling my dress down.

"That's impossible, Brook, and you know it."

"Fuck. This was the long way?" I smirked at him.

"It was the best bloody limo ride I've ever had." He smirked at me as he threw his T-Shirt back on. I grabbed his button-down and threw it at him before reaching into my purse and pulling out a pair of lace bikini panties. I held them up and waved them around. Cade smiled in response.

He watched me clean up and pull the panties over my shoes, before I fell to my knees on the floor of the limo to hike them the rest of the way up under my dress.

"Always prepared, eh?" He shook his head with a small smile.

"A girl's gotta do, what a girl's gotta do to take care of her man." I reached out to touch him. He was buttoning up his shirt when Peter pulled up to the red carpet. I could see Noah through the windows and ran a hand quickly through my hair.

"And you do that *so* well, my love. Mickey will be upset when he sees what we've done to his *artistry*," Cade scoffed.

I leaned in to kiss him quickly before placing my hand on the door and motioned for him to scoot back far enough so the fans wouldn't see him in the limo with me.

I'd just begun to open the door when I turned back to him one last time.

"Not as mad as he's gonna be when he realizes why it's so fucked up." I laughed and then stepped outside, donning my sunglasses and waving as I moved toward Noah.

The screams were thunderous as Noah's arm slid around me and we began the dance of autographs and photo calls. "Sorry I'm late, Noah," I practically had to yell over the din.

"Brook, where's Cade?"

"What's it like to kiss Cade, Brook?"

"Ugh! Cade!"

"Isn't Cade coming?"

Cade, always, Cade. Over and over they screamed at me. I smiled up at Noah as they snapped photo after photo.

Well... he just, uh... did.

Caden

I SAW BROOK TAKE her seat next to Noah in the front row with two empty seats next to her.

"I'll sit next to Brook," Denise murmured as she touched my arm. "Pinnacle's orders that you two don't sit next to each other for the entire night." She looked at me apologetically. "Sorry, hon."

She'd met me backstage and was going to escort me to my seat when the bloody mess started. So many screaming kids, I felt like my head was about to explode. I was terrible at these things and I didn't really have anything prepared in case I would win anything. The kiss award would take care of itself without words. I grinned as I thought about it.

"I have to sit by her before the Best Kiss thing. We might not win, but um... if we do, we haven't talked about what we're doing."

Denise rolled her eyes at me. "What? Didn't you two ride over here together?" she admonished.

"Uh... yeah. We didn't talk much, Denise." I rubbed the back of my neck when she looked at me, her mouth opening to speak and then shutting again with a snap. *Enough said, I guess.*

I took my seat on the end and then Denise sat between Brook and me for most of the show. I won the bloody Best Actor award and didn't know what to say in acceptance. I mumbled something and watched as Brook put her hand over her face, so it must have been really pathetic.

Brook was still laughing when I took my seat, but when Denise got up to go to the bathroom, she moved over to sit by me, finally.

"I can still smell you on me..." she whispered, and instantly my body reacted and I lost my breath.

I smiled and leaned toward her and put a hand over my mouth as I spoke to her.

"Brook, stop if you don't want me to attack you when we win that bloody kiss award."

"Mmmm, as good as that sounds, I don't think we should kiss, Cade."

I heard the uncertainty in her voice and looked at her and she glanced at me out of the corner of her eye.

"What? I thought…"

"I know, but I want to keep our relationship private, and I'm overly emotional tonight. I just… I'm not sure I can handle it in front of all these people, okay?"

I sighed as they announced the nominations and the screams drowned out her voice as she spoke, so I just nodded.

Davina Duchman was presenting because the studio figured we'd win and wanted to promote our new movie, which was another reason not to kiss on stage. I heard our names called out and it was like she was having a spastic fit.

"Oh my God, oh my God, oh my God! Caden Carlisle and Brook Halloway!"

Applause and endless screaming ensued. We both got up and walked up the stairs leading to the stage and I still didn't know what was going to happen, but I thought I'd play along as much as I could.

Davina hugged both of us, before we took to the podium.

I pulled out a piece of paper from my pocket and removed my gum, wrapping it in the paper.

"I have to remove my gum to give Brook a proper kiss…" I said into the microphone and the fans all screamed even louder.

I shook my arms, and dropped my head, rubbing my hands over my eyes before I raised my head and looked at my girl. I nodded to her, letting her know I was ready and she placed a hand over her mouth.

I closed my eyes and waited. This was her call… so I let her take the lead. I felt her move closer, her perfume assaulting my senses when she did so and she inched in closer and closer, her forehead coming into contact with my face. I took the cue and bent my head lower, to bring my mouth within reach for her. All she had to do was tilt her face to mine and our lips would meet.

Seconds passed and the screams increased and my hands moved to her waist to pull her closer and end her hesitation. Suddenly she turned toward the mic and grabbed the silly award.

"Thank you! But we've got to leave you wanting more! Wait until you see the kisses in the next one!" she said, leaving me there wanting… waiting. My jaw tightened and she pulled my hand.

"Come on, Cade," she said to me so softly that no one but me could hear and dropped my hand to keep up the illusion as we went backstage for pictures and interviews. "Sweetie, come on."

Her eyes looked at me apologetically. She knew I had wanted this public display of affection and wanted it badly. Finally there would have been some public acknowledgment of her feelings for me. I'd told the world a million times I loved her, but she hadn't reciprocated yet.

I wished all of the crowds would disappear and I could take her in my arms like I wanted to.

I appreciated all of the fans and their adoration, but on this day, the day before I was leaving her for three months, there were other places I'd rather be.

We posed for pictures and had a small interview backstage, before making our way around toward our seats in front.

Brook stopped me. "Cade, you need to go to the bathroom and fix your shirt. The buttons are crooked." She smirked at me and then left me to go out to her seat. I looked down and sure enough, my shirt tails were uneven.

Shit.

I felt like a complete wanker, but the reason my shirt was askew was so worth it.

I smiled as I hurried into the bathroom and rushed to correct the problem. My face was flushed, but I needed to get back out there because Brook was nominated for Best Actress and our movie for Best Film. I didn't want to miss either one.

Brook was nervous about the Best Actress nod. She didn't feel comfortable in situations with huge crowds any more than I did, and this was her first nomination. I mean, look how I screwed my acceptance speech for Best Actor. Literally.

Watching her stumble around with her words, I couldn't help feeling a little trepidation for her. At least she remembered to thank the fans and the cast. She was dealing with her sprained ankle and she accidentally dropped her popcorn award. I couldn't help but laugh out loud at the way she tried to go after it but then came back to the podium to tell everyone that she was awkward as everyone was expecting. She was so adorable but I knew she was embarrassed as hell.

I had a camera in my face the entire time she was onstage, and I knew I was doing a poor job of keeping the love from showing, but I was beyond caring.

Brook's face was flushed when she came back to join me, and the rest of the cast in our seats to wait for the Best Picture nomination. She rolled her eyes at me and grinned.

"I broke my fucking popcorn." My eyes met hers and I laughed with her.

"Mine will probably go in the dustbin unless you want it?" I asked under my breath.

"Are you kidding? Could they make an uglier award? We *have* to keep them, Cade. Maybe you can ship yours to Lillian?"

"I'm sending it with Denise. I don't care what she bloody does with it."

Toward the end of the evening, the entire cast went up on stage to accept the award for Best Film, including Martin Deering. We were all content to let him make the acceptance speech before going backstage for one last interview with *E!News*.

I barely spoke during it, Brook said even less than I did. We let Gavin, Jennifer and Noah take it. We were just happy when it ended so we could leave. I hugged everyone goodbye. Brook would still see most of them in L.A., but I had no idea when I'd be back.

Brook nestled on my lap in the back of the limo as we raced through West Hollywood to the restaurant I'd made reservations at for dinner.

This time, we were both content to hold each other, soaking each other in, every touch reverent and lasting. I rubbed her back and she'd place an occasional kiss on my neck as we sat in silence, our fingers laced together. I kissed her forehead as I leaned my head against hers, willing myself not to get emotional.

I knew her well enough to know that her mind and heart were racing as much as mine were. We were struggling but trying to be strong for the other.

Both of us were looking forward to the rest of the night and ready to savor each moment, but dreading the morning to come; dreading the next three bloody months.

I closed my eyes at the thought.

Chapter 7

Don't Forget to Remember... It's Only Us

Caden

I KNEW BROOK WOULD want me to play a song for her tonight.

It would be difficult, but it was something she loved, and I'd give her anything she wanted; especially tonight. Anything that would ease the pain or create a moment of happiness was what I hoped for.

We were in a secluded u-shaped booth at a new Italian restaurant that was among a few that my manager had recommended, sitting as close as we dared and clung to each other's hands under the white table cloth that hung long enough to cover our laps. I decided that since I was leaving the next day, I wanted to take her out, not hide in a hotel room all night. My hand felt clammy, and I didn't know if it was because I was worried about getting caught or because of the agitated state of my emotions. I wondered if she noticed.

Of course, she noticed. She knows everything... even when I don't speak.

I picked Ciccone's because we had some beautiful memories from our time in Italy the past few days and I wanted the mood to continue.

And then there was a restaurant in Vancouver we used to like and go to quite often, starting with pre-production on the first movie. We'd come so far since then; when I was already hopelessly in love with her, and she was still running from her feelings.

Denise made the reservations and took care of everything I wanted for later in the evening; the flowers, the champagne, the hotel suite with the hot tub, and the other basket of necessities for pulling an all-nighter with Brook.

I hadn't taken my guitar to Italy, and so she'd had the hotel ship it to her L.A. office. She asked Peter to deliver it to the hotel during the MTV Movie awards before it was time to come back to pick Brook and I up.

The restaurant was new and trendy, with shiny black and white tile in a diagonal design on the floor, open walls made of some sort of metal mesh and crystal chandeliers. The lights were dimmed and candles flickered on all of the tables. It was soft and romantic and that was perfect.

I couldn't order wine because Brook wasn't old enough, but drinking wasn't on my agenda for the evening anyway. I wanted a clear mind so I'd remember every moment of the next twelve hours. My eyes roamed over Brook's face, her blue eyes looking into mine as she bit her lip, then her eyes dropped and she squeezed my hand.

"You look gorgeous," I said softly, longing to lift her hand so I could kiss the inside of her wrist or lean in and pull her closer to my body. Her scent enveloped me and was one I knew well; one I'd miss every day that I was gone. My chest tightened over my lungs and it made it difficult to breathe.

She smiled softly at me when she lifted her gaze again. The waiter came to get our drink order and left the menus with us. I was reluctant to let go of her hand, so I flipped one menu open between us so that we could share it, each of us holding one side.

She laughed softly, perusing the offerings. "Mmmm... What are you having?"

"Well... what are *you* having?" I asked with a smirk. She always ordered better than I did and I always ended up sampling from her plate. It was easier to share behind the closed doors of our hotel rooms, but I could sneak a bite or two if no one were looking when we were out. It had become a game between us.

"You could always order the same thing. That would be the safe thing, wouldn't it?" Her hair hung in a chestnut curtain around her face as she bent over the menu. She was cutting her glorious hair off for her role in the Runaways in a couple of days. I knew she was nervous about it. I was nervous about it too, but I'd never admit that to her. My hand itched to reach out and brush it back from her face.

"What fun would there be in that? Or... if I dislike mine, we can simply trade." I smiled at her and she shook her head at me and smiled wide, her eyes sparkling.

"Yeah, we can do that." My heart warmed at how easily she'd give up her choice for me.

"Look, they have broccoli ravioli," I wrinkled my nose and she laughed at me. "I find the prospect of it *quite* revolting."

"No broccoli for you, that's for sure. Meat and dessert, coming right up," she said as her elbow nudged my side. It brought me so much pleasure that she knew my habits so well.

We ended up with meat lasagna for me and grilled swordfish for Brook, undoubtedly to be followed by Tiramisu. It was one of my favorites and I'd managed to get her to share with me in the past.

When the meal came, Brook picked up her fork and held a bite of her swordfish out for me and I leaned over to take it.

"Do you want to talk about the movie? I mean; I know that we've been sad, but I don't want to discount what a great thing this is for you, Cade. Are you looking forward to it?"

"What part exactly? Leaving you or not seeing you for three months?" I said sardonically, as I forked up a bite of the lasagna and held it out for her to take.

She cocked her head to one side and shook her head. "No, but I mean... we haven't talked about it very much, and I don't want you to think that I'm not happy for you. I'll miss you so much, but I'm proud of you, too. I know you'll be wonderful in it."

I sighed. It was obvious she was trying to be strong and make it easier for me and I loved her for it. I was making the same effort for her, and it was bloody difficult.

"I'm not that excited about it." I paused and watched her face. "I thought you sensed that. Davina has a reputation for being difficult to work with."

She shrugged. "Not exactly... I just figured you thought talking about it would hurt me, but I want to know. If you want to tell me," she said in a low tone.

"Nothing really to tell, love. I'll be counting the hours until it's finished," I said cryptically and then tried to change the subject. "You have that magazine shoot coming up, right? I can't wait to see those pictures. I'll Google it the minute you're finished with the shoot. Surely someone will leak them." The corners of my lips lifted at the prospect.

"Yeah." She played with her fork. "The last hoorah before my hair gets chopped and dyed."

"Don't worry about it, Brook. It's hair. It grows back," I reassured her.

She looked at me steadily for a moment and then took another bite of her meal. "I know... it's just..." her words fell off.

"What is it?"

"You said in France that the thing about me that you liked best was my hair."

I laughed. "Yes, and I recall you said you liked my nose best. Of all things... my nose!"

She had the grace to blush and I reached out and brushed my knuckles across her cheekbone. "I was afraid my feelings would show if I said the wrong thing," she explained with a small laugh. "I was flustered!"

"Brook, I love you no matter what your hair looks like, okay?" I only had to say that. Imagine the ruckus if I'd have told the truth? I adore absolutely *everything about her.*

"The Allure shoot isn't the only one I have while you're in New York, and you have a couple, too, don't you?"

I nodded, "Yeah."

"So... every time I'm looking at the camera, I'll be thinking about you," she said softly.

My heart thumped in my chest and I squeezed her hand. Leave it to her to say the perfect thing.

"Brook." I paused and met her eyes with mine. "Me, too. I'm thinking about you all the time, anyhow," I said and forgot about the rest of the people in the restaurant as I finally allowed myself to bring her hand up from beneath the table and kiss it.

We finished dinner and shared the dessert, but we barely ate, picking at the meal for over an hour.

"I'm sorry I didn't eat very much. I guess I wasn't that hungry."

Me either.

My hand still held hers beneath the table and I wasn't planning on letting go of her until I absolutely had to.

"Are you ready to go?"

"Yes, please," she said as she nodded and leaned into my arm.

I sighed as I tried to dispel the tightening in my chest and struggled to overcome the rush of emotion that threatened to choke me.

Tonight was going to be both glorious and heartbreaking. Beautiful and painful, but I wanted to feel it all, to savor each moment, to feel *everything* there was to feel... with Brook.

Brooklyn

THE PRIVATE BUNGALOW at the Beverly Hills Hotel where we'd gotten ready for the awards show had been cleaned up and the big bouquets of white roses and freesias were on the side table and in the entryway. They lent a fragrant scent to waft in the air, which mixed with the vanilla from the candles that were flickering here and there around the rooms. And red rose petals were scattered across the white duvet on the bed.

I turned and watched Cade enter behind me, before turning to look around the room. My mouth fell open, but I couldn't speak.

I guess I shouldn't have been surprised, considering how romantic he had shown he could be over the months... Nevertheless, I was speechless.

He walked to me slowly and brushed my hair back with both hands before he bent to take my mouth in a gentle kiss, softly brushing his lips back and forth with mine. He couldn't help but deepen it enough so that his lips softly tugged and sucked on mine and I reciprocated unabashedly. My breath left my body in a rush as my heart swelled and ached at the same time.

"Cade... God." I could barely get the words out. "This is... amazing."

"Do you want to take a bath?" he said softly against my lips. "I want to take this slow tonight, Brook. I want to talk and hold you, and make love to you. But I want it *all*, is that okay?"

I felt a single tear fall from my lashes as I nodded and wrapped my arms tightly around his waist, burying my face in his chest as I willed myself not to cry. He held me close and kissed the top of my head while his fingers drew small circles on the small of my back. This room was beautiful and all about romance, and we'd make love, but tonight wasn't about sex... it was about absorbing the love.

Help me get through this without completely losing it. He needs me to support him, not fall apart.

I was glad Nathan had managed to do as I asked and got the new iPods, set up the account, and had them ready for me when I stopped home to get my things. Nate had them both formatted although I didn't have time to wrap Cade's but was able to tuck it inside his duffle while he was out of the room during Mickey's visit. I noticed my journal inside as well, and so I inserted a letter I'd written, knowing he'd be reading the journal on the plane and would find it quickly.

The duplicate iPod Nathan had gotten for me was waiting inside my purse, and the dock set up on the bedside table. As I moved out of Cade's arms to sit on the bed, I noticed his guitar leaning up against the wall.

He knows I'll want to hear him play for me tonight. I drew in my breath.

Jesus... he always knows.

I looked up at him and offered a sad smile as he came across the room to touch my chin with his fingertips. I reached for his hand so I could place an open-mouthed kiss on his palm.

"Thank you," I said as my eyes met his. I saw all the love and pain that I was feeling reflected in Cade's deep blue eyes. He swallowed and nodded.

"It's my pleasure, sweetheart."

My chest tightened and my mind screamed. *The sadness is going to drown both of us.*

I tried to smile and stood up, still holding his hand; my throat throbbed and my eyes burned. I prayed I wasn't shaking.

"A bath sounds nice. And the rest... I agree with you." My voice trembled and cracked on the words. "Do you think if we try, we can slow down time?"

He folded me in his arms, pulling me tightly to his chest. He sighed heavily against my temple.

"Oh, Brook. I'd be happier if we could stop it *completely*. I'm bloody *aching* over this." He lifted me so that my face was level with his and my hands wound around his shoulders, to fist in his hair. I knew he loved it when I did that and he closed his eyes before resting his forehead on mine. "I just... don't want tomorrow to come." Emotion clouded his velvet voice; evidence he was struggling right along with me.

His mouth finally opened over mine and his tongue slid into my mouth. I pulled his head closer so I could melt into him, matching him kiss for kiss. He tasted delicious and I held his head with both hands. When he finally moved his mouth from mine, I found myself sitting on the vanity in the bathroom, not even aware of how I had gotten there. My hand ran down his chest, feeling the hard contours beneath the two layers of his shirts.

He smiled softly before leaving me to turn on the water in the large bathtub. There were more rose petals in the bottom of it that began to float on the water as it filled.

"You're going to join me in that big tub aren't you?" I tried to tease him as I quickly brushed a tear from my face.

He added some scented bath foam to the water and then came back to lift one of my feet to begin unlacing my shoes. He removed first one then the other. He was so gentle and tender in his movements, his eyes hardly ever leaving my face. I was aching, the sadness so overpowering I could barely breathe.

"Eventually." He smiled gently and then bent to kiss me again before lifting me down from the counter and turning my body so that he could run the zipper down the back of my dress. He moved my hair aside and kissed the back of my neck, the wetness and feel of his lips giving me goosebumps as his hand ran lightly down my back where the skin was exposed. "Do you need something from your bag to put your hair up?"

He was so amazing. Leave it to Cade to think of that.

"Yes. There's a clip in the zippered compartment on the side." He placed one last kiss on my shoulder and left the room.

I closed my eyes as I fought the tears that welled inside. I heard him moving around as I stripped out of my dress and underwear and slowly lowered myself into the warm, scented water. The tub was large and was still filling, the bubbles rising, dotted with the red rose petals.

I leaned back and closed my eyes and then felt his hands in my hair, pulling it up and securing the clip.

"I'll be back, love." Cade walked out of the room and then I heard his guitar; the soft strumming of the chords he was playing coming closer. The tune was upbeat, happy and I smiled as he came into the bathroom. He'd removed his jacket and button-down, leaving only the white T-Shirt. He sat down on the bench across from the tub as he continued to play the guitar. His eyes roamed over my face and watched as I turned the faucet off with my foot.

"That's beautiful," I said, and he smiled.

"Exactly," he answered and then started to sing to me. He was gorgeous as always and I knew I'd be happy to watch him play for me forever. Listening to his sultry voice singing just for me was the most I could ask for in the world, and I was thankful for the gifts he brought to my life.

The song, called *Beautiful.* It was so right for the situation, and I knew Cade was trying to reassure me that he'd be thinking of me and that the time apart wouldn't change his feelings; that the love between us was unshakable. His voice was strong and clear, his eyes intent on mine.

He smiled wide and I couldn't help smiling back as I felt a blush come up under the skin of my face. I was hypnotized.

I was speechless. Just... amazed at how he could turn a sad moment into one of utter joy. My heart ached at the prospect of not being with him, but he was letting me know that distance wasn't what mattered; he was mine and nothing would change it.

"Beautiful you..." As Cade sang the last lyric and strummed the last chord, I held my hand out to him. He carefully set the guitar down and came to sit near the bathtub, taking my outstretched hand and bringing it to his mouth. He kissed the inside of my wrist and then pressed his open mouth to the palm before letting it settle on his cheek. He pressed his face into my hand, his big one covering my smaller one.

"No, beautiful *you*," I said softly.   "You're so amazing, Cade. Thank you. That was gorgeous."

He stared into my face, his gaze never wavering from mine, his thumb rubbing circles over the top of the hand that he held.

"I want you to be happy, Brook. I mean, when you're filming, I want you to enjoy it. This film is something you wanted so badly and you should embrace it. Let yourself have fun. I don't want missing me to ruin it for you."

I nodded. "I know, but I'll still miss you."

"Okay... I'll let you miss me a little. I'm counting on it, sweetheart."

"Are you going to follow your own advice?" I asked. I raised my eyebrow at him because I knew he was preaching something to me that he would struggle with himself.

"Well... I'll do my best, of course," he said with a sad smile. I wanted to make him happy, to take the pain from behind his eyes.

"I thought you were coming in here..." I coaxed him. We both laughed softly as he kissed my hand again and got up to strip off his clothes so he could join me. I couldn't tear my eyes away from him as inch-by-inch all that beautiful flesh was exposed to my view. "Mickey was right," I teased, "I am a lucky, lucky bitch."

I was rewarded with a big smile and the beautiful sound of his laughter and my heart tightened inside my body.

The tub was large enough for us to face each other lying on our sides and he pulled me closer and brushed a wet tendril off of my face. We lay looking at each other and softly touching.

"I don't want to sleep tonight, Brook."

"I know. Me either." I bent to kiss his mouth very softly. "I love you so much."

"Not as much as I love you." He looked at me seriously, and his brow dropped over his eyes. "So, don't forget."

I smiled at the irony of it and shook my head; I started to protest, but he put a finger to my lips to silence me.

"No arguing," he insisted as he nuzzled my nose and I reached for his mouth again. I sucked his lower lip into my mouth and I slowly pulled it with me as my mouth moved off of his.

"The song was perfect, Cade," I said as his mouth lifted from mine.

His eyes dropped and his jaw jutted out a little before he finally spoke. "I knew you'd want me to play for you tonight, and I searched for music while I waited for you in Italy."

"But... you didn't... take your guitar when you went to Cannes," I said slowly.

"You don't miss much, do you love? I bought one in Italy so I could mess around with arrangements on different songs. I wanted it to be perfect for you, tonight."

"*Everything* you do is perfect, Cade. That's why I'm such a mess." I ran my fingertips along the stubble on his jaw as I watched his expression. His blue eyes were dark and intense. "I didn't see a new guitar in Italy, either, so..."

"No, I gave it to the hotel owner's son the day you arrived. I wanted to surprise you. I found a bunch of songs that... well, that echoed everything I was feeling. But um... I really struggled with the choice."

My eyes widened. "There are more?" I asked hopefully. His hands were roaming lightly over my body, down my waist and hip and up again. Those hands did delicious things to me.

"Yeah, but the others are full of sadness and loss, and I don't want to make you sad."

I swallowed. I understood what he meant, but I didn't want him to feel like he had to hold back what he was feeling.

"Whatever you want to play, I want to hear. We share everything, right?" My voice shook and my chin trembled as my eyes welled with tears. "I've got a serious case of sad already, and I want you to sing whatever you feel, okay?"

He swallowed hard and his hands on my back fluttered across my skin, making me tremble.

"This reminds me a lot of our first time in London," I whispered against his beautiful mouth as I remembered that incredible night. My hand ran down his chest and around his waist and his legs tangled with mine. My body was reacting in ways I couldn't help, even as my heart ached.

"I know. It was a dream; so beautiful. You're a miracle to me, Brook." My hand moved up to the back of his neck and he moved until he was over me and his mouth was diving into mine, our tongues laving each other, tasting; like we were starving.

We *were* starving, desperate to be close to each other. We kissed and caressed each other until the water chilled to the point of making me shiver. His kisses left me breathless, trembling and always wanting more. He was so passionate, yet tender and I never wanted to stop.

"Cade... I'll miss you so much."

His arms tightened as he lifted us both until we were standing and could step out of the tub.

"I know, Brook." His eyes answered me without my even saying the words. "The kisses are enough to live on without anything else," he whispered against my neck and jaw.

Feeling me shiver, he rubbed his hands up and down my arms before he reached for two large white towels and wrapped one around me, and the other around his waist before scooping me up bridal style to carry me into the bedroom.

When he sat me on the bed, I got up and went to my purse to remove the iPod and connected it to the dock. The music softly filled the room and then we crawled under the covers without drying off and pulled the covers over our heads, giggling. He gathered me close to him and I curled into what had become my spot in the crook of his arm with my head on his chest.

"See? Going to bed naked and wet is good, yes?" The steam from our bodies was rising and filling the space and taking the chill off of our skin left by the tepid bath water.

His chest rumbled underneath my cheek when he laughed. "Yeah, incredibly; it does. If it weren't for the bloody time difference, we could do this together on the phone while I'm in New York. Three hours might make pillow talk difficult; as much as I want it."

I nodded and tightened the arm that was around his waist. "The time difference will be a pain, but we can text during the day while we're working. Not much probably, but as often as we can."

"Yeah, I'll be texting you so much, I expect my phone keyboard to literally melt, love."

We spent more time just lying together, talking about the upcoming films. We talked about Patrick Armstrong and my new film,; cutting my hair and all the physical stuff I'd have to learn. I told him I'd get the sheet music to the song and learn it. Cade had helped me with my guitar skills quite a bit, but I knew I had a lot of work to do to get as good as him, but that part of it would be fun.

He told me about his co-star, albeit only when I asked about her. I wanted to make him feel like I was okay with it even if in reality, I cringed at the thought of him kissing some other girl on film. But, hey, it was his *job*. He'd said it a hundred times, and he was right. I'd just have to deal with it.

"I don't know that much about her really. Beyond on stage at the MTV awards, I only met her the one time in L.A. and I was preoccupied, if you'll remember. My girl was piggybacking around with some wanker, so my mind wasn't really focused on Davina Duchman."

He was teasing me, but I could see it had hurt him.

"I'm sorry," I said softly, my heart thumping at the pain he had over it.

As fast as lightening, he flipped me over and his body covered mine and I gasped. "You better be," he said in a low voice as he nuzzled against my neck, but I could hear the amusement behind the words. My hands ran up his back into his hair and I turned my face into his. Obviously, he was as aroused as I was and I could feel the proof of it pressing against my hip.

"Making love makes the time go too fast, Brook," his lips brushed mine even as he gyrated against me, and I breathed against him as my air left me in a rush. I reached up and pulled his earlobe into my mouth, sucking and nipping at it with my teeth.

He shifted me so that I was completely underneath him and my legs came up on the sides of his hips. His hardness pressed against me as he dragged his mouth across my jaw and down the curve of my neck.

"Mmmm..." I moaned.

Cade brushed my hair back and I drowned in his blue eyes before he rested his head on mine, his lips continuing to torture my neck, sending shivers through my entire body. I pulled his head down so I could kiss him and he groaned against my mouth, giving in to the inevitable, our hips surged together.

"I said, I *don't* want to make love..." He groaned in protest, but his mouth took mine hungrily. I opened to him and moved my mouth with his over and over, until I couldn't breathe and my heart was beating wildly in my chest. He lifted his mouth slightly to take a breath now and then, but we continued to devour each other's mouth again and again.

We fit so perfectly together; making love was effortless, natural; necessary. As necessary as breathing.

Emotion welled within my chest and my throat ached, even as he set my body on fire.

"Jesus, Brook. Tonight will disappear in an instant and these three months will feel like forever."

I closed my eyes at the pain in his voice. Tears squeezed from between my lashes despite my resolve not to cry.

Cade was right. Losing myself in him would make time fly, but it felt so right and we both needed the closeness of it.

His mouth moved to my breast and I arched against him, wanting the blissful torture to continue, yet needing his mouth on mine and his body intimately connected with mine. I wanted to be connected with him in every way possible. Our mouths moved perfectly together as he filled my body with his and his fingers threaded through mine, his other moving to twine in my hair to hold my head.

"Cade..." I cried into his mouth even as my free hand pressed into the muscles on his butt to bring him deeper into me. I just wanted to be closer. His movements were slow, measured, like he wanted to savor every touch and memorize my response. It was amazing, beautiful and...us. Just us. "Oh, babe," I said breathlessly.

We made love for hours, with our hands, our mouths, our bodies. We worshiped each other again and again, never wanting to let the other go, needing the constant contact as some sort of shield to the coming goodbye... and the aching loneliness that loomed like a tsunami over us.

When finally we lay spent, gasping for breath in each other's arms, I turned my face into his neck and gave in to the sobs I'd been holding back. His gentle hands brushed my hair back as he hovered above me.

"Brook. Look at me." My shoulders were shaking softly and I knew I didn't have the strength to look up and see the anguish on his face. I could tell from the thickness in his voice that he was succumbing to the overwhelming emotions as well.

My arms wound around him and I pressed into him even tighter and I felt his lips on my face, tracing my cheeks and my tear-dampened eyes, until finally moving to my mouth to brush back and forth over it.

"Brook... babe, we'll get through this because we have to. You know how much I adore you. You're all I think about."

I nodded and tried to control my voice enough to speak. "I know. It's the same for me."

He rolled to my side but continued to look into my face, lying on his side facing me, touching my hair, trying to soothe me and kiss the tears away. I finally brought my eyes up to his. He was so gorgeous, his face soft and sated from our lovemaking, but full of pain and love. We just lay there looking at each, other and I wondered what time it was, how many hours and minutes I had left with him.

He must have read my mind because he shook his head. "I don't want to know. I don't want the sun to rise, Brook."

My eyes closed. "How do you do that? How do you know me so well?"

He smiled softly. "Hmmph. You're part of me." His thumb rubbed across my lower lip and pulled it down before he leaned in to kiss me softly on the mouth. "And, I love you more than anything on this earth."

Another tear slipped from my eyes, and he bent to kiss it away. "These songs, Brook... they're all of our songs..."

I closed my eyes and nodded. "I know."

"I mean, the song you sang in London, the one I sang at the wrap party... everything, even some that we only talked about." His eyes held an incredulous look like he was amazed that I'd remember them.

"Yes." My throat ached, and I couldn't say much, so I just reached out to trace his jaw with my fingers and nodded softly.

"You're so beautiful. You touch me in places that no one ever will again. You're so perfect for me, do you know that?"

I couldn't help but laugh a little through my tears. "So, you keep saying."

"And *will* continue to do so until you believe it." He kissed my nose and my forehead and I snuggled into him, content just to hold him, smell him and feel him wrapped all around me.

***

SOMETHING WAS SHINING in my face and I wanted it to go away. I threw my arm over my eyes and tried to go back to sleep.

Sleep.

My heart constricted in my chest as I realized where I was and that I didn't want to be sleeping. I sat straight up in bed, my chest heaving with my frantic breathing as my eyes searched the empty bed and room around me. My eyes stung, my throat hurt... "Cade?" I started to cry. "Cade!" I yelled.

He rushed out of the bathroom and I saw that he was already dressed in gray pants and a black T-Shirt. He took one look at me with the tears running down my face and sat on the edge of the bed so he could pull me into his lap.

"I'm so sorry..." I sobbed against his chest. "I didn't mean to fall asleep, to... to waste our time together."

"Love, it's okay. I was tired too."

"But did you sleep?" I looked up into his face as his thumbs brushed away my tears.

"Um, no, honey, but it's okay." I shook my head as my face crumpled.

"No! I'm *so pissed* at myself," I said in disgust and as usual, he tried to comfort me.

"Babe, don't be. It allowed me to watch you sleep, Brook."

"So what? Are you Ryan now?"

He only smiled sadly. "Only where you're concerned, Julia."

I slid my arms around his neck and cried into him. "Oh God... I can't do this. I thought I could, but I just *can't*, Cade."

His arms tightened around me, and he buried his face into the side of my neck and shoulder, one hand coming up to cradle the back of my head. He was breathing heavier, but he was silent, just holding me in his arms like he'd never let me go.

My phone vibrated and I knew it would be my mother. She was going to help get Cade to the airport without anyone knowing. Well, at least that was the plan. The whole world was watching the airports, knowing he'd be traveling today. It had gotten so damn insane.

I pulled back so I could look into Cade's face. His eyes were liquid with unshed tears and I knew he was hurting as much as I was. I leaned my forehead against his cheek as I sat in his lap and inhaled his scent with my shaky breaths, trying to get control of the crying.

"What time is it?" I asked, not wanting the answer.

He waited and swallowed. "Just after eleven."

I sucked in my breath. It was worse than I thought. I grabbed on to him tighter as a new flood of tears ran through me. "Oh, God."

He just held me and let me cry.

I knew he had to leave by twelve or he'd miss his plane. I glanced around the room and noticed his bags were already packed. His guitar was in its case waiting as well.

"I thought you were going to play me another song." I sniffed back the tears and tried to smile at him, but I knew it was a pathetic effort at best. *I can't hide from him. He knows everything.*

He sighed. "Is that what you want?" he asked quietly.

"I don't know what I want right now... except that I *don't want you to go.*"

Again, his arms pulled me close and he nodded against my shoulder. I knew he was crying with me this time. I was so damn selfish. I should be making this easier for him, helping him to do what he had to do, and instead here I was this quivering mass of tears. He deserved better from me.

"I'm sorry. I'm not being fair, Cade. I know you have to go, and I'll be fah... fine." I pushed off of his lap and moved to my open bag to gather out the clothes I had brought.

"Well, I bloody won't be," he said miserably.

I pulled on some panties and a bra, knowing that Cade was watching as I did so. After I had donned the jeans and the T-Shirt, I went to the bathroom to study my reflection. My eyes and mouth were swollen, and my hair was a wild mess.

I was a mess. I ran my hands through my hair and under my eyes to remove the ruined makeup. Ruined by lovemaking and tears.

When I came back to the bedroom, Cade was sitting on the bed next to his open guitar case, and holding the instrument on his lap.

"I'm the one who will be the mess. The minute I leave, you'll turn into a tough futuristic babe, yeah?" he tried to tease me, but the tears in his eyes kept it from having the effect he wanted.

"Hmmph! Hardly," I said as I sat down next to him and ran my hand down his arm. His expression reflected that he realized my weakness where he was concerned.

I wish I felt tough.

He started to pluck at the guitar softly. A soft haunting melody and I knew this song would be sad, full of the loss he talked about last night. When he began, the lyrics made my heart stop.

"Is this from the same band as the one last night?" I asked.

"Yes, it's called *Shattered. Yesterday I died, tomorrow's bleeding...."*

I looked down in my lap and struggled with my emotions as I listened to his vibrant voice sing the words that echoed how I felt. I bit my trembling lip then tears fell from my traitorous eyes. He knew how this was affecting us both, so I brought my eyes back up to his. I wanted to see his beautiful face for every second left to me. I didn't need to hide my feelings from him... I *couldn't*, even if I wanted to.

The music slowed as a tear fell from his eye and he lifted his hand to brush it quickly away before continuing, the music increasing in speed and volume. His voice became stronger as he sang and he never took his eyes from mine. I had to put a hand to my mouth to keep from sobbing aloud. I didn't know how he did it... singing with tears on his face. He was so much stronger than me... even if he thought I was the strong one.

The last few notes died out and as he put the guitar back in the case, I knelt in front of him and wound my arms around his body, my head buried in his chest as we clung together, his hand stroking my hair. I felt his lips pressed to the top of my head as he breathed me in.

"I love you. Always," he said against my forehead.

"I know. I love you, too." After a few minutes, I moved out of his arms and sat next to him on the bed. I needed to talk to him.

"You know all the songs on the iPod?"

"Yeah, I noticed that it was a new one. Did you lose your old one?"

I smiled and shook my head. "No. It's new." I reached out and took his hand. "I sent Nathan a list of the songs I wanted to load on it, and had him set up a new account, and buy two new iPods."

His brow dropped and he shook his head in question. "Two?"

"Uh huh. One for me, and one for you. I put it in your duffle yesterday when you were out of the room. The account is set up using my email address, but you'll have access to it as well."

His eyes searched my face as comprehension appeared on his features. "Music is a way we've always connected…"

I nodded. "I just thought that we could download songs for each other on the days we can't talk… or maybe, every day. I can load them in the evening, so you'll see them when you wake up, and you could do the same for me in the mornings. That way…" I fiddled with my fingers in my lap, but he reached over to take my hand and raise it to his mouth, "we can add to our playlist together. And will you add the song you sang last night and this morning?"

He sighed. "Brook. It's… *brilliant!* Perfect. Thank you for thinking of it, my love."

My phone went off again and this time I had to answer it. He didn't want to let go of my hand, and my fingers fell from his as I crossed the room to get it.

"Yeah?"

"Hi, honey. Is Cade about ready to go? I'm waiting down by your car. We need to go soon Brook, or Cade will miss his flight."

Tears filled my eyes again and my voice trembled. "Um... yeah. We'll be down shortly, Mom. Thanks for being here."

"Are you two okay?" she asked hesitantly.

"Um, no... .but, as good as can be expected."

"Okay, honey. See you in a minute."

I turned around to find Cade right behind me and he gathered me close, lifting me up and holding me tight. I rested my forehead on my shoulder and fought back the sobs.

"Would it be easier for you if I go down alone, then you can come after I've gone?"

I shook my head as the sobs finally broke from my chest. "Don't be crazy, Cade. I'm spending every minute I can with you."

He kissed me long and hard before setting me on the floor and gathering up his things and I shoved my feet into my sneakers. He picked up his guitar and offered to take my bag for me with his over his other shoulder. He threw his head back and took a deep breath to steady himself before reaching for my hand, and we left the room without talking all the way down to the parking lot.

My mother and Denise's assistant, Zoey, were waiting to rush us behind the open door and tinted windows of my mom's Suburban.

Zoey started talking. "Are we ready to do this? Cade, I'll go to the airport with you and make sure security is on hand when we arrive."

Cade nodded and turned his back on her to hold me close. We clung to each other for five minutes without talking, both of us tearing up behind our sunglasses. My hands splayed out on his back and he bent his head to mine.

"I love you so much..." he whispered against my hair.

My arms tightened and I nodded. "Yeah. Me, too." I knew that if I didn't make a break for it, I would lose it and there were probably paparazzi lurking somewhere, trying to get pictures of everything. "Cade, I gotta get to my car. Will you call me tonight?"

His fingers brushed my chin and he lifted my face so he could give me a small, gentle kiss. "Every night, love." I nodded as my fingers closed around his for the last time and I brought his hand to my mouth one last time before I made a dash to my car.

Once I got inside, I flung my arms around the steering wheel and struggled not to let the sobs that threatened overtake me while I waited for my mom to join me. I tried to concentrate on breathing in and out, in and out.

It seemed to take hours, and the tears slipped silently from my eyes as my chest burned me alive. I felt like my fucking heart was ripped out of my body. I heard a knocking on the window and I pulled my head up to see Cade trying to get my attention.

He motioned for me to roll down the window so that he could talk to me.

"Are you okay?" His face held a worried expression and I knew he couldn't say all he wanted. I found it hard to speak, so I just wiped at my eyes and nodded. "I'll call you when I get to New York." Again I could only nod. "Love you." He mouthed at me, and then extended his hand toward the window one last time before hesitating and walking away.

I watched through blurry eyes as he got into the SUV and Jean climbed in the driver's side to take him to the airport. My mother finally got into the car with me, looked at me with sad eyes and placed a hand on my back.

"I'm sorry, honey. One thing is certain. He loves you, Brook."

I nodded, my head was still buried in my arms as a sob finally broke from my chest. "Mom, can you drive? I can't see. I... I ca... can't even breathe."

Chapter 8
Leave The Memories Alone

Caden

I FELT EMPTY. My heart lay cold and lifeless in my chest, as I sat in the first class cabin waiting for the bloody plane to take off and transport me to the empty wasteland that would consist of the next few months. I usually loved the energy of New York City, and when Denise lined up the audition for this new movie a year ago, I was excited for the opportunity to work with this director. But now, neither held the same appeal. The engines roared to life and the plane finally lifted off the runway. The waiting was the worst. At least once I arrived in New York I'd be one step closer to getting back to Brook.

It was a good script with several subplots that gave it quite a lot of depth, and the director was young enough that maybe he'd be open to interpretative discussion. If it weren't for my aching heart, I would have embraced this opportunity with relish.

The walk through the airport had been worse than I'd ever experienced before. For the first time I resented the fans; I hated them as they yelled and asked for autographs and pictures. I felt intruded upon and utterly violated as they all tried to peer into my life and invade my personal space.

The paparazzi ran after me like lunatics, asking me point blank if I was bloody shagging Brook. It made my head explode. Literally asking me if I'd fucked her. It was all I could do not to turn around and pound them. What was worse, I knew Brook would face similar situations during the next few weeks as we tried to navigate through life without each other. I felt furious that I couldn't protect her from all of that. I felt completely helpless.

For Christ's sake! They were such ruthless bastards.

The air rushed from my lungs as I pressed the heels of both hands against my eyes.

Maybe it hadn't been such a good idea to stay together at the hotel in light of the fact everyone seemed to know about it. Social media was exploding in the span of an hour and a half since I'd left her crying in her car. My eyes burned behind my closed lids.

My throat ached and my chest constricted as I remembered her tear stained face and finally her head buried in her arms, her body shaking with sobs around the steering wheel of her car. Diane had been so nice, hugging me goodbye and telling me that Brook would be okay. I'd turned my tortured gaze to her on my way into the SUV, and she brushed my hair back to try and comfort me. Nothing could bloody do that.

Leaving never got any fucking easier, even knowing how much we loved each other. Not being with her for so long, and seeing how much she was hurting... I was going to lose it. I felt myself breaking.

The book in my hands felt hot as I looked down upon it. The fabric covered journal, embossed with her name and the watermarked image of orchids in shades of gray on the black background had been my lifeline to Brook during those awful months when Wendy had pulled her tirade. It would be again now. This and the music that Brook had sent with me would have to be enough to keep her close.

I closed my eyes as images of us making love all night to those songs ran rampant in my head.

What a beautiful sentiment. The iTunes account made for the two of us so we would be able to send each other musical messages when we were unable to talk to each other. The time difference was going to kill so many opportunities. I'd be working for several hours before she'd even be out of bed and then sleeping or trying to, during Brook's evening hours. I smiled when I gave up that illusion. The hell I wouldn't be up late and on the phone or Skype as often as she would agree. I knew her production schedule included a lot of nights, so that would be another obstacle.

I sat up in my seat as I realized that while Brook told me the email address for the music account, she neglected to give me the password. I'd need to text her when I landed in NYC.

Denise was already in New York and would be there the first few days when we went through pre-production. She wanted to make sure that the PR people weren't doing anything shady and also to negotiate the schedule to see if she could get me at least two or three weekends off. She was a good friend and I was grateful that she was so adept at her job as my manager. If anyone could shove it up Pinnacle's ass, it was Denise. And she had the help of Jeanne and Joel. I smiled despite myself.

The flight attendant brought me a beer and after I'd downed half of it, I opened the journal, longing for Brook's words. If I couldn't hear her voice, at least I could read her words.

I set my beer on the tray table and flipped the cover open. As always, the scent of her perfume assailed my nostrils and made my heart beat faster. There was a letter in the front that hadn't been there before and I was curious as I unfolded it. Of course... it was from Brook. She must have slipped it inside last night. My hands were shaking, slightly, as I slowly unfolded it.

> *~Cade,*
>
> *Last night meant everything to me and I'll cherish every moment we've shared. Having you with me, so close to me, and knowing how much you love me, has been the greatest gift of my life.*
>
> *I'm so proud of you and know you'll be amazing in this new film. I'll miss you and ache for you every single second you're away from me. You have all of my heart, forever. Remember... I love you, so much.*
>
> *~Yours Always,*
> *Brook*
> *P.S. PW = CadeNBrook*

My heart swelled at her words and also the choice of password. One of the gossip gurus had combined our names for our rumored couple status and while neither Brook nor I were particularly fond of labels, we agreed that this was one we would be able to live with.

CadeNBrook I shook my head and ran my hand through my messy locks. Bloody perfect. How could I expect anything less?

I flipped open the cover and rested my hand lovingly on the page, my fingers tracing over the words. Brook's rough handwriting filled page after page as she poured her emotions out to herself, and to me. Her love was so precious and had become a tangible part of my existence. My heart raced as I began to read.

April 15

We worked on the coffee shop scene today. Most of the extras were local, and I could see them all stare at Cade as Martin prepped the scene and the makeup and hair people did a re-touch. The women were so obvious; standing close and never taking their eyes off of him. It was SO annoying, but I hope I didn't let it show. That would have been embarrassing.

Cade and I had practiced the lines over and over the night before, even though this was one of the scenes we did at Cade's audition. Both of us knew the dialogue forward and backwards, but I made the excuse that we should run the lines so that I could be with him last night. Every cell in my body was screaming one thing over and over... STAY. I feel guilty because of my relationship with David, but I can't begin to help what I'm feeling.

Cade touches me... without touching me, holds me without holding me. I can't fucking explain it, but I'm aching for him. Yearning for his kisses and his touch... I feel him on my skin just from the way he looks at me. I feel like there are magnets in my chest that pull me to him. God, I wanted the scene to continue, but I could only flub my lines so long before Cade gave me a strange look because of all the rehearsal.

At the end of the scene when we hugged, I never wanted to let go. I love being close to him. One take and we nailed it, but at the end his eyes dropped to my mouth and the pull was so strong, all I wanted was his mouth on mine. I thought I would die when the scene was done and we hadn't kissed.

That beautiful mouth haunts my dreams nightly. So many nights I lay here listening to music, wondering what he's doing... if he ever thinks about me like this. This song playing now... God, it's so perfect for how I feel about Cade. The longing I feel consumes me, sometimes more than I can deal with.

The air left my lungs and my eyes closed as her words and emotions took my breath away. In the margin, Brook had written *Incredible Love by I. Michaelson.* The song flashed through my head as I tried to remember the lyrics.

Incredible love... you fill me... spill me... kill me.

Brook was right. That was so bloody us, I thought. Right from the moment I'd first laid eyes on her.

Ingrid Michaelson was one of my favorite singer/songwriters. I loved the soulfulness of her lyrics and rich melodies of her music. She'd gotten more famous, but I listened to her stuff before anyone knew her name. I'd played that song many times, thinking of Brook. During the early days of working on pre-production, we'd talked about anything and everything, not the least of which was our favorite music, books, and movies.

Brook and I shared so much and were so in sync. No one could ever be more amazing or more perfect for me. Getting to know her just made me more and more certain that she would be the love of my life. Even that early in production and despite her relationship with that wanker, David, I knew I had to do whatever necessary to make it happen. Whatever necessary.

All the women screaming after me became a joke because the one that I wanted above all others seemed elusive and untouchable. She had been so young, and I felt insecure about whether I should even approach her. There were so many times when I thought it might never come to fruition.

But now, almost a year and a half later, here in my hands was the proof that she was not left untouched by the love I felt and showered upon her. I loved knowing the words stating her love, were written at the same time I was struggling to control my own feelings. It was a deep connection and it meant the world to me.

I vaguely remembered hearing *Incredible Love* last night while we made love, but I had been so lost in the passionate haze, and the pleasure of her body, and the sadness that enveloped us, that I couldn't be sure. I pulled the iPod out of my duffel and searched through the songs. There it was. I put the buds in my ears and let the music transport me back into her arms and back to the day when she'd written the entry in her journal.

The ache in my chest began to subside slightly. I'd miss her like hell, but at least I could be certain that she loved me. She loved me beyond reason, just as I loved her... and the knowledge gave me the strength to get through the next weeks.

My heart swelled as I let the lyrics rush through me, the music so sensual as it surrounded me.

Brook felt these things for me before I'd told her that I loved her... I had to have faith that if the bond between us was so unspoken then, now we could survive anything. After all we had been through, all we had felt and said to each other, nothing in the world would bloody come between us.

Nothing.

Brooklyn

"BROOK... HONEY, it will be okay. That boy loves you."

I sat despondently in the passenger seat of my car as my mother drove us back to my parents' house. I'd put my sunglasses on to hide my swollen eyes. I felt so tired.

"I know he loves me," I said softly though I was filled with sadness. "Three months seems like forever. Our production schedules are so screwed that we'll have a hell of a time seeing each other at all until the end of August for Comic-Con." I leaned my head on the window and closed my eyes and willed myself not to cry. "I already miss him."

"What can I do to help?" Mom asked and reached for my hand. She squeezed softly, but I didn't find comfort in her attempt. Only one touch, one voice, one face would comfort me.

It wouldn't do any good to lament a situation that I had no control over so I quickly brushed the tears from my cheeks and answered my mother.

"I think I'd like to look for a place of my own, Mom." When my mother gasped and began to speak, I quickly continued. "I want a private place that Cade and I can be together. It's time that I took that step anyway, don't you think?"

"You're so young," she began.

I rolled my eyes and sighed. "I'm almost twenty, mom. Plus, I'm older in my head than most people my age. You've always said so."

"I know, but still..."

"But nothing, mom. I need this. Decorating and setting up a place will give me something to concentrate on other than Cade being gone."

"Are you planning on having him move in with you?" she asked hesitantly.

I thought about it for a moment before I answered. Nothing would make me happier than having him live with me, but we still had Pinnacle to deal with. "Um... we haven't really discussed it, but I can't see us being apart when we're in the same city. I doubt we can officially move in together even though I know that Cade gave up his apartment when he went back to London... last January."

"He was in so much pain. I know you both were."

"Yes... but it's made us a lot stronger. I can't say that seeing him kissing another chick for this film is going to be a breeze, but I trust him completely. Pinnacle is going to try to spin the shit out of any photos of him with his new co-star, and Cade's worried how it will affect me. So I have to be like iron." A new sense of control and determination came over me.

"What did you tell him, Brook? He always puts your feelings first. Even your father has noticed."

I smiled, the corners of my mouth lifted sadly. "Yeah and there isn't anything I wouldn't do for him either." I ran a hand through my hair and turned my body more toward the center of the car. "I told him that I love him more than anything, that I'm proud of him and that I know he'll rock the shit out of this movie. Because he will, Mom."

She didn't say anything, just nodded with a big grin on her face. She'd support us, no matter what we were planning, which was a relief. It was apparent from her appearance today at The Beverly Hills Hotel, so I felt the time had come to tell her about the engagement ring. My hand went up to lovingly touch the diamond heart hanging beneath my shirt. I pulled it out and stroked it between my fingers.

"Mom..." I paused when she looked at me and smiled after seeing the necklace in my hands.

"That's certainly beautiful, Brook. It's obvious how much he adores you. You should have seen his face today after you started crying and he still had to leave you. My heart was breaking for both of you."

My chest constricted at the memory of him tapping on the window, the look on his face so lost as he slowly moved away from my car.

Jesus. I closed my eyes.

"I know. It kills me when he's hurting. I'm hoping that after this summer, things will be easier, and we'll have less time apart. He... Cade asked me to marry him, Mom." My eyes snapped to her face, and I held my breath waiting for her to blow her top and tell me I was way too young to get married.

She didn't. She just smiled and nodded her head. "I know. Your father does too, Brook. We were wondering how long it would take you to tell us."

My eyes widened and I shook my head slightly, almost imperceptibly.

"What? But... how did you know?"

She sighed as she turned into our neighborhood and drove down the street to our house. "He came to us and asked for our permission."

Thud. My heart stopped and my breath left my lungs.

It was so... *Cade*. "When?"

"The day after Thanksgiving. Before you woke up, honey. He asked us if he could talk to us when I was making breakfast. He was so cute, running his hands through his hair over and over... so nervous. He sat down and told us how much he loved you and wanted to take care of you, that he valued you above all everything else in the world. Your father always liked Cade, honey, but that morning, Brook, his chest puffed up like he was his own son. I've wanted to tell you for months."

My hand covered my mouth as my eyes welled. I couldn't speak.

My mother pulled into our garage and shut the car off before she turned to me.

"He told us that he'd already asked you and you said yes, but he wouldn't even think of going through with anything until he knew he had our blessing. He showed me the ring, Brook. It's gorgeous."

I felt a sob rise in my chest as she put her arms around me. "Mom... I... can't believe this! I don't think I can breathe if I don't marry him."

"I know. He told us something so similar. He said he didn't want a life without you, Brook," her voice caught as we both cried together.

"What did you and Dad tell him?" I choked out.

"I just hugged him and your father said that nothing would make him prouder than to welcome Cade into our family."

"Oh, my God," I cried and laughed at the same time. "He's so flipping perfect, isn't he?" I pulled back from her and tried to wipe the tears from my face. "Isn't he?"

"Yes, perfect," she agreed, "but we are hoping you'll wait a while."

"Cade isn't rushing me, Mom. In fact, he rarely speaks of it, but I do know that it would make him happy to see that ring on my finger. He's such an honest person he wants to be real and tell everyone we're together."

"I can understand that. He deserves that, Brook. If you love him, you should want the world to know too."

"I do. But we've got these damn contracts for now. We're planning on being more open during the third film and the managers and lawyers are dealing with it all. Hopefully, it can be sooner than later. We just have to get through the next three months."

***

I WOKE THE NEXT morning early to the sound of Cade's voice on my alarm. I had the Allure photo shoot and hair and makeup call was at 9 AM.

Hair.

My stomach lurched at the prospect of chopping it all off for my next role, but it had to be done. I knew that I'd never throw myself into the role if I didn't fully commit to it, besides sometimes those movie hair people didn't exactly make that shit look real. This cover was coming out in November, just before *Don't Forget to Remember Me* hit theaters, so I still had to look like Julia. Only hotter, I hoped.

Leave it to Jeanne to make sure all of my ducks were in a row. She was my organizer and kept me on track, so yes, this shoot had to be today. I wanted Cade to see these pictures and miss me. Okay, more than miss me. I'd settle for aching uncomfortably. I smirked at myself. Maybe that was mean but I needed him to want me and miss me as much as I missed him.

I searched for a sexy song to send him that he could listen to when those pictures hit the Internet. No doubt within twenty-four hours. That fucking shit pissed me off, but it was expected.

I found the perfect song and typed out an email to Cade to go along with it.

> *-C*
> *The lyrics to this are so effing hot and it's exactly what you do to me. If you find the photos tonight, listen to this song. Know that this is how I feel and you are who I'm thinking about, with my eyes focused on you, and this music in my head, my body on fire for yours and my heart full of love for you. You're mine and I'm yours...*
> *I want you... Love you... need you...*
> *-B*

I added *Oh My God* by Pink to the iPod library. I knew he'd get it when he woke up. My heart raced when I saw a message from him waiting in my inbox, the subject line, Leave the Memories Alone.

I opened the message, my heart thumping in my chest as I read words.

>*Babe,*
>*I don't want to see the way it is, as to how it used to be...*
>*I'm missing you desperately. Even one night without you in my arms is too many. I'll remember everything about you... Your beautiful face, the way you smell and taste... How you feel in my arms. I love you more than anything.*
>*Don't ever forget that.*
>*Always,*
>*-C*

God. As I downloaded *Leave the Memories Alone* on iTunes. I was running late, so I'd have to listen to it on my way to the shoot. That song plus the one I'd just sent to Cade would be playing in my head all day. I smiled as I imagined his reaction. It was super hot, and I hope it worked him up.

I got up, went into the bathroom and turned on the shower, letting my thoughts drift back to the conversation I'd had with Cade the night before as I stepped under the hot spray.

He'd made it to New York and met with the director and production manager for dinner. His co-stars would be on set later in the week, but Cade had some scenes to film on his own first. My heart tightened a little at the thought of him being away from me and working with someone else on a romantic film. I wished it weren't romantic. I had some damn space odyssey dystopian thing and he had a romance. Awesome. I let the water soothe me as I washed my hair and remembered his voice on the phone the night before.

I had snuggled into my bed wearing one of his T-Shirts that he'd worn the day before; his scent floating around me and his velvet voice in my ear. So sexy...

"Brook, I miss you... I bloody hate this."

I sighed and rolled onto my back, searching for the words he needed to hear.

"Me too, but we'll be okay. I still love you... even if it is from across the country," I said softly.

He sighed heavily on the other end of the phone. "Yeah, but it sucks to be without you, love."

I felt my body flush at the words and my heart swell. "I know. I feel it too, but I am trying so hard to stay positive. Feeling like crap only means I love you. I'd feel worse if I didn't miss you this much. So I want the ache. I want it," I whispered.

"Ugh... God, Brook," he moaned into the phone and my body tightened and throbbed at the sound. "Believe me, I ache too. In *several* places."

I laughed, happily. "I'm wearing your T-Shirt. It still smells like you. I never want to wash it."

"Mmm. I miss you."

"Just think how much I'm going to climb all over you when I see you next. Mmm..." I teased. "And the pictures tomorrow; are just for you."

"Has it only been fifteen hours since I've touched you? It feels like fifteen fucking years."

"Uhhh, Cade. I hope it gets easier."

"Impossible."

I smiled into the phone. "Tell me what you've got going on tomorrow."

He proceeded to tell me about the production schedule and meeting the co-stars, and how Denise was working to get him some time off, maybe around the Fourth of July. My mind was already reeling about how I could get some time off to surprise him in New York as well, knowing that we couldn't go ten weeks without seeing each other. We stayed on the phone for almost two hours and it was very hard to let him go, but I heard him yawn and knew he'd have to be up fairly early. Given the time difference, he'd only have three or four hours of sleep.

"Baby, you need to sleep. I'll call you tomorrow."

"I don't think I'll sleep without you, Brook."

"Do something to relax. Take a shot of something, take a shower, or..."

"Your hands are the only ones I want on me, if you're suggesting what I think you're suggesting." He laughed softly.

"It's just a thought," I said softly and smiled into the phone. "Better your hands than someone else's."

"Brook." His voice hardened a little. "That isn't going to happen. You aren't seriously worried about that are you?"

"No. I trust you, but there will be women throwing themselves at you, and your new co-star will probably—"

He cut me off. "Stop it, right now. None of that matters anymore here than if you're right in front of me. Don't you know how much I fucking love you?" His voice was angry and shaking slightly.

"Calm down, sweetie. I know. I'm sorry. I shouldn't have said that. I guess I'm a little insecure. It's sort of me against the entire world when it comes to you."

He sighed loudly. "Yes it is. And the entire bloody world doesn't stand a chance in hell, Brook, okay?" He paused for a few seconds.

"Just... please don't make me feel like you don't trust me. I've got issues too. David is in L.A. and I'm not. Don't think that hasn't crossed my fucking mind." I could hear the exasperation laced in his voice.

"David? Who is he again?" I tried to tease him and laughed quietly, hoping Cade would join in. He didn't.

"I'm trying to forget."

"Okay, baby. I'm sorry. Love you," I promised. "Go to bed now and tomorrow when you see pictures of me on those gossip bastard's websites, I'll be sending you a message, before and during the shoot, okay?"

He finally laughed then. "Yeah, okay, my love. I'll send you a song for when you wake up. By the way, I read the journal on the plane and saw the note in the margin about Ingrid Michaelson. We have that incredible love."

I remembered writing how my body and heart had ached for him while that song played in my room that night.

"I love that song. Fill me..." I moaned at the memory.

"Yes... Spill me..." he said softly in return, both of us echoing the lyrics.

"Oh my God. I have to go... you're killing me."

"What a way to die. I love you so much. Goodnight, honey."

"Love you... you hang up first."

"You hang up first..." he laughed.

"Okay, but only because you need to sleep. I really love you, Cade. Have fun tomorrow."

"Love you too, baby." I hung up the phone and rolled on my side and missed him.

Caden

THE DAY WENT BY relatively quickly, laced with hot text messages to and from Brook. I had a shit-eating grin on my face the entire day since this morning when I got that damn song.

Bloody Hell, it was hot.

It had me jazzing all day to see the damn photos as soon as possible. I never thought I'd be happy to have something leaked online, but I couldn't fucking wait.

The director, Alan Cortman, and I spent part of the day going over production and I had some wardrobe fittings. I didn't know why they bloody needed that shit, and wondered why I just couldn't wear my own clothes. The character was basically an unkempt slob and hell if I couldn't do that without any fancy help.

I was able to go back to my hotel late afternoon and went to PopSugar and Googled Brook. There she was in her signature tight jeans, and an I Love New York T-Shirt, sunglasses and her earbuds from her iPod hanging from her ears. She looked right at those damn paparazzi and smiled wide for the cameras.

The first message delivered to me and hinted to the world. I fucking love New York. *Bloody Brilliant.*

The earbuds were probably pounding out Oh My God, Oh My God, Oh My God... My body swelled and throbbed painfully at the thought. Damn if she couldn't make me come from three thousand miles away. I smiled to myself and tried to spend the remainder of the afternoon going over the script.

I wished I was able to run around the city, but I realized it wasn't possible. I'd asked Daniel to visit on the coming weekend and so maybe I'd get out a little then. I was trying to fill up what little free time I had so the time would pass more quickly.

The storyline of *Only Us* was a good one with many layers and I tried to look forward to it and dive into it full on. I ordered room service and went over the script for a couple of hours before my phone vibrated.

Shoot ended a couple of hours ago. Let me know when you see them. They're all for you. OMG! XOXO

I moved to the desk and turned on the laptop and Googled Brook and Allure Magazine. The pictures popped up immediately.

Holy Hell!

I sat down and stared. She was so fucking beautiful, her light eyes magnificent against her pale skin, dark eye makeup, and windblown hair. I felt my dick harden and I thanked God that she was mine. Shot after shot, she was smoldering, her lips full and open... wanting. *Dear God.* My mouth went dry and the blood raced all around my body at the speed of light. I sat mesmerized by her eyes, her hair and her bare skin.

Fuck me.

Every shot was hot and showing skin. Her shoulder was bare in some of them, but the ones with the short skirt and the thigh-high boots were my undoing. I saved all of them and put one on my desktop and just stared at it, until I remembered that she wanted me to play that song as I looked at them.

I opened iTunes, started the song and then took out my phone to text Brook.

Oh my fucking God. You are the hottest, most beautiful thing I've ever seen... I love you so bloody much. I'm such a lucky bastard.

Forget the bloody script. I wasn't moving from this computer for the rest of the night. The song flooded through my head... and I sat back in the chair and ran my hands through my hair, my body throbbing to the point of pain. The song was sex set to music, and Brook was smoldering in the photos.

Jesus Christ. She knew how to torture me, and make me want so fucking bad I could barely stand it. She was a temptress and I loved every bloody minute of it. She made me happy, despite the distance. My heart was so full, thudding so fast it would fly from my chest and my body so turned on, I couldn't bloody breathe.

My phone vibrated on the desk next to the computer and I opened the message from Brook.

**That's what you do to me. Oh my God'em, oh my God'em...
OH MY GOD!**

The breath rushed from my lungs and I smiled to myself as I searched for a song to send her that would make her scream for me.

Two could play at this bloody game.

Chapter 9
Crazy Love

Brooklyn

THE NEXT TWO WEEKS passed by in a blur of music, tears and hard work. The day after my Allure shoot, I had my hair cut and dyed. I tried to be brave about it, but afterward, I fucking lost it. Cade's sexy song selection for the day hadn't even helped. He'd sent me *Freek* by George Michael in response to the Pink song I'd sent him the day before. It was super hot, but I was in a funk over my stupid hair.

The dark color made my skin look even paler and my blue eyes pop, but I hated it. I never wanted to go out in public again. The paparazzi followed me out of the salon and were relentless, asking me personal questions about whether I had relationship with Cade.

We both decided that maybe it wasn't such a good idea to stay together in Beverly Hills in light of the new wrath of shit raining down on us about it, but I wouldn't trade one minute of it for anything. It was beautiful and painful, but like everything else with Cade, completely worth it. That night he listened to me cry on the phone for two hours, telling me I was beautiful over and over again, his velvet voice trying to comfort and reassure me. We hadn't had more than a ten-minute conversation since that one, and I was missing him in a major way.

He'd been very busy and so had I, meeting with Patrick Armstrong and some of the cast, getting final costume fittings, makeup tests and fitness training for hours on end. I spent endless hours trying to get the mannerisms, facial expressions and general quirks for my character down and it was time-consuming and exhausting.

Cade's friend, Daniel Mayfield, came to the States to spend his first weekend with him so he'd have someone to explore New York with. Cade said it had been a good time and the first and last time he'd been able to go out without huge mobs of girls chasing after him. It was completely insane and I worried about him.

He'd seen some of the Internet pictures of my new *look*, for lack of a better word, and he'd been so supportive. Deep down, I knew he had to hate it. Hell, *I* hated it, so how could he help it?

Our schedules were so nuts that we lived on the song exchange and countless text messages. Our managers were working on the plan to distance me from David publically at the same time as Pinnacle was doing their best to hook Cade up with his new co-star, Davina Duchman. It was expected to promote his new film,, but it literally made me crazy.

It was weird seeing *"Cade gives Brook an Ultimatum!"* on the same rack as *"As things heat up with Davina, Cade dumps Brook!"*

Fucking polar opposite bullshit. Could that be more of an oxymoron? I wouldn't be surprised if Davina were chasing after Cade, but the less I knew about it, the better. It didn't help my piece of mind that she dumped her husband just in time to hit the set of *Only Us*.

Hello? Coincidence much? Hardly.

I couldn't help the insecurity that made my heart drop. She was beautiful and worldly in a way that only age and experience could create, but I had to focus on my own film and did my best not to think about it.

Jeanne and Denise had the ultimatum article leaked so there would be sufficient time until Comic-Con and getting back to the set of *A Love Like This* next September to make it all more believable. They were planting the seed that David and I were finished and then bracing the world for Cade and me to come out as a couple when we got back to set. It would appear that I made the choice to be with Cade after enough time had passed to realistically put Pinnacle's botched beard scheme to bed.

The real ultimatum was the one Cade gave Pinnacle to let us be together by the time the third film went into production, but what the hell? Whatever worked so that we could eventually be more open about our relationship was fine by me. All of this crap was exhausting and I was so over it.

I was on a break with another young actress; Stacy Mills. We were sitting on the ground in the shade sipping cokes and going over our next scene, when my phone rang. It was Cade, but it was unusual he'd call in the middle of the day. He never did that so I answered as fast as I could. I stood up and moved away from Stacy, making sure she didn't see Cade's name flashing on my phone and careful to turn my back so she wouldn't hear the conversation.

"Hey…"

He was breathing hard. "Cade?"

"Brook, thank God. I really needed to hear your voice." I could hear the tremors in his tone but his voice was quiet.

"What's wrong?" He didn't answer and I felt the panic beginning to rise inside my chest. "Babe, are you okay?"

He sighed and I knew he was either running his hands through his hair or covering his eyes with them. I'd seen him do it so many times when he'd been frustrated or anxious.

"Not really, no.   Bloody hell! The fans here in New York are complete lunatics. The security team has tried to keep them off of me, but they are fucking *everywhere*." His voice was loaded with incredulity and a hint of anger and even fear.

"Oh my God. Do you want me to have Joel call Pinnacle? I mean... what can we do? What just happened?"

He laughed nervously and took a deep breath.

"Where are you?" The questions spilled out of me.

"All I was doing was going to the set, Brook. Hundreds of bloody girls started screaming and running after me down the bloody street. The guys had to get physical with them. One of the guys shoved and literally pinched them to keep them off of me. They were touching me, pulling, and clawing at my clothes... Jesus, I've never seen anything remotely like it. It's... madness. I utterly *hate* being here."

I let my breath out in a rush and I felt my eyes begin to prick. "Oh my God, Cade, I'm so sorry. I wish I could come up there and beat their moronic asses!" My heart was breaking for him and I couldn't stand the thought of all of those women treating him like that... like he wasn't a human being, but just an object that they wanted a piece of. I tried to joke to help him relax.

He laughed softly, finally calming down a little bit. "I'd love to see that Brook. Actually, it is weird that when you're around, the girls are more respectful. Why do you think that is?" I pictured the soft smile I knew would be turning his mouth up at the corners as the soft words tumbled from his beautiful mouth.

I struggled to swallow the rising lump in my throat, although I didn't have much luck. My skin flushed with warmth. "Because their stupid fantasies die with a dose of reality, maybe?" I knew my voice was trembling but there wasn't a fucking thing I could do about it.

"Hey... don't get upset. I'm sorry. I shouldn't have called you with this, sweetheart. You definitely are my reality, my love."

I was feeling anxious, afraid for his safety and my mind raced on what could be done or how in the hell I could get out there. I needed to wrap my arms around him, to stroke his hair back and feel his heart beating next to mine. Like I was the strong one; what a gigantic joke.

"Brook, are you still there?"

"Yes. Sorry, sweets. Of course you should have called me! I'm just... so scared and just... *pissed* that this is happening. What a hellacious nightmare! I wish..."

Cade sighed and finished my thoughts, "We could be together? Yeah, me too. I miss you," he said softly.

"Would it help if I came out there? I mean... I can't promise, but I can try."

He groaned. "God, that would be amazing, but don't jeopardize your film, babe." A few seconds ticked by in silence and I wondered what was happening. I could hear the screaming in the background and I grimaced. "Denise is trying to get some time off for me too, but I don't know when it will be. I bloody hate not knowing when we'll see each other again."

"Yeah. It hasn't even been that long and I'm not doing so well. The songs are helping, but I miss being with you." The cast was moving around and my production assistant was waving me back from break.

"Ugh! There are no words. It's only been eight days. I say *only* because I'm counting down to the end. Eighty-one days to bloody go."

I closed my eyes at his words, before opening them and running after my cast mates.

"I *do* know, I'm counting, too. Shit, Cade, I have to go. We're being called to set. I'm... scared for you, I wish we could talk later, but I'm working late tonight. I'll send you a note and a song when I'm finished, but you should be sleeping by then. Should I call Jeanne and tell her to get on Pinnacle?"

"Honey, there's no need. Denise already called them, but we may need to call Joel if they don't increase security."

"Okay. I'll have him call you. Please be careful. I love you."

He sighed. "I love you, Brook... and you look hot in those leather pants. I'll ring you tomorrow, love. "

I laughed, knowing which photo he was referring to. "You Googled."

"Of course," he chuckled, and I could hear that he was more centered and felt better from our talk. I felt a great deal of pride that I had the ability to calm him and make him smile. My heart swelled with emotions. Jesus, I missed him.

"Love you. Bye."

"Bye, love."

Caden

THE REST OF THE week Brook and I barely spoke, but the songs kept coming. Sometimes I was so tired at the end of the day I just wanted to fall into bed, but I always found myself looking up whatever I could find of her online, new pictures and news about her film, and I never missed a day of sending her songs. Each and every morning I would wake up and find a note and song from her too, but I missed her voice and the feel of her soft skin beneath my lips. I sighed as I opened the newest one. It was short, but the words overwhelmed me, and my heart ached.

> *-C*
> *My arms may be empty and aching, but my soul is so full of you. I'm yours & you're mine. I love you...*
> *-B*
> *The song is... Soulmate by Natasha Beddingfield*

I closed my eyes. Jesus, she was amazing. In all the madness and despite the distance and our incredibly crazy schedules, Brook was still my center; the anchor of my chaotic existence.

Only Us was going well. The days were packed and long. Only one thing was missing. The director had bounced me about the obvious lack of chemistry with my co-star, insisting that the fans would be looking to see the screen set ablaze like they did in *The Future of Our Past*.

Bloody Hell. I couldn't fucking *manufacture* it, but if I were honest, I didn't want to get to know her. I didn't have the same desire to spend time with her like I had with Brook. Frankly, she left me cold, and I couldn't even be sure it was because of my blazing love for Brook that kept me distanced or just the fact that Davina had such a plastic personality. Either way, it didn't matter.

Davina tried to talk to me and break the ice on several occasions and I'd been avoiding her. We had a kissing scene coming up in filming this Friday and I knew I'd have to try harder if it was to be at all believable. Leave it to Pinnacle to make sure the kissing rubbish was scheduled at the front of the production so it would hit the stands as soon as possible and they could start weaving their hype and lies.

My heart constricted. I had to tell Brook because I didn't want her bombarded with the press and Internet barrage, and no doubt Wendy wouldn't pass up that opportunity to bring it to her attention. Brook would say she was fine with it, but I knew it bothered her just like it would me if she were making out with some other bloke; on screen or off. We could say it a million times... *It's just a job*, but it was still hard to see it unfold.

Brook's movie, was coming out around the time *Only Us* was, and I'd have to watch her naked with some other guy, so maybe a kiss or two wasn't so bad. I tried to rationalize it all away. She was almost nude with me in our series, so it wasn't likely Jeanne would be able to negotiate her out of nudity for this film. Ugh! I should have thought of that.

I clicked reply on the email and attached the song.

> *B-*
> *You give me crazy love, Brook... It makes me crazy and makes me calm, it's everything... all I need in the world is you. Listen to the lyrics, love...*
> *The song is Crazy Love, by Van Morrison.*
> *-C*

I took out my phone and dialed Denise on my way down the hall to the elevator. I knew when the doors opened John and Brian would be there to ward off the screaming masses, so I stood and looked out the window of my hotel as I waited for her to answer.

"Hi, honey. What's up? Are you okay?" Denise always sounded upbeat but her voice held a slight strain, and I was sure that was caused by the numerous calls I'd been inundating her with. It was due to the stalking incident, the issues she was trying to work out with security, and also my incessant pestering for time off.

"Yes. I'm just checking in. I'm getting ready to face the mobs again," I sighed into the phone and leaned my head on the window.

"I know! It's bullshit, Cade. I'm working on it. I told Pinnacle we needed to get the streets blocked off further back from the set and add two more guys to travel with you, at the very least; but they're pandering."

"Jesus, Denise. I shouldn't have to have an entourage of security! This film isn't even that big for Christ's sake," I said in frustration.

"I'm doing what I can, Cade. Your safety is my first concern. I'm sorry if it cramps your style." She sounded irritated.

"I don't mean that I'm ungrateful. I just think it's bloody ridiculous. And..."

"And?" she asked impatiently.

"I'm anxious for a trip out to Los Angeles," I said softly.

"Cade, it hasn't even been two weeks. You have to deal with it for a while longer. How are things with Davina?"

"Horrible. Do we have to go there?" I begged.

"She seems like a nice young woman and from what I've seen a pretty decent actress."

"She's... boring. I have nothing in common with her. Talking with her is like pulling teeth. It's bloody uncomfortable. It's all I can do not to bolt in the opposite direction, between takes."

"You're being melodramatic," Denise warned. "Are you sure you just aren't coming up with reasons to keep a distance between the two of you?"

I groaned into the phone because she was probably right.

"Maybe a little, but I can't help it."

"Look, you know she isn't going to be Brook. Get over it, babe,"

Denise said flippantly. "You have to deal and get your head in the game."

I rolled my eyes even though Denise couldn't see me do it. "No, she's definitely not Brook. I'm sorry. I'll try to be more receptive to getting to know her if you'll get me out to L.A. I've never been this miserable on a job."

She laughed. "What you are is pathetic, Cade. We can't have the press documenting your trips to Los Angeles after we just broke that *ultimatum* story. You know that."

"So charter a plane. I don't care what it costs."

"Money isn't the problem. Schedules, remember?"

"Yeah, I understand. I have to go to work, Denise, just do the best you can."

"I will, hon. Have a good day, and Cade?"

"Yeah?" I stopped.

"Can you pretend it's Brook with you in those love scenes? That might make it easier for you."

"Yeah, right. That would only be possible if I could shut down all five of my bloody senses. All *five*."

"Like I said...*fucking* pathetic," she laughed.

"You don't know the half of it. Later."

Brooklyn

A MASS OF PAPARAZZI waited as I pulled up at my new apartment at the end of the day's shooting. It was Thursday and I was hoping to spend a quiet night at home. With any luck, Cade would have some time to talk tonight. Missing him was even worse than I'd imagined.

I took a deep breath and opened my door, stealing myself for their harsh words and thousands of flashes. They were more frantic than usual, and I heard one theme over and over again... screaming in my head, my heart ready to explode and my lungs gasping for breath.

"Brook... how's Cade? Have you heard? There was an accident on set!"

Oh, my god! My heart fell.

My feet flew up the stairs to my apartment and my hand took out my phone to call Cade. I slammed the door shut behind me and I felt my knees give way beneath me as I fell to the floor, but managing to hold the phone to my ear. It rang and went to voicemail.

My hands were trembling so much I could barely push the numbers as I dialed Denise. Once again, it went straight to voicemail. Frantically, I tried Cade's number again, and again; voicemail. I rolled onto my side and sobbed into my hands.

Oh God. Please let him be okay. Please let him answer! Tears were streaming down my face and my chest constricted. My phone rang and it was my mother.

"Mom! I heard Cade was hurt, and I can't reach him! Oh my God. I need to go to New York," I cried into the phone. "Right now!"

"Baby, calm down. We'll find out what's going on, but you can't go running off without knowing what's going on."

"Mom! He isn't answering his phone and I can't reach Denise either! I can't just sit here, not knowing! I have to go!!"

"Brook, calm down. I'll call around and see what I can find out. You call Jeanne and have her call the studio and try to get some answers. I'll call you back, honey. I'm sure he's fine."

I was gasping for breath as I tried to form the words. "Mom... Oh God. I'm scared. What if..."

"We don't know what happened or if it's even true right now, Brook. You aren't doing Cade any good by freaking out. Just breathe and we'll get to the bottom of it."

I dialed Jeanne the minute I hung up with my mother.

When she answered, I was frantic. "Jeanne! " "I just heard Cade got hurt on set, and I'm going out of my mind." I wiped at the tears rolling down my face, and my voice broke.

"Holy shit, Brook! Have you tried to call him?"

"Yeah. All I get is voicemail. Denise, too. I need to go to New York, Jeanne. Can you help me? Please?"

"Brook, I'll see what I can find out. Let's wait on the trip to New York, for now. This may be nothing. It might even be a seed to see if they can get a reaction out of you. Nothing will confirm your relationship more if you go running off to New York at the mention of a rumor."

"I need to be with him. Even if he's okay, I need to fucking see for myself, Jeanne!" I knew I was losing it, becoming hysterical, but there was nothing I could do about the anxiety and fear I was feeling.

She hung up and I did the only thing I could do. My eyes were blurred with the force of the pain, but I took a bag down from my closet shelf and started shoving clothes into it as fast as I could. My phone vibrated on my bed and I grabbed it, hoping it was Cade, but it wasn't, but at least it was Denise.

"Is Cade okay?" I cried into the phone. "Just tell me he's okay," I rasped out.

"Brook, he's okay. He's bruised and sore, but he's fine, honey." Relief flooded over me and once again my legs gave out beneath me as I dropped my head and sobbed.

"Oh sweetheart, he's okay..." she said softly. "I'm sorry, Brook."

I was gasping for breath. "W-what happened?"

"It was fans, Brook. A dozen or so broke through the barricades and stormed him on set. He took off running and tripped over something."

"Oh, Jesus," I cried and anger rose inside me like a sickness. "Something has to be done about those freaks, Denise! Where were his bodyguards and why can't I reach him?"

"They were with him, but he was on set. They don't surround him during filming, obviously. Cade broke into a run to get away from them and tripped. When he fell, his phone went flying into a brick wall and was shattered. I'm getting him another one and I'm on my way to him now. When I get there, I'll have him call you on my phone, okay?"

I took a deep breath. "Yeah. I need to see him, Denise. I'm trying to get out there." I got up and started packing again.

"No, Brook. Cade already told them he's not working this weekend. You have some scheduled filming, so I'll get him out to you. He wants to come to L.A., okay? He has some scenes in the morning, but then I'll put him on a plane."

I sat down on the bed and held a hand out in front of me. I was shaking so bad that it amazed me that I didn't drop the fucking phone. I took a deep breath, trying to calm myself. "Okay. How long until you get to him?"

"Maybe ten minutes. They have a medical team checking him out at the hotel, but they told me he's fine. I'm going right over there. I'll have him call you as soon as I get there. Try to calm down, Brook."

I sat on the bed and tried to get control of my emotions, the fear still ripping through my body. I felt helpless being so far away and not able to see for myself that he wasn't hurt. I sat here, trapped; powerless to offer him comfort, unable to put my arms around him and whisper that I loved him.

I was still shaking as I went to my laptop and turned it on; longing, yet terrified to see what I could find about it online. All I could find of what happened, that he was basically attacked on set and his bodyguards weren't able to keep the crazy bitches at bay as they chased him through the streets. I went to the refrigerator and poured a glass of Perrier and took a big drink of it as I paced back and forth for what seemed like hours; I knew it was only a few minutes when my phone finally rang.

"Cade?"

I quickly answered and strained to hear his voice above the thundering of blood in my ears.

'Yeah, it's me, love."

I felt my fragile hold on my emotions begin to slip. "Oh thank God." My voice cracked and I sank down on the couch. "Are you hurt? Those crazy bitches! I swear to God…"

"Hush. I'm okay, Brook."

I started crying, a mixture of relief, fear and frustration washed over me like a wave. I felt weak, defenseless and sad. "No! This shit shouldn't happen! I was so worried and then when I couldn't reach you… Oh, God…" I started to sob in earnest again, shaking as I sat alone in my apartment. "What would I have done if something happened to you?"

"Brook. Nothing's gonna happen. I'm okay. I have bruises and the right side of my body is sore, but nothing's broken. I won't even miss any work." Cade tried to lighten the subject and he even laughed, but I couldn't stop crying. "Baby. Stop."

The tears continued to roll as I listened to that beautiful voice. He was safe, but I was still losing it, the magnitude of what could have happened looming in my mind. The madness of everything that we dealt with came crashing down around me, threatening to crush the air from my lungs until I was gasping for breath.

"Brook, honey, it's okay. Please, babe."

"I need to see you, to touch you... to make sure you're okay," I whispered.

"Okay, we can do that. I'm dying to see you, too. It's been eighteen fucking days and I miss your beautiful face. I miss how you smell and how you feel against me. I have to film in the morning, but I'm chartering a plane. I'll be with you by dinnertime, okay?"

"Okay," I sniffed. "I'm sorry I'm such a whiny baby."

"I like it when you're a baby. You're *my* baby. I love you so much."

"I can't wait for this to be over, Cade. I only found out because one of the photographers stalking me asked me if I knew you'd been hurt. I almost lost it right in front of them... I could barely make it into my apartment before I broke down. It would have blown our cover straight to hell."

He groaned on the other end of the line. "To hell with it anyway. Our *cover*, if you can call it that, was blown the morning I left The Beverly Hills Hotel, and I don't bloody care. I'm sorry you had to go through that, my love. It makes me so bloody furious. Those parasites!" he breathed. "The fans are bad enough, but the press constantly in your face... I want to fucking kill something."

"They're pretty bad, I guess." My eyes were swollen and my throat still ached. "Do you have ice on your hip, Cade? Does it hurt bad?"

"It hurts, Brook, but I'm fine. And I get to see my girl tomorrow, so things are starting to turn around."

I laughed softly into the phone and walked into my bedroom to curl up on my bed.

"That's the sound I want to hear," his voice full of laughter. "Denise will probably want to leave and will be taking her phone, so I may need to go. She's getting me a new one before I leave for L.A. tomorrow, so I'll call you from the airport, alright? Thanks for the beautiful song today, Brook. I loved it."

"I've loved every one you've sent, too. I love you."

He sighed and his voice throbbed when he answered me. "Oh, I miss you, babe. Tomorrow night you'll see how much."

"Mmmm... that sounds nice. I'm so glad you're okay. Thank you for calling."

"You don't have to thank me. I'm counting the minutes until you're in my arms. Goodnight."

Chapter 10

Juxtaposition of Jealousy

Brooklyn

OKAY. I'D HAD ENOUGH. I couldn't watch Davina fawning over Cade anymore tonight. There was some big awards event in New York he had to attend. I didn't know what it was, and I didn't care. He hadn't really mentioned it, but it was obvious. Every picture I'd seen of Cade included her; the way she was always following him around, sitting next to him and hanging on every fucking word he said in interviews. It was all over the TV, social media, and rag mags. It made my damn head hurt.

I sighed and ran my hands through my hair in agitation. *Only Us* had been filming for a month and I'd been spending almost every free minute following him in the press, which had to be the reason this was eating the hell out of my insides. What else could it be?

Snap out of It, Brook. You know he loves you. It's all for show.

I mean, we spent countless hours trying to get into our character's head, so it was only natural that he'd have to do that with her, too. My heart fell. He and I had completely immersed in our roles. We even joked about it, but I had to examine what the hell was really going on. Was I being sucked in by the role or by a pair of fantastic blue eyes?

As I watched the news clips of the two of them, I wanted to pull my hair out; it felt like my fucking skin was falling off. *Shit, I felt like running out the damn door.*

My eyes narrowed as I took in the scene. He looked casually hot, as always. He was wearing a black suit, but carrying the jacket, he'd removed the tie and the sleeves of his white button-down were rolled up. Davina's red-nailed hand wrapped around his bicep caused a throb somewhere that I didn't want to think about. The fact that he didn't even know how amazing he was was the hottest thing about him; talented, gorgeous, interesting and so incredibly smart. There ought to be a damn law against someone having all that going on. It wasn't fair and none of us had any sort of defense against him. I couldn't blame Davina for being sucked in by all that he was, but it made me sick to my stomach.

In watching him with Davina, I noticed Cade's demeanor was polite and attentive. I mean he didn't exactly drool all over her, but he didn't snub her either. I didn't expect him to, but it hurt to watch. Davina was a beautiful woman and Cade was seriously hot. It was only natural she'd be attracted to him and the press pushed them together. It was all part of the job.

Job, job, job, my head hammered at me. I knew I had to suck it up and trust him. I'd been trying since the first story broke, but the truth was, all I wanted was to scratch her eyes out. She was lapping up the publicity with fervor.

Suddenly my throat felt dry and I reached for the can of soda. I'd spent more time than I would admit researching her and she had more men than I had birthdays, and a reputation for hooking up with actors, directors, and producers. I huffed. Anyone that could further her career, obviously. Anger rushed through me like fire. I didn't want her using him to further her own pathetic career.

I stopped myself and tried to step back and look at the situation objectively. How *was* I feeling? *Was it protectiveness toward Cade or jealousy toward Davina?* Either way, it didn't sit well. I hated anything that I didn't have control over. I was the queen of control and made it a point never to let anything own me. *Ever.*

Nathan had come over with Chinese food and was unpacking it in the small kitchen of my apartment, while I was glued to E!News. Thank God the segments were short, but I was sick of the media blowing it out of proportion.

I absentmindedly picked at the material of my jeans as I sat with my eyes glued to the screen, my hands were shaking. How in the hell was I going to get through two more months of this?

Okay, I was seriously screwed.

I pulled my knees up and leaned on them, barely noticing Nathan entering the room, setting a box with a fork sticking out of it on the coffee table in front of me and then taking a seat next to me on the couch. He forked a mouthful of his food and then stopped. "You okay, sis?"

"I'm okay," I said and smiled as brightly as I could manage. He shook his head and dug his fork in for more food.

"Rough day?" Nate asked, glancing at the screen.

I shrugged. "Um, not too bad. Just long. Thanks for coming over. I wouldn't have eaten anything, and just lazed around like a slug all night."

He laughed lightly. "No problem. It was my excuse to bail on shopping for new furniture with mom. She's trying to set me up with what's her name's daughter."

"Hmmm," I muttered under my breath. "I always hated shopping. I'd rather work if those were my choices, but—" I stopped and shoved his arm, grinning. "You could stand to get laid."

Nathan huffed out a disgusted laugh. "Whatever. Speaking of that; why aren't you in New York with Cade at that thing?" Nathan asked, in a gentle tone. Obviously, he could sense my tenseness.

I shrugged, not willing to tell him the real reason; that the studio wouldn't let me. "I don't know. Not in the mood, I guess."

"Yeah, that isn't like you. I thought you and Cade were the king and queen of secret meetings," he said and took a drink from his glass.

"Yeah. I guess. But I've got a busy week and so does he. I have to shoot tomorrow. There just wasn't enough time to make it work." My eyes fell on the screen as he stopped to talk to a reporter. My jaw jutted out involuntarily and I shifted uncomfortably as Davina showed up beside him to the delight of the interviewer. "Besides, the studio would have a shit fit if I showed up and ruined their little Cade and Davina lie."

Nathan followed the direction of my eye line and then glanced back at my face. Something like recognition flashed across his features. "Yeah, I understand."

I rubbed the back of my neck, feeling the perspiration accumulating a light sheen. It wasn't hot in my apartment but I felt like my skin was on fire, and I hoped it wasn't flushing red. I got up and went to the corner of the room where the guitar Cade had given me for my birthday was leaning up against the wall. I picked it up, and returned to the couch.

"Aren't you gonna finish your food?" Nathan asked, looking

hopefully at the carton I'd left on the table.

"Go ahead." I sat down; just holding the guitar, then ran my fingers over the strings. It made me feel close to Cade when I played it.

"Cade told me he's working with you a little bit." His eyes looked at me knowingly. And my eyebrows went up. *Was Cade talking about me with my brother?*

"Yeah, but I don't get a chance to practice that much," I murmured as I watched Cade say something to the reporter and Davina burst out laughing.

Okay, I'm out. Fake bitch.

I started to get up, feeling uncomfortable with the turn in the conversation. Somehow, the interaction between Cade and I was something just between us. It felt personal and I didn't want to share, even with Nathan. I reached over, grabbed the remote and switched off the television.

"That was last night, right?" He nodded toward the TV. He meant the outing with Davina.

"Yes. Gag me. If I see anymore of her fawning all over him, clawing at him with those devil nails and saying how beautiful he is in every interview, I'm going to barf. She's annoyingly obvious."

"Have you met her? She looks awful. I mean she's hot and all, but..."

I strummed through a few chord changes on the guitar to interrupt him. "Only once. Can we drop it? I don't want to think about it."

"Yeah. Sure."

Nate finished his food and after he left, I was alone with my thoughts, remembering how I'd felt on set with Cade. I sighed. How could I expect another woman to be immune to him? I set the guitar on the table and lay down on the couch, letting my mind wander to another time jealousy had eaten me alive. Back when we were filming *The Future of Our Past*; I didn't have a right to be jealous because I was still seeing David. I closed my eyes and let the scene replay in my mind.

We'd been at a party, and Cade had been playing music with Dawson and Daniel, and Wendy had been stuck to him all night while I observed and mingled with the others. It was a day when I had been shooting without him and we hadn't talked. I was anxious to get some time with him. He'd glanced in my direction a few times, his expression always apologetic because Wendy's constant clinging didn't give us any time to talk. Finally, he came over anyway.

"Hey, Brook," he said softly. His blue eyes sucked me in as always, pulling me straight into his soul. Not that he ever tried to hide anything from me. He didn't. He was so open and giving. I felt like I'd known him forever. I'd told myself that it was because he was so damn beautiful that I felt like a rag doll around him, but in truth, it was him. How he was inside. How we were together and how he always made me feel. He made me feel happy, smart and beautiful. He made me laugh.

"Yeah! Hey, Brook," Wendy chimed in, leaning into Cade as she did so. I tried to paste a happy smile onto my face, but it felt frozen and my cheeks quivered under the effort. Her voice grated on me like knives.

"Hi," I answered her but my gaze shifted back to Cade as I leaned on the front of the bar. "You were really good tonight." I couldn't help the way my voice got softer and felt a rush of pleasure at the crooked grin that split his face.

"You think so? That means a lot to me." His eyes were boring into mine and it was like everyone else disappeared. I felt myself

falling and I put out a hand to steady myself.

"Hey, Cade, I told you how excellent you were. I think you're amazing." Wendy, obviously tipsy, fell into him and he put up his hands to steady her and push her away from him a little.

"Thank you, Wendy. Do you need to sit down?" he chuckled.

I put an arm through hers, and together we turned her around and took her to the couch to set her on it. She flopped down and reached for Cade's hand, looking up at him expectantly. He moved back a little. "We'll get you some water, okay? Just a moment."

Cade nodded his head away to communicate with me that he wanted to speak with me alone so I followed him across the room. My heart thumped in my chest even though we'd spent countless hours together. He still affected me in ways no one else ever had. Not even David. A new rush of guilt had rushed over me and I felt the skin on my face flush.

When we moved toward the balcony doors out of earshot of everyone else, he reached out and ran a hand down my arm. "Are you okay? We haven't talked much tonight and I... well, I found myself missing your words." He smiled sheepishly and ran a hand through his hair as I looked up at him. His bronze hair was messed up in the perfect Cade way and he had two days' worth of stubble on his face. Those intense blue eyes that I swear could look right through me... So beautiful.

Oh my fucking God. Was it seriously possible for anyone to be that fucking beautiful? I'd wondered.

I looked down at the ground because I was afraid of what would show in my eyes. "Yeah, me, too. What did you do today?" His hand had moved down my arm to my hand and I longed to close my fingers around his. They were warm and full of electricity. I shook my head slightly to get my focus back.

"Hung out with the guys." He shrugged. "Basically did nothing the whole day, except work out and lay around. Bloody boring." His finger touched my chin to get me to look up. "Honestly, I found myself wondering what you were up to and when you'd be finished. I missed seeing you."

A swell of elation came up inside me, and I smiled in spite of myself. "Yeah." If only I could tell him that I missed him too, that I thought about him constantly and I couldn't wait for the fucking shoot to end so I could get back to the hotel and call him. "It was a long day. I was actually going to leave soon. I have to go over our scenes for tomorrow."

His brow crinkled and he raised an eyebrow at me. "That isn't like you. To go over our scenes without me, I mean."

I nodded. "I know." I glanced at Wendy, across the room on the sofa. "Because, Carlisle, the scenes with you need lots of work," I teased and shoved him with my shoulder.

He smiled. "Yeah, yeah, sure. Ten films and I'm still ridiculous."

"Shut up! You know I'm kidding. But you're obviously otherwise engaged, tonight."

"I like the practicing, actually," he murmured softly, and my heart fell to my stomach as he ignored my reference to Wendy.

I liked practicing, too. I'd been so scared at how much I obsessed about the time I spent alone with him.

With Cade beside me, it had been the first time that night I was feeling like I didn't want to throw-up. Talking with him had a calming effect and every day I looked forward to the evenings when we would get together and hang out.

He glanced down at me again right before Wendy bounded up

and launched herself at him, throwing her arms around his neck and pulling him down, almost off balance. His right arm moved around her to keep her from falling to the floor.

"You forgot about me over there!" she pouted.

"Easy Wendy," he said, his eyes still on my face. "You need to stop drinking now, okay?"

"No, I don't. Things are just getting fun. Right, Brook?" Wendy quipped with a laugh, holding Cade even tighter. I balked and turned away.

"Um, actually I was just leaving. I'm... really tired. I barely get a day off."

"Well, that's why you make the big bucks. Can we shop tomorrow afternoon?" She'd asked as Cade set her back on her feet. I felt the hair at the back of my neck rise in protest.

"Uh, if I get done, sure. I'll call you." I tried to smile and hedged toward the door of the suite, knowing there was no way I wanted to hang out with her and listen to her babble on and on about herself and Cade. "See everyone later," I called out so the others would hear and waved before walking out the door. I felt an unfamiliar ache in my chest as I walked to my room and my eyes welled with tears. Leaving Cade in Wendy's clutches was not what I wanted to do, but I didn't have any right to do anything else. I was committed to David and Cade was free to do as he pleased.

I'd gone back to my hotel, pulled out my journal and wrote about Cade for two hours, interrupted by a call from David, which made me feel like hell, because I couldn't bring myself to tell him I loved him, when he said it to me. During the call, I'd been flipping through the pages that started out as director's notes but had turned into my journal and eventually into my thoughts and secret letters to Cade.

The one I'd given him for Christmas.

After I'd hung up the phone, I'd touched the pages of the book, reading again some of the feelings I'd so carefully placed on the pages, and then grabbing a pen, I wrote the word one more time...

Cade.

Wendy was a pussycat compared to Davina Duchman. The thought of Cade getting close to anyone else had always hurt, but I could tell Davina was devious and she had plans to further her career by latching on to my guy. Who in the hell had a name like that anyway? I sighed and rolled over, throwing my arm over my eyes, chastising myself for my hatred of a woman I didn't even know. I'd promised Cade I wouldn't wallow. It's just a movie, just another part... she's just another actor. No big deal. Right?

Suddenly, it occurred to me. I needed another journal. Writing down my feelings helped to channel the longing and sadness before, it could again. Tomorrow, I'd get a new one.

Caden

BLOODY HELL! The night went on forever. Davina clinging to me, like some sort of human parasite, drove me mad. Especially without Brook there. I mean, normally, I'd be flattered by the attention, but knowing this rubbish would be all over the media and Brook would see it, it was the last thing I wanted.

"Cade, Earth to Cade..." Davina invaded my thoughts again.

"Oh, sorry, Davina." I looked at her face. She was very beautiful, but shallow and lacking warmth. She held an expression of agitation. I was sure she wasn't used to anything less than complete and total attention from the men lucky enough to be in her presence. However my thoughts were on Brook. I tried to mind my manners and concentrate on what she was saying.

"Did you hear anything I said? I was asking you if you wanted to ride to the set together tomorrow? I looked at the call sheet and it appears you and I have to be there early due to those damn wires. So what do you say?"

"Oh. Yeah, sure." I took a pull from the beer in my hand and motioned back toward the table where a good number of the cast and crew were sitting. "Want to go back with the others?"

"Not really," she purred and ran her hand along my arm. "I'd like to get to know you better. You spend all of your time locked up in your room."

I drew in a deep breath and tried to figure out how I was going to turn this conversation to Brook. I had to drop the seed to get this bitch off of me. I was sick of peeling her off me every time I turned around.

"Um, mostly, I spend a good amount of time working on the script for my next film. With Brooklyn Halloway," I said bluntly, meeting her eyes without flinching.

Her eyes narrowed slightly, but she leaned toward me and licked her lips. "Oh, she's just a girl, and that Remembrance thing was her first big break, right? She's so young. I bet her attention span is like that of a gnat."

I almost laughed out loud, choking on my beer. *Brook* had the attention span of a gnat? "Um, she's actually very mature for her age. She's over the age of consent, by the way," I said shortly.

"How fortunate for you," Davina shot back nastily.

"Yes, isn't it?" I smiled, more slyly than I wanted, but goddamn it! Enough was enough.

"Well, keep in mind this film is the priority. You wouldn't want a leak of some fling with Brook. It could turn into something damaging. Besides, she's dating some kid in L.A. David, something or other, isn't it? She's been with him practically her whole life. So cute."

Inside I wanted to yell and scream at Davina, but the studio had constructed such an elaborate ruse, of course, she bought into it with the rest of the world.

I shifted uncomfortably in my seat and turned, preferring to look behind the bar since suddenly it was much more interesting than what she was saying. It wasn't like Brook hadn't told me about how she met David, but for some reason when she told it, it didn't sound like some sickly sweet romance. It was more like; *Yeah, we hang; he's cool.*

Davina's comments were like a resounding reminder that David was in L.A. with Brook when I couldn't be. Not that she'd see him, but it still didn't' sit well.

She never made it sound like she'd ever been madly in love with him, but maybe she was sparing my feelings. Maybe I was still sensitive that David had what I loved, what I coveted, for almost a year before Brook and I got together that made me hate the poor bastard. It wasn't even his fault.

Bloody hell. I guess I asked for this.

"Hmmm..." I answered, because I didn't know what else to say, and I didn't want to let her instigate a comment that I'd regret.

Brook never lied to me about her relationship with David so I knew going in, but it didn't stop me from falling in love with her, and it worked out well in the end.

"Want to leave?" Davina said suggestively. "Afraid of a real woman?"

I huffed in agitation as she leaned in and tried to wrap her hand around my forearm. I pulled it back before she could.

"Oh, come on. Loosen up, Cade. We don't have to go back to the hotel. We can find a club with open mic night and you can play. I'd love to see you play in public. You really are amazing, you know," she said in a sultry tone, but it left me unmoved. The talk about Brook and David was making me uncomfortable and I longed to be on a plane to L.A.

"Uh, thanks. I really thought that music would be my career," I said, offhandedly and glanced at my watch. It was two in the morning. "You know, I think it's getting late and we do have those bloody scenes to do tomorrow."

Davina reached out a finger and ran it down my chest over my T-Shirt. "Get rid of the others... I don't have to go just yet. Let's practice."

I smiled at her and ran a hand through my hair. "That's um..." I laughed uncomfortably. "You've had a little bit too much to drink, and you wouldn't want to do anything you'd regret in the morning." *Or, that I'll regret for the rest of my fucking life.*

Davina took out her phone and started typing. I felt a sudden rush of panic wash over me.

"Who are you texting?" She raised her eyebrows as she finished sending and then raised her eyes to mine.

"My manager. I'm going to see if we can get some time off. God knows, I love the time on set, but let's face it, you and I don't know each other that well and I think we need a little alone time, don't you?" Her well-manicured eyebrow shot up and reminded me of one of those over-exaggerated lightning bolts animators use in cartoons. "I mean, I saw that Remembrance thing you did with Brook Halloway and if you can get that hot and steamy with a young little thing like that, imagine what you can do with a real woman." She smiled slyly.

I stiffened and my heart sank to my stomach. I wanted to scream at her that I got it. Did she have to bring Brook into it?

"I'm not dumb, honey. I know you and she had a thing. It's obvious by how you're jumping out of your skin right now, but get over it. A man in your position can't be ruled by silly romantic fantasies."

Suddenly, I wanted to get out of there; frantic in my need to text Brook and make sure she knew the truth of this situation.

Davina's phone buzzed and she read the message and then turned the screen so I could read it.

Sure, I can talk to them. I'll let you know.

The thing that didn't occur to her was that I didn't want to spend time alone with her. All I could think about was the trip to L.A. "Look, Davina, that won't work for me, " I began, but she interrupted me.

"Stop. We'll go out and have a great time. No big deal. We're friends. We can *all* be friends," she said suggestively. "I'm not opposed to sharing, though frankly, I don't see the appeal."

I shrugged and downed the rest of my beer. "It's getting late. I need to get to bed."

"Look, Cade. I can understand that you've been spending all this time with Brook and being around me might make her uncomfortable... but she was only hanging out with you for the role. It's her job. I can tell you that everything I hear around Hollywood is that Brook's heart is with David, so I'd hate to see you get all wrapped up in her for nothing. And, as I said, your world has little place for romantic dreams even if you have her temporarily swooning over you. You have a job to do, too; with me. Let's make it believable, shall we?"

She looked sincere as she said the words; words I didn't want to hear. She reached out to touch my arm and it was all I could do not to pull away. Her revelation wasn't anything I hadn't told myself a hundred times during the first film, but the days of uncertainty were behind me. I leaned my head on my other arm as I looked at her, steadily.

"Thank you, Davina. I appreciate your concern, but I assure you, I know all of this, and I'm not *wrapped up* in anything," I lied through my teeth for the contract and because I hadn't discussed "coming out" with Brook. The last thing I wanted was for Brook to think I was insecure about her now fake relationship with David or that I didn't trust her.

I pushed roughly away from the bar as Davina watched, then walked over to the guys. I fell into a plush chair next to Daniel and he just looked at me in consternation. It was obvious he could read my mind.

"What's with that sappy face, dude? Did you strike out with Davina?" He teased, with a laugh.

"Pfft. Who was trying?" I answered shortly, more perturbed than I wanted to admit. He was one of the few who knew the truth about Brook and me. "I'm just tired. Can we call it a night? We all have that stupid shit tomorrow."

Daniel looked at me knowingly and leaned back on the couch. "Sure, Cade. Heard from Brook tonight?" I shook my head in quick answer. "How come?"

"How the fuck should I know? It's not my day to babysit. Why does everyone always think I know everything about her all the bloody time?"

"Whoa. Because... you *do*, Cade. I mean, I've never heard you talk about Brook like that before, mate. You worship that girl, so what the hell? What gives?" He nudged my arm with his elbow.

"Nothing! Nothing gives. Just..." I sat up and motioned for my bodyguards to come closer. "Can you guys get Davina out of here?" I put a hand over my eyes and pinched the flesh at the bridge of my nose. "I don't want any hassles right now. Romantic or otherwise."

"Yeah, she's a man-eater," John said under his breath. "I saw how she was working you. I doubt romance has anything to do with it. You'd wake up with your dick missing."

I burst out laughing. "Yeah, and I might need it later."

He turned and motioned with his arm and called out to her. "Davina, let's go. Cade is tired and he asked me to make sure you get back to your room."

Davina draped over me in a big hug and brought her hand to my face, but I pulled back. "Night, baby," she said. Daniel rolled his eyes over the top of her head and I stifled a smile.

"Good night. See you on set."

Daniel took Davina's arm and started to lead her out of the door. "Yes. Call me later, if you want. I'll be up." She smiled lazily, but looked put out that I'd asked her to leave.

Immediately after, I left myself and in a matter of minutes I was in my room stripping off my shirt on the way to the bedroom. I threw myself down on the bed in the dark.

"Bloody hell," I said into the silence of the room. I reached my hand into the pocket of my jeans and pulled out my phone. I knew I wouldn't find a message from Brook because it hadn't vibrated. I knew she hadn't called because her ringtone had been silent all night. My thumb ran over the screen as I scrolled through the hundreds of texts we'd exchanged over the last month. I longed to send a message.

What was she thinking? I was well aware of the pictures had been clandestinely taken on fans phones and paparazzi on the sidewalks. Ugh! I was seriously screwed. Either way, I couldn't win. I struggled with what to say, as I pulled out my phone to send a text to Brook.

It wasn't the same without you tonight. Sweet dreams.

I waited a few minutes, staring at the damn thing and willing a message to come in with all that I had. It never did.

Fuck, fuck, fuck!

I threw my phone down, unbuttoned my jeans, pushed them down and kicked them to the floor. I rolled over and grabbed a pillow, bunching it up in my arms. Morning couldn't come soon enough. I just needed to look in those gorgeous blue eyes. Then I would know what she was thinking. Then I would have some peace.

***

I WOKE UP THE next morning with a feeling of dread for the day ahead. Somehow I'd made it to set for the 5 AM call and the love scene, while awkward and uncomfortable, had wrapped in only three takes. Thank God.

I was dragging, but I rushed back to my suite, showered and dressed quickly. I didn't bother shaving; just jammed a blue stocking cap on my head and shoved my feet quickly into my Nikes. The limo ride to the airport and the flight on the private plane was painfully long. I'd held off texting Brook more after she didn't return the others from last night. I felt sick; my heart heavy, even as I willed the miles and time between New York and Los Angeles to melt away. I was worried at what I'd face when I got to Brook, but I couldn't wait to get there, nevertheless. The three hours on the plane felt like years.

Upon landing, I'd called Jeanne, who filled me in on Brook's schedule. She only had a rehearsal today, so hopefully she'd get done earlier than usual. I knew Jeanne would be waiting for me because she'd agreed to take me to set. After I climbed in the car, Jeanne gave me a rundown of Brook's day. She met with her director and the special effects team early, and then they were taking test shots for camera angles, the lighting tests and to see how well everything would mirror the storyboards. I ran a hand through my hair as I stared out the window. I didn't care about this shit.

Today the sun would shine in New York, but for the rest of the week the forecast called for overcast skies; which would justify my escape to L.A. if I were questioned.

I barely spoke to Jeanne in the car and I didn't say much more on the way to Brook's set. I knew my one-syllable answers were awkward, and she longed to ask me what was bothering me, but I wasn't in the mood for small talk. My mind was consumed with the fact that Brook hadn't returned my texts. That wasn't like her. Not like her at all.

I didn't expect to see Brook right away but she was there as Jeanne and I walked into the studio. Her face was stoic as she spoke to her director, Pat Armstrong. She glanced at us approaching out of the corner of her eye. Her jaw jutted out as she turned back to her conversation with Pat. She was dressed in jeans and an oversized flannel shirt with her hair drawn back in a ponytail. Nothing like the futuristic costume I was expecting.

"Uh oh. Brook's on the warpath," Jeanne murmured as we drew closer. "I thought she'd be happy to see you? Do you know what's up her ass?"

"She's your client, Jeanne. You supposedly know more about her than I ever will," I snapped back.

She stepped back and stared at me with her eyebrows raised. "Great. You're both on the rag. Today should be a real joy," she said in droll annoyance.

"Humph…" I snorted and turned in the direction of the others, my eyes gauging Brook's expression as I walked toward where she was standing with Pat.

"Hey, what's going on?"

"Nothing at all. Just… this is like a slave train. I want a damn day off. That's *all* I'm asking for!" Brook said and huffed off without properly greeting me. "I hate this fucking movie!" she said under her breath. Her director chuckled as I waited for an explanation.

"Well? What brought that on?" I questioned though I knew Brook's sour mood came from my well-reported excursion the previous night.

"She wants time off this weekend and next weekend, but I can't change production. I don't get it. She's been so easy going. I thought she understood how this stuff works."

"She does." I shoved my hands in my pockets and watched Brook stomp off, feeling my heart drop to my stomach. Obviously she was mad about something, and I knew what that something was. I was getting so tired of the charades. If we were alone, she'd just yell at me and be done with it.

"Your client is acting like a spoiled diva, Jeanne. Fix it," Patrick commanded.

Jeanne went toward Brook and held up her hand to halt her, but Brook kept walking. I stood watching and frozen next to Patrick, who shook his head in exasperation.

"She knows a lot of people are involved and the budget is what it is. Was she difficult on the Remembrance set?"

I shook my head. "It's not like her to blow like that. Something must have happened. I'm here this weekend, so that explains why she wants time now, but what's happening next weekend? Why does she want time off then?"

He shrugged impatiently. "Damned if I know. Ask Jeanne. And tell her to get Brook's ass back on my set! Pronto!"

I shoved my hands deep into the pockets of my black jeans. "Will do. Sorry Patrick. I'm sure Brook will get her head back in the film," I said apologetically as he turned to walk away.

My breath rushed out as I watched Brook argue with Jeanne, not sure if I should interrupt. Soon, Brook was grabbing her hair with one hand, looking over her shoulder at me before storming off toward a trailer at the other end of the lot. Jeanne came toward me with an apologetic look on her face.

"What's her problem?"

"Really? Are you serious, Cade?" Jeanne's eyes widened incredulously as she pulled out a cigarette and a lighter from her purse. "Davina and the photo-fest. You two should be more concerned with anyone seeing you on this set, Cade. Jesus."

I bloody knew it already, but I was floundering for what to say. "I thought you said she'd handle that rubbish! And, why does she need two weekends off?

"She wants to go on a trip, alone."

"Alone?"

"Yeah." She blew smoke out impatiently. "You have to work, anyway." It was just one more way to dig in the knife a little deeper.

I scowled. "So does Brook, Jeanne!"

"Uh huh. Don't get your boxers in a bunch." She took another drag from her cigarette. "Want one?"

I shook my head. I was trying to quit, but damned if I didn't need it. "I don't want her traveling alone."

"Why don't you rant at Brook, instead? It's moot anyway! Go! I need her calm and on the other set ASAP. Go work your magic." She nodded in the direction of Brook's retreating figure. "I don't need this temperamental bullshit right now."

"Wha... uh," I stammered. "I might not be able to help. I'm the reason she's upset."

I couldn't say that it disappointed me that Patrick Armstrong wasn't letting Brook off work, but then again, if he did, I might be subjected to watching her parade around with that ignorant twit, David, and a paparazzi free-for-all to follow. Personally, I didn't understand how she could have ever found him the slightest bit appealing. There was a distinct gap in their intelligence levels, and he wasn't even a nice guy; they just didn't fit. She was a thinker, and he was an asshole.

"Talk to her. Calm her down. That's what you always do. So do it." She looked at me pointedly. "*Now*."

I nodded and took off in a jog after Brook. It was the excuse I needed to talk to her alone. When I was within hearing distance, I began calling after her. "Brook! Wait!"

She stopped for a split second when she heard my voice behind her, but then kept on walking, picking up her pace as she got closer to her trailer.

"Brook! For Christ's sake!"

"Leave me alone. I've got work to do." She flung over her shoulder at me and kept walking as if the fires of hell were on her heels.

"Will you just wait?" She kept moving, not even slowing a little. I reached out and grabbed her arm, turning her but she jerked her arm away like my touch burned her. She was breathing hard and she looked up at me in a glare, her nostrils flaring.

"What's going on?"

"I just... I want some time. I need a break from... all this. Go back to New York."

My jaw set. I knew she meant me. She needed a break from *me*.

"We both know you don't want me to go back to New York."

"Arrogant, much?" She scowled at me.

"Why are you doing this? What has changed since we talked last?" Both of our voices were raised and I was concerned that the others could hear what was becoming a private conversation.

"Apparently every damn thing!"

"What in bloody hell are you talking about?" My own blood pressure was starting to rise. She had to know that any time I spent in Davina's company was purely work related.

"I guess the studio is fine with you hanging out with Davina all the time?" she laughed, but it sounded more like a sob. "I knew it was coming, but already? I thought we talked about everything. Why is this the first I hear about it? From *Wendy* and the stupid rags?"

I shrugged my shoulders and ran a hand through my hair, half turning away from her. I shook my head. I mean what in the hell was I supposed to do? I should have known that vapid bitch was stirring the pot.

"Yes. Wendy's always such a good friend. Have you lost your senses?" I was getting angry at the sheer stupidity of Brook's doubt. "This is crazy, Brook. Why are you even talking to Wendy?"

Brooks jaw jutted out in defiance, but she didn't speak.

"You know the studio insisted on it; it's no different than your charade with David. Davina knows about us," I said softly. "Why are you so pissed off, anyway?"

"I'm not." She angrily brushed an errant tear off of her cheek. "I mean, I don't know."

"Look, I'm dealing with the same things you are. Even more. The time we've been together means everything to me. But—!"

She was upset and couldn't meet my eyes and I couldn't stand it. My throat was tightening up, making it difficult to talk. I wanted to throw her over my shoulder and haul her off where no one was looking and leave her in no doubt of my feelings for her. But I couldn't.

"But, I can't let this, whatever it *is*, take over. I can't lose my grip on reality. The reality is, that we have months of separation in front of us! We can't lose it over a couple of weeks, and a couple of staged outings."

Her mouth dropped open and she sucked in her breath before turning and resuming her run away from me toward her trailer. "I don't have time to talk about it now."

"No, Brook. I won't let you accuse me of this and then run away. We're going to talk. *Now*." I grabbed Brook's arm and jerked her toward the trailer, opening the door and staring pointedly at her until she acquiesced. As she stormed in, I noticed several members of the crew watching us from a distance as I followed. I didn't give a fuck what they were thinking. I shut the door and closed the window shades so no one would be able to see what was going on between us.

"Patrick wants me on set!" Tears were running silently down her face when I turned to her. I opened my mouth to speak but shut it as I considered what I wanted to say. I needed to calm down. I was older and more experienced with the ways of Hollywood, and she'd seen how women acted around me. I sighed heavily, trying to calm my temper.

"Who bloody cares? Look, we'll have many films to make without each other. That's our life. You have to trust me. What is it you expect from me, Brooklyn?" I asked softly.

She brought the back of her hand up to her nose and she closed her eyes. When she spoke, her voice cracked. "I don't know, Cade, okay?" She looked at her lap and took a shaky breath. "I want us to be like we've been. I miss you. You're my best friend. It's not as much fun this time."

I closed my eyes. "I know, it's the same for me. Why are you letting something we prepared forget to you?" I asked simply, but the fact was I ached for her; body and soul. "We tell each other everything, so why do you just believe this bullshit as gospel without asking me first? We knew this would happen; we talked about it. A few bloody photographs and you forgot those conversations?" When she didn't say anything or look at me, I continued. "We should let the world know about us, but you and your team don't want that." I drew in a breath so deep I thought my lungs would bloody explode. "If you want to have a normal relationship, we can't care what people think or what the studio will do."

Finally, she turned to me and lifted her blue eyes to mine. "I know. I'm not handling these feelings very well, but I have more to lose. You already have your career, Cade. I'm trying to build one."

My chest constricted at her words. I was stunned she doubted I'd consider her career as important as mine.

"I can touch you and kiss you as Ryan on a screen, but it's me, okay? It's bloody *me*! That said; I can't live in a dream world, hoping you'll eventually come to the same conclusion that we need to tell the studio to fuck off and screw the consequences. I mean, who in the hell are we fucking trying to convince?" I knew the tone in my voice was getting urgent and elevated but I couldn't help it. "Do you think the fans don't already know?"

Her blue eyes widened and became big limpid pools. "Cade, please! Jeanne is advising me we need to keep our relationship private. Not just for me, but for you. I'm just... I'm trying to sort through it all. "

"Well, do it faster, will you? Because it's bloody ripping my guts out! I'm sure she has outings set up with your co-star, yet you're pissed at me because Davina followed me out with Daniel? Can't you see how hypocritical that is?" My heart was bursting in my chest and I could feel my eyes prick with unshed tears. I turned away so she wouldn't see.

"I saw the interview; I saw the pictures! My head knows it's all bullshit, but it still hurts to watch it! This type of jealousy hasn't happened to me before you, and I hate it. I'm so screwed up and I don't know what the hell I'm doing. I just—"

"Think about what you just said. It hasn't happened to you before. Why do you think that is? Because it's fucking *us*, okay?" I was so frustrated I wanted to scream. I fisted both of my hands in my hair and softened my voice. "It's because it's you and me. It's a first for me too, and I don't just mean with other actors in roles. I mean, it's *never* been more than a job for me before!"

I hadn't given much thought to her new co-star. Pinnacle was using Brook's thrust off our films to put her on screen with a few bigger names in support roles, and a new unknown actor opposite her on lead. They were smart; using her success to help launch the career of a new actor they could capitalize on. However, I didn't give him much thought. I was more worried about David being in L.A. with her when I wasn't around. Surely he'd try to get her back, and it was always in the back of my mind. It was the reason I wanted to come to her set, instead of having her come to mine. I wanted to see what was happening. "Think about me for a change! The press paints horror stories about you and this guy, plus… " I decided to put it out there. "David is here. He'd be stupid not to try to get you back while I'm gone."

She bowed her head and her shoulders shook with the force of her tears, but she was silent. I could only hear her sniffles and gasps. My heart ached and I reached out to enfold her in my arms. She melted into me and I turned my face into her glorious, though now a shorter, mane of hair. I sucked in her scent as if my life depended on it and kissed her temple.

When I pulled back, I tilted her chin up so I could look in her face and brushed her hair back. "But I have to trust you, and I need you to trust me. We've still got a couple of months apart and I don't want to spend it fighting with you. The separation is harder when we're fussing with each other. If you don't want me to do any appearances with Davina, then I won't."

Her little face crumpled and she shook her head. "You can't do that. That's not fair. I know you have the same obligations that I do. I think I was more upset at myself today than at you. I get pissed that I can't control my feelings."

"Some things are bigger than we are."

"When did you get so damn smart?" She tried to smile and I couldn't help a small grin, but I shrugged.

"It's not easy for me, either. I had to accept that you'll be surrounded by a bunch of new men and that you have to get naked on screen with someone else."

"She's getting naked with you, Cade! Did you forget what you filmed this morning?"

I inhaled. "So what? It's not the same thing." I knew my statement might piss her off, but I had to be honest; I didn't think about Davina half-naked with me, in the same way I thought of Brook half-naked with another man, but I tried to turn it into a joke. "I've got those knickers on the whole time. If you want to flash your knockers, that's your decision." I tried to coax a laugh out of her. "But it won't be as much fun with what's-his-name. What *is* his name, again?"

I pulled her into my embrace again and kissed her temple, smiling against her skin. I couldn't tell if the sound that erupted from her chest was a sob or a laugh. I rubbed up and down her arms and her back, bending to kiss the curve of her shoulder.

"The only decision I have to make is whether I can put up with your silly worries. Okay?"

"Okay," she said softly and sniffled as she wiped the tears from her face. "Me too, I'll try."

"Well, then, it looks like we have absolutely nothing resolved and we're back at square one. I guess I'll take it because it means more time with you. Now get your sweet ass ready, Miss Halloway." I brushed my fingers under her chin and she nodded, her eyes pulling me in, in ways I couldn't even reconcile. She was so beautiful I could hardly breathe. "Get on set and get it in the can, so we can have an evening together."

"Okay."

We broke apart when there was a knock on the door and she looked up at me apologetically, her hand reaching out to touch my stomach. She backed away and called out. "Come in."

I tried to blend into the background and sat on the sofa in Brook's trailer as the costume assistant helped her dress and the hair and makeup people worked on her. We tried not to talk about anything personal while they were around; trying to keep the conversation about work, acting as if my visiting her on set was completely ordinary. The curious glances of the crew signaled their doubts that this was only a friendly visit, but I was beyond caring what anyone else thought. Curiosity and speculation were normal, but I still slipped each of them a hundred dollar bill with a few words; "No pictures. This is not a big deal. I'm visiting a friend."

When everyone left, I grabbed her arm and shut the door so I could plant a brief kiss on her lips before she preceded me out.

"Give me a hug, *friend*," I murmured sardonically, but loud enough for the retreating crew could hear.

Her expression twisted in amusement, but when her feet hit the ground my arms enfolded her in a big bear hug and hers slid up around my neck. When I felt her fingers in the hair at the back of my neck, it was all I could do not to crush her mouth beneath mine. I wouldn't do that until she asked me to, until she'd also made the choice to be open about us. The hug was a big enough risk.

My hand went to the back of her head and wound around the golden silk as I pulled her tighter into my embrace. "It's going to be okay, Brook. Whatever happens, I'll always be here for you." I whispered into her hair. "When I'm done in New York, I'm gonna buy us a house in L.A. Even if it isn't official, I want you to move in with me, okay?"

She nodded and hugged me tighter. "The press will find out."

"I don't care. I hope they do. I'm going to speak to Denise and have her plan a few things to leak to give a few obvious hints."

I waited for Brook to protest but she didn't. I pressed my lips to the top of her silky head.

"Tell Patrick everything is fine and call me when you're done, yeah?"

She smiled up at me as she started to pull out of my arms.

I should have shut my mouth right there, but there was part of me that wanted a leak to the press that I was in L.A. and with Brook on her set. I was tired of sneaking around, but now wasn't the time to be defiant. "I think we need to lose the crowd tonight. Let's just watch a movie and order room service."

Her smile widened and she nodded. As I watched her disappear through the door to her sound stage, she carried my heart in her hands. Though we only had a few hours together, I'd take every second I could get.

I walked back toward the SUV where Jeanne was waiting; yammering on her cell phone to someone. When she hung up, her eyebrow shot up sharply. "Everything good? Think you could have worked a little harder to let the cat out of the bag?"

My lips lifted in the start of a small smile. "Take it easy, Jeanne. Brook and I are still fighting over that one. She's winning."

"She'll get a few films under her belt and will then be in a better position to do what she wants."

"Really? I've made a dozen films and they still have my balls."

"Only because of Brook, Cade. The suits know you're protective and they use it to their advantage."

"They don't pay us enough to take this bullshit."

"Maybe not on one film, but they keep signing you. They hired her for a second gig and it will help secure her future with other studios. Remember that."

Her comment annoyed me. The last thing I cared about was cash, but I couldn't argue with Jeanne's logic. "Yeah, yeah. Something's gotta give."

I'd figure it out later, but right now I was already looking forward to room service and a movie with my girl.

Chapter 11

Not so Comic-Con

Brooklyn

I RUSHED OFF SET and threw my backpack into the back of the beat up Honda Civic I was driving to stay incognito; frantic to get on the road... frantic to get in the arms of the man I was dying for. This fucking summer had dragged on and on and it still wasn't over. After this weekend, we still had three more weeks until we hit the set of *A Love Like This* when we could finally be together again.

I sucked in my breath, filling my lungs to the point of pain as I shoved the key in the ignition and turned the car on. As I plugged in the iPod and cranked up the tunes, all of the songs that Cade and I had compiled on our CadeNBrook playlist over the summer would surround me for my three-hour drive down to San Diego. So many beautiful songs, most of them about longing and missing each other, the lyrics full of meaning to both of us that had helped ease the ache of the separation. *Helped* but not completely obliterated it.

Fuck. I glanced at the clock on the dash. It was 10:30 PM, which meant I wouldn't be down there until at least 1:30 in the morning. I hadn't seen Cade since that weekend he'd come to Los Angeles after he had been mobbed by fans. That was almost nine weeks ago and I was dying to get my hands and mouth on him. My body was literally shaking in anticipation. Our managers hadn't exactly pulled through on setting up time together.

My phone buzzed and I pulled it out of my pocket and opened the message.

I'm sorry about our row. Be careful while you're driving. I can't have you getting in an accident since I'm planning on making it all up to you in a few short hours.

Yes, I was sorry about our fight, too. The distance, the time apart, the paps hounding both of us, and the ridiculous tabloid headlines had all done their best to rip us apart and hang rumors over us at the same time. I sighed and shook my head in disgust. We were both impossibly sensitive and both had a tendency to overreact at times. Cade could be stubborn as hell, and God knew, I had a few volatile moments where I'd snapped his head off. The past months apart had been so emotionally charged and the pain of the long separation had really fucked us both up.

That was over now. I smiled and threw the phone on the passenger seat, holding off on my response.

Short? Hardly. Just for that we'll see how short the hours are, baby, I thought with a smirk, as I got on the interstate and merged into traffic.

It was dark and as I left the bright lights of Los Angeles behind me with the random towns and steady stream of headlights coming at me, I sat back in my seat and let the memories roll over me.

It was bizarre that the only place I could find any peace was racing down the highway, alone in my car. Cade was a prisoner in his hotel room in San Diego, waiting for me to be with him. I was already a prisoner where he was concerned, heart and soul, but that was the easy part. He'd been there most of the day because he had an interview for the October or November issue of *Vanity Fair*, and knowing Cade, he was pacing the room like a caged animal in anticipation of my arrival.

There were many times over the course of the past few months when I'd questioned if we should stay together because of everything we had to go through. The paparazzi's constant stalking and taunting, the fans crazed and frantic to the point of endangering Cade's life; had at times, made me pull away from him. It was a pathetic attempt to give him ease from the torment and to find some small shred of peace myself, but it backfired horribly, only making us both miserable.

I shuddered as I remember kissing his bruised side and feeling him wince in pain as we made love that one weekend he'd come out to be with me. We spent the whole time locked behind the closed doors of his hotel room, in bed, holding each other and making love, barely able to let go of one another. We even showered together so we wouldn't have to be apart, but it was a delicious problem to have. I smiled and my heart raced at the memory. All he wanted to do was touch me, but I couldn't stop thinking about his injury and all of those mobs of women chasing him down like a dog. It was scary and worry hung over us both like a hurricane that never dissipated.

The paparazzi had been ruthless in the past months. The horrible things they'd printed and the questions that they'd asked me had been *beyond* invasive; cruel, even. I couldn't even get a latte without being bombarded.

It bothered Cade to see how they hounded me in the same way that it had bothered me to watch the fans stalking him. Both of us more worried about the other, it had become a unhealthy and painful habit to watch what was going on with each other online when we couldn't talk to each other.

The separation made me doubt just about everything and made him anxious and upset whenever I would withdraw. It was sort of a vicious circle of anger and pain. We had lots of tearful conversations where I'd question our relationship and what was in our best interests, leaving him hurt and yelling at me over the phone or Skype.

"Just fucking make a decision, Brook! This is killing me for Christ's Sake! Either you want to be with me or you don't. I can't bloody breathe it hurts so bad! Just please make a decision!"

I could still hear the anguish in his voice as he'd said those words. If I were honest with myself, the publicity with Davina still hurt even after our weekend when he completely reassured me. Though I knew it wasn't real, I still struggled and pulled away from him. I suppose it was a natural reaction, a way of self-defense, considering how many women wanted him.

Fuck, I couldn't help it. I felt like I was suffocating, helpless while Davina Duchman's intentions were clear. I might as well have been on the other side of the world, and although I'd come to love my new movie, I felt like it was a big weight around my neck. During the times when all I wanted was to get to Cade and I couldn't, I felt trapped and frustrated.

I almost didn't go down to Comic-Con because I'd heard that Davina was going to be there. Cade and I hadn't really talked in two weeks because of everything happening, and sometimes it just seemed easier not to.

There was a story about David going to my house that had the shit hitting the fan. Cade went *insane* over it and even though I told him it was all bullshit, it put us into a funk. We both became defensive and overly sensitive. It was crazy. We knew it... yet it still created problems.

This morning, my decision not to go to Comic-Con was relayed to Cade after Jeanne had called Denise. It wasn't long before my phone, which had been dormant of his calls for at least ten days, began to ring. Part of me was pissed he called me after so long, but a bigger part was just glad that he finally did.

"Yeah?" I answered the phone, knowing it was Cade. It took a few seconds for him to speak.

"I know things have been weird between us, but it isn't the end of us. We're still us. You and me. Just us... like always. Please come to San Diego."

Tears flooded my eyes, and my heart squeezed in my chest, knowing he was absolutely right. No matter how pissed or scared I was, I would always belong with him. I couldn't deny my heart.

"Okay," I'd said brokenly into the phone.

"Tell me you still love me," he'd said softly and my heart lurched.

"You know I do. It's beyond my control."

"I love you, too, love. I've missed you. Not talking to you has been unbearable."

"I don't mean to let all this crap come between us, Cade. It's just so much to deal with."

He let out his breath in relief. "I know. I hate it just as bloody much, but it will never make me doubt the decision to be with you," he said achingly. "Even when I'm brooding and hurt, always know that I love you and want you. I'm sorry for all of this rubbish."

I sighed deeply. "I'm sorry, too. I just hated to see you so tormented and I felt that if the speculation could stop, so would the bullshit. It hurt me and I reacted by pushing you away. I guess it made me feel overwhelmed. I was wrong."

"So will you come to Comic-Con then?"

"I have to film late tonight, so maybe I should wait until tomorrow morning," I hesitated because I still didn't want to see Davina there. It was stupid and childish, but I didn't want to deal with hearing things that the fans or the paps would undoubtedly be screaming at us. "But I know if I wait, there really is no point. All the Remembrance stuff is tomorrow. When are you promoting Only Us?"

"Brook. Davina isn't coming down, okay?"

He read my mind.

"What? Why?"

"I don't know why and I don't care."

Jealousy still reared its ugly head somewhere deep down inside of me as my brain raced to figure out why she would suddenly decide not to be there.

"Love, please stop. I know what you're thinking, Brook. It's no different than you asking me to believe that little weasel isn't stalking you around L.A. I told you that yes, she showed some interest, but I squashed it months ago. This is bloody hard, but I need to see you. Just come to me tonight. Please. I'll wait up for you. I'm aching to see you, love."

I closed my eyes, melting at his words. I loved him; I missed him and I knew that even though we'd argued over the last few weeks, that there was no other place I wanted to be there with him.

"Where are you?" I asked and tried to push down the ache in my voice.

"The Hard Rock Hotel. Will you come tonight then?" he asked anxiously, waiting impatiently for my answer.

"Yes." I nodded, even though he couldn't see the gesture and pushed the hair off of my forehead. "I'll leave as soon as I can get off set, but I don't have many clothes with me. Just some extra stuff I keep in my trailer. If I go home first it will be even later when I get to town."

"I don't care about what you're wearing, you know that. I'm just... well, thankful you agree to come down here. We need this, Brook. No amount of time, space or misunderstandings could ever change how it is between us."

I sighed. "I know. I'm sorry," I said again. "This summer has been so hard. I see what you go through and know what I deal with, and sometimes I just wonder if it's all worth it."

He was silent on the other end of the line for at least a minute and the worry began to well within my chest.

"Cade?"

I could hear him breathing and finally he answered, his words completely unexpected and his voice harsh. "If that's how you bloody feel then don't come. If I'm not worth it, then don't fucking come, Brook!"

The phone had gone dead then and I stood there staring at it in disbelief. I had been trying to explain why I'd been distant, not saying that he wasn't worth it, so what the fuck just happened? Holy shit, I'd asked myself. What had just happened? I panicked, my heart dropping into my stomach as I dialed his number immediately, but it went straight to voicemail. My shoulders slumped as I shut my phone off and walked back toward the set, fighting the tears and struggling to focus on the scene I had to do.

I hadn't been able to reach him all day after that, even though I tried several times. I barely made it through my filming and on my *last break I called him again. He finally answered and relief washed over me.*

"Cade, please don't hang up. It came out wrong. That wasn't what I meant and I really want to see you. We are both so raw everything gets so screwed up. Please forgive me." My heart was pounding in my chest in the sudden fear that he would still be angry and not want to see me and maybe hang up on me again.

He let his breath out and I knew he was probably running his hands through his hair or tugging on his eyebrow like he did when he was thinking. "Okay. I'm sorry too. I shouldn't have hung up on you." I couldn't speak as I brushed an errant tear from my cheek and dug my sneaker into the ground. "Just get down here as fast as you can. Everything will be okay once we're together again. This has been too bloody long. It can't be this long again."

The trip was never ending, my anxiousness and exhaustion making it even worse that it really was. When I finally got to San Diego and found the Hard Rock Hotel, I parked in the garage and flew up the stairs to the eleventh floor. Our old routine returned with ease, without a second thought.

I stuck my head carefully out of the stairwell to see if anyone was around before pushing the door wide and breaking into a run. It was early Thursday morning and so thankfully the hallways were clear. I swiftly got to Cade's room and knocked once, the blood rushing in my ears and my hands clenching in anticipation.

I heard shuffling behind the door and five seconds later the door opened and I was falling into his open arms.

"My fucking God, Brook. Oh God!" Cade said as he pulled me into his room. My bag dropped at our feet and he just held me close, crushing my body up against his, his hand cupped around the back of my head as he breathed me in. I turned my face into the curve of his neck and wrapped my arms around him in anxious desperation to be closer to his body. *Jesus, I never want to let go.* His familiar scent assaulted me; all warm, spicy and man. He held me like that for a minute, both of us absorbing the other as much as we could.

"Cade," I choked out his name just before our mouths locked together in a long, deep kiss. I felt the desperation in him by the way he held me and the way his mouth sucked on mine, our tongues laving each other as we stumbled backward into the room without ever breaking our kiss. His hands tangled in my hair and mine in his as we strained frantically against each other. He lifted me and my arms and legs wrapped tightly around his body while his arms held me so close it felt like we were one person.

"I'm sorry, Cade. God, I'm so sorry," I cried; the tears raining down my cheeks. Love, happiness, sadness, desperation, passion and longing all flooded through my entire being at once. I couldn't breathe but I wasn't sure if the gasping was originating with Cade or me. He was as overwhelmed as I was as he carried me into the room and to the bed.

"Baby, Jesus Christ. I missed you." We fell onto the mattress and frantically ripped at each other's clothes, anxious to feel skin on skin. "I love you," he groaned against my breast as he lifted my T-Shirt up and over my head. I was sobbing into his shoulder unable to stop the shaking that wracked my body. He rose up slightly and looked down into my face as he pushed my hair to the side while my fingers still frantically tugged at his shirt and the buttons of his jeans.

"Shhh, Brook. Don't cry, my love." His blue eyes burned me alive as he suddenly slowed down, his movements deliberate and purposeful while he touched my face with the back of his hand and then slid it down my neck and to cup my right breast. Pausing to capture its weight in his hand, he brushed his thumb lightly, ghosting over my nipple. I felt it harden underneath his touch and I watched his eyes close as he felt it.

"Bloody hell. I can't take being away from you anymore," he whispered as he bent his head toward mine and resumed the delicious kisses. He started out slow and nibbling but within seconds we were back to devouring, so hungry and thirsty all at the same time. My hands resumed their task of tearing at his clothes while I sucked his tongue into my mouth. He groaned and pressed his erection into my hands as I opened his pants.

"Oh, Cade. Uhnnn, I want you... I've missed you so fucking much. I don't want to wait, I can't wait. Please," I begged as my hands closed around his length. He grunted and struggled to help me push down his jeans, the urgency to be closer afflicting Cade as much as it did me. We were both starving for each other, the more than two-month separation driving us on frantically.

He peeled my remaining clothes off of me, his hands deft and swift, all the while his mouth hovering over mine, and giving in to kissing me when I tugged his head down. I fisted my hands in his hair and pulled on the roots slightly. He groaned and spread my legs with his, rubbing up and down my wetness.

"God... it's been so long. I can't stand it," he almost growled. "Dear God, I want you, love... I've missed you so much. *Too* much, Brook." My heart ached at his words because I knew exactly what he meant. The love we had for each other was so overpowering it somehow overshadowed everything else in our lives. Nothing would ever mean more than being with Cade. We both knew it. Finally being with him had all of the doubt and disillusion that built up over the past weeks disappearing into thin air.

He was right. Everything would be fine as long as we were together.

Cade lowered himself to the bed so that his elbows rested under my arms, his hands holding my head as he sank into my body. I arched my back and rocked my hips into his, aching as he filled me to the hilt.

"Ohhhh..." I said softly against his mouth just before his tongue teased my lips apart. I pulled him into me, inexorably deeper, relentlessly wanting more and more of him, encasing him again and again as he moved inside me and against me. His movements were long and strong like he was savoring every inch of our bodies together. Our kisses were like wine, so sweet and hot, sucking and licking, taking and giving. I was losing myself and I only wanted to drown even deeper. I clenched my muscles around him wanting him, needing him to feel me and to give him the same pleasure he was giving me.

"Jesus, babe. Whatever you're doing, keep doing it. You feel so bloody good. You have me on fire, mmm," he moaned against my neck, his open mouth dragging across my skin. He excited me like no other and the throbbing started and I couldn't stop it.

"Let's burn then. I want you to come inside me," I gasped and scratched my nails down his back and grabbed his muscled ass.

"Brook... God," Cade groaned and kissed me again, the plundering of his tongue in my mouth and the luscious kisses only serving to push me closer to the edge. Steady and strong he drove into me again and again, his breath rushing out in bursts. His effort to hold off for me was obvious. I would have been fine without climaxing. I just wanted to be close to him, but he knew how to coax it from me.

My body started to shudder and contract around him as I gave myself over to the flood of sensations. "Uhhhh..."

"Yes, love... I can feel you starting to come. I love that I do that to you. Oh, babe..." His body tensed and shuddered as he thrust one last time while he came deep inside my body. I found myself wanting every drop of him that I could get and I rocked my hips and squeezed around him. "Uh, Brook," he breathed out and collapsed upon me.

We lay still connected together, Cade panting into the pillow and me stroking my hands lightly up and down his back. I raised my head to bite into his shoulder. He laughed lightly and raised his head so that he could look down into my face.

"Do you bloody get that I can't live without you?" He quirked his eyebrow at me and grinned as he thrust hard against me once more. I reached up and ran my hand through his gorgeous hair.

"Yes. I'm sorry..." I began.

"Shhh." Cade nuzzled my nose and kissed me lightly on the lips, brushing his open mouth against mine. His sweet breath rushed over my face and I raised my mouth for more. "Shhh... Just kiss me. You taste so good." He kissed me again deeply then raised his head and gazed into my eyes, his blue eyes still glazed over with passion.

I looked up at him seriously for a moment before he slid out of my body and to my side, pulling me against his chest and into the crook of his arm. I closed my eyes, the exhaustion catching up to me; my body relaxed and sated in the arms of the man that I loved. "I just..."

"I know. We don't have to rehash it. It's been hell on both of us. But it's almost bloody over. I'm counting the days."

"When are you supposed to go back to New York?" I asked hesitantly.

"Friday. They want me to fly back from San Diego and not go up to L.A." His hand brushed up and down my arm, his touch soothing and comforting, but he sighed heavily.

I lifted my head and rested my chin on his chest. "What is it?"

"I just... I'm tired of this whole bloody charade. I want to be honest. And tomorrow will just be more of the same. Then they ship me off and away from you as quickly as they possibly can." His frustration was clear. "I just feel like it's never going to bloody end."

I looked at him through the darkness in the room, with only the light from the television casting a glow on his features. I'd missed his beautiful face despite all of the time I'd spent looking at photos of him online. He was even more beautiful in person. I kissed his chest lovingly and then rested my chin back where it had been. "Well... it's going to be different when we film *A Love Like This*. You made that deal, right? I mean... we won't be able to be obvious, but at least we will stay together in Vancouver, Cade. That's *something*." I let my fingers trace figure eights on the muscles of his lower stomach, mesmerized but the trail of hair leading beneath the edge of the sheet low on his hips.

He cupped my face with a gentle hand. "I *want to be obvious*, love. I want to shout it from the bloody rooftops. I want everyone to know you're mine, sweet."

I sighed and crawled up his body, snuggling into his neck and kissing the side of his face. "I know you do. Why do you love me?" I asked incredulously. "I don't deserve you."

"Hmmph." I couldn't see his face but I knew he was smiling as he kissed the top of my head and his arms tightened around me. "I'll tell you what you deserve, yeah?"

I laughed lightly. "Yeah. So what do I deserve?"

"Everything that I can give you and more." A smile filled his voice and his hands ran over my body.

"Why are you so perfect? I love how you talk to me, what you say... the sound of your voice. I really missed you."

"Brook, if I were perfect we'd *never* bloody argue! Last I checked, we argue," he scoffed. "A *lot*."

"It's 'cause *I'm* such a bitch. It has nothing to do with you," I laughed softly.

"Whatever," he replied in exasperation.   I could almost hear his eyes roll in the darkness. "You're tired. We can fight about this tomorrow, okay? Go to sleep, my love. In a few short hours it's back to the madness."

"I missed your sweet British ass," I smiled, hugging him closer and closing my eyes.

He chuckled softly, his chest vibrating beneath my cheek. "Ah, Brook." He yawned and I knew he was as tired as I was, probably even more due to the three-hour time difference. "My British ass missed you too, love."

Caden

I STRETCHED IN THE bed, alone. My phone was ringing and I scrambled to get to it.

"Yeah?" I mumbled into the phone and flopped back down on the bed. There was a note on the pillow where the indent left from Brook's head was still plainly visible.

"Hey. Where are you?" Denise's voice was tense. "Jesus Cade, Brook and Noah are both here already and you're ten minutes late for the photo call before the first press conference," she lamented.

I was reading the note and barely registered what she said.

Hey, sexy beast. Love you, want you, need you. Always.

***Now get your ass to the convention center, pronto. I'll
make it up to you later.***

She had scrawled a smiley face by the letter B across the bottom in
her messy handwriting. I smiled and rolled off the bed.

"Cade!" Denise yelled into the phone. "Hello?"

"Yeah, okay, Denise. I'll be down shortly. Did you send a car?"

"What the fuck? What do I usually do, Cade, if it's not take care of
your ass?"

"Do you kiss your mother with that mouth?" I teased. I was
smiling as I pulled my jeans on, almost dropping the phone in the
process, and searched for my T-Shirt.

Bloody hell, I don't have time to pull different clothes out of my
bag, let alone shower. I groaned as I caught a glimpse of my disheveled
self in the mirror and I wet my hands and ran them through my hair
trying to make some sort of order out of it. It was pretty much a lost
cause and forget shaving. There was absolutely no time for that.

Oh well, good thing that the fans are used to me looking like I just
fell out of bed. Today I did, for Christ's sake!

"Fuck you. You make my job so damn hard sometimes!" she
ranted.

"Relax. I'm already on my way downstairs... so is the car there or
not?" I grabbed the plaid button-down I'd worn last night and threw it
over my T-Shirt and shoved my feet into my favorite Nike's.

Denise sighed loudly. "What do you think? I'm in it, waiting.
Security should be waiting for you at the elevator."

I saw three large blokes I didn't recognize down the hall just after
I left my room.

"Yeah, I see them. Is Brook already there?" I smirked, knowing she was and thinking I would get chastised from Denise for even asking.

"Yes. She has her shit together, per her usual. Very professional, even if she looked a little, um..." she cleared her throat, "unkempt."

"Yeah, well, that makes two of us." I almost laughed out loud.

"Awesome. So everyone will know you were together all night."

I ignored her comment and moved on, walking out of the elevator with security and through the lobby of the hotel. The fans started screaming the minute they saw me through the glass windows. I shoved my sunglasses on and tried to prepare for the onslaught.

"Hey, I'm professional. I was tired and overslept. Who cares as long as I show up? I hate this bloody rubbish and you know it. I have to do the dance now, see you in a few." I hung up and shoved the phone in my back pocket as the doors opened and I was met with the screaming throng of women. I stopped to sign a few autographs, but the girls kept screaming my name and shoving more and more books and pictures in my direction. Finally, I had to get into the car with Denise and the closed door muffled the loud voices.

I ran my hand through my hair as she shook her head at me.

"Christ, Cade. Good thing you're so beautiful, because you're a mess." She rolled her eyes in admonishment.

"Whatever. Look, this is a job, nothing more. I don't enjoy this process," I sighed as I leaned my head back against the seat. "So? What needs to happen?"

"Well, you have the press conference, a couple of panels, the private interview with Entertainment Weekly, the photo call with the entire cast outside the convention center and then the re-screenings of The Future of Our Past and Don't Forget to Remember Me, this evening." Denise was reading out of her day planner, periodically biting on the end of her pen.

"Oh... that's *all*?" I asked sarcastically.

Bloody hell, it was like we were monkeys in a cage at a circus.

She shrugged. "That's the price you pay for being a huge star," she said offhandedly. "The crowds clamoring for you translate into my next salary negotiation so can it. Brook and Noah are already in the hall waiting and getting photos taken. You'll join them, but Cade, remember to keep your distance from Brook. Pinnacle has asked that Noah sit between the two of you."

"That's silly. I mean, there is no love triangle in this film... especially with me and Noah." I mocked and tugged at the neck of my T-Shirt. It was hot in the limo and I was anxious.

"Um, yeah, right. Sure, Cade. You're hilarious."

I smirked but I wasn't amused. "So, what does that mean?"

"You know what it means! You and Brook seem to have uncontrollable urges to ogle and stare each other." I smirked and put my hand over my mouth as she continued. "We get it, but try to keep it under control. Noah in the middle should help. At least, that's what Pinnacle is hoping for."

I sighed as all the frustration that I'd felt the past nine weeks swelled within my chest. "Screw Pinnacle, Denise. In three weeks we'll be back in Vancouver and they've agreed to let us stay in the same hotel, so isn't this a lot of wasted subterfuge?" I scoffed. "Haven't Brook and I been through enough? We almost broke up several times this summer. I mean... really?"

She had the grace to soften her features as she watched me, hesitating slightly before speaking. "I know and I'm sorry. But even during the next shoot, it won't be like you'll be able to be obvious, Cade. That's part of the compromise. The good news is that you'll be with her most of the time."

Yes, and then after three more months it was just another ride on the same damn publicity train when I went to Europe and Australia for my next film. I put both heels of my hands to my eyes and scrubbed, knocking my sunglasses off and onto the floor of the limousine.

I didn't bother voicing what I was thinking or feeling. As close as Denise and I were, and for all the time that she had been my manager, even she couldn't understand what it was like to feel like a lab rat. No one could. No one; but Brook.

The limo pulled up to the backside of the convention center where the police had the street blocked off. We were ushered alongside one of the main doors so I could get through without dealing with the mobs of people again.

"The press had been instructed to avoid any personal questions, especially about your relationship, so hopefully that won't be a problem."

I got out of the limo, greeted by my bodyguards. "Oh, so you mean they won't ask us if we shagged last night?" I asked, disgust filling my voice as I remembered all of the comments Brook and I had to endure over the summer, beginning all the way back in June at the airport as I went to New York for the first time. "You have more confidence in them than I do."

Denise put her hand on my arm but didn't say anything as we walked in the door and down a long hallway. Another door opened and I could hear the screaming getting closer.

"Noah!! Brook!! Ahhhh!!!!"

Jesus, here we go!

"Ladies and Gentlemen, please welcome, Caden Carlisle!" A nameless announcer boomed over the din, but then the screams increased even more. I walked out onto a raised platform where Brook was standing with Noah, his arm tightly around her, and her arm around his waist in return.

Brook's eyes briefly darted to meet mine and then away, while Noah nodded to me in silent greeting.

"Hi. Sorry I'm late," I murmured, taking my place on Brook's left side. Immediately my arm went around her and pulled her slightly away from Noah and closer to me. I'd be damned if I could help myself. The hand I'd slid behind her back reached out to wrap around the arm she had around Noah. I pulled it back slightly, in silent request she remember who she belonged to. I glanced down at her face and although she wasn't looking at me, I recognized the gentle smirk that spread across her lips at my action.

The cameras flashed for a few minutes, the reporters getting their fill as we all smiled and posed for them.

"I fucking hate this shit," Brook said under her breath, never breaking the smile formed on her lips. Noah seemed a natural, eating up the adoration being thrown our way.

It was a bloody long morning, being bombarded by question after question; even the dreaded relationship question and I dropped my head and tried to hide a smile as Brook let the guy have it.

"Okay, seriously? You did not just fucking ask me that, right?" The subject was dropped after that, Denise stepping in to remind the reporters those types of questions were off limits.

I stole a look at Brook and on several occasions while Noah was answering questions, we'd talk softly, leaning into each other. I could feel Denise and Jeanne's eyes boring into us, but I didn't bloody care. Brook seemed oblivious as well, which suited me perfectly. At least the long separation made her less sensitive to keeping our relationship a secret.

I laughed out loud when a reporter asked each of us what scene we were looking forward to shooting in the coming movies and Brook's response was such an in your face response that left everyone there in no doubt as to her meaning.

"Um... Well, we're um... gonna make a baby," she said with a smirk and sat back in her chair, running her hands through her short dark hair as she tried to keep from laughing. It was bloody brilliant and the crowd went wild. Anyone who read the books knew what the third film would entail.

Thinking back on the last two months, I could only remember one time when the crap going down with the tabloid articles was even remotely funny. It was when that stupid European rag reported that Brook was pregnant. I panicked at how that would affect her so I'd called her right after I'd heard it, keeping my voice light-hearted. I knew if it were true, she would have told me herself.

"I hear I'm having your baby..." I teased through my chuckles.

She had laughed in response. "Are you sure it's mine? I want a maternity test." We both giggled and talked well into the night, and we paid for it later when both of our asses were dragging the next day.

"What about you, Cade?" The same reporter asked and someone screamed a response from the audience.

I struggled not to laugh, but a grin split my face because I couldn't bloody help myself. My cheeks actually ached with the strain of it.

"Um... getting her pregnant, I suppose." I leaned forward and stole a glance at Brook around Noah to find her smiling, trying to stifle her obvious laughter with her hand, her shoulders visibly shaking.

Somehow we made it through all of the bullshit, but didn't have much time to speak to each other. I reminded myself over and over that Pinnacle wanted the focus placed on Noah's increased role in this film so they could feed their funnel of star power for upcoming movies. I did a fair job of pushing down the anger I felt that we had to hide our feelings for each other, but I wasn't mad at Noah. I could see he'd developed a crush on Brook during filming, but he was acting very professionally and respectful. He was a good guy and I admired his acting ability and his commitment to the franchise.

I was fine... until the bloody E!News interview. Then I saw red and had to get the fuck out of there. Seeing Brook lean into Noah and throw her arm around him like she'd never do with me in public had my blood boiling and my chest constricting. I felt suffocated and I wanted the hell out. I wanted to be anywhere but there.

Brook glanced at me and saw me stiffen. Her eyes widened and as I turned and stormed out, praying to God that I'd have some sort of relief, some small reprieve from the crowds and the clawing. I needed a cigarette... I needed air. Now. I shoved on my sunglasses and my black hoodie, pulling it up over my hair as I moved through the crowds.

As if by some miracle, most of the people paid me little attention, those who did let me pass with only one or two who tried to stop me. As I passed, I put up my hands and said softly, "I'm sorry, I can't just now. Please forgive me."

Maybe those were the magic words I'd needed all along.

Brooklyn

CADE WAS STANDING back, watching my interview with Ben Lyons from E!News and I could see him visibly stiffen with each passing second. I was doing what I was told to do to promote the film and refraining from any and all comments about him, so why was he shooting daggers at me with his eyes? Clearly, he was upset that Noah was with me, and he wasn't.

Jesus, after last night, could he seriously be upset?

"So do you have a new love interest in the next film?" the interviewer asked, shaking me out of my focus on Cade and his tantrum. I laced my arm through Noah's and leaned into him.

"You'll have to see the film," I said, forcing a smile but felt my heart sink as Cade turned quickly and stalked off. Despite the heat of the day and the suffocating atmosphere in the convention hall, he threw on his black hoodie, pulled it up over his wild hair and shoved his sunglasses on his face.

Fuck! Fuck! Fuck!

Cade was obviously braver than I, taking off through the massive crowd at the Comic-Con event. I knew he was upset, but was he crazy? The mobs of fan girls would tear him apart if he wasn't careful. One of the bodyguards moved to follow, but he held up his hand and glared, effectively halting the security guy in his steps.

Jesus, didn't he learn his lesson in New York? Instantly I was worried that he'd be mobbed, chased or worse, injured somehow.

I wanted to go after him, but we couldn't take on that type of publicity. Pictures of me frantically chasing him through the crowds would be headline news and it would wipe out every piece of the illusion we'd built up to this point. I'd have to wait until later, but my heart ached in my chest because I knew he was hurting and there wasn't anything I could do about it now.

Noah patted me on the back after we were finished with the interview.

"What?" I asked, wondering if he'd seen Cade's reaction.

"He'll be okay, Brook. I think he's just had enough of this crap."

I looked into Noah's warm expression and was thankful for his friendship.

"I know," I sighed and ran my hand through my hair and held it at the back of my neck as I looked down at the floor. "I'm gonna go see if Denise or Jeanne can help track him down. I want to talk to him."

"We have that last interview with Entertainment Weekly at 4:00. It's most of the cast. He won't miss that Brook. Maybe you should give him some space to get his head on straight," he said reasonably, and I nodded my head in agreement. "He seems so out of sorts."

I saw the logic in Noah's suggestion. Maybe Cade was doing this to get me to blow our secret. Suddenly, I was angry. "Yeah, he is, and you're right, he probably does need some time. Thanks, buddy." I punched his arm playfully, although my insides were clenching and I was getting nauseous.

"He loves you, Brook. Don't worry."

I nodded but bit my lip. Yeah, he loved me, but the pressure of all of the mobs, the tabloid's constant rumor mill and the sneaking around had made both of us crack on more than one occasion. We were bound to do so again. That, on top of the months apart, was enough to break up any normal couple, and we were under a global microscope.

Jesus, it was impossible to deal with, and we'd been doing it for so long. But after last night...

My eyes scanned the crowds for Cade as we walked across the floor of the massive hall between four of the bodyguards. He was nowhere to be found. Noah and I went back to the lounge they had set up for the cast to wait the ninety minutes until that final interview. Maybe after that, Cade and I would be able to talk and sort this shit out. Ninety minutes would feel like forever under the circumstances. I'd tried to call, and texted him but all I got was voicemail, and he hadn't returned any of the messages. Shit.

I found a chair in the corner that was off by itself and curled into it, wanting to be alone. I shoved my ear buds in, turned on my iPod, and rested my arms on the back of the chair, burying my face in the crook of my elbow. The time couldn't pass fast enough. I hated this fucking shit. I closed my eyes, trying to relax and steady my uneven breathing. I would talk to him... and he would understand that I was just doing my job.

Someone pushing on my shoulder startled me. I lifted my head and tried to open my eyes. Jeanne was still shaking my shoulder to rouse me.

"Huh?"

"Brook, we have to go. It's time for that last interview."

"Sorry, I guess I was more tired than I thought. Have you seen Cade? He disappeared a while ago." I felt anxious; my stomach fluttering because I was scared of the answer. I realized I must look like hell as I rubbed my eyes and got up out of the chair.

"Denise called an hour ago and said he was really upset and wanted to leave. To go back to New York."

I drew in a deep breath and grabbed her hand. "She stopped him, though, right?" I asked anxiously.

"Yes. She managed to calm him down but said he was extremely moody and agitated. He wouldn't talk to her about why. Do you know what caused it?"

"Uh huh. It's my fault."

We started walking across the convention center surrounded by my bodyguards. More conversation was impossible as fans started screaming at me as we made our way the short distance to the private room where the interview was being held. "All this stuff is getting to us," I muttered as we walked into the room.

Jennifer, Noah, Cade and me, along with Martin Deering and the new actress, Leah St. Claire were scheduled for the interview, but Martin had taped his segment separately and had already left.

When I walked into the room, the three of them were already sitting on the small white couch across from the interviewer; Leah sidled up to Cade. Of course, I thought.

Another nameless interviewer, with the same tired bag of questions I'd already answered ten times, no doubt. Ugh.

Cade was bent over his knees with his forearms resting on his legs, but he glanced up at me and ran a hand through his hair. Jennifer moved to make room for me between the two of them while Leah stayed plastered to Cade's other side. I prayed this interview wouldn't be long because I was feeling weird about the whole thing now. He didn't say anything, so I nudged him with my elbow.

"Hey."

"Um, hey." His response was relaxed but distant. He had a bottle of water in his hand and he twisted the top off and took a long drink as the interviewer began asking the questions. After a few about the set, the new cast members, and if we were ready to get back to set, she turned to Cade and me.

"Brook and Cade, both of you talk about how *Don't Forget to Remember Me* is your favorite book of the series. Can you tell us a little bit about that and why that one really does it for you?" She was nice and didn't seem like she'd be asking any of the personal questions that I dreaded. We'd been bombarded and I was struggling, openly bitching some guy out earlier, but this seemed okay.

I began with my answer. "For me, it was just because it sort of felt like it was the first movie. I mean, since Julia didn't know Ryan anymore. We got to build more layers into the characters. It was, it was, you know, I guess... that's why it affected me the most."

Jesus, stutter much, Brook?

Cade listened with his head bent down the entire time, and then it was his turn to answer and I held my breath.

"My opinion of the whole series is... it's about the relationship between the two characters that can't be shaken, no matter where they are, or what happens to rip them apart. The devotion and attraction were undeniable. Even when Julia didn't know who Ryan was. That was what I was trying to draw from and relate to," he took a deep breath and shrugged, "You know, when you find yourself becoming or being so in love with someone... and... it sort of transfers. You know what I mean?"

I sucked in my breath, hoping no one noticed.

Leah pointed to a TV above Cade's head where the interview was being shown live. He was distracted and he turned toward me.

"What?" He seemed exasperated at the obvious interruption, but we all laughed in embarrassment.

"Cade, you're on a, you're on a roll, I think you should keep going." I smiled at him.

He sighed and tried to continue, "Okay, you find yourself in love with someone, you become sort of ultra-aware of yourself, and that other person, even if there are obstacles that keep you apart. You know they're 'the one' for you, and that's it. That's.... Ryan and Julia. "

I was trying not to listen too closely to his words because I knew he was talking about his feelings for me during the filming of *The Future of Our Past* when I was still with David, and also now, with the act we were putting on for the press. I knew it hurt him, so I absentmindedly played with Jennifer's ring, and he, apparently being hypersensitive to what I was doing, stopped.

"That's it!" he breathed and started laughing; I burst out laughing too.

Jesus, couldn't anybody see what was going on between us? This subject was so sensitive and we were sworn to secrecy; which made us both clumsy and uncomfortable. Maybe that was the reason Pinnacle was so worried. I dropped my head into my lap and covered it with my arms for a split second before I got control of myself and sat back up.

"God." Cade let out his breath and shrugged, "I can't concentrate anymore." We laughed again nervously and he took a moment to regroup and continue.

"Getting into Ryan's head, I obsessed over being in love with someone I couldn't be close to, and then you keep elevating the other person higher and higher..."

Is that how I made him feel back then? Like he wasn't good enough? He was so good and I didn't deserve him. I felt horrible and I had to interject; "Julia feels unworthy of this 'perfect stranger' who happens to be her doctor, who swoops in and takes care of her."

Cade turned and looked straight at me.

"But Julia is really the strong one."

"You guys are gonna blow it." Jennifer was whispering to me again, and Cade took a breath so deep that his shoulders rose and we heard the breath rush from his lungs. His brows raised and his lips twitched.

The interviewer smiled and looked from one of us to the other. "You guys seem close."

"No. Whenever anyone asks if we have chemistry, I'm like, no way! She's a complete pain in the ass!"

"Yeah, right!" I couldn't help but blurt out, and he glanced at me and we both laughed again.

Somehow we made it through and at the end of the interview we all filed out to the curb of the convention center among the bodyguards and masses of screaming fans to wait for the cars. We were all lined up for the photos and Cade and I didn't protest when Cade's arm slid around my waist, and I reciprocated so we were standing close enough, so our bodies touched. He felt so good and I tried to rub the side of his waist, hoping he knew what I was feeling about what went down in the interviews.

Out of nowhere, Wendy appeared on my right as Cade stood on my left. I didn't even know she would be in San Diego, so I was totally surprised by her presence.

She grabbed me in a huge hug and the cameras flashed.

Cade took a hold of my arm and roughly pulled me out of her embrace, casting a dirty look in her direction before letting my arm drop... I hoped, before anyone noticed. "Stay the hell off of her, Wendy," he almost growled under his breath.

I looked up into his face and he looked uncomfortable and pensive.

"Jeesh, Cade. Possessive much?" Wendy blasted at him.

"We don't need your bloody bullshit. Just keep the hell away from her, Wendy. I'm serious. No one is buying your rubbish anymore."

Wendy mocked Cade by smiling up into his face and looked like she was ready to speak, but he leaned toward me and I moved closer to him, turning my back to her without a word to her.

"It's okay. Relax, Cade."

"She's poison. I don't want her anywhere near you."

If this weren't a photo call, I'd think it was just another setup photo op for Wendy to be in the press. No one could ever say she wasn't on the ball, even if she was the most irritating, two-faced bitch that I knew. I was still uncomfortable around her after all we had been through, but supposedly she was dating some new up-and-coming director. Yeah, right.

I knew it was just to save face after we basically banished her from the set when her filming had ended last April. She had to be attached to someone before we went back to set so it wouldn't look like she was still pining over Cade. And the more potential a new relationship had for moving her career forward, the better it would be for her; damage control for the press and her reputation. This wouldn't last and I was sure she'd be sniffing around Cade again soon enough. The new guy didn't have a fucking clue that he was only her latest tool.

Cade and I got into different cars that would take us back to the Hard Rock Hotel. I couldn't wait to talk to him and I pulled out my phone to send him a text the minute I was alone.

Meet me in my room. I need to talk to you, please.
Love you.

Thirty seconds later, my phone vibrated in my hands.

Yes, we do need to talk, Brook. I love you, too,
but this charade is too much for me.
I'm sorry.

I ran up to my room as fast as I could. I was shaking and worried, but this needed to happen as soon as possible. It was normal for Cade to get mobbed by fans, so I knew he'd be a few minutes behind me, so I stripped off my clothes and hopped in the shower. The hot water felt wonderful on my tense muscles and I prayed it would help me to relax before he got up to my room.

I threw on some clean jeans and a T-Shirt and as I was running a comb through my hair, he knocked on the door.

I opened it and he looked stoic, but I was still so happy to see him. I stood on my tiptoes and slid my arms around his neck and tried to place a soft kiss on his lips. He was pretty much unresponsive, except for his hands lightly touching the sides of my waist. His lips were unmoving under mine. What a difference a few hours made.

My heart fell and he removed my arms from around his neck and walked into the room. When he turned to face me, I could see that he was still angry, so I just waited for whatever was to come.

"What the fuck was all that about today, Brook?" The tone of his voice was hard, guarded and pain flickered in the depths of his blue eyes.

"Do you mean my interview with Noah? That's what they told me to do, Cade. I thought you knew that!" I wrung my hands in front of me, struggling to figure out what to say next. "You don't think...?"

"Fuck, no. But you didn't have to hang all over him, did you? Do you know how I bloody feel? Denise and Jeanne are working to ease our relationship out into the public. Tomorrow there's another magazine breaking a cover article about my 'secret feelings' for you, and you have to keep making it look like it's one-sided! How bloody long will I have to play the fool in this mess? It's fucking *People* magazine, for Christ sakes! Don't you get it? Did you forget about that?"

He was pacing back and forth as he spoke to me, his hands running through his hair over and over, and the look on his face was so hurt, it broke my heart. *People* magazine had slipped my mind and I balked.

Out of so many, it was one that was taken seriously, they were known for not printing unsubstantiated information.

I took a couple steps toward him, but he held up his hands to stop me.

"I'm sorry, Cade. I guess with everything going on, I did forget. I never want to hurt you."

"Yeah, well, you do! Over, and over again! Hmmph!" His breath left in a whoosh as he walked to the bed and sat down, bringing his fisted hands over his eyes; he rubbed them back and forth before he continued. "I know that it's for the movie, but the whole world is watching us."

He hesitated and I froze where I was standing.

"Like at the MTV Awards before I went to New York... We were supposed to kiss, finally giving a clue to the truth of our relationship, finally allowing me to validate all of the feelings that I have professed for the past fucking year and a half! Then with minutes to spare, you decided not to go through with it. When do I have something to say about any of this? I feel literally ridiculous! I look like a bloody moron!"

"You never seemed upset by it... I... I just thought that we'd be hounded even more than we already were, and..." I stopped and looked at the floor, my eyes filling with tears. "That beautiful night... you were... mad at me?"

I could understand why he was so hurt. He felt like he was admitting every feeling he had for me, over and over, and all I did was deny, deny, deny. My heart ached in my chest, I couldn't breathe.

He sighed. "No, not later. I was leaving you and I didn't want to think about it then, but it has all built up. What about today in that damn interview? I was pouring my fucking heart out like a lovesick idiot, and you and Jennifer were playing around like little girls. I was talking about how my feelings for you were what I base Ryan's emotions on, feelings I've had since the bloody audition! I was bloody talking *to you*, Brook! Telling you how much I love you, and you weren't even fucking listening!"

I started at the tone in his voice. I couldn't remember ever seeing him this upset and angry except when it had been about David.

His face was flushed and his eyes were glassy. I knew he was holding back tears by the way his fists clenched and his breath came in short bursts. "Brook, I'm sorry, but if things don't change, I just can't do this anymore. I'll have to distance from this," he said painfully. "It will kill me, but I can't keep looking like an idiot if you don't feel enough for me to be honest about it." His tone was defeated and I was sure that my heart stopped beating in my chest. I couldn't breathe.

Did he just say he was leaving me?

I willed my feet to walk and I moved to sit next to him on the edge of the bed. I tried to put my arms around him, but he flinched away from me. I felt the sobs well in my chest as my hand hovered in the air he'd just vacated. He'd never refused to touch me before. Even in Tokyo, he'd held me and kissed me despite everything. I realized now, how serious this was to him and I was scared. I needed to make him understand.

"I'm so sorry. I understand why you're mad, but..." My voice broke on the words and I had to stop for a moment. "But, I love you more than anything in the world. I thought you knew that. Haven't I done enough to make you sure of me?" The sobs broke from my chest and I huddled over my knees, my head in my hands as I cried. "Why do you want me to risk my career?"

He sighed but didn't say anything... and didn't touch me.

I raised my teary eyes to his and I tried to wipe the wetness from my cheeks with both of my hands; the emotions building; my desperation to make him understand overwhelming me.

"What do you think? That this hasn't been hard on me too? This whole thing has been hell for me, too, Cade! All the tabloids hooking you up with Wendy and now Davina! Over and over again, I had to deal with that fucked up bullshit! The paparazzi stalk me everywhere I go, constantly asking me, to my face, what I thought about you and your new co-star... and at other times hammering me about the relationship between us! They even asked me if we fucked!" I threw my hands in the air and then through my hair. "If we *fucked*, Cade! All the while I had to keep any emotion from showing on my face, when I was dying inside! I sat back and ate all of the jealousy and insecurity I felt whenever I heard you'd gone to dinner with Davina, or you were seen getting close off set, that she was hanging out in your trailer between scenes... and all of those fucking pictures of the two of you kissing! You know why? Because I told myself that we were solid! That it meant nothing to you, that you loved me, and it was only about the stupid film! And then, when you got hurt and I couldn't get to you, I thought I'd go out of my mind."

Cade didn't move, but his nostrils flared. "The kissing thing was from set. We were acting!"

I nodded. "I know, but it still hurt." I wiped at my tears again but they were endlessly raining from my eyes. "I was only doing my job today... just like you were, Cade! It has nothing to do with our relationship. I was just hugging Noah, and you don't know deep down, based on all we've shared, that I love you more than I can even deal with?" I cried.

"It's not about Noah and hugging him. It's about me pouring my bloody heart out, and you continually denying any feelings. It's fucked up, and I'm done with it!" he shouted back.

I felt myself crumbling and my voice lowered, cracking. I could barely form the words around the aching in my throat.

"I wish it was enough to know how much I love you. God, why isn't it enough? Don't you know yet, how you consume my... Entire. Fucking. Life?" I was almost screaming at him in my anguish.

He finally turned his pained features to look at me, and reached out to me, but this time it was my turn to withdraw from him. I got off of the bed and went to stand across the room with my back to him as my shoulders started to shake in silent sobs.

"And here we are, fi-finally together after over two months, and you want to fight with me?" My voice broke as I turned to face him. "I don't want to fight. All I want to do is hold on to you and never let go," I said softly, almost a whisper.

I covered my face in my hands after I said the words, my heart literally breaking in a million pieces and the next thing I knew, Cade's arms were around me and he was kissing my temple. My arms went around his waist and he crushed me to his chest as I continued to cry my heart out.

"Oh, Brook. I'm so sorry. I'm such a selfish bastard. I didn't consider all that you've had to deal with... you're always so strong. All I could see was how much I was hurting. I'm sorry, my love. So sorry."

Both of his hands moved to the sides of my face as his thumbs wiped the tears from my cheeks and he tilted my face up to his.

"I'm sorry too. I n-never meant to hurt you. It's like ripping my own heart out," I said brokenly. "I don't want to do this anymore."

He pulled back to look into my face, a worried expression flooding his features. "What?"

I saw the panic in his eyes and rushed to explain. "I don't want to do this anymore. You're right. We have to be able to show how we feel. I understand why you need this."

He closed his eyes and he sighed in relief.

He kissed my eyes, nose, and cheeks before moving to my mouth in a soul-wrenching kiss. All of the anger, pain and jealousy we felt, every emotion we'd had to bottle up over the past months manifesting in the urgency in our kiss and the way our arms wrapped around each other. Over and over he kissed me, and I wanted more.

Before I knew it, our clothes were scattered across the room and we were lying on the bed. Our bodies were joined in the same desperate urgency of our kisses. We forgot meeting the others for dinner, forgot the movie showings that Pinnacle wanted us to attend as part of the convention... we lost ourselves in each other. The overwhelming feelings of love and the months of pent up longing we had for each other, our only focus.

As our bodies moved and sweated together, we were sating not only our maddening desire for each other but also the utter desolation we had both suffered at our separation. The physical separation as we filmed on opposite sides of the country and the forced lie to keep our real relationship at bay for so long had taken a huge toll on both of us.

We gave to and took from each other until our bodies were sated and our hearts were healed. When it was over, we were both clinging to each other, looking in each other's eyes, running soft caresses over each other's exposed bodies. Cade brushed my hair off of my face and whispered that he loved me over and over as he placed soft kisses on my mouth.

"Don't you know how much I love you, Cade? My heart breaks when you doubt me." I still had tears spilling from my eyes as I looked at him.

His arms gathered me close and he buried his face in the side of my neck. His hot breath washed over my skin as he exhaled and then placed an open mouth kiss on the sensitive skin below my ear.

"My heart knows it, Brook. But it's been impossible for me to pretend that I don't love you and it completely devastates me that it seems like it's getting much easier for you. I want to take your hand and go out to dinner, to go to a ball game, to just be bloody normal. I'm afraid all of the rumors floating around will rip us apart. We have to get our heads around this before it gets out of hand. We know all of the headlines are rubbish and it still hurts us. These last weeks were unbearable."

I knew he was right, but somehow it all seemed less invasive and hurtful as long as he was by my side. I took a deep breath and let it out in a shudder. My hand stroked the hair at the back of his head as he held me tight. "Besides what Jeanne and Denise are doing to feed the press little bits of the truth, I think we need to do something drastic. Once we get back on set."

"What? Do you mean without the managers?"

"Yes. Okay?"

I wondered what he was thinking, but at the moment the details didn't seem to matter. I was just happy we'd made up. "Okay." I turned my head toward him to place several soft kisses along the strong plane of his jaw, the stubble longer now and soft against my lips. "I can't breathe when you're mad at me."

Cade sighed deeply. "I can never breathe when it comes to you. When I'm with you, you take my breath away. And when I'm without you, I'm suffocating."

His velvet voice saying those perfect words had me holding him tighter and fighting the tears again.

"Please don't go back to New York. Come home with me to L.A."

"You mean sneak back?" he asked quietly.

"We need to figure this out and we can talk about it over the weekend. Besides, I'm not ready to let go of you yet." I said against the skin of his chest as I lay next to him. His strong arms tightened around me and his lips brushed against my forehead. "I have my car, so I'll have to drive it back. Can you call Peter and have him drive down here to pick you up?"

"It would be faster just to hire a car from here. I'd like to spend the drive with you. I don't want to waste those hours alone in a bloody car. I still have to be back to New York, soon."

I thought about it for a second or two and bit my lip as I tried to figure out a way to get my car back up to L.A. without anyone being the wiser. My hands fluttered along his forearm as we lay quietly together.

"Maybe we could ask Noah to drive my car back up?"

"Do you think he would?" Cade asked hopefully, and hugged me closer, kissing my cheek. When he lowered his lips to mine, I pressed my mouth more fully to his for a brief, but deep kiss.

"I do. He's become a good friend."

I reluctantly untangled myself from Cade's limbs and walked to get my phone so I could dial Noah's number. I told him that Cade and I weren't going to attend the screenings like we were supposed to. We'd make an appearance at them and then sneak out when the lights went down. I'd slip Noah my extra key and a note about where I'd be leaving my beat up old Honda. He readily agreed. Cade dressed in a hurry and went into the bathroom to call Denise and ask her to send a car.

"I thought Cade was leaving?" Noah had asked on the phone.

"Change of plans. Change of, well... a lot of things now, Noah," I said softly as a sudden calm settled over me.

"Okay. That's good, Brook. I'm... well, I'm happy for you guys."

"Thank you, Noah. I really mean it," I said sincerely.

***

I LEFT MY CAR parked and let Noah know where to find it and was soon diving into the back of Cade's limousine and his waiting arms. He pulled me across his lap and his mouth found mine hungrily. I'd never get enough of him, for as long as I lived. I knew it, and I'd accepted it as something beyond my control. It was a scary prospect to a degree, giving that much of your heart and life to another person, but I realized as I melted into him, that it was a battle I'd lost eighteen months earlier and nothing would ever change it.

Shit, it was a battle I'd lost before I was even born.

"Do you think anyone saw you, love?" he breathed into my open mouth.

"It doesn't matter. I don't care anymore, Cade." My hand held his face gently, stroking his chin and I pulled back to look into his eyes, my fingers pushing his hair off of his forehead. "What do you need now?" I searched the clear blue eyes that looked into mine and then dropped to my mouth. He was sexy and I loved him; which made me want to rip his clothes off. His mouth dipped and his tongue laving mine as I answered his need with my own.

"Mmmm... to make love to you," was all he said, several minutes later after his mouth finally lifted off of mine. I chuckled softly in response.

"No, I didn't mean that."

He drew in his breath and pulled back to look at me seriously, brushing my hair behind my ear on the left side of my face, and then lifting my chin with his index finger. His brow crinkled slightly and the vein running up the center of his forehead pulsed. "Um, I just want to be with you and to love you openly. The whole world knows anyway and I just want to be honest," he said seriously. "What do you want to do?"

I swallowed and looked down at my lap. His hand closed around my fingers and he lifted it to his mouth, his lips ghosting over my knuckles. Even the softest touch of his lips could send shivers through me and I trembled. He smiled softly against my skin as he felt my reaction.

"I don't want you to be hurt. I never wanted that." The words throbbed across my voice. "I want to make you happy so I think you should tell me about the thing you want to do once we get back on set. I just hope we can keep the intimate details about our relationship to ourselves. Some part of it needs to be just ours. You belong to the world already, so I need to have some part of you that's only mine." I raised my eyes up again to find him smiling, his hand still in my hair, stroking and threading through the strands.

"It's beautiful that you would speak my thoughts. Of course, I understand but you should know you have all of me. This is ours." I nodded and leaned my forehead on his shoulder before he continued. "The producers don't have as much leverage for this series since we're on the last movie. I'm defying them by driving up to L.A. to be with you."

"Two weeks until you're finished with Only Us?"

"Yes, but I'll come back next weekend too, Brook. I'm done letting them run us and keeping us apart."

I smiled up at him and then snuggled into the curve of his neck and against his chest. His arms tightened around me and my breath left in a whoosh. "Hmmph! I know you want us to be photographed, but we're supposed to keep it under wraps until Don't Forget to Remember Me is in theaters, and that's still four months away."

"I know. But if something should just happen to slip through the cracks... well, that's no one's fault, right?" Cade smiled brightly, his eyes dancing.

"Like what?"

"Maybe if we can't exactly say we're together, we can let a few pictures speak for us. We'll arrange a photo shoot with just us; that doesn't involve the films or the studio."

I liked Cade's plan. If we could pick and choose carefully and let just the right amount of information out, little by little and under our control, not Pinnacle's, that would be ideal.

"We don't have to confirm it for sure, but I want to just stop denying it," he said softly. I'd been the one saying we were friends, never Cade, and I understood what he needed. Enough time had passed since David was out of the picture, too, so that was no longer a concern.

My heart swelled and I realized that I wanted the same thing and finally, I was more than willing. The pain in his face at the hotel earlier was something I never wanted to see again.

I moved over his lap until I was straddling his hips and he smiled up at me while I wound my fingers in his hair. "Me, too." I nodded.

The lopsided grin that I loved lit up his beautiful face and his eyes widened. "Yeah? Bloody hell... really?" he asked incredulously.

I nodded slightly and bent my lips to his. "Yes," I whispered against his lips. "I won't deny it again. I promise, Cade. I love you so much and I never meant to hurt you. You're the last person in the world I want to hurt. It's like hurting myself."

He groaned and cupped my face as he kissed me over and over. It wasn't long before Cade's hands were roaming my body and ripping at my clothes as he lowered me onto the seat beneath him and we started making out in a mad rush.

"Brook... I love you. You're the most precious thing to me. I always want to take care of you, keep you safe and make you happy. I can't bloody wait until we're married."

His words made my pulse race and my heart swell as our bodies surged towards one another. We devoured each other, body and soul, like it was our last night on earth. Both of us desperate and hungry as we kissed again and again, kissing frantically, clinging to each other. His mouth followed every inch of skin that he uncovered as he undressed me and yet it wasn't enough. I wanted more and I could feel his need consume him as his breathing increased and he pressed his hardness into my soft heat.

When we were both panting and naked, he stopped, running his talented fingers down my body and into the wetness between my legs and I moaned against his mouth. "Uhhh... Cade," I panted as my hands closed around his shaft, moving on him, urging him to take me, even as his fingers moved in soft circles and small thrusts on and into my body, brought me to the edge of ecstasy.

"Brook. Baby... tell me what I need to hear. You know what it is, love. Tell me and I'll give you everything you need. "

My mind raced with a hundred things he could want me to say and I longed to tell him each and every one of them. I gasped and my fingers pulled his hair, dragging his mouth toward mine and I licked his top lip lightly and then pulled his lower one into my mouth to nip and suck on it. "It's only you... forever. You're the only one, the only one that will ever touch me like this for the rest of my life..."

His mouth crushed into my lips, parting them and plundering with his tongue and his fingers teased the tender peak of one of my breasts until it ached and caused a new surge of wetness and throbbing between my legs. My mouth opened to his, sobbing my need into him. I couldn't get close enough, sucking on his tongue like he was sucking on mine, moving against him and showing him how much I needed him.

He was so perfect, so delicious and my heart swelled. He had me panting against his mouth, begging for him to possess me, when finally his legs parted mine and he sank slowly into my body, filling me, stretching me..."Please don't ever leave me. I have to have you, always," his velvet voice begged, even as it seduced me.

We made love to each other, worshiping each other with our hands and mouths, our bodies joined as closely as we could possibly make them. His thrusts were long and hard as his body brought mine into shuddering rapture and he followed when I clenched and released around him over and over again.

"I won't!" I gasped against his shoulder as the last of the shudders racked through both of us. "I can't live without you now." I breathed against him, kissing the side of his face as he finally relaxed against me and he surged against me one last time.

His mouth moved up my neck to my mouth, and he kissed it softly. He moved around my face, kissing my closed eyelids and then nuzzling my nose, his mouth hovering just inches over mine.

"Oh, honey. Jesus, Brook," he breathed. "You're my whole life. I'd give it all up just to be with you."

I knew he meant it with his whole heart and soul because it was like I was saying the words myself.

I wrapped my arms tighter around him as he moved with me to sit up on the seat, his body still embedded deep within mine. I moved to lift off of him and he held me still.

"Where do you think you're going?" He smiled against the skin of my breast, lifting one of them to take the nipple into his mouth. "I'm not done with you yet, my love. Far from it. I want to be inside you for fucking ever." He continued to suckle my skin, causing me to writhe against him, which excited him as much as it did me.

I reminded myself that I was the luckiest woman on Earth as his body swelled even more within me and his arm around my waist urged me to move. Every woman wanted him and yet he wanted me. It was a gift that I would never take for granted.

My hands wound in his gorgeous mane as I tugged on the bronze strands. "You are, Cade. You are," I whispered before our mouths resumed the passionate dance that was us. Our bodies and souls entwined, this was us.

"Yes, forever Brook... This is us."

Chapter 12
Together Again

Brooklyn

SOMEHOW WE'D MADE it through the summer, and the final *Remembrance Trilogy* film was set to start in three days, so we were all on our way back up to Vancouver. Pinnacle chartered a private plane to take most of the cast up at one time; including Wendy and her new *boyfriend*.

Yeah right. I wasn't born yesterday. I was sure it was designed to be a huge smoke screen in her attempt to keep some dignity in the eyes of the world after her blatant play for Cade had failed. Her exit from the previous set last spring didn't get a huge amount of publicity, but her hasty retreat was certainly the subject of speculation and gossip by the crew and cast.

I'd managed to stay away from her most of the summer while I worked on *Dystopia*. I spent most of the free time with Nathan and communicating with Cade. Wendy made that half-assed attempt to suck up to me at Comic-Con, and I'd been surprised by Cade's vicious smack down. He even asked Jeanne and Denise to arrange our interviews without her to avoid any confrontations. The *Entertainment Weekly* interview was done in two parts so that we didn't even have to see her, but then she ambushed us on the sidewalk outside the event. That weekend had been supercharged enough, considering Cade and I had barely seen each other all summer and our emotions were pretty raw. I shouldn't have been surprised his fuse was short about Wendy.

Cade was sitting next to me holding my hand; his thumb caressing the inside of my wrist. I glanced over at him and smiled. Since Comic-Con, we'd seen more of each other because he'd come back to Los Angeles to be with me the final two weekends of filming in New York. It might seem silly to some, running back to my side when we'd be together for three months beginning only two weeks later, but after that horrible fight and our decision in the back of the limousine, we just needed the validation of being together.

My heart swelled as I thought about it. I promised I'd stop denying our relationship and we decided that we still wouldn't come right out and confirm it, but we weren't going to put much effort into hiding it either. I'd stayed with him at his hotels, we'd gone to Daniel Mayfield's concert, and we were photographed together on two or three occasions out and about in L.A. I didn't even try to sneak around that much when leaving his hotel. While that caused problems for Joel, Denise, and Jeanne, it made Cade happy and that had become my first priority.

Most of the cast knew we were a couple anyway, and the deal Cade had made with the studio would ensure that once we got to Vancouver, we'd be in the same hotel. Once again, our management team was taking care of us. They booked an entire floor for us and would post security at the entrances to the stairwells and the elevators so we'd have complete privacy. The rest of the cast was staying at a different hotel a few blocks away. It sounded like heaven, and I was thankful that Jeanne and Denise were our friends, not just our managers. The closeness gave them more room to yell at us for not being as careful, but they really cared about us and were also sick of the "lie."

The plane banked and the engines whirred as we made our approach. The lights were low in the cabin and the one overhead reflected off the golden highlights in Cade's hair. It wasn't as long as it was when we started *The Future of Our Past* because he was just coming off another film. Martin had a dumb idea of putting extensions in it, and Cade quickly put the clamps to it. I'd laughed my ass off and Cade told him he wasn't "*bloody Fabio*" and said surely Ryan could get a haircut. I bit my lip, to stifle a giggle as I remembered, and then his eyes narrowed on my face.

"What, love?" His blue eyes sparkled and his lips lifted at the corners.

"Just..." I shrugged, "what a difference a year makes, huh?"

"Yeah, but it's been more than a year. We were together already by this time last year." His fingers laced through mine tightened. "The best times of my life."

"And the worst," I said softly. Turning toward him in my seat, I reached out with my free hand to touch the stubble on his jaw; so gorgeous, without even trying.

"Hmmph." He pushed his breath out in a huff and then smiled. "Yeah, but worth it. Haven't you ever heard that the depth of the love is measured only by the depth of the pain?"

I shook my head and looked at him intently. He always said the perfect thing. "Only you would say something like that, but yes. I get that too."

"I wish I could take credit, but it's in the script." He pulled my hand up to his mouth and kissed the back of it. "I love you," he murmured against my skin, his hot breath causing my own to catch in my throat.

My heart started racing just like it always did when we were close or when he looked at me like that. "Love you, more."

He laughed. "Don't start. You won't win that fight."

"I'll tell you a secret. Fighting is not what I'm in the mood for." I raised my eyebrow at him with a smirk.

He chuckled softly. "Me either. I wish we'd bloody get there already."

"I have a surprise for you." He turned toward me so that we were almost facing each other and tugged me closer. I didn't want to tell him until tonight in the room, but I couldn't help myself.

"Really? Did you get me out of the screening tomorrow?" he asked, his eyes full of mischief. He hated watching himself on screen, but this was the first chance we'd have as a cast to see the entire second movie after editing. "Or is it a very *sweet* surprise?"

"Don't get too excited, babe. It's not *that* type of surprise; however, I can see that happening, if that's what you want." I bit my lip and then gave up as my lips parted in a big smile.

"Mmmm. Stop teasing. Tell me."

"Imagine Dragons are playing in Vancouver tomorrow night." His eyes widened and his brows rose in the adorable way I loved.

"Yeah? I'd love to go, but I doubt they'll let us off the leash that soon."

"No, they wouldn't let us go alone. We have to take the entire damn cast, but I had Jeanne get tickets for one of the upper balconies, so that security can keep us separated."

"That's brilliant. I love Jeanne!" Cade teased.

"Hey!" I shoved his shoulder, a mock pout settling onto my face. "It was my idea."

He pulled me into his arms and kissed me full on the mouth. It felt good, but I was surprised. "Cade!" I gasped out.

"Shh... Just, shhhh." His mouth was on mine, warm and insistent and I allowed him to pull me closer. My hand lifted to his face to curl around his jaw and his hand moved up to hold on to my wrist. He licked my top lip as he pulled away and I wanted more. I lifted my face and sucked his lower lip between both of mine.

"Uhhh, Brook. You're so good to me." His mouth hovered over mine and I wanted to melt into him, but had to remember where we were. I pulled back slightly and leaned my head against the seat, still unable to pull my eyes away from his.

His eyes watched mine for a minute and then he got a little crinkle between his eyes as his brows dropped. "I have to tell you something, love. While you were in the bathroom, Wendy slunk up here and gave me an ear full."

My breath caught and I visibly stiffened. *When would it end?* He could see me tense and his hand tightened on mine.

"Don't stress. She was just pointing out that we weren't doing a good job of hiding our relationship based on our actions." He gave a low chuckle. "She said she was only pointing it out *as a friend.*" My mouth tightened into a thin line and he rolled his eyes slightly. "She said she wanted us to be aware of how it looked to others."

"How considerate of her," I said in disgust, pushing back into my seat. "Interesting how she couldn't point it out while I was sitting here, isn't it? She pisses me off!" I straightened in my chair. "What did you say?"

"Not much. Just that it wasn't her concern and we weren't idiots.

Basically to sod off," he said calmly and shrugged. "Besides, she brought that guy so I don't know what the bloody hell she's so worried about us for."

"That poor bastard. He's only here to keep people from thinking she's crushed over you, obviously."

"He's utterly ridiculous if he allows her to use him like that. She's hardly worthy of our pity. Anyway, Wendy's a bloody boring subject. Let's talk about something else."

I smiled. "Yeah? Like what?"

His eyes got serious and the smile left his lips. "Like what I'm going to do to you later when we're alone. Finally back together... *day and night*. Mmmmm. I missed you more than I can articulate."

The velvet voice oozed around and over me: causing my insides to melt and the delicious throbbing to start. I felt my face flush and my breath rushed out before I could stop it. We'd made love last night and again today before we left to go to the airport, but I was hungry for him like I hadn't had him in a year.

His eyes darkened as he looked at me, and he licked his lips. He was super hot when he did that. My eyes dropped to his perfect mouth. "God, Cade." I ran my free hand through my hair and shifted uncomfortably in my seat, trying to assuage the want that was pulsing through me. "Cut it out."

He pulled my hand up to kiss the inside of my wrist again. "I'll take care of you later, love. I'll make the ache go away, I promise," he whispered and leaned over to brush his lips along my cheekbone and up to my temple. His breath was hot and sweet as it washed over my skin. The scent left his taste on my tongue and I trembled.

"Will it ever go away? You can make me so hot with only a word or a look." I blushed as I whispered the words, our eyes locking and holding. He was still leaning toward me and the corners of his lips lifted in a small, satisfied smile. "I mean... it's uh, really... it makes me feel completely helpless," I admitted.

"Brook," he breathed. "You're not the only one who's bloody helpless. You make me ... *insane.* I can't even think of anything else. You consume me, day and night. No matter if you're right beside me or thousands of miles away. I always want you. To feel you, touch you... taste you."

My heart thumped in my chest, thinking about how hard these past months had been.

"Uhh..." His words always left me breathless. He was so romantic and beautiful. "I love you."

"You'd better. I'd be in a world of hurt if that weren't the case." He sat back and pulled at the front of his jeans. "Maybe more than I already am, if that's at all possible."

Heat pooled between my legs at his movements and excitement flooded over me, just as it did every time I knew he wanted me. I found myself wishing it was two hours later.

"What are the odds we can ditch the cast dinner tonight?" I asked quietly, glancing up into his face, with hooded lids. I knew he could read the same desire on my face that I saw on his.

"Ugh, love. I wish. It would be rude of us, yeah?"

"I guess," I said, resigning myself to the unavoidability of the situation as the plane touched down on the runway. "Here we go again."

"Yeah." Cade grinned wide. "Five months with you constantly. It'll be torture; that."

I was forced to smile in agreement as he nudged my chin with his thumb.

Denise's head popped up and she shot Cade a look. "Cool it, Romeo. Don't push our luck, please."

"Sod off, Denise," Cade murmured with a grin. Denise and I both laughed.

Caden

IT WAS PITCH BLACK in the room. Brook had thrown her shirt over the alarm clock on the nightstand, so I wasn't sure what time it was. It had to be very early morning because we'd come back from the cast party around midnight and then made love. My body quickened just from thinking of the way she had melted into me and the hot way she always responded so completely, surrendering her body, heart and soul to me. My heart swelled along with my groin.

I listened to the sound of Brook's even breathing and realized how comforted I was, just to have her near me. I rolled on my side toward her and reached out my hand. Her skin was so soft, like velvet or cashmere under my fingers. I couldn't resist touching her whenever she was near me and my fingers softly ran down her bare arm that was clutching the covers up to her chest.

The summer months in New York had seemed like forever. I'd been miserable. There were always people around, but I felt completely isolated because Brook wasn't there. The time difference and our schedules kept us from talking as much as we wanted but I burned up my cell with texts whenever I could. The fans had been ruthless and I barely left the hotel other than the first weekend when Daniel came to town or when the studio demanded I make an appearance with Davina. Those were the longest fucking three months of my life.

Leaving Brook crying at the hotel the morning I left for New York had ripped my bloody guts out. I'd thought about that a hundred times since then, agonizing that we had many of those times in front of us, and wondering if it would ever get easier.

I drew in a deep breath, expanding my lungs to the point of pain and closed my eyes and leaned my head closer to hers, resting on her pillow beside her. I nuzzled her forehead, anxious for her sweet scent and the warmth of her skin under my eager mouth. She shifted and turned toward me, cuddling closer as my arms slid around her naked body.

"Cade..." she murmured breathlessly as I pulled her against me. Her hands glided across the sides of my body and around my back, her nails scratching my skin on purpose and I tensed at the shivers it caused. I was hungry; as hungry as if I hadn't had her in ten years. I grabbed her hips and shifted her beneath me and automatically, Brook lifted her legs around my waist. I brushed her hair off of her face and pressed her into the bed, grinding my pelvis with hers. She rocked her hips in response.

Christ, you feel good.

"Brook. I want you, and I can't do without right now. I'm starving for you," I groaned into the curve of her neck. "I love you."

Her hands slid up my back and fisted into my hair to pull my head back so she could take my mouth with hers. Her tongue snaked out and licked along my top lip, yet her mouth ghosted over mine, making it go dry in anticipation for the passionate kiss I knew would follow. I swallowed and tried to reach for her mouth with mine. "You don't have to do without, baby. Never."

"Brook. Give me your mouth. Now," I demanded and she did so, willingly. God, it was hot.

Her mouth opened to me as her hands in my hair tugged me closer still. My tongue plundered the softness of her mouth and she moaned into me. My hand moved down her body, over the side of her perfectly round breast and further still. Down over her hipbone and the curve of her thigh, and I curled my fingers and raked softly back up again until I closed over her breast. The tender nub came to life under my thumb as I grazed over it again and again.

"Uhnng..."

"God, you're all I want."

"Yes. Always, yes." She arched into me, seeking to take what I longed to give her, her hands clawing at my ass and pulling me toward her. I let the head of my dick find her opening, navigating the soft folds to enter just a little. The heat and wetness I found there left me gasping against her mouth.

"Oh, babe. God, Brook," I moaned as I sank into her at the same time as her lips parted underneath mine and she sucked my tongue into her mouth. My need for her was feverish and the kisses and her body clenching and sucking on mine did little to ease my hunger for her. Instead, it only made me want more and more.

I slowed my pace, wanting to get deeper, closer. My hands wound in her hair as I pushed into her again and again, the sensation building and tightening. My stomach muscles tightened at the blissful ache caused by the feel of her surrounding me, and the sound of her soft moans as I made love to her. I softened my kisses and lifted my mouth from hers, still pushing, seeking more sensation, longing to bring her more and more pleasure. I opened my eyes to look lovingly into her face. The strength of my love overwhelmed me and my eyes blurred causing the shadowy outline of her beautiful face to swim before me in the darkness. Her eyes closed and her lips parted when her breath left her in a rush.

Her legs tightened around me, her heels digging into the muscles of my ass, urging me on and her head lifted from the bed.

"Kiss me, Cade. I want to taste you. I missed you, so much."

My mouth crashed into hers and we kissed again and again, our bodies moving, hands touching, breaths catching. Every time with her was like the first time... like the last time, like I'd never touched her, yet like I'd touched her a million times. As I moved in and out of her slick hot flesh, I could feel her legs start to tremble and her walls tighten and milk around me, the emotions I felt overtook me.

"Uhhh... Cade, Cade, Cade..." She panted in time with my thrusts and it pushed me to the edge, and I fought it. I wanted more. More time with her like this... forever would never be enough.

"Brook." Her name ripped from my chest in a low growl. "I want you... I *need* you to come for me." I put one arm beneath her left knee and hitched her leg higher, so I could get even deeper. I rubbed my pelvic bone against the sensitive flesh of her sex and she dug her nails into my back, dropping her forehead to my shoulder. "That's it. Yes, Brook," I whispered against her neck and then sucked the sensitive skin into my mouth. She shuddered and arched, the delicious throbbing around me let me know without a sound that she was coming.

With three more hard thrusts, I let myself go and the force of it left me gasping for breath. "Ahhh, Brook... Ughnnng..." I buried myself and stilled as the orgasm racked my body. Her hips still moved against mine, and I knew she was trying to get every last drop out of me. It filled my heart up to the point of bursting, even as the physical ecstasy shook me to the very core.

When it was over, both of us lay entwined in each other's arms. I bent to kiss her lips softly and then turned my face into her neck as my arms tightened around her so tight I thought I would crush her ribs. My eyes were burning and my throat ached. I felt her hands brush my hair back tenderly and she kissed the opposite temple.

"Cade?" she asked softly. My only answer was to run a series of kisses along the cord in her neck and hold her tight. I was reluctant to remove my body from hers. "Sweetie, what is it?"

I shook my head and squeezed my eyes shut, causing a single tear to push from each one of my eyes.

"Tell me." Her gentle fingers brushed the side of my face over and over again, catching one of the drops as she did so.

"I just… I missed you so bloody much," I said, my voice thick and cracking. "I was in hell. I'm so glad we're back together for now. At least for a while."

"Babe." She reached up and kissed me on the mouth, sucking my lower lip in between both of hers and then moved to brush her lips along my jawline. "We have months together now, right? Please don't be sad."

I finally pulled up to look into her face and moved to her side, sliding out of her body and pulling her to lie on the pillows facing me. I lifted my hand and brushed her hair back. It was shorter now and even though I missed her long tresses, she was still my beautiful Brook.

"Brook… I know. I just hated being away from you." Her brow crinkled a little and I reached out to smooth the frown away with my index finger.

"I feel the same way. The time with you goes so fast and the rest drags like it will never end."

"Yes, exactly. You're so special. There is no one like you in the world."

Her eyes crinkled and her lips lifted in a soft smile. "Lucky for you," she teased, but I was having none of it.

I nodded seriously. "Yes, it is. I love... making love to you."

"Cade." Her voice was suddenly tight. "You know how much I love you, right?"

"Yeah." I nodded. The tightness in my chest and throat were making it hard to speak. I licked my lips and swallowed once, closing my eyes to the pain. "Remember you told me once that loving this much hurts and it would hurt more?" I opened my eyes to see her reaction.

She nodded. "Before we were a couple, I still missed you. I missed you so much that even I was surprised by the strength of it. But after this, being away from you is just... unbearable. It's insane how miserable I am when we're not together." I pushed a dangling tendril behind her ear. "I'm considering giving up film."

She gasped but I put a finger to her lips to keep her from speaking and shook my head. I'd thought about it a lot and I was serious. I didn't give a bloody hell for the money or the fame. Not when my heart hurt so much. "No, Brook. Just listen. It keeps us apart too much. When the series is done, it will be years before we'll be allowed to work together again and I don't want to lose that much time with you. It's too painful." I searched her blue eyes as they welled with tears. "Isn't it?"

"Very. I missed you, but I don't want to hear that you're considering giving up acting. *Ever.* You're so gifted at it; more than the world, or even you know."

I stared into her eyes and then used my thumb to wipe a lone tear off of her face.

She moved to the curve of my shoulder and curved her arm around my waist. I pulled her close until her head rested on my chest and I closed my eyes, relishing in the feel of her skin on mine.

"Promise me you won't do that, Cade. Please."

I sucked in a deep breath and my chest rose beneath her cheek. "Nothing is more important to me than being with you, love."

Her little hand slid up my chest, over my shoulder and finally found my cheek. "We'll work it out. Whatever, we'll be together as much as we can. I don't think we should turn down roles or stop acting because of schedule conflicts, Cade. We still have to be true to ourselves or we won't be happy as a couple."

I listened in silence, wondering how this much wisdom could come from a woman barely twenty. I knew she was right, because she was saying the same bloody words I'd said in the logical part of my brain over and over.

When I didn't speak, she sighed. "Sometimes we'll have to be apart physically, but you're in my heart. Nothing can change that." I tried to concentrate on the soft patterns her fingers were drawing on my chest. "I worry too."

"What about?" I asked so quietly I almost didn't hear my own voice.

"What do you think? The women, being away when you need me, the temptation you'll face."

"Well, stop. There's no need." I could read her so well. The slight stiffening of her body and the silence all led to the same place. I knew she was thinking of the new movie that I'd just been cast in. I was cast as a womanizing businessman, and there would be several women on set and sex scenes with some of them. I ran a hand over the silken skin of her arm that was wrapped around me, slid my fingers up over her shoulder then down her back as I leaned over to place a kiss on her temple. She'd read the script back in Los Angeles so she knew what it would require of me. "I've told you before. I don't fall in love with my co-stars, Brook. It's you. I loved you before we were even born. How many times do I have to tell you that?"

"About a million."

I smiled into the top of her head and my arms tightened around her slim form, my leg slipping between the two of hers as I settled us both in for sleep. "No bloody problem. No problem at all."

Chapter 13

Gold

Brooklyn

WE WERE LATE, and I was still so tired. Cade and I stayed up all night. I was helping him run lines for some of his scenes with Leah St. Claire, though making love was something we rarely passed on, and so we barely got any sleep at all. Sleeping was the only good thing about being separated this past summer. When we were together, it was the last thing on our minds.

I groaned and sat up, running my hands carelessly through the tangles in my hair. The sheet slipped off of my body as I clamored out of bed and padded into the bathroom. My muscles ached in protest. At least I'd have the nagging pains to remind me of his use of me last night.

I smiled and almost laughed at the happiness I felt at being with him again. *God. I love feeling him on me all day, even when he's not even touching me.*

The bathroom was hot and steamy, and there were two wet towels lying haphazardly on the floor. I reached in and turned on the water, stepping underneath the hot spray and grabbing the shampoo that Cade had left there all in one motion, thinking that I needed to hurry and get ready.

The screening was at two and even though I'd seen the rough cut of the film a month earlier, none of the cast, including Cade, had seen the finished product. Martin was anxious for our reactions, and truthfully I was a little nervous. It was silly really, I thought as I rinsed the shampoo from my hair. I should be getting used to this stuff, but like Cade, I didn't enjoy watching myself on film, but this time... *ugh*. There was that one almost naked scene with Noah. The logical part of me knew it was stupid to feel paranoid and nervous about the scenes Cade hadn't seen yet. After all, he was in most of my scenes, so what the hell was my problem?

I shook it off as I stepped out and wrapped myself in one of the oversized white towels provided by the hotel. I ran my hand through the short hair on my head and groaned. Cutting it shorter for *Dystopia* seemed like a good idea at the time, but now I was kicking myself because I'd have to spend the rest of the day getting extensions put in and having it dyed back to my character's chestnut brown color. Jennifer complained nonstop about the wig she had to wear in the first two films, so I had a good idea of what was in store. I pulled on the strands to measure how long it was, and moaned. It would take two years to get it back to the way it was. *Moron*, I chastised myself.

Even though Cade had been supportive of my decision, he had to hate it, even if he was too sweet to admit it. Shit, *I hated it*, but there was no use crying over it now.

I heard the click of the outside hotel room door open and within seconds Cade was calling my name. "Brook, I have food and coffee!"

I walked into the sitting room to find him pulling pastries out of a bag and setting them on napkins, along with the paper coffee cups on the table near the couch.

"I see it's your usual choice, hon; health food," I teased dryly. Cade glanced at me, his blue eyes roving over my wet hair and the towel that I was grasping around my body. A crooked grin split his face, flashing his white teeth, but he looked as tired as I felt. The stubble, the messy sex hair, still slightly damp from his shower, was gorgeous even if he made no effort. I licked my lips as I picked up a cherry Danish and bit into it. "However, today I have to agree with your choice." I held it out for him. He opened his mouth wide and took half of it in one bite, pulling me close to him at the same time.

"Mmmm. Well, time doesn't allow for egg white omelets today, so I did the best I could." His hands slid down my back and over my ass to pull me in tighter and bent to drop a series of kisses along the side of my neck and down to the curve of my shoulder. "Delicious," he murmured.

I was still holding the remnant of the Danish and the towel with the other, so I couldn't put my arms around him. Instead I turned my head and nuzzled the side of his face with my nose, and then pressed my lips to his jaw, silently hoping he'd turn his face and kiss me like I wanted him too.

"I agree." He pulled back and kissed me softly on the mouth one time.

"We don't have time to get into this now, love. Peter is waiting downstairs. We've got to be at the theater in thirty minutes or so."

"I could have sworn you were going to try to get out of it."

"Yeah, but I'm anxious to see how it turned out."

"That's a first. Is that how you managed the food?" I asked as I took the last bite and went into the other room to get dressed.

"Yeah. We drove around looking for a place until we found this little bakery. Peter went in and got it while I hid in the back of the limo. Bloody lucky those windows are solid black. The screamers were still hammering on them even though they didn't know that I was inside for sure. How in the hell do they always know where to find us?"

"This is the information age. Tweet, tweet, tweet." I mimicked the sound.

"Yeah. If I thought we could buy the company and shut it down, I'd do it in a heartbeat. But another would spring up instantly." He flopped down on the bed and crossed his legs, leaning back on his elbows as he watched me pull on a black lace thong and matching bra. "Not fair, Brook. You're just being mean now."

I raised my eyebrow and laughed. "Hey, no one is holding you there. You can leave if you don't like the view."

"I like the view. Too much," his voice was low and hungry. When I looked at him, his gaze was intense; watching every move I made. The look on his face was full of desire and it made my stomach muscles tighten and the throbbing start. It was so bad that I could feel my heartbeat throbbing in the core of my body.

"I like the one from over here too, so we're both in the same boat." I pulled on a white sleeveless T-Shirt and dark jeans before digging back in the suitcase for my dark gray hoodie. "I love you, you know."

His lips lifted in a small smile. "I know. It never bloody stops."

The phone rang in my purse and it was Jeanne, I flipped it open at the same time that I sat on the edge of the bed next to Cade and ran my hand along his jaw in response to his sweet words.

"Hello?" I answered.

"Where the hell are you guys? Get your asses over here, Brook.

You're late!"

"Humph!" I expelled my breath "Good morning to you, too, Jeanne. We're on our way. Give us ten minutes."

I shut the phone without waiting for an answer and Cade rose from the bed at the same time. I walked across the room and pushed my feet into my chucks before running into the bathroom and putting on a little eyeliner and lip gloss.

"Come on, Julia. Let's not keep them waiting," Cade teased in his American accent. I loved his voice and the sound of that accent transported me to a memory of our first film. I began to associate that accent with when he was allowed to touch me and kiss me... when we could lose ourselves in the world we wanted to be in, and not the one that kept us apart.

"Promise not to run off with Ethan right away, huh?" I was teasing but I bit my lip as I looked up at him. His eyes darkened and his lips twitched slightly in the start of a smile. "Plenty of time for that later when I'm strapped in the salon chair while they torture me."

"Fuck Ethan." His arms slid around me and lifted me up before his mouth devoured mine in a deep and very passionate kiss. My hands lifted and slid into his hair as my lips parted to admit his probing tongue into my willing mouth. I lifted my legs and wrapped them tightly around his waist and I could feel the evidence of his arousal grinding into me, his hips pushing forward as if he couldn't help himself. I pushed back and he dragged his lips from mine and buried his face in my shoulder, his breathing heavy and still holding me tight.

"Ugh... hell, Brook," he groaned against me.

"Yeah," I agreed and nuzzled into him but he didn't raise his head, despite my attempts. Instead, he leaned down and loosened his arms as he set me on the floor and ran a hand through his hair.

He laced his hand through mine and led me without a word to the door.

Caden

MARTIN PUT HIS hand on my shoulder as I left the theater. Brook was walking in front of me and Noah was talking to her. The rest of the cast filed out behind us while he and I shared a conversation about the film and it's coming promotional tour. Three months from now, he and I would be going to Japan together after *A Love Like This* wrapped for part of the promotional tour for film number two.

"What did you think, Cade?"

I turned toward him, but out of the corner of my eye I was watching Brook's interaction with Noah. She and I agreed to take our own limousine to the concert downtown, even though many of the other cast members were joining us there. Peter was waiting at the curb with the door open for her. Noah was very excited about what he'd seen in the film and he should have been. He was very animated and he had Brook laughing hard. I tried not to be annoyed.

"I thought it was great, Martin. I'm looking forward to seeing the final cut after the soundtrack is added, but overall, I think it was something you can be proud of."

"We all can. Editing it all together is the real work. No offense." He laughed out loud.

I shook my head. "I don't know how they do it. It's amazing."

"See you on set tomorrow."

I was distracted because I wanted to get into that limo and felt that it was going to take my intervention to get Brook into the car.

"Sure thing, Martin. When we met two years ago, I wasn't sure how these films would turn out, but you've impressed me. I'm really going to miss working with you, and sorry to see it end." I shook the hand he offered and lowered my voice. "Brook and I really appreciate your understanding of our relationship. "

Martin swatted his hand as if batting at a fly. "Bah! You two kids deserve a break. Just take care of her. The rules, be damned; you're only young once. But, I've noticed Brook is very sensitive, even though she tries to hide it. The gossip affects her, but I guess I don't have to tell you how it is."

I smiled and ran a hand through my hair and down to rub the back of my neck. "No. That's for sure. Are you coming with us to the concert?" I asked.

"No. I'm just going to go back to the hotel. My wife and kids came up for the weekend, so we have plans. My wife gets tired of me being gone, so this is an attempt to soothe her ruffled feathers before we really get into filming."

We walked up to where Noah and Brook were talking and she turned toward us, a bright smile splitting across her face and her arms opened. She hugged him hard. "Martin, it was so wonderful! Even better than the first one!" Her voice thickened slightly as Martin hugged her.

"You're a great cast," he said sincerely. "But the chemistry between you two blows off the screen. It's believable." He winked at Brook and she smiled.

"We were lucky you were the director, Martin" I murmured.

Brook moved to my side and my arm slipped around her to pull her close, my hand resting on her hip and I felt her head tip to rest against my arm. The familiarity of it was not lost on the others that were filing past us into the waiting cars, but this time, they were all told about the situation and the need to keep it under wraps. At least Pinnacle had done that for us. We could be open with each other on set if nowhere else.

"What's this 'were' bullshit? We still have one film to make." We laughed. "You guys go and have a good time and stop thinking about the films. Pre-production starts tomorrow, so we have plenty of time for that."

Noah walked beside us as we left the theater. "I wish I had more time on screen," his mouth tightened but then he smiled and shrugged. "That's the breaks, I guess."

"You'll get a lot more jobs after this, Noah. You're just getting started," Cade encouraged.

We were still in the lobby, but the paparazzi were flashing photos of the others as they got into their cars and they pulled away. When only Peter's limousine and one other SUV waited at the curb for Noah and Martin, we said our final goodbyes and started to leave. Noah took the lead, followed by Brook and myself, then Martin. We rushed out and dove into the back of the car as quickly as we could. Peter closed the door behind us.

"No doubt our shared limo will make the blogs and live TV in thirty minutes," Brook said in disgust as I settled in next to her. In seconds she was straddling my lap and kissing my mouth gently. My hands slid up her body from her hips to her shoulders and down again as she gently sucked on my lips.

I felt the dull ache in the pit of my stomach start and my dick started to harden instantly. "Brook, stop. We don't have time. God, you feel so good," I said despite my protests.

"I love watching you kiss me on film. The piano scene was *wow*," she whispered. "It was so hot. I swear the screen melted."

"Because it was real. I was telling the truth when I said I didn't know how to live without you," I said against her mouth, then bent to kiss her hard, my tongue sliding into her mouth hungrily. She opened and her hands threaded through my hair as we kissed deeply. Her tongue met mine and I sucked it into my mouth. She moaned into me and my hips involuntarily thrust up into her. She was so hot; I could feel her heat through both layers of our jeans. " I'll never be able to, Brook."

"I love you." She moaned softly as she ground her hips into mine. I felt a growl well within my chest, but she swallowed it with a kiss so it only came out a soft moan.

I pushed my hands greedily under the hem of her shirt, seeking the soft warmth of her skin. I shoved it up quickly, letting my hand close over her lace-covered breast. The nipple was hard under my thumb and I ached to push her back into the seat and ravish her. "Babe, you're so bloody hot... I can feel you through our clothes."

She smiled against my mouth and then nibbled on my upper lip. I let my teeth graze at her lower one. "That's 'cause I'm on *fire*..." she chuckled softly and I had to join in at her reference to the concert we were on our way to attend, "for you."

I grabbed her hips and surged against her again, leaving her in no doubt just how aroused I was.

"Mr. Cade, Miss Brook; we've arrived at the concert hall. " Peter's voice came across the intercom, effectively halting my movements. I dropped my head to her shoulder with a frustrated sigh.

"Bloody hell." I looked up into her flushed face and sparkling blue eyes. The dark hair made her eyes pop even more and I could drown in them. "I can't decide if you're an angel for arranging this concert or the devil for working me up when we can't assuage the need."

"Poor baby..." Brook smirked as she pulled her shirt back down against the protests of my seeking hands. "Cade, stop. Come on. We have to go. You wanted to see this concert."

In a flash, I flipped her on her back and ground my pelvis into hers, my hand closed over her breast to massage and tease her nipple, and my lips assaulted the curve of her neck in a series of soft, sucking kisses that I knew drove her crazy. "This," my hand slid down her body and began rubbing her sensually through her jeans until her hips started undulating in response. "This is what I want." It didn't take long until she was gasping and trying to pull my mouth up to her own. She was moaning against me when I pushed away and started to straighten my clothes. I left her panting, wanting more and she gasped in response.

I shoved my stocking cap on my head and threw the hat she'd brought with her in her direction. Her eyes narrowed at me but she took it and scrambled into a sitting position.

"Don't forget two can play at that game, love. I'm not going to be the only one uncomfortable as hell all night." I knew I surprised her and I reached over and pushed the intercom button. "Peter, we're ready now. How does it look outside, mate?"

"There are a few photographers, but the bodyguards are waiting, sir," he answered. "I'll come 'round and open the door."

I took Brook's hand and kissed the top of her knuckles. "Are you mad at me or mad *for* me?"

She touched my face. "You know I'm going to have to get you back," she said with a sultry smile. I could see the desire in her face, her cheeks were flushed and I was mesmerized by the knowledge of what I could bring her to. It was intoxicating and my heart thumped in my chest, pushing blood around my body and infusing the obvious parts of my body. Her little hand closed around me, pulling and squeezing relentlessly. Her eyes were wide and I gasped in response.

"Mmmm... that's *mine*," she said softly, as Peter opened the door and I startled. I was thankful that my shirt was long enough to cover the results of her sweet torture. "Don't *you* forget it."

"Tonight is going to be fun in so many ways." I smirked and motioned for her to precede me out of the limo. The cameras were already flashing so we exited quickly, walking quickly past the paps and into the building.

I threw my hoodie up out of habit and hunched down on the way in. It was hard to keep an eye on Brook with my eyes downcast, so I watched her feet move a few feet in front of me, followed by the two bodyguards that had been newly assigned for this film.

Once inside, it was easier.   The entire cast was already in the balcony off to the right of the stage and it was roped off so no one else could enter. Jeanne had done an amazing job, getting us located where we would have our own private bathrooms and there were three attendants on duty to get us drinks or food if we wanted. I settled in to Brook's left in the front row of the mezzanine.   I drew in a deep breath. It had been so long since I was able to go to an event like this and just be normal. The band was already playing and the entire arena was filled with the unique melodies and full percussion. Brook knew I'd seen them in concert before and that they were one of the only contemporary American rock bands that I really enjoyed.

"I'm not sure they wanted us to sit together, babe," she said under her breath, leaning in slightly.

"I don't bloody care. You did this for me, so there is no way I'm not sitting with you. We agreed we'd be a little more open, didn't we?

The others are here, so relax love."

She glanced at me and my face was turned toward her. I didn't care who saw me gazing at her in adoration.

"I am. I'm glad we're here." I wasn't sure if she meant the concert or back together in Vancouver. For me, the latter sent a sense of relief through me. I took a deep breath and reached for the beer that had been placed in front of me and I felt her hand scratch along my back. A rush of pleasure flooded every cell of my body. Brook's gentle hand on me, and how she was allowing herself to openly touch me filled me with happiness. All I wanted in the world was to be with this woman and to be open about it.

I stayed where I was, leaning up in my chair and watching the band to encourage her to continue roaming her hand over the muscles of my back. I closed my eyes at the pleasure such a simple action gave to me.

Over the course of the night there were more touches and glances. I found myself smiling so much my face hurt. The music was excellent, but the best part of the evening was that it felt like a date. Even though we knew each other intimately, this was exciting in new ways. I reached over and brought her arm underneath mine so I could entwine my fingers with hers.

When she leaned in to whisper in my ear, I relished in her breath rushing over mine. The others milled around us. Ethan was sitting behind us and Dawson took the seat on Brook's right, effectively shielding her from Wendy, who was draping all over her new man. The guys had become good friends and I'd been honest with them about my complete aversion to Wendy and her lying mouth being anywhere near Brook. Jennifer was dancing in the aisle and the new actors were mixed in around. We should have probably spent some time getting to know them, but my focus was only on Brook. Leah was there and she tried to get my attention once, but sitting in the seat to my left. I made casual conversation, asking her if she'd been to Vancouver before or if this were her first time seeing this band.

More and more I felt Brook melt into me and I started rubbing the inside of her palm with my index finger. She shifted slightly in her seat but didn't say anything. Finally, they started *Gold* and the auditorium went wild. The screaming was deafening. I dropped my head toward her and leaned in so close I could press my lips to the skin below her ear, I could literally feel her pulse quicken beneath my mouth. Her breath stopped and her hand tightened on mine. After our little exchange in the hotel room and then the limousine, I was waiting for this song to put an exclamation point on the evening.

"Cade..." her voice was aching. "Stop. You're killing me."

"Then it will be a sweet death, love." I kissed her again, softly, coaxing. "Kiss me," I commanded. "I want to feel your tongue in my mouth, Brook. I need it."

"But—"

"Shhh. Don't think." I didn't care if the world saw, and I didn't want Brook to care.

She turned her head toward mine and I fell into her deep blue eyes, made darker by the lack of light. Brook's hand came up to clamp onto my jaw as my mouth opened over hers.

Uh... that's it. The rhythm of the song vibrated all around us, and I kissed her deeply, hard and hungry, the urgency in my body, craving hers. I knew I couldn't kiss her for long, so I wanted to make it count.

I pulled away and then kissed the corner of her mouth once more. Her breath rushed out as she breathed my name. "Cade... ugh..."

"I know. I'm so turned on, Brook," the words were low and ripped from my chest.

Her hand left mine to move onto my lap and close around my raging erection. I groaned. At the same time I covered her hand with my own to stifle her movements I placed the rumpled ball of my hoodie in my lap with my other hand. "Brook... Jesus. Please let me calm down."

She nodded slightly and reached for her glass with her right hand, glancing at me through half closed lids over the rim of her glass. I knew that look and it said she was going to be wild when we were finally alone. I loved that part of her that couldn't help herself.

I resumed my gentle teasing on her palm, rubbing little circles that I knew would remind her of my fingers on other parts of her body. My mind was racing and my body was pulsing with a life of its own. I leaned in once more, my voice intent, low and aching. "I'm going to take you so hard tonight. I want to feel you come all around me, in my mouth, under my hands. I'm bloody dying right now. You're mine. Forever."

Her mouth dropped open and her eyes widened as I sat back into my seat. We were both vibrating, on fire... yearning for the end of the bloody concert so we could be alone.

Her fingers tightened around mine. "Yes. Anything you want," she said in a low, breathy tone.

"And anything *you* want. I love you so fucking much; I can't bloody breathe." She swallowed hard and then turned her face toward me, her breathing increased. Her eyes were glistening, intent and suddenly I wanted to be the hell out of there.

"I'm right there with you. It scares the shit out of me how much." Her need was tangible ache in her voice.

I squeezed her hand. "I know. It hurts; it's that incredible. I want to kiss you."

"Cade... when can we leave?"

I glanced over my shoulder and my eyes collided with those of Leah St. Claire. *Fuck!* I'd forgotten all about her sitting next to me, and my stomach lurched sickeningly. Now, I'd have to worry about her leaking this to the press, and if Denise could contain it. I blinked, deciding not to make a big deal out of it, and resumed my search for the bodyguards until my eyes met those of the one in charge. He nodded toward the door in question and I nodded my assent. After he spoke to the other three and opened his phone, they all rose and I pulled Brook to her feet with me. "Now."

The others looked at us as we passed, some with questions on their faces and others with nods in understanding. Ethan patted my shoulder as I walked by him and pulled Brook behind me. Two guards in front of us led the way, and there were two others followed closely behind us. I let go of her hand and slid my arm around her back and side of her waist to pull her close. She turned her face into the curve of my shoulder in silent need as we walked quickly through the halls to the exit in the alley where Peter would be waiting. I turned to kiss her forehead before I could stop myself.

On cue, Peter was there with the limousine placed perfectly so that we could quickly get in through the open door of the car as soon as we stepped outside. I followed Brook in and the door closed behind us. I was already closing the partition and she was shedding her sweatshirt. I struggled to pull mine off at the same time that I buzzed Peter.

"Can you just keep driving, please?"

"Of course. Anywhere special?" he asked in response.

"No. It doesn't matter." I pulled my T-Shirt over my head and Brook fell to her knees in front of me, between my knees. She reached frantically for the button to my jeans and then slid the zipper down. I pushed her shirt up and she obediently lifted her arms so I could remove it. Soon she had me free of my boxer briefs and took me in her mouth, her left hand snaking up over my abdominals and reaching further up my chest. Her mouth was so hot and felt incredible; I just fell back in helpless surrender. Seeing her so intent on giving me pleasure with her beautiful eyes looking at mine as those sweet lips closed around my dick, it was my undoing.

"Shit, Brook. Uuhhnnnggg... " Her fingers clutched at the skin of my chest and my hand closed around hers. I pulled it up and placed my open mouth on her wrist and sucked. I wanted the taste of her skin. I wanted to devour her like she was devouring me. She sucked and licked, her tongue swirling around wildly until I couldn't stand anymore. My muscles tightened in my stomach and she moaned over me. "Cade, I can taste you... let it go," she begged but I wasn't ready for this deliciousness to end. I fisted my hand in her hair and gently raised her head at the same time as I sat up. I twisted her head to the side so I could take her mouth with mine. I was starving for her. I wanted to wrap her around me and never let go. My other arm snaked around her and I lifted her to lie back on the seat.

My body was so aroused that I thought my dick would explode with the slightest touch. "Brook, baby..." I moaned as I dragged my mouth from hers and started to undo her jeans. She lifted her hips, her eyes never leaving mine and I peeled them off after she kicked off her shoes.

Mine were still on, just open, but I couldn't wait to remove them completely. She spread for me and I found her opening, plunging in hard and fast. She closed around me hot and tight and I stopped for a moment so I could get control of my body. I could come so easily. Her hips rocked into mine in protest. "Cade... I want you. Move in me."

"Jesus, Brook. I don't want to come yet. You feel so good." She ignored my plea and clenched around me and surged her hips.

"If you're not going to give me what I want, then I'm going to take it," she said urgently, breathlessly as she continued her movements. I struggled for control but her movements were driving me crazy and her hands in my hair urged my mouth to hers.

Fuck it.

I let myself go, mirroring her movements, but pushing in hard and then pulling out fast. I kissed her again and again; trying to concentrate on the kisses instead of the way her body was milking mine. When she sucked my tongue into her mouth with the same rhythm that her body was sucking on mine, I lost it.

"Uhhhggg... .noooo... ." I gritted my teeth as pleasure ripped through me, but I needed to see her come with me. I dropped a hand between us and went to work on her sweet flesh. She was so swollen, so I knew she was close. I kept thrusting into her until her body trembled around mine and I knew I had her.

"Cade... God, I'm coming..." She breathed out as her body shook and then stiffened against me.

"Yes. I feel you. It's so beautiful. I love you, Brook," I panted into her shoulder. Her fingers raked down my back so hard I thought she would draw blood, but I didn't care.

Our bodies were still moving, but slowing and my mouth found hers, kissing her softly as I pushed her hair off of her face. Her legs and arms wrapped around me tight and she kissed my shoulder wetly, biting and nipping in the end.

"I love what you do to me."

"Say that again," I begged. Even in the aftermath of such passion

I wanted her words. "You're so beautiful, and everything I want in the world. Tell me you love me."

"You already know it," her voice cracked on the words. "It's so intense I sometimes think it might kill me."

"Like I said, my love, it's the sweetest kind of death. If we have to die, then let it be like this."

Chapter 14

Harping on Vanity Fair

Brooklyn

HE WRAPPED ME UP. Literally engulfed me; heart, body, and soul.

It was to the point I could barely remember what life was like before him, what it felt like not to love him. Now, amidst all the chaos, I didn't think I could exist without him.

I smiled into the darkness of the deep night. It was pitch black within the suite, the curtains drawn tightly over the windows and I'd thrown a towel over the clock on the nightstand. The wind whipped the rain into the windows on the 19th floor of our hotel as the strong arm that was wrapped around me tightened. Cade's legs entwined with mine, my naked body completely engulfed in his as he stirred against me. I spent the past several minutes listening to his steady breathing, his gentle presence the only thing I needed to gain peace from the craziness that was our lives. It was hell, yet it was heaven. I wouldn't trade a second of our time together; especially after the months we'd just spent on opposite coasts of the country.

Cade moved against me and I pressed further back into him. He moaned softly, the sound so velvet and close beneath my ear as he buried his mouth in the curve of my neck. I could feel his arousal nudging at the back of my thighs, and my body responded of its own volition. His arm moved and his fingers grazed the nipple of my right breast. "Mmmm... Brook."

I turned my face over my shoulder, yearning for him, and pressing into him again, my hand grazing down his hip and around the back of his ass cheek to grip him and pull him closer. I was going to treasure every second of our time together, this last few months of working together. I tried not to think about this being our last movie together.

"Mmmm... *Cade*," I said in a breathless whisper, a soft smile dancing over my lips. His hips surged against mine, the delicious satin of his erection pressing into the space between my legs. The ache was starting, the heat and wetness pooling deep inside of me.

"Baby... God Brook, how do you make me want you so much? I always want you; even when I'm bloody asleep. You'll be the death of me." Hearing his amused, yet delicious words, feeling his arms and legs around me, his nimble fingers pulling and teasing my nipples as he began to play my body like only he could... his desire seeking mine was more than I could resist.

"Uhhhh!" I gasped as he slipped inside me. My body moved with his, urging him on as he filled and stretched me, pushing deeply into me. I arched back toward him to take him in fully and his mouth moved hungrily on the skin of my neck, dragging down to the curve of my shoulder. His mouth opened hotly on my skin to bite gently on my flesh as I clenched around him and pulled one of his fingers into my mouth to suck it gently. I had come to know how much that stimulated him and Cade rewarded me with a low groan from somewhere deep inside his chest. I could almost feel him vibrating against my back.

"Uhhh, you feel so good," he breathed against me, his breath washing over my skin in a hot rush. "I want to get closer, love." He pushed into me again, as his hands roamed over the front of my body. I held my breath because I knew what was coming. He never forgot to touch me, to make sure that he gave me as much pleasure as he possibly could.

"Yes, closer... " I said softly, and pulled away so I could turn toward him. Instantly, my body felt the loss, but Cade gathered me close and lifted me closer, moving so he was sitting up and pulling me with him so that my legs straddled his lap and my knees rested on the bed on the outside of his slim hips. My arms wound around his shoulders, and my hands threaded through his hair as he found my entrance and filled me again. The position was so intimate, allowing deeper penetration as our hips moved into each other and our eyes locked. The strong arms around my hips held me tightly and he moaned and panted with each thrust. The open mouth kisses he was running along the curve of my neck and shoulders left me gasping. My head fell back and the breath rushed from me as the intense tightening in my lower body began to build. He licked and nipped at my tender skin. It almost hurt, it was so urgent, but it was delicious and I wanted more and more.

"Yes... Cade. That's it, baby." Our hips ground and rocked into each other, easily finding the rhythm that had us both gasping.

"Brook... I can't... I can't stop it. Bloody hell, tell me you're with me," he moaned in a low growl. "Oh, God."

That voice moaning my name in the throes of passion were my undoing and I fell apart. I bent my head to find his mouth with mine, his tongue thrust into my mouth and we sucked on each other I fell over into the waves of my orgasm, even as his arms tightened and his body tensed against mine.

Our bodies were still moving together, the tremors still racking through both of us, as our mouths separated and his forehead rested on mine. We were both panting and licking at each other's mouths, our hands stroking each other's hair.

How do I love you this much, hmmm?" Cade continued to kiss me and moved to lay me back down on the bed, his body still connected with mine. Brushing my hair back over and over. "So much," he whispered against my mouth.

I brushed his lips with mine and kissed him gently before I looked up into the beautiful face with wonder. His blue eyes were dark and soft. The sun was just starting to come up and there was just enough light to see his face, his pupils were wide and dilated and he nuzzled my nose with his own. I was so content I felt like purring like a cat. He represented everything I needed in the world. My heart swelled and I swallowed to hold in the emotion.

"You always... amaze me."

He smiled. "I thought you were going to say that I always... *make you come.*" He chuckled softly and kissed the side of my face and then pulled my lower lip in between his to suckle softly. He was so gentle.

I smiled and touched his face. The stubble was getting softer after 24 hours of growth. "Mmmm, you'll get a big head." I laughed. "Oh right. You already have one." I surged my hips against his once more before he pulled out of me and moved to my side.

"I don't right now. You wear me out, woman. We've got a big day. We should try to sleep a couple more hours, yeah?"

I turned toward him and he pulled me into the curve of his shoulder, close to his body. "Are you afraid you won't be your normal gorgeous self? Just so you know... it's inevitable." I smiled and he huffed.

"Whatever," Cade huffed. "And no, I don't give a shit how I look most of the time, but this is a message to the world. I want it to be perfect."

Yes, today was our secret shoot with *Harper's Bazaar*. We'd done the interview three weeks earlier right after we got to Vancouver and the magazine was sending a crew up to take the photos that would print with it. I smiled at the memory of the interview. It was fucking perfect. When the guy asked me questions, I knew he'd be asking Cade some version of the same thing, and even though we'd been unaware of what he would ask, I knew our answers would be the same or similar, and that was sort of the point. *Hey, world... you wanna know? Well, here you go.*

Jeanne and Denise had been brilliant, completely taking control of what Cade and I wanted to accomplish. We'd had enough of Pinnacle pushing us apart and after how hurt Cade had been at Comic-Con, I was done playing their games. We both promised to keep our relationship quiet, but I'd promised Cade I'd stop denying it. This was the little positive reinforcement he needed and a very clear communication of what was real. And this was all *us*.

We wanted this series of photos and the interview to tell everyone what we couldn't say aloud. Our fans had to realize we were together by the chemistry that showed in photos and on screen. Even when we were trying to hide it so they sure as hell were going to get confirmation this time. We were trying to confirm it this time... loud and clear.

Cade's chest rose as he drew in a full breath. He turned and kissed my forehead, leaving them there when he spoke. "Bloody finally."

I closed my eyes. He'd waited patiently for almost two years, and it had caused him a lot of pain. "I love you," I said softly and turned my face into the base of his neck. "I'm sorry I've wanted to keep it quiet. It's just—" I hesitated.

"I know, love. You're going to be so beautiful," he said so softly I wasn't sure if it were real or a dream. "So beautiful."

I pushed up off his chest to look down into his face, my eyebrow raised wryly. "How many times do I have to say it? It's *you*. You're the beautiful one."

"Brook, when we're taking those photos today, I want you to think about how it felt just now when we were making love. Know that when I'm looking at you, I'm feeling you, thinking of possessing you. Remember how it felt to have me inside you just now. Feel how full my heart and soul are with you. I want it to show."

I sucked in my breath and then tightened my arms around his body as his heart beat beneath my cheek. Again, for the millionth time... his words left me breathless. "Cade," I reached out to touch the strong line of his jaw and run my fingers along it softly, "I always feel it. Every single time you look at me, I feel it. The world feels it, too. It's palpable." My eyes shot up to his, and his gaze was burning into mine. "I still don't understand how I got so damn lucky."

The corners of his lips lifted slightly and my heart thumped in my chest. He shrugged almost imperceptively. "You ran away and I couldn't live without you. You left me no choice but to come after you. No matter how long it took, how much it hurt, there is no choice but to be with you."

My heart thrummed wildly inside my chest as my love for this man overwhelmed me once again.

Caden

BROOK WAS FILMING with a scene with Wendy and my stomach clinched. We'd stayed pretty much away from her like the plague. Ever since the plane trip up to Vancouver I'd managed to steer clear of her except on set. She was still trying to get back into Brook's good graces, but she wasn't buying her bullshit anymore.

I'd just come from an appointment with my personal trainer and he had worked my ass off. I kicked off my shoes and ran my hand through my hair, still damp with sweat.

It was late afternoon and Brook wouldn't be back for a couple of hours yet. I was restless. I felt like a bloody prisoner during this film. After the rubbish with the stalker fans in New York we still had to maintain some privacy, and I felt like I lived in this stupid hotel room, even though the studio execs were more reasonable. Sometimes it was tolerable, but other times, I felt like pulling my hair out.

Brook's room was next to mine, but we had the entire floor to ourselves. Except for the bodyguards that were posted outside the elevators, we were pretty isolated. Isolation was fine. I didn't miss people that much, but I missed freedom. I didn't blame the fans. They were always respectful. Well, except for those couple of times in New York City, but in general, all they wanted was to talk to us, get an autograph or photograph.

The paparazzi were another story entirely. Those bastards were ruthless and had no respect for anything and there were untrue stories about one or both of us almost daily. All they cared about were hits to their sites, or copies sold. Bloody bastards. I honestly didn't know how they slept at night when they made their living as they did. I'd played around online and it was obvious that most of our real fans wanted us to have peace. Sure, they wanted to know what was going on; they were vested in our movies, I was sure were waiting for confirmation of our "couple" status. So many times when they caught us out or waited for us to come and go from the set and they yelled questions; I just wanted to say, "Yes, we're together. I adore her," and be done with it. But even then, would the paps leave us alone? Doubtful. My experience with them and any relationship I had in the past said it would only get worse; They'd just be searching for ways to tear us apart with sensational headlines, twisting facts and quotes, printing untruths, and photo-shopping pictures. Part of me felt selfish for wanting to be public about our relationship because I knew it would expose Brook to more.

The intimate details of our relationship were sacred, so we'd decided to keep those between us, but at least we wouldn't be saying we were just friends or denying our relationship anymore. Frankly, it bloody exhausted me. I wanted to be normal. I wanted to take her out, kiss her in public, and scream from the rooftops that she was mine. And she would always be mine.

I smiled to myself and picked up my guitar, my fingers automatically strumming out chords of one of the melodies that always ran around in my head. I hadn't had time to write anything new for ages and that was a part of my life that I wanted to explore. As a cast, we didn't have as many jam sessions during this film either. After being apart for three months, Brook and I holed up alone most nights, and the rest of the guys in a different hotel made it less convenient.

My phone started playing Denise's ringtone and I put the guitar in the bed and answered. "Hey."

"Cade, did you get it?"

I rolled my eyes and laughed. "Obviously not since I don't know what you're talking about. What am I supposed to have gotten?"

"Well, it's supposed to be there. What time is it?"

"It's 3:30."

"Well, call me when you get it," she said excitedly. "Oh my fucking God, Cade. It's so amazing. You'll be so happy."

"About *what*, Denise? Bloody hell!" I laughed in exasperation.

"Oh, sorry. Harper's sent the finals on the pictures and the interview! I had a copy sent to you by Federal Express. They'll verify the content before it prints, but the photos! Oh. My . God! You both look *so* gorgeous. And if you don't want the world to know you're completely gone for each other, then these are an epic fail. Seriously, Cade. They brought tears to my eyes." Her voice thickened on the other end of the line.

"Are you crying now?" I chuckled.

"Stop teasing me. You'll get it when you see for yourself. It's clear Brook loves you, too. So clear."

My heart swelled and I smiled. "Yeah," I said softly. "Finally."

A knock at the door made me jump. "Hey, someone's at the door, maybe that's it. Hold on."

I opened the door and one of the bodyguards handed me an oversized packet. "Thanks, man," I said and let the door close before moving back to the table in the sitting room and setting it down. "Yes, Denise, I think this must be it." I quickly opened the package and gently lifted out the contents.

There was a cardboard sleeve that was taped on all sides and a manila envelope with the words, *Interview: Carlisle/Halloway/Dec. Issue* scrawled in black Sharpie. *Confidential and Contents under Copyright Conde Nast 2015,* was stamped in red across both.

I set the envelope aside and slit the tape around the cardboard with my fingernail. The knowledge of what we were trying to accomplish with these photos made my heart beat slightly faster in my anxiousness to see them. I should wait to open them with Brook, but I was too anxious to see the look on Brook's face that Denise had just described.

"Well?" Denise said impatiently.

"I'm just pulling them out." My breath left my body as my eyes fell on the top photo. It was Brook and I lying on a bed of flower petals; we were staring into each other's eyes and my left hand was touching her arm. "Bloody hell. Denise... " My words fell off as my hand hesitated over the photo. I couldn't take my eyes off of Brook's face. How in the hell I kept myself from kissing her in the moment this photo was taken, I'll never know. She was so beautiful and the way she was looking at me slayed me. It was so intense and even though there were literally thousands of photos that had given hints to our feelings for each other, they were all times when we'd been trying to hide them. In these pictures, we let them show. We *wanted* them to show.

Her left hand was resting on her stomach and her forehead was resting on my bent arm that was also holding my own head. The red of the roses was picked up in the velvet bodice of her dress, but her face, her porcelain skin... she was perfect. My heart thrummed in my chest as I glanced at that left hand. The only thing that would have made it more perfect would have been to see my engagement ring visible there.

"Caden! What is it?" Denise's voice was panicked. "Is it okay? Cade!"

I cleared my throat and sank down on the bed next to the photo. "Um... it's just... I'm... completely *speechless*. There are no words."

"Jesus, you scared me." I heard her sigh in relief and I moved the top photo off to the side and shifted through the others. "So they're good then?"

"More than good."

"Okay, call me after Brook has had a chance to look at them and when you both get a chance to read through the interview. I don't want any hiccups on this project. Jeanne and I have a tight reign on this article and we want it to deliver just what it's supposed to. The Vanity Fair article comes out just before that, so have you seen that interview?"

"Not yet. Was it supposed to be sent like this one?"

"I'd think so. We need to see it before it prints in any event."

"Right."

"How did the horseback shots turn out? I know Brook was adamant about the horse segment," Denise said, and my hands searched through the stack of pictures and found two shots she was referencing. Brook was staring into the lens on both, and the whole focus was the long expanse of her leg and her eyes. Those amazing eyes: so intense. "Really good. One was labeled with a headline, "Fairytale." I guess that's the headline of the article, yeah?"

"Probably. Listen hon, I have to run. Call me later and let me know if you get the stuff from Vanity Fair."

"Okay, talk to you later, then. And, thanks, Denise. To Jeanne, too." I hung up and threw the phone down, moving to lift one of the photos to look at it more closely.

I grinned widely when I saw the picture of Brook and me on the magnificent black stallion. She had the great idea to do that and Jeanne had insisted it be part of the photo shoot. I remembered how much she loved that horse. I'd have to get an acreage and then see about buying it for her for Christmas.

"Official fuck you to Pinnacle and their ridiculous demands!" *Brook had laughed as she said the words. "What better way than to shove it all back in their faces then to have Julia on the back of a horse with Ryan? I love it!"*

I was laughing out loud at the memory when the door burst open and the object of my thoughts sauntered into the room. She looked tired, but she gave me a smile as she threw her hoodie down and kicked off her shoes.

"Hey, sexy. What's so funny?" she asked casually and then her eyes widened as she saw the pictures strewn out on the table. "Oh, my God. They're here." She came forward and I pulled her down on my lap as she looked through the photos. "They're amazing."

I nuzzled into her neck and her hair was matted slightly, and there was the faint taste of salt on her skin. "Yes. You're so beautiful in them."

"I'm looking at *you.* Jesus, Cade. Oh, my God! You're so... *hot.*"

Brook reached forward, pulling down the two pictures that were labeled *cover one* and *cover two.* In one, she was dressed in a sexy top and leather pants and practically plastered up against me, my hand resting on the bare skin of her midriff and the other, in the custom gown that they had made for her, in a light off-white, lacy and elegant. It could have been a bridal gown if she had a veil and my heart had dropped when I'd seen her in it. I was dressed in a tuxedo and we were holding hands and staring into each other's faces. It was intense and conveyed just the message I wanted. This one had been my idea, because when we did get married, the pictures wouldn't be public.

"That , beautiful," she observed and then ran her hand over the image of me. "You're so gorgeous." She turned in my arms then and laced her fingers through the hair at the side of my head as she pushed it off of my face. "So gorgeous," she murmured against my lips before we kissed deeply, our mouths hungry for each other. I wrapped my arms tightly around her. "My man in a tux. I don't think I'll ever recover from that."

"I quite like this mutual admiration society we've got going, love." I smiled against her mouth as we drew back to look into each other's faces. Her eyes were sparkling as a small smile danced on her kiss dampened lips.

"Look at this one." I pulled the 'bed of flowers' picture from the bottom of the pile and moved it to the top.

Brook stilled as her breath rushed out. "Holy shit. Just... *wow.*"

My hand was drawing circles on the back of her shirt and she leaned back into me slightly. "Exactly. That's my very favorite. I never want to stop looking at your face. The love there... it's incredible."

"It is." Her lips found my temple and she brushed them across my skin. That photo was the last one that we shot and afterward, we could barely keep our hands off each other until we got back to the hotel that night. Heat rushed under the surface of my skin at the memory. Brook read my mind. "That night was incredible. You were so... "

"Hungry," I said softly.

"Mmmm, yes. That's a good word. I like you hungry," she teased.

"That works out well then, doesn't it?" I ran my hand down her leg and squeezed the muscle of her thigh as she sat on my lap.

"Yes, and I could easily let myself get caught up in it right now, but I'm gross. It was a long day, and I need a shower." I could hear her stomach grumbling and smiled. "Looks like I'm hungry, too," she chuckled softly.

"Okay, I'll order something while you get cleaned up. What would you like?"

"*Food*." Brook kissed my mouth quickly and then got up and went to gather clean clothes from the dresser. I laughed at the way her eyebrow raised as she looked at me. "Whatever you order is fine, unless it's Figgy pudding." She laughed and I couldn't help but join. "You didn't peek at the interview, did you?" I gave her a cheeky grin and her eyes widened. "Cade?" she questioned.

"Who, me?"

"Better not have. I'd have to punish you."

"Damn it!" I teased. "Now I wish I *did* read it!" My eyes roamed over her body, and stopping on the bare skin exposed above the waistband of her jeans underneath the hem of her shirt. "But, no, I didn't. I promised I'd wait." We hadn't discussed the interview right after we'd done it and agreed that it would be more fun to wait and read the other's responses without knowing what the answers were ahead of time.

She giggled as she took note of where I was looking and purposely pulled off her shirt and disappeared into the bathroom. The expanse of bare skin across her slender back called to me. "Don't worry. I'll still punish you if you want me to, baby."

I couldn't help but laugh out loud and picked up the phone to order room service as the water turned on in the bathroom. I ordered beer and burgers and then grabbed the still-sealed envelope and went into the bathroom. I could see Brook's naked body through the steam that had accumulated on the glass door of the shower.

"Mmmmm... Yum," I said softly, then slid down the wall next to the shower, now torn between reading the article and staring at her delicious nakedness.

She glanced up from soaping her body and admonished me. "Hey, none of that until after we read that interview and eat. I didn't have lunch."

I felt tension grip my chest. Wendy.

"What did she do?" I asked with a great deal of trepidation.

"Nothing really, it's just so damn uncomfortable being around her. Timing sucked because she just got fired off another movie." The amusement in Brook's tone was clear and I drew in a breath. I was always on guard when it came to Wendy. After everything she'd put us through, I'd never trust that bitch. "To be fair, she's a good actress, but she's a trouble-maker. Cade?"

Brook's voice snapped me out of my thoughts. "Um, yeah." I ripped open the top of the envelope and pulled out a stack of paper held together by a spring-loaded clip. "Do you want me to start?"

"Sure." She was shampooing her hair now and my gaze lingered on the curve of her breasts as she raised her arms. Her pink nipples, and the roundness waiting there for me to open that door and reach out and touch. I shook my head. *This is not what she wants me to be doing.*

I cleared my throat and began. "With *The Future of Our Past* the young actors found themselves thrust into the spotlight. Now, while their characters are torn apart in *Don't Forget to Remember Me*, they couldn't be closer." I smiled because I couldn't bloody stop myself. Fuck! If they only knew, we'd been *close* for months more than anyone knew.

Brook grabbed a towel that was hanging over the shower and opened the door. She was smiling too, and taunting me with her nakedness. She knew how helpless I was when she got all flirty and tempting.

"I'd like to get closer. You?" She raised her eyebrow and licked her lips once.

"Stop being so naughty. Do you want to read this, or what?"

"Okay. I couldn't resist." She wrapped the towel around herself and began running a comb through her hair, sitting on the edge of the tub as she did so. "What about the newlywed thing? That dude, Mark, told us that he was going to reference it to the picture of the white dress."

"Um, okay... I'm looking." My eyes scanned the page. "Hey, that asshole said you lead me around by the nose. What a wanker," I said, amusement lacing my tone. I let out my breath. "Hmmph. I think that was pushing it. I wanted to be public about us, but I don't need people thinking I'm a pussy."

Brook laughed out loud and nudged my knee with her foot. "You're just too nice in those interviews, babe. It's just a perception people get. They scare the crap out of me, so I come off like a standoffish bitch. Everyone assumes it, even before they even meet me. It's the deer-in-the-headlights look." She tried to widen her eyes and stare blankly at me, but she couldn't stop the huge grin on her face and we both ended up giggling. "You're so humble and oblivious to how beautiful you are."

"Pfft! Whatever." I looked back down to the pages. "They're so wrong about you."

"As long as you think so," she said softly and then moved to sit next to me on the floor, the towel barely clinging to her damp skin. She leaned her head on my shoulder, and I bent to place a kiss on her wet hair. "I love you."

"Yeah, I missed you today. I was worried that hag would bother you. I'm glad it turned out okay."

"I can handle her now. Keep reading." Her hand wrapped around my bicep and squeezed. The clean scent of coconut from her shampoo was all around me, and I inhaled deeply.

"Okay, so it talks about us being here in side-by-side rooms, with the entire floor to ourselves."

"Good old Jeanne. That should send a message even though the fans already know we're in one hotel and the rest of the cast is down the street. She's great."

"You said I spend more time on my hair? Seriously?"

"Cade. Come on. Did you deny it? Plus, I lost half of mine."

I smiled. "Not really. I just said that I don't like people messing with it."

"Shit, *you* mess with it. Constantly. "

"You agreed I'm more athletic. Good girl." I smiled.

She only laughed. "Wouldn't want you feeling inferior. How did you answer the questions about who Googled themselves more?'

I nudged her with my shoulder. "I told the truth. I said you, of course."

She gasped. "Me? Uh uh... you're always looking yourself up."

"I knew you'd say me. Do you really think I'm superstitious and not a good sport?"

"You *are* more superstitious than I am. I could give a fuck about most things and you know it. But I never said you were a bad sport. I just said I was more uh... relaxed." She bit her lip to hide her smile as she started to stand up and then began to run into the other room. "I was referring to the need to be open about the relationship. I'm fine with keeping the secret, and you aren't. I couldn't say that, so I improvised."

I longed for the day when we could be honest about everything. I quickly set the article to the side and reached for the edge of her towel, and yanked it from her retreating form. She squealed and I jumped to my feet and chased her back into the bedroom. My arms caught her and I fell with her onto the bed. We were both laughing, but quickly sobered as our mouths found each other.

"Sorry, love, I just can't help myself. Here you are all naked... and mine so... " I knew the food would arrive soon, but I looked into her eyes and brushed her hair back off her face. I saw the look there, the same one I'd seen in that photograph and my heart leapt in my chest.

"Yes. Yours."

"Are you sure you want dinner?" I asked against her mouth, and it came alive under mine. All thought of burgers and beer was forgotten. Even when the knock on the door came, we ignored it. The only sounds in the silent room were panting breaths, soft moans, and hungry mouths as we claimed each other yet again.

Brooklyn

I WAS SITTING IN the makeup trailer as Mickey worked on my face, my heart thrumming in my chest at the contents of the envelope on my lap. Jeanne sent it to me through the production company using a bonded messenger. It hadn't hit newsstands yet. I had only looked at the cover and hadn't read the article.

I glanced up at the man working to make my face perfect, and then he moved to start working on my hair. "Damn girl. You were a stupid bitch to cut you hair. These hair extensions are a pain in my ass!"

"Hey, dipshit. I hear that from you daily. I get it. Move on." I rolled my eyes at his reflection in the mirror. He huffed.

"It's me that has to deal with the repercussions, not you, missy. Couldn't you have thought of what I'd have to go through before you whacked the shit out of it?" he complained. "I kept hoping your man would hate it enough to dump your skinny ass and give someone else a chance at that hotness." He smirked at me and I smiled happily back at his reflection. He knew that Cade and I were solid, but he loved to tease me.

"It's not that short, and nope. He's off the market indefinitely, Mickey. Although," I quirked an eyebrow at him, "I might have a seriously delicious treat for you today."

His eyes lit up. "Is he coming in to see me?"

My jaw jutted out as I tried not to start laughing.

"Um, no. But this is close. Before I show it to you I want you to promise not to damage it, Mickey. You can't keep it either, only look at it. It comes out in three days, so I have to keep it under wraps."

"What is it?" Mickey asked anxiously.

"Do you promise?" I persisted.

"Bitch, if you don't get on with it, I will not be responsible for my actions!"

I burst out laughing. "I love you, Mickey. You're so hilarious!"

"Brook!"

"Oh, okay." I pulled out the November issue of *Vanity Fair*. Cade was on the cover and his intense gaze ripped right through me. Jesus, he was beautiful. I pulled it to my chest to hide it from the anxious man practically jumping up and down next to me. He reached for it, and my arms tightened around it. "Mickey. Take a deep breath," I teased. "This is probably the most beautiful picture of Cade I've ever seen, so be prepared. I don't want you hyperventilating on me."

"I'm fucking prepared already! Just let me see it!" The man was beside himself with excitement.

I lowered my arms and his gasp was audible.

"Holy *Jesus*." His hands reached out to take the magazine from me, bringing it up so he could examine the cover photo more closely.

"I know, right?" I asked breathlessly. He was sexier than hell, in bed no less and his blue eyes blazing.

"Oh. My. God!" Mickey took the magazine from my hands and looked at it in silent awe. "That boy is... "

"All mine," I said quietly and glanced down at my hands.

"Like I said Brook, you are one lucky bitch. If you hurt him, I will hunt you down and shave your head. More than it already is."

"Shut up, Mickey. It's not *that* bad. Now give it back. I need to be on set in twenty minutes."

"I want to read the article and look at the rest of the pictures," he whined but handed it back to me reluctantly. I tugged it hard to get him to let go completely, "For crying out loud. You see him every day."

"So?" He pouted.

As Mickey went back to work, and I flipped open the magazine; my phone rang. It was Jeanne.

"Hey. Thanks... " I began but she interrupted me.

"Brook. Have you read the article?" she asked anxiously.

"Not yet. I was just about to. Why?"

"Cade is going to be so pissed." I felt my face flush. If there was something in the article that was wrong, it was too late to do anything about it.

"Why, Jeanne? Just tell me."

"Well, Cade did that interview at Comic-Con the morning before you went up there, and well... "

My heart was beating faster and I stood up from the chair, leaving Mickey to throw his hands in the air at his lack of subject matter. "Jeanne, please."

"It says that he's not in a relationship, that he's single."

I took a deep breath. Considering all of the articles that came out around the time of Comic-Con and since where Cade's feelings for me were plastered across them for all the world to see and then all of the photos of us together than had come out just after this interview had taken place, I could see the problem. I also knew that I didn't really care, but that Cade would. He wouldn't want any contradiction to the Harper's article, and he was adamant that while we didn't exactly confirm anything, we'd stop denying the relationship. This definitely fucked that up.

"Ugh… "

"No shit! The worst part will be is that the *Harpers* article is coming out in two weeks and we don't want that message to be discounted because of this one."

"What can we do?" I started to pace back and forth across the table. "How did this happen?"

"Brook!" Mickey called, and pointed to his watch. I waved him off impatiently.

"Obviously, the writer of the article did not verify the contents with Cade just before publication as is what the protocol is. He's going to be in deep shit from his publishers. Especially since the same company publishes both *Vanity Fair* and *Harpers*. It's a huge cluster, and I'm sure the execs over there are pissing in their pants."

"Oh, God," I said shortly. I wanted to run my hands through my hair but stopped when I realized I'd screw up Mickey's work with the extensions. "Well… they have to do something if they ever want Cade on a cover of any of their publications ever again." My mind raced and the silence on the other end of the phone meant Jeanne's was too.

"I'll call them. We need to get the *Harpers* pictures out there before this article publishes. I think that's the best solution."

"Will they do that?"

"Brook, the entire Harper's spread was to let the world know you and Cade care about each other. We can't have the *Vanity* article screwing that up. They'll do it because I'm sure it won't keep fans from buying the magazine for the interviews. Even if it does, it's their problem, not ours."

"Okay." I sat back down in the chair so Mickey could resume his work but he shot me a snarky look. "Tell Denise to let me break it to Cade. He's going to be so upset, but I'll try to explain it to him."

"Actually, she and I have already talked. That was our plan: to have *you* tell him." Jeanne laughed nervously over the telephone.

"Hmmmph," I sighed but smiled. "It'll be okay. He won't blame you two. I'll handle it. I promise."

When I hung up the phone, Mickey was staring at me. "I'll bet you'll handle it."

"Yes." A blush rushed up under my skin, which was surprising, considering Mickey knew the status of Cade and I. "He knows who loves him, and soon fans will know, too. This is just a little, unexpected bump. I'm sure it'll be fine. We've got the best team behind us, and we have each other. No matter what."

Chapter 15
Remember Remembrance

Caden

FILMING WAS GOING well, and as much as I hated the thought of our time filming together ending, I was anxious to get out from under Pinnacle's preverbal thumb and start our life. Out in the open.

Brook had a screen test for a new film, so Martin had graciously given her a break from filming while I was to work on some of my scenes with Leah St. Claire. I didn't want her doing the movie because I didn't like the director, nor did I trust the male lead who had already been cast. Sheldon Richards was a plonker who used his good looks and star-power to leave a stream of women in his wake. He preyed on the younger actresses and crew who weren't aware of his reputation.

Tonight, during dinner and then on the way back to our hotel, Brook and I had a row about it. She didn't want me on set for the test, bloody hell if I wanted to stay away. I knew it was part of the job, but there was a part of me that didn't want that shit to go down without me around.

"Cade, we talked about this! You know I don't like you on set when I'm doing these kissing or almost kissing scenes. Can't you just let it go?" she said impatiently, pulling away to sit by the window of the cab and away from me. I ran my hands through my hair in frustration.

"Get over it, Brook. I'm going to be there."

"Like hell! You always respected this before, so why now? This is going to be fucking uncomfortable as it is! I've been dreading the goddamn thing for the last two weeks! I knew you'd do this. You kiss actresses! *You* get over it!"

It wasn't long before we were pulling up to the hotel entrance. There were ten or so paparazzi and a few fans on the sidewalk in front. Immediately the flashes of the cameras started and I shoved on my sunglasses and pulled up the hood on my sweatshirt.

Brook didn't wait for me or even for her bodyguard to open the door. Instead, she pushed it open and flew into the hotel. I followed closely behind, worried someone would try to stop her, grab her, or hurt her in some way. At the sight of me, the screams intensified and the press started firing questions, but I ignored them all.

"Cade! What are you doing here?"

"Is Brook your girlfriend?"

"Mr. Carlisle! Cade, look over here!"

"Brook! I'm sorry! Just stop!" I called before I stopped to think of the implications of my words or actions. Surely these photos would be all over social media in a matter of seconds, and then the hotel would be inundated with more and more fans and press people.

She tossed me a glaring look over her shoulder, and her chin jutted out as we waited for the lifts to come. There were two or three other people waiting as well, all casting curious glances in our direction and the reporters continued to rant and the fans screamed at the top of their lungs. I hated this shit. I could do without this part of fame. "Brook... " I began again as the lift dinged when it settled on the floor and the doors started to open.

"Cade! Just wait until we get up to the room and away from all these people. *Please.*" She was visibly pissed, her bitch face firmly in place, so I followed her into the lift with the three others and shoved my hands in my pockets. I stared at the black and silver marble tiles on the floor of the lift as my mind raced and the seconds dragged. I could feel Brook fidgeting at my side.

When we reached our floor, I dug the key card out of my back pocket as she stormed down the hall in front of me. She leaned up against the wall and waited as I opened the door. I pushed it open and let her go in ahead of me.

"We're together in this hotel, but can you stop fucking leaving our dirty laundry out there for the lousy reporters? I can see it all now; Cade and Brook fighting on the sidewalk!" she said angrily, her blue eyes spitting fire as she turned on me. "Breaking news!"

"Oh for Christ's sake, Brook!" I threw the card down on the side table and kicked off my shoes. "Who bloody cares what those bastards print? We know the truth! I am fucking sick of the whole charade!"

She glared at me and then stormed into the loo, slamming the door behind her.

"Oh Holy hell," I muttered and flopped down on the bed we shared, covering my hands with my eyes.

I could hear the shower running but no other sounds coming from the other side of the door. I got up and grabbed a beer from the wet bar and chugged half of it down before flipping on the telly; trying to find something to watch. I found nothing that caught my interest. I didn't feel like playing my guitar or reading. I threw the remote down and leaned back against the cushions of the sofa in the suite and I waited for Brook to finish her shower.

We were real. We knew each other inside and out and we were both stubborn as hell; naturally we butted heads on occasion.

The water shut off, and I could hear her shuffling around and obviously taking her sweet ass time about it. No doubt, it was her way of torturing me more. I got up and knocked lightly on the door.

"Brook... babe, can I come in?" I leaned my head on the wood and sighed. "Brook. I'd like to take a shower. I'm exhausted. Please?"

"Last I remember you had your own room!" she yelled from the other side of the door.

"Okay, really? Over this?" I was frustrated, my own anger building.

The lock rattled and the handle turned before she pulled the door open so I could enter. She was in a white bathrobe with a white towel wrapped around her head. She turned back toward the sink to begin brushing her teeth without a word.

I watched her through lowered eyes and then turned the water on in the shower and started to peel my clothes off and leave them in a pile on the floor. She didn't look at me, just kept brushing her teeth as if I wasn't there. After I was under the warm spray, it started to ease the tension caused by our squabble I took a deep breath and spoke. "Tell me why you don't want me there."

She glanced toward the shower in the mirror and shrugged. "You know why. I can't make out like I mean it with anyone other than with you. Least of all, some guy I've never met. Why would you want to see that? I mean, wouldn't it have been hard to get it on with Leah or Davina if I were watching?"

I squeezed some shampoo into the palm of my right hand and began to work it into my hair, feeling the hair gel start to soften and disappear under my fingers. "I tried to pretend it was you with Davina; I told you that. And with Leah, it's hardly anything."

"Pfft!" Brook huffed. "Yeah, hardly anything except her grinding on your crotch, and sticking her tongue down your throat. Yay!" Sarcasm dripped from her words.

I understood what she meant, but there was a part of me that needed to be there. It wasn't just the scene; it was Sheldon Richards. I couldn't stand the thought of anyone's mouth on her but mine. My mind protested, knowing it was ludicrous.

"Cade, please. This is going to be hard enough without having to worry about hurting your feelings. You know I didn't want this audition, anyway." Her voice was resigned. "I tried to get out of it, but Jeanne insisted. The whole thing just feels fucking wrong to me, and a big part of it has to do with you." She paused putting lotion on her legs and shrugged. "But work is work, and we'll both be kissing other people, so better to get this over with. Don't you know this guy anyway? Aren't you friends? Won't that help?"

Friends? Right. I abhorred the bastard.

She was leaning both hands on the ceramic top as I turned off the water and grabbed a towel, beginning to dry the front of my body.

When I didn't answer, she persisted, using my next film against me. "Right? I mean, I read the *Coming Home* script and that's heavy shit. I have to deal with that and I'm not looking forward to it, either. The script Jeanne just sent over has loads of sex in it, so what can we do?"

"I won't be around for that because I'll be filming *Coming Home*, so it won't be as difficult."

Brook shot me a dirty look. "Then why do you want to be on set for this test? It makes no sense, Cade!"

I was gonna have to tell her about Richards. "Sheldon Richards is a predator and I don't want you around him. I'm calling Jeanne and telling her to tell them you won't be auditioning." I wrapped the towel around my waist and walked past her into the bedroom of the suite.

"What did you just say to me?" she asked angrily, and followed me. I dropped the towel and got underneath the covers of the bed. I could feel the heat of her eyes rake over me. "Well, it's not your decision. If Jeanne listens to you, she's fired! Besides, you don't seem to have a problem getting naked on film."

I turned my head so I could look at her. "I don't want to fight."

"Then don't."

"I love you, you know. I just want you to be safe."

"I know." She walked around and slid in beside me after pulled the towel from her body. I reached over and switched off the lamp beside the bed and then gathered her close by my side. Her skin was warm and smooth, as I ran one hand up and down her arm and then down to her hip. I turned toward her and began to kiss the skin of her shoulder.

"I hate it when we fight," I said softly, my mouth moving over the skin of her chest and collarbones up her neck until I found her mouth. "Bloody hate it."

"I know."

"I still don't want you to do it," I whispered against the warm skin covering the pulse in her neck. "I don't."

Brooklyn

MY SCREEN TEST WENT well. It was a big exclamation point that we only had a few weeks until we were finished. A trip to Paris for the last couple of scenes, and we'd be completely done. Over the course of three films, the separation between films was tempered with the fact in a few months we'd either be promoting the one we just finished or filming the next in the series a few months later. We'd have one last promotional tour, one last series of awards shows, and then bam. Done.

My lungs constricted in my chest as I watched Cade pluck at his guitar in the corner of the living room of our suite. His beautiful profile was pensive, sad and detached from the tune his fingers were automatically coaxing from the mahogany instrument. I wondered what was racing through his mind. He was always thinking and one of the things I loved most about him. My heart surged and the throbbing began in my throat again.

It was silly to be sad, because he was mine, even if *Remembrance* was almost over, which meant the day-in and day-out of his presence would be sporadic at best. Already he had two new movies lined up, and I had one. My eyes blurred. For the first time since my first audition, I didn't want to work. I wanted to run away and hide. But, always with Cade.

I crawled to the end of the couch and leaned on the arm closest to his chair. He swallowed, and it looked like he was going to speak but thought better of it. I stretched out and reached toward him, but he was far enough away that my fingers barely grazed down his back. He was wearing the jeans with the rip in the knee he'd had on the first time I saw him at the audition and his vintage Led Zeplin T-shirt. I'd slept in it last night when Cade pulled it over my head. I'd been shivering in his arms but it hadn't been from being cold.

"Hey you..." I murmured, so softly I wasn't sure he heard until his fingers stilled and his head turned to rest his chin on his left shoulder.

"Hey." Cade's eyes didn't meet mine, but his velvet voice was shaking slightly. I knew he was in the same place as me. "We're back to this, are we love?"

I blinked at the tears welling in my eyes, not wanting to let this turn into a sad-fest, but somehow knowing that when Martin yelled cut for the last time, we'd both crack open and bleed. If I could manage it, I'd keep it in until we were alone, but I wasn't sure if I'd be strong enough. And forget the wrap party; I'd never be able to get through it in one piece.

My mind flashed back to the end of the first film when I found my boy alone on that balcony and he said the words that changed my life; *"God, Brook. I just... I can't do this."* He'd been so emotional. *"I can't say goodbye to you tonight. I don't want this to be over."*

"Yeah, what goes around comes around." My voice was cracking and Cade set the guitar in the corner before he moved to the couch next to me. I scooted to the back when he lay down next to me and folded me into his warm embrace. The first traitorous tears fell as I breathed him in and settled into what had become my place of solace. Cade's elegant fingers splayed out on my back and hips, our legs entwined and his lips on my forehead. "I don't want this to end, Cade."

"You'll always be my Julia."

I sucked in my breath as my eyes slammed shut and I willed myself not to let the sobs escape, but my arms tightened and I buried my face in the warm skin of his neck. His lips moved in a series of tender kisses on my temple, alternating with his nose nuzzling against me. I could feel him breathe and it hit me how important that sensation had become to me.

"Cade." It was like a prayer. His name was my alpha and omega, summing up my entire fucking life with amazing simplicity. There was no hiding from him. He knew me inside and out. I needed him. I could exist without him, but it wouldn't be living.

"It'll be okay, baby. You'll still have me, just not around to annoy you every day."

"I like it when you annoy me." A small laugh choked out around the enormous lump of emotion in my throat.

He chuckled quietly, but the sound wasn't quite genuine. "No, you don't. You'll be so into your new gig, and you won't even miss me."

The back of his knuckles brushed against my cheek and I turned my face into the caress, the tears squeezing from my tightly clenched eyes. I shook my head, willing this pain to go away and trying to keep the tremor from my voice. "Stop saying shit you know isn't true."

His chest rose beneath my cheek in a huge sigh and he shifted slightly to bring us ever closer, more entwined as the fingers of one hand slid into the hair at my nape and his thumb brushed over my cheek again and again. I could feel the burn of his blue eyes on my face, even though my eyes were closed, and the beat of his heart next to mine. He was wrapped around me and it still wasn't close enough for either one of us.

"Brook." His fingers continued their gentle assault on my cheekbone until finally he nudged my chin with his thumb. "We've done this before. We're always *us*. Nothing comes between us. It never will."

I nodded and snuffled, still unable to open my eyes. He was trying to be positive, but my sadness would be mirrored in his beautiful face. "I know. But this is...this is..."

"This is just the end of a job, not the end of you and me."

He was right; I knew it. Logic screamed at me that this was the start of the rest of our lives, not the end of anything, but all my heart could recognize was that he'd be away from me so much more.

Somehow hearing the words fall from Cade's lips made it too real, and I lost the battle with the tears and his arms tightened around me even more.

"Listen, love; it's only a film. We're the real thing. You won't be able to get rid of me that easily. I'm sort of looking forward to it, actually."

I pulled back and opened my eyes. I must look horrible with my eyes are puffy and my nose running. "What?" I frowned in bemusement.

Cade smiled, his lips lifting in the crooked grin I loved as he nodded. "Yeah. I mean, not about being apart, but um...when we're together after this madness ends, there'll be no mistaking that we're together."

I huffed. "Pfft! Everyone knows, Cade. Jesus, it's no secret anymore."

"We still haven't come out, formally. It will piss me off if you stay away from premieres and set visits just to keep from confirming. And I sure as fuck will not stay away from you." He grinned at me. "So, don't do it either."

I rolled my eyes. He'd already proven it when he'd flown to Los Angeles for my screen test with Sheldon Richards, walking off set, and leaving Martin to deal with a lost day of production. It was against my will and it was a surprise when he showed up in the middle of it, but damned if I wasn't happy as hell he did. "Yeah, I remember."

"You were glad to see me. I know you were, so no arguments. You do a piss-poor job of convincing me you don't want me around." His mouth found mine in a soft kiss, pulling one lip in between both of his, just before his teeth sank into the tender flesh.

My breathing quickened as the air charged. "Do I?" I said as my lips began playing with his. "Are you sure?" I bit him back as his mouth played with mine. Cade yelped and pulled back with a surprised expression, his eyes wider.

I could feel the tears clinging to my lashes, but the look on his face made me smile. "Ow! That hurt!"

"No shit?" I tugged on his hair harder than I needed to bring his mouth closer once again.

"Ow!" Cade said again. "I can play this game, too!" His fingers closed around my right nipple and squeezed, his eyes widening with mine, a smirk creeping slowly along his lips as I winced from the pain.

I grunted and pushed hard against his chest, toppling him off of the couch and onto the floor. He landed with a thud and I burst out laughing. "Oh, yeah?"

"Yeah!" Cade reached up and grabbed the leg of my sweats and then closed his fingers around my ankle to pull me down, shift me beneath him and start tickling me ruthlessly. "You're gonna get it, now!"

I gasped and struggled, giggling uncontrollably. "Stop! You know I can't stand it when you tickle me, Cade! Stop! Stop!" I screamed and tried to pry his hands away from my ribs but it only opened me up for more torture. "Please! Oh, God! Stop it, Cade!"

Cade laughed and kept it up, leaning over me and pinning me down. "Give!"

"Agggghhhh!" I screamed again as he continued his merciless onslaught. "Cade!"

"Give, Brook!" His face was animated, openly laughing at me now and clearly enjoying my predicament.

"Alright! I give! I give!"

Suddenly he stopped, still pinning me down, his body over mine. "What do you give?" he said softly, his tone serious and sensuous as his blue eyes burned into mine, still blurry from laughing so hard.

The fingers of my right hand reached for his jaw, skirting over the stubble, now softer from a full day's growth. "Everything."

His brow crinkled and he looked at me skeptically, cocking his head slightly. "That sounds good, but—"

"Don't you trust me?" He felt so good, his breath on my face and arms around me. I relished in the closeness as his lower body settled into the cradle of mine. "You're bigger than me anyway."

"But you're more devious. I know how your mind works. You'll suck me in, get me all soft and gooey, then move in for the kill." Cade rested his elbows beside my head and bent to kiss my mouth as my heart threatened to burst from my body. His lips brushed mine. "But if this is dying, kill me now."

"I'll miss you. Miss this." I brought my knees up beside his hips, which brought him more intimately against me. I reached up and our mouths moved in intimate unison, tongues moving together as the kiss deepened and the ever present passion flamed between us as his body moved against mine. When his lips finally lifted, we were both left breathless as he rested his forehead on mine.

"This is the stuff I think about when we're apart."

I wrapped my arms and legs more tightly around him and buried my face into the crook of his neck. "What will I do without you?"

"Love, let's not be sad. We still have three weeks of shooting and I want to make the most of it. And after, it won't be so bad, I promise. We'll see each other as much as I can make happen. I'll have Denise work with Jeanne on the schedules. And I bought the house in L.A."

I drew in a sigh and let it out. "I know, but I'm used to being with you constantly."

"Yes, I've spoiled you rotten and enjoyed every bloody second of it."

My fingers raked down his back and he hissed as they settled on his firm ass, pressing his hardness tighter against my sex. "Mmmm.... yum," I whispered and his mouth devoured mine again and again. I never wanted it to end as I responded passionately. The rush never left. Every time he touched me, it was amazing. I moaned in protest as his mouth lifted from mine and my hands grasped the back of his head, telling him I wanted more.

"Fuck Brook. This sucks, but haven't you got somewhere to be?"

I pulled back with a sigh, my heart dropping. "Shit. Thanks for reminding me." I frowned. "Wanna come with?"

I had the final costume fitting and I couldn't miss it. I'd have to wear one of those fake bellies. We'd be filming in a week and frankly, I was anxious for him to see it.

"Um, no. I'm just gonna hang with my guitar ."

"You're choosing that over me?" I teased as I found my shoes in the corner and shoved my feet inside. Nick would have the car waiting soon. "I see how you are. Please come, Cade." I didn't want to spend any time away from him.

"I don't want to see you in that getup, Brook."

I was taken about, perplexed. My expression twisted. "Is that what this is about? Why, for fuck's sake?"

"I just think that I should wait. For the film."

I rolled my eyes and crinkled my nose, checking my cell phone for messages. "Cade. You're being weird. It's just a costume."

Cade moved back onto the couch and retrieved his guitar from its resting place. "No, it isn't. It's you *pregnant*."

I pulled on my grey zippered sweatshirt and plopped down next to him. "Are you serious? You weren't this goofy when I had to get the wedding dress fitted."

He reached for my hand and brought it to his mouth. "Because I knew it wasn't something you'd really choose. Humor me. I just don't want to see you like that until we film."

"Cade...for *Only Us* what's-her-name had a pregnancy suit. Were you this ridiculous with her?"

"Davina." Cade supplied her name then bit his lip and his eyebrows lifted. "This is you."

"Hmmp," I sighed. "So you're planning on avoiding me during set up, too?"

He nodded. "Yeah," was the simple answer.

"Why? Because I'll look like a whale? Next you'll be saying you don't want to rehearse."

"That's not it, but probably not."

"You're crazy." I ran my hand through my hair and leaned in to place a quick kiss on his mouth. My heart thumped in my chest as I gazed at his handsome face in wonder. He was so damn romantic.

"Crazy for you." I smiled and ran a hand through his hair before walking to the door.

"Love you."

"I know." He nodded with a brilliant smile and strummed *Brahm's Lullebye* on his guitar.

"Bleh! I hate that stupid song!"

His delighted laughter followed me into the hall where the bodyguards were waiting, as patiently as ever, as I shoved the sunglasses over my eyes.

Caden

IT HAD BEEN ONE hell of a week; the press junkets, the traveling, and the crowds. I'd just come off of presenting at the Oscars with Davina. Jesus, I was tired. I'd wanted Brook to meet me in Los Angeles for the awards, but she chose to stay in Vancouver. I missed her, but I couldn't really blame her. Even though it nagged in the back of my mind that she was still keeping us a secret, I realized with all the interviews I had on the radio and other media, I wouldn't have had time to be with her anyway. It was necessary, and I cared about this new film, but bloody hell it wore me out. The screaming fans everywhere I went, while a measure of my success, had gotten worse.

I was dreading the end of *The Remembrance* movies, as much as I was looking forward to moving beyond it. It had owned me for the past three years, but without it, my life would be so different without Brook's constant presence. Life would calm down as time moved on. I doubted that I'd ever see a greater success than I had with this job. To think I hadn't even wanted to move from action movies to romantic drama. I should thank Denise. Without it, without that obscure audition with an unknown actress my whole life would be so different. Meeting Brook was destiny. These books were written, produced, made and marketed, only for us, so we would meet, fall in love, be together. It was fate, pure and simple. I knew it as surely as I was breathing.

The end was emotional and bittersweet. I tried to be encouraging and supportive of Brook when she was feeling melancholy, but the truth was; I was a mess. I'd grown used to having her with me constantly, and even though we worked on other projects during breaks, there was always another of these films on the horizon that would bring us back together for months. Now, that was over.

I now had four journals sitting on my bedside table, one from each film, which held all of her notes. Director's notes, notes to me. The first was the most precious because it represented that first, fragile year, but the others were memory books of our time as a couple. She was amazing. Was then, was now, and would always rock my world without question.

I wasn't sure I was ready to see Brook in her pregnant costume. Even though I had it in my head that we'd be together, get married, and have kids, neither of us was ready to think about it. I wasn't sure how I'd react seeing it on her. On the plane, I'd re-read the scene in the book. I couldn't picture it, but I was certain, whatever it looked like, it would make me even more anxious for the charade to end, for the world to see and finally know without doubt, she belonged to me. Her choice was *with me*. I sighed deeply.

I was sick of the haters, the hackers, and all the bullshit. I was even sick of the jobs that would take us to different parts of the world. I wanted to be normal; with Brook.

I left Davina in L.A. the minute we were finished presenting. I had tomorrow off, but Tuesday we were filming the last scenes of A Love Like This and tonight, I wanted to see Brook.

The soft sounds of her breathing soothed me as I came in and threw my jacket on the sofa, followed quickly by my white shirt as I kicked off my shoes. I undid my pants on the way to the bedroom and shed them before lifting the covers to slide into the bed beside her.

Her body shone translucent where the moonlight landed on her skin. She stirred softly as I slid in next to her, letting her scent envelope me as I reached toward her, my fingers aching for her flesh.

"Cade?"

My heart leapt in my chest. Even asleep, my name was on her lips.

"Yeah, babe. It's me. Come here."

I opened my arms and she curled up next to my body, her head coming to rest in the crook of my shoulder and her fingers playing lightly on my chest.

"I missed you," she murmured softly and again my heart thudded inside me.

"Did you miss me enough to wake up for a minute?" I pushed her hair back and let my fingers twine around the silky strands. So soft. So Brook.

Brook propped up on one elbow and leaned in to kiss my mouth in a feather kiss. "Yeah. What's wrong?" She blinked twice and wiped her eye.

"I lied to you last week."

I turned toward her and slid one leg between two of hers. She had on sweat shorts and a tank top, unsure if I'd be home tonight.

She was puzzled; her blue eyes almost black in the shadows. "What? About what?"

"I am *not* looking forward to this. I'm miserable."

She let out her breath in relief before melting into me, our arms automatically closing around each other. She felt so damn good. "I know."

"You do?" I asked.

She huffed in the darkness. "Cade, come on. We've been inseparable. I can barely breathe just thinking about it. We share everything so why would you think I couldn't tell?"

"I'm wrecked. I wanted to be strong for you, so you wouldn't see it."

"You don't need to hide from me."

"I know. I love you."

Brook's fingers drew circles on my chest and I began to relax. I would miss this part the most. I took knowing she'd be in my arms every night for granted. I knew she was tired, and I was exhausted. Tonight it was enough just to hold her close.

"Me, too."

I smiled into the darkness. "Did you want to rehearse the baby scenes, Brook? It was selfish of me to discount that maybe you needed to."

She shrugged in my arms. "I don't *need* to. But winging it isn't what we do. We never have." Her voice was sleepy.

"Yeah, but the script is weak in that scene anyway. Not at all the way I'd imagined it to be."

She let out a soft sigh. "We'll be fine."

"I've rehearsed it in my head a hundred times, Brook."

Her fingers stilled and she snuggled closer, her arm going up around my neck. "Me, too."

"Screw the script. We'll make it perfect."

"Yeah. Just remember to call me Julia, *Ryan*."

I couldn't help but chuckle and I felt her smile against my skin. I quickly flipped her on her back and lowered my mouth to the sweet skin of her neck, dragging my open mouth lower, tasting her so thoroughly, taking control and pushing away my exhaustion. Jesus, I already missed her.

"How about a little love for your doctor, *Julia*?"

"Mmmm...Yeah, I need some medical attention." We both laughed softly before our moods turned serious.

My body pushed into hers impatiently, seeking the amazing heat of her flesh surrounding mine. We were both so hungry, our bodies moving together in a familiar, yet desperate way. I'd never be able to live without this woman and it always felt like heaven and hell whenever our time together was dwindling.

Brooklyn

"OH, MY GOD! Brook! I'm gonna cry like a baby for his momma's tit!" Mickey fanned at his face with his hand, and I burst out laughing. I'd just spent two hours in the makeup trailer where he'd shooed everyone else away while he worked to make me look all disheveled and sweaty, then patted my fake stomach. It looked real; I looked really pregnant, and now all that was left was to hit the set.

"Mickey!" I laughed some more. "I'm going to cry myself!"

"Bitch, don't you dare! I worked like a dog on that face! It's perfection!"

"How can I look any worse? I'm gonna have to cry during the scene."

"I'd be crying my ass off if I were having a baby with that, too. Jesus fucking Christ! I've been crying for almost three years already! Maybe he'll let me touch up his makeup?" Mickey wagged his brows and sighed. "At least I might get to touch him one more time. Maybe I can kiss him goodbye!"

I laughed harder, knowing what Cade's reaction would be. Priceless.

"Uh, probably not?" My eyebrows shot up in amusement.

"Nom, nom, nom....God. I have to stop! I'm going to hyperventilate and have to do something in the back!"

I was dying to the point of holding my fake belly as it shook against me. The tears started to accumulate, threatening to spill from my eyes. "Stop, Mickey! My stomach hurts!"

"You're still the luckiest bitch on the planet! The lovemaking scenes, oh my God! I swear I'd give anything to be you."

I wiped at my eyes and hugged him. He hugged me back full force. "I love you, Mickey! Thank you for making this so much fun. I've been a little sad."

"Awww, baby, I can understand, but you're takin' Cade home with you, so what's to be sad over?"

"Just the end. You know. I'll miss everyone. I'm certain I'll never have so much fun in hair and makeup as I've had with you."

"Just name your first born after me! I don't ask for much!"

Sally came in to get me. "Martin called. They're ready for you." She smiled. "Are you ready to have a baby?"

My heart fluttered. "Ready as I'll ever be."

Soon she had me into the cotton hospital gown costume over a flesh-colored camisole and boy shorts. I looked like a whale, no getting around it.

The birth scene was intimate and since it was the last scene we were shooting, I knew I'd be an emotional mess. Cade asked that the set be on lockdown, as if it were a love scene. It was 2 AM and I hadn't seen Cade all day. He'd stayed away from me all day, saying he was working on music, but I knew he was dreading tonight's shoot as much as I was.

As I walked toward set, Martin and two or three crewmembers were checking the lighting, but nothing existed but the beautiful man that waited for me, dressed in surgical scrubs and hat. His eyes on fire, with the love I knew was more real and sacred than anything I'd ever hoped for, never left my face.

Cade took my hand when I was close enough. "This is it," he whispered, too soft for the audio to catch. My heart swelled and fell all at the same time, the moment so bittersweet. My throat hurt and I struggled not to cry my eyes out. "You look perfect."

I shook my head, a tear slipping from my eye. I quickly brushed it away, managing a tumultuous smile. "I'm fat."

His hand squeezed mine, he smiled, and shook his head. "You're beautiful."

Cade *was* as perfect as the character he'd embodied, even more so. I'd known it the moment I met him.

And the miracle was, he really was mine and would be forever.

Chapter 16
When Cade Met Sheldon

Caden

WHAT THE HELL KIND of a name was Sheldon for a man? I wondered in irritation. The name was weird, though it was my abhorrence of the man that dictated my disgust. I'd just arrived on the set of Brook's new movie, and Pinnacle didn't want me to be there, but I didn't give a rat's ass. The studio's reign over my relationship with Brook was coming to an end, but the contracts still bound us until *A Love Like This* released three months from now.

I'd always found the sod irritating, but now I hated his guts. My eyes narrowed as I watched from behind the director's chair, following his every move as he leaned in and spoke to Brook. She was beautiful, her cheeks flushed pink, and she was laughing at something the wanker said. The skin on my neck and face began to burn uncomfortably, and my fists clenched involuntarily.

My presence at the screen test should have told the other actor to keep his distance from Brook when they weren't on set, but the familiarity between them grated on my nerves. I was in physical pain; as if a knife had been pushed into my gut.

I'd wanted to surprise Brook, and so I'd jetted off my own set the first chance I had without telling her to expect me. I missed her and the late night Skype sessions helped but didn't take the place of holding her and waking up beside her. It had been three weeks since we'd been together in Los Angeles and I could barely stand still in my anxiousness to let her know I was there, but I'd agreed to wait until this scene was wrapped. Maria Denton, the director on this gig, was particularly anal, and while she produced quality on film, she was annoying as hell to work under with. I'd done one film with her three years before, and I couldn't wait for the damn thing to wrap.

During my break between films, I'd managed to purchase a house in L.A. and Brook and I covertly moved in together. Denise and Jeanne did an excellent job of scouting properties and arranging for Brook and me to check them out during a few middle-of-the-night shopping excursions and Joel had drawn up a non-disclosure for the real estate agents and agencies were required to sign before they were even told who the client was.

By some miracle, we'd managed to skirt the paparazzi's intruding lens for most of it, though when the bill-of-sale was recorded on public record, the tabloids blew up in speculation. Brook and I didn't go out together, but they became merciless in chasing us around Hollywood individually. I expected it; it was my property, but in the five years I'd been working in Hollywood, I hadn't moved from London, so there were sound bites, articles and magazine covers screaming everywhere I looked.

The Pinnacle execs weren't happy that I didn't wait until the last movie premiered, but screw it. It was much more likely we'd be discovered if I were constantly sneaking in and out of her condo or parent's house. The privacy fence and lush foliage of the property would help. The amped up press made Brook wary and she was still wavering on keeping the relationship a secret, though Joel assured me the most the studio could do was keep a chunk of the salaries.

Standing here watching this sod move in on my girl, made me all the more determined to come out with it. I was fed up.

"Maria, how many more takes will be necessary?"

She was a small woman, dressed in jeans and a hooded sweatshirt, her hair pulled into a knot at the top of her head, and tortoise shell glasses sitting on her pert nose. "Who knows? If I didn't know better, I'd think Shell didn't want to finish. But my production budget for the day is basically blown, so I need to get it done."

"Shell," I murmured in disgust. "What kind of fucking name is that for a man? His manager did him a disservice by not suggesting he change it to something tougher. I'm surprised he even gets cast for characters who have a dick." I ran a hand through my hair, in exasperation.

Maria laughed out loud. "If we don't get it this time, I may call it a day and just see what we can piece together in editing."

"I know that's not how you work." I smirked at her.

"True." She shoved her glasses further up her nose. "Fall back into the shadows, please. I don't need another interruption so I'd rather Brook not see you until we're finished."

"No problem." I took four steps back until I was cloaked in shadows. The scene was an office scene and while Brook had mentioned the script, I hadn't read it through. She was dressed in a business suit, as was the wanker to her left, though Brook's jacket was fitted, hugging her curves and topped a short pencil skirt and stiletto heels. She looked amazing as the makeup artist came to retouch her face and fluff and spritz her hair.

"Do I want to watch this?" I murmured under my breath.

"Places!" Marie called loudly and the crew got ready and the support staff left the set. "Quiet on set! Action!"

As the scene unfolded in front of me, I became more agitated, though I put on a good front; my hands in my pockets and my stance full of forced nonchalance. This was just another job; my mind screamed as his mouth smashed down on Brook's, one hand fisting in the back of her jacket and the other sliding over the curve of her ass. My heart tightened and my lungs constricted inside my chest. My expression tightened and the muscle in my jaw worked overtime as my teeth clenched. I tried to inhale deeply, hoping to ease the feeling of claustrophobia I felt. This was an open set, on a big soundstage, but I felt like I was in a coffin.

"Mr. Carlisle, would you like anything? Coffee? Soda?" A soft voice whispered.

I glanced down at a young production assistant, clearly star-struck. I noticed the name on her badge and shook my head. "No thank you, Sharon. I'm good."

"Okay. Do you think I could get an autograph? When the scene wraps?"

"Sure."

The girl smiled brightly and scurried away after one of the producers shot her a dirty look.

The next thirty minutes moved at a snail's pace as it became apparent to me that Sheldon was throwing his lines. Apparently, he was enjoying kissing and feeling up his costar.

When the director finally called it a day, it was my opportunity to move into Brook's eye-line, and I didn't waste any time doing so. Making sure Sheldon Richards was aware was almost as much a priority as getting my arms around my girl.

When Brook's eyes met mine, her eyes widened and her face lit up in a joyful expression. "Cade!" she exclaimed happily. We both moved quickly and it wasn't ten seconds until she was in my arms with her feet dangling off the floor. "Why didn't you tell me you were coming?"

I hugged her tight, pushing down the urge to kiss her. Torn, I knew the studio could do little about a friend visiting a friend on set, however, with the short time remaining until we were free, I didn't need to antagonize the situation. We'd have two days together and so I'd bide my time. My eyes met the steel gray gaze of the other man, and I nodded in his direction as I reluctantly released Brook. Her small hand trailed down my chest to rest for a split second on my abs.

"To what do we owe this honor?" Sheldon said his annoyance barely veiled.

"Hello, Shelly. I was in the neighborhood." I dismissed him and turned back to stare down into beautiful blue eyes.

Brook bit her lip at the nickname, laughter dancing in her eyes.

"Cade," he acknowledged. "How nice. Maybe we can all have dinner? Brook and I made plans to go to a little bistro down the street."

My back stiffened, and Brook's expression turned pensive, her eyes imploring me not to make a scene.

"Really? I wouldn't want to intrude."

"That's crazy. We're all friends here, " Brook put in. Her words were rushed; her voice tight.

"Are we?" I asked.

Sheldon strode closer, his pace slow and deliberate. "What are you doing here, *again*?"

I huffed. He was just as irritated when I'd been there for the screen test. "As if I'd explain myself to you. If you'll excuse us, I have some things to discuss with my, uh, *friend.*"

The other man's mouth thinned a little then he smiled slowly. "Uhhggg," he cleared his throat "Fine." He nodded in Brook's direction. "I'll call you about dinner in an hour or so."

Brook bristled, clearly not sure how to deal with the situation. By now my blood was boiling. Why was she even hesitating?

"You do that, Shelly."

She looked back and forth between the other man and me; clearly struggling.

When her eyes met mine, my eyebrows shot up and I shrugged slightly, hoping she understood I was irritated about her hesitation. I'd understand not wanting to blow off Noah, Gavin, or Jennifer on our set, but she barely knew this asshole. It pissed me off.

"Shell, would you mind if we rescheduled?" She was pensive and pandering, which made my anger elevate.

What the hell? Was she asking his permission?

I sucked in a breath and squared my shoulders. "Look, Brook, clearly you're busy. I guess I should have called before showing up."

Brook bit her lip and started to wring her hands a bit. "No, Cade. I'm glad you came." She reached out and rested her hand on my forearm. "Shell and I can have dinner another night." She glanced his way, imploring with her eyes. "Right?"

He laughed shortly. "Sure, no problem." He moved toward her and wrapped his hand around her upper arm, before turning and starting to leave set. "See you tomorrow, kid."

My eyes locked with Brook's, mine harder than hers.

"What's wrong? Why are you pissy? It was just dinner." She took a step toward me but I put up my hand to stop her progress. "You were rude!"

"Let's just... get out of here," I said shortly.

Her brow dropped and her expression turned to anger.

"Okay, fine. I have to change."

"Yeah." I remained rooted where I was, my hands still shoved in the pockets of my jacket.

"You don't want to come with me to my trailer?" Her words were stiff.

"Well, someone might get the wrong idea," I said sarcastically.

Brook huffed. "Whatever, Cade. Since when did you care what people think?"

"Never. But obviously you do."

"Whatever." She strode past me, knocking into me as she moved.

Fuck it. I walked after her. She was right. I didn't care. I wanted people to know and I was done hiding the truth so wankers like Shelly Richards had room to move in.

I felt every pair of eyes following us as we left the sound stage and walked outside toward her trailer. I took notice that Richards was sitting right next to hers. It wasn't anything out of the ordinary to have the two leads trailers in close proximity to each other, but my blood was boiling already, and it only added to my aggravation.

Brook stomped up the three steps and pulled open the door and hurried inside, only noticing I was following when I grabbed the door before it slammed.

"What the hell? I thought you weren't coming?"

"Sorry to interrupt your plans with *Shell*. I guess showing up here puts a cramp in your determination to keep me a secret."

Brook turned on me. "Where do you get off? I was working! You expect my understanding with you and Davina and whoever else you have to parade around, and you act like a two-year old when it's *my* set! Are you gonna pout about it?"

I laughed angrily and flopped down on the sofa against one wall of the trailer. I didn't take my eyes off her as she moved around and started to change, pulling a pair of jeans and light rose-colored sweater out of a drawer. I leaned my elbow against the back of the sofa, and my fingers absently plucked at my right eyebrow.

"Maybe," I snapped.

"Great."

She flung off her jacket and blouse, exposing her white lace bra, then turned her back and unzipped the matching skirt, pushed it down and stepped out of it. Her panties matched and even that grated. Jealousy ate away at me. "Nice matching underwear. Very nice."

Brook turned abruptly and glared at me. She was beautiful, her body perfect, a slight tan to her skin. They obviously had her in the tanning beds for this role. "I always wear stuff like this, so stop insinuating. Anyway, it's part of the costume."

"Wow. That makes me feel so much better."

She bent to push first one leg, then the other into the dark blue denim, shaking her head. "Now you know what I went through. Except Shell doesn't follow me everywhere I go."

"Really? What about dinner, then?" I was agitated and I shifted on the couch. "Got any beer? Scotch?"

Brook threw the sweater over her head and shoved her arms into the sleeves, walked to the small refrigerator and opened it, reached in and pulled out a Coke. "No, alcohol in here." She held it out to me. "Sorry."

I took the can and popped it open. "Answer the question," I said steadily, my eyes trained on hers while I took a drink from the soda.

"Dinner was to discuss a scene. I wanted to go over the script, and figured you wouldn't appreciate it if I met him in his room as we used to do." She moved to a makeup vanity and sat down, picking up a hairbrush and began to comb through the silken strands roughly. "He's been nice to me. It was embarrassing how you treated him."

My mind shot to the many nights I'd spent in her hotel room or her in mine going over scenes, and using rehearsing as an excuse to make-out when we shouldn't have. Those were amazing memories and I'd have to be insane to think anyone else wouldn't want to get close to her like I had. I sucked in a breath and set down my soda on the floor next to the leg of the sofa.

"I don't give a shit about him. People know I'm in here now. Oops." I was feeling defiant, like a petulant child. I was older than Brook by four years, and prided myself on my professional ethics. I should respect her wishes to keep the intimacy of our relationship private, and it wasn't like me to act like a jealous idiot. The Harper's article screamed we were together, and that should have satisfied me, but I was tired of worrying and sneaking around. And going forward, it would ease my mind if people on her movies knew she wasn't single.

Brook threw the brush down and it slammed into perfume bottles and makeup containers on the top of the desk, twisted on her stool and looked at me. "Did you come all this way to fight with me? I don't understand why you're so mad. You knew it'd be awkward if you're around when I'm filming love scenes. There will be more tomorrow, so you should just stay off the set."

"Get over it, Brook. I'm going to be there."

Her blue eyes widened incredulously. "Why?" Her voice elevated again. "This is uncomfortable as it is. I've been dreading these scenes for weeks, and you show up right when this is on deck?"

"Yeah." I scowled. I'd wanted to see her, but I'd managed to get a copy of the shooting schedule from Jeanne and it was no coincidence I was here now.

"How convenient."

I leaned back on the sofa again. "Isn't it? I guess I'm jealous. I don't like it, but it is what it is. I remember how it was with us. This is a romantic movie, like we had, and I don't like what's-his-name. I saw how he was looking at you, and I don't trust him. He has a reputation of bedding his costars. It would be easier if he knew we were together."

Brook suddenly jumped up, grabbed her bag, coat and shoved her feet into her boots. "Well, you're being ridiculous! I'm outta here. I hope you enjoy your time with Sheldon. Maybe you can call Marie and the three of you can make it a threesome!" She pushed open the trailer door with enough force to slam the door against the outside of the temporary dressing room.

I was in pursuit before the door even closed; my shove on it echoed Brook's. I was rewarded with another resounding bang as I flew down the stairs and across the lot. She was running toward the black SUV waiting to take her back to her hotel. "Brook!"

Her bodyguard was waiting and held the door open as she climbed inside. He was a big, burly, bodybuilder type. I didn't recognize him but he obviously knew who I was because he nodded and waited for me to climb in after her.

"Awesome," she spat. "Did you pay this guy off or something?"

I ignored her jab. The bodyguard got in the front passenger seat and the driver asked Brook if he should proceed. She was keeping a good distance between us by staying close to the opposite door, her arms folded across her chest.

"There will be photographers at the hotel," Brook objected, pissed off when I didn't immediately answer. "Cade."

I nodded and brushed off her concern. "Mmm huh. Probably."

"What, did you leave a trail of crumbs from the airport to make sure?"

My jaw stiffened. "That's a good idea. I'll remember that for next time." I could feel animosity seeping off of her.

"Is there a problem, Ms. Halloway?" the driver asked, glancing in his rearview mirror. He and her bodyguard were both very professional but it was clear they were there to do her bidding, and not mine, though that fact didn't unsettle me. I was beyond caring what anyone thought. "Should we get another car for Mr. Carlisle?"

My response was to settle in and buckle my seatbelt, silently daring her to contradict my right to be in the car with her.

She shook her head, but didn't say anything. Soon the car was moving. It was clear it would either be groveling or a down and out fight once we hit her hotel room, but I was done sneaking around to see her.

I didn't consider she'd be angry that I was here. She seemed happy to see me when I'd arrived on set; until this. "Do you want me to leave?"

"No. I just want you to respect my space. I don't want you watching me while I'm working. We discussed this before. It's not any different from you getting it on, on screen."

"First of all, it's not getting it on. It's *acting*."

"Thank you for making my point."

I understood what she meant, but there was a part of me that needed to be there; the part that couldn't stand the thought of anyone's mouth on her but mine.

"It's different with this guy. He's notorious for being a dog."

"Cade, can you listen to yourself? It's acting for me, too. Besides, Sheldon is gross. He sweats all over me.

"Dogs don't sweat; they piss on things." I couldn't hide my antagonism.

She paused and shrugged. "Work is work, and we will both have to kiss other people in the line of duty, so better to get the first one over with."

"Hmmph!" I huffed. "I saw the way Shelly was looking at you."

"Stop. He doesn't matter."

By now we'd arrived at the hotel and somehow managed to get in through the door by the restaurant kitchen without anyone seeing us; though the chefs, dishwashers, and wait staff all watched our every step. Bill led us through the kitchen and into a stairwell off to one side that we could take to Brook's room on the eleventh floor.

I hoisted her on my back and she laughed. "Maybe you'll be kinder to me after this. Did you gain weight?" I was teasing but she knew I was still upset about the scene with Sheldon.

"Cade. Seriously, do you think everyone doesn't know we're together? You're here. No one thinks we're just friends. Especially Shell."

When I kept quiet as I climbed the stairs, Brook continued.

"Besides, all I can think about is that scene from *When Harry Met Sally*. You know the one?" She started reciting the scene. *"You do not have great sex with Sheldon. Sheldon can do your income taxes. If you need a root canal, Sheldon's your man... but humping and bumping is not Sheldon's strong suit."* She giggled. "Right?"

It was funny, sure, and I chuckled despite myself, but I wasn't easily sidetracked. "Brook, I know this guy. Don't let the pussy name fool you. He tries to get naked with every woman on set."

Bill was smiling wryly as he opened the door to her floor, and I moved through it.

"What room?"

"1120. Right by the elevator." Brook pointed to my right. I could have let her down, but didn't.

"Where's that prick's room? Is there a connecting door?"

Brook burst out laughing as we entered her room.

"Now who needs to get over it? Come on!" she teased, her eyes flashing.

I peeled off my clothes and checked my messages while Brook took a quick shower. She joined me in the bedroom afterward, removing the towel from her blonde hair and starting to run a comb through it.

I pulled back the covers on the bed, and sat down with my back to her. I could feel the heat of her eyes rake over me. "You don't seem to have a problem getting naked."

Her nearness calmed me down. "Not with you," I murmured.

She sidled up on her knees behind me and started to run the comb through my hair with her right hand, the other resting on the muscles of my left shoulder. I could smell her shampoo and the sweet scent of her skin. And her soothing strokes were relaxing me as she continued for a few moments, neither one of us speaking.

It wasn't long before her warm breath rushed over the skin of my neck and her hot little mouth opened over the skin where my neck and shoulder joined. She sucked and bit me gently and it sent goose pimples rushing all over me. My body sprang to life, thickening and hardening within a few seconds.

"Brook…" I pulled her hand in front of me so that I could kiss the inside of her palm, bringing her body flush against my back. "I love you, you know. I don't like being away from you. I hate being in the new house without you."

The fingers of her other hand threaded through my wet hair and pushed my head slightly to the side so she could run a series of kisses down my neck.

"I know," Brook whispered against my skin and another rush of gooseflesh rushed over me. I pulled her around until she was straddling my lap and my hands were untying the knot on her robe until it tumbled open to reveal her luscious body to my view. "I miss you every day. I'll be home in a few weeks," she murmured against my temple. "Then we have the Movie Awards in L.A. before our last press tour. It's a month together before you leave."

"A month together flies by."

My hands pushed it open farther, my hands cupped her breasts, brushing over the nipples that instantly hardened beneath my touch and then sliding lower to her hips and behind her back to pull her closer to me as my mouth found one of the delicious mounds.

"Mmmm, Cade," she moaned as my erection pressed into her soft swells. "I miss you, too."

"I hate it when we fight," I said softly, my mouth moving up the skin of her chest and collarbones up her neck until I found her mouth. "Bloody hate it."

"The distance makes it worse, but making up is nice."

Her fingers pulled my head closer as we finally started to kiss those deep, soul-searing kisses that said we couldn't get enough... that we were starving for each other. It amazed me how it never lessened and I thrilled each and every time her little tongue sought mine out and started the passionate dance I loved. I sucked her lower lip into my mouth just to give us both a breath before I took it in wild abandon once again and turned to press her into the mattress with my body.

Brook's knees came up around my hips and I could feel the moistness of her calling my body home. It was easy and perfect as I slid so effortlessly into her, sinking and falling as I lost myself in the woman I loved more than anything. I loved her beyond the pains and glory of fame; beyond everything real or surreal that was a part of our messed up, blessed, and cursed lives. I loved her beyond anything. The love was strong enough to survive anything.

Chapter 17
Another Best Kiss

Brooklyn

UGH. NOT THIS SHIT AGAIN...

"Brook, you know you're going to win again, so suck it up already." Jeanne's voice droned over the phone. My stomach turned at the thought. It was bad enough to have to attend to present the clip of *Don't Forget to Remember Me*, but the kiss...would this shit ever end? The award shows were months behind release, and the releases were a year behind production. We'd just wrapped *A Love Like This*, but the focus of this year's award shows was on the second film.

"Can't they rig it so we won't win? I'm so over these things."

"I thought you liked the glitz of this job."

"It's wearing off." I was tired of the press chasing me, and I'd just had an incident with Sheldon Richards two days ago when he'd asked to meet me to discuss a possible role in an upcoming film he was producing. It was a joke. I should have taken Cade's concern seriously. After his visit, I took more notice of how Sheldon treated the women on the set. Not only in the cast, but also the production staff. It was obvious Cade wasn't just jealous. The man was nothing more than a skirt chaser who wouldn't take no for an answer. He'd made a big effort to get me in bed on set, but I'd kept my distance and holed up in my room.

Now, back in L.A., our film done; he hit on me. Huge. My face flushed with heat, and my heart pounded just thinking about it. Not because of Sheldon, but because of Cade. It seemed innocent enough, and he'd been nothing but nice to me during filming. Despite that, I was panicking. Cade and I were closer than ever, and I shouldn't have brushed off his warning about that asshole.

I hadn't told Cade because all it would do was cause him to worry and he'd probably find Sheldon and cause a scene. I felt stupid for even going, and nothing happened. Cade would be leaving on another job soon, and the last thing I wanted was to upset him. I wanted to enjoy the time we had left. We promised not to have secrets, but Sheldon Richards was insignificant to me, and my life with Cade. The fingers of my right hand fiddled with the engagement ring on my left.

We were settling into the new house, and making appearances here and there around Hollywood and L.A. The appearances were nothing too over-the-top; just out for tacos, to the grocery store, or driving to my mom's house. Our relationship wasn't official yet, and we found that letting the press see us together did little to dispel their interest. Cade thought if we just came out with it, they'd back off... that wasn't the case. Now they were stacked five deep at the entrance to the house. We'd started staying home more and more as it got worse.

"Look at the bright side; you'll get to show up with Cade." Jeanne broke me out of my thoughts. "That will make him happy."

I sighed and rolled over on my stomach and stared into the big brown eyes of our new puppy, Lucky. He was a mutt we'd gotten from a shelter when my mom refused to let me take Molly. He was adorable as he looked at me apologetically as if he understood exactly how I felt. I reached out to scratch his silky black head and his eyes started to droop immediately. He had taken ownership of both of our hearts at first sight and was perched in his place of seniority on my pillow.

"I know," I retorted sulkily. Cade would be happy, but my life had been almost normal the past couple of weeks. I was hanging out with my brother and spending time with my parents. I'd forgotten how much I'd missed it. Not that I didn't miss Cade. I did. It was fucking ridiculous.

"The official "coming out" was supposed to be the premiere of the third film. I'm still not sure about this." I was feeling uneasy. Unsure if I'd be able to look Cade in the face and hide the incident with Sheldon.

"Get your game face on. It's almost over."

"The hell it is. I've got another *eighteen months* of this crap if we keep getting more of these dumb nominations."

"Ugh!" Jeanne protested. "I'm sorry I do my job so well. You're welcome," she teased, the amusement trickling in with every syllable.

"Ha ha. You're hilarious. If I didn't love you so much, I'd rip your hair out."

"I can't take all the credit. These films blew up because of you and Cade."

"Yeah; it had nothing at all to do with the plot or the big studio money behind the promotion. Not a bit," I mocked. "It was filming this movie; I loved. I should have listened to Cade when he told me two years ago fame wouldn't be what I expected."

"Aw, honey, just take it one day at a time. The stylist has three outfits for you to choose from and they'll be there tomorrow around noon and Mickey's coming. I've made it as painless as I possibly can."

"Oh, boy. Mickey's coming? Can't wait to see Cade's reaction!"

"I thought you loved Mickey?"

Lucky whined and crawled onto my lap. I lifted him up and kissed his sweet face three times.

"I do, but he loves *Cade*. Doesn't he, Lucky?" I asked my sleeping puppy.

"What about the red carpet?"

"What about it?" She couldn't have missed the disgust in my voice.

"Brook," she said sternly.

I cringed. I knew we'd agreed to walk the carpet... finally giving the fans what they'd been waiting to see, but it went against everything I believed or wanted. Even if Cade and I didn't confirm our relationship for sure, speculation was everywhere. At first he'd been elated, but now he acknowledged it only made the stalking worse. There were women who hated me just because he was with me, and I loathed dealing with them. No matter how good I'd gotten at hiding how much it affected me, it still stung more than I wanted to admit. And worse; I hated how it worried Cade.

"Can't we just sneak in right after the awards begin, and then leave after we present the clip?"

"Uh...*no*. Best Actor is the last award, and what are the chances your boy won't win?"

Jesus. I knew she was right. I rolled over on my back taking Lucky with me. He snuggled onto my chest. I let out a deep sigh, trying to concentrate on the soft golden glow reflected through the closed blinds and the shadows being cast on the ceiling.

"None, what-so-ever," I admitted. "The hormones in the room are always enough to make me gag... and the screaming... make it fucking stop."

"The screaming is for you, too."

"Humph!" I scoffed. "Marginally, maybe. I see some of the same faces at these things, and I wonder if they have a life beyond worshiping Cade? I mean, seriously?"

"You aren't jealous, are you?"

I laughed. "No. It's annoying, that's all. Some of them are great, but others, just... Ugh!"

"Have you and Cade worked out what you'll do about coming and going?"

"We're gonna figure it out when he gets here." Cade was flying in from a short visit to his parents in London, mostly, in effort to divert attention of the press, and allow me to come and go from the house undetected for a while. It was technically his house, but they were on watch for any appearance from me. No doubt that was the money-shot; absolute proof Cade and I were together.

"Why don't I believe that?"

"We have to practice. I mean, in case we win." I chuckled softly, and Jeanne's face showed her amusement.

"Yeah, sure you do. When does Cade get in?"

"He texted he was on the ground, so any time now. I'm sure he's tired, and probably starving." My voice softened and my heart sped up. Just a few minutes now...

"Hmm, yes. At least you have twenty-four hours to um... ah, rest up." Jeanne laughed as she headed for the door.

"Right. We'll do loads of resting." I laughed along with her. "I'll call you tomorrow."

Caden

MY STOMACH WAS FULL, Lucky was sleeping beside the bed, and my girl was draped over me. I was lying on my back in the middle of our new bed, Brook's naked body felt like silk against my skin, and her head rested just below my rib cage, her arm flung over me. I lazily stroked her long hair down her back.

"Hard to believe it's been a year since you cut your hair. It's almost as long as it was when we met."

"Mmmm… don't remind me. Ugh. That first separation was a bitch. I missed the crap out of you. I guess some things will never change."

I smiled into the darkness. "A lot of things won't, babe. I miss you, too. Even though we have the house, it still feels like a long-distance relationship because of the traveling."

"I know," she said softly, her mouth tracing a line of soft kisses up my chest until her head was resting beneath my chin and I wrapped my arms more tightly around her slight form.

"I still think I should stop acting and devote myself to music and you." Brook would think I was joking, but I wasn't. I had enough money I'd never have to work again, and there were times, I didn't want to do even one more film. "I'd have a lot more time in L.A."

"Sounds good. Like heaven, but I'd still be traveling. And after a while, you'd have tours. What would change?"

She was right.

"Did Denise give you the line-up for tomorrow night?"

"Not really. I only know that they want us to walk the carpet together. At last." Pinnacle had vacillated between the MTV Awards and the premiere, but they probably realize trying to hide our relationship was a lost cause at this point. My chest lifted beneath her as I breathed in. Her scent surrounded me, and my heart tightened. I was finally at peace with the situation because everyone knew, and that was the way I liked it. Little by little, we were confirming it. Her presence at the premiere of my last film left

little doubt every news outlet and gossip rag blew up with speculation.

It was unbelievable that some of the fans were saying Brook was with me for PR reasons. It was hilarious, in a twisted sort of way. If she came with me, they said it was PR and she was trying to take emphasis away from my co-stars, and if she stayed away, she wasn't supporting me. Damned if she did, and damned if she didn't. Finally, I had to agree with her. Fuck them all. I knew the reasons and I knew she loved me; *more* than loved me to put up with all the bloody bullshit.

My fingers drifted down her arm to her left hand, and found her engagement ring; her *secret* engagement ring. I moved it back and forth on her finger, well aware that she wore it whenever she was alone, and or just with me. I longed for the day it would she would wear it constantly.

"Someday soon, babe" she murmured softly, and I smiled again. She was reading my mind.

"Not soon enough for me, Brook."

"You've always been impatient."

"Oh, sure; because three years isn't long enough to wait or hide my feelings. Since the day we met, I was totally over the moon for you."

"I've always loved you, too."

"I know." Warmth spread inside my heart at her teasing words.

Brook raised her head and rested her chin on my chest, her eyes sparkling in the darkness. "Remember the first time we made love in L.A.?" Her fingers traced little figure eights in the hair on my chest. It was something that had become a habit of hers whenever we talked in bed and I loved it.

"Of course. Two years ago. After the first movie awards; when you attended with David." I wasn't sure if the burning in my gut was resilient jealousy or just that the memory of it was still so real.

"Mmm... but that whole weekend was heaven. Remember the pool?"

"Of course. I remember it all. I replay it all in my head when we're apart. So many things remind me of you."

"You're such a sap." She was teasing as her fingers found my jaw and skittered along the stubbly skin. "I love the stubble. So sexy."

"You've distracted me long enough." I placed a soft kiss on her mouth, and reluctantly pulled back. I would be exhausted if I didn't get some sleep, but we had to discuss the kiss. "What do you want to do tomorrow night?"

"I don't know. Skip it?" Her voice was amused, but I knew she meant it.

"I think we should just give them what they want to see."

"Don't you mean what you'd like them to see?"

"Yes, exactly. It's no secret anymore, anyway. I just want to kiss you like it's us, and not an act. I think we should just do it. Forget that millions of people are watching and go for it, full on. Let them know it's not a one-off. I'm tired of denying each other, because that's what it comes down to."

Brook was silent and I could practically feel her conflict. She drew in a deep breath.

"I know you don't want to, babe. It's okay."

She met my eyes and shook her head. "Cade, it's not that. But it's one piece of you that is mine. It's so intimate... I guess, I just don't want to share everything. Something has to be ours."

When she put it that way, my heart melted. Hearing that it wasn't just the momentum of her career or studio regulations that made her want to keep things quite, resonated. I nodded, fully understanding. "Every piece of me is yours."

"You know what I mean. The whole stinking world thinks they know you, and so many try to tear what we have apart; I just... I don't want to give them more ammunition. This part of us is private, and I like it that way. I'm scared if we come out with it, something will happen."

I rolled her over quickly and she gasped in surprise as I loomed over her. My fingers were eager for her flesh, my mouth hungry for her mouth as I explored her softly. Her hands drifted gently down my back before sliding up and into the hair at the base of my neck. My dick hardened and swelled as the delicious pulse began, but my heart was also aching.

I let my nose trace along her jaw, and she moaned softly, quietly echoing my own need, her sweet breath washing over my face and calling my mouth to hers.

"Nothing will happen," I whispered against her mouth. "I hate being away from you."

She shifted underneath me, and her hands tightened in my hair; pulling my mouth to hers as we kissed deeply, our tongues moving together slowly, slowly savoring the magic that was us. My hands cupped her face as our kisses grew passionate and my body pushed into hers. No matter how many times I made love to this woman, it would never be enough. I marveled at the magnitude of the thought.

"Cade." The word was reverent, her voice breaking slightly between her panting breaths. "You feel so good."

"I swear, I do *not* want to do this anymore." I buried my face in the curve of her neck, my elbows under her arms and my hands wrapped around the top of her head, cradling, my thumbs brushing across her cheekbones. Even as our bodies wrapped around each other, our legs entwined, emerged as I was in her, it wasn't enough.

"You don't?" Her question was wary, even with the passion between us, pushing deeper, partly because I needed to, and partly to punctuate my meaning. I studied her face as her mouth fell open, her hair splayed out beneath her head. I slowed my strokes and pulled back to look into her eyes. I knew she felt the same pain but seldom voiced it. She was stronger, more able to keep it from showing to the world than I.

"I'm tired of not having you with me, of leaving each other. I'm sick of lying in interviews."

"We don't lie." Her eyes filled with understanding and began to shimmer with unshed tears. Even as we continued to make love, and she clawed at my back and ass, begging me to ease the one ache we created in each other, that always hung over us.

"We don't tell the truth, either."

"Just kiss me. Touch me. Cade, we're together. The moment is perfect."

She was right. No matter what we had to give the world, this closeness we felt, the amazing and overwhelming love... even the aching sadness when we were apart was something we gave only to each other. It didn't matter if anyone else knew, or understood. It would *never matter* what anyone else wanted or expected.

Brook cried into me; her soft moans echoing my own, our bodies fell apart. Afterward we lay together, neither willing to separate, our hands still worshiping, our mouths still clinging desperately together, I realized it was always so bloody perfect, and it always would be.

Chapter 18
World On Fire

Brooklyn

"CADE! PLEASE!"

"Please, what? What the fuck do you expect from me? I trusted you!" He stormed at me. I'd never seen him so upset. His face twisted as he rushed around the house. Lucky cowered on the sofa.

My heart exploded in pain. "I expect you to listen! Just listen!"

"No! I don't want to listen! They have more than fifty pictures of the two of you making out? I have to see it when the whole fucking world sees it, Brook! You did this to us! *You*! Now we both have to live with it! I don't want to hear the details! I'm already in bloody hell!"

My heart felt like it was about to explode as I watched the man I loved break. Tears glistened in his eyes as his jaw jutted out as he rushed around throwing his guitar in its case, and gathering clothes from the floor and a couple of drawers.

"Oh, fuck it!" He threw the clothes down and headed for the door to our house; his phone now lying shattered into a million pieces after he'd flung it against the wall a few minutes before. It was the only time I'd ever seen him do anything violent.

I rushed after him and wrapped my arms around him, locking my fingers together as I cried into his back. He stopped; unmoving. His chest was heaving so much it was almost enough to lift me off of the ground. I felt sick.

"Cade, stop! It's not what you think. You know those bastards take a hundred pictures in three seconds! *Please!* I'm begging you! Let me explain. It's not what you think. Don't go. I love you."

"Don't you dare say that to me right now!" His back stiffened in front of me.

He didn't move, but I could feel the anger and pain writhing inside him; threatening to explode. "Please," I cried softly against his shoulder. "Don't leave me. Please, I just... I just need you to listen." My own body was shaking so violently I thought I'd break.

"I... *can't!*" The words wrung from him. "All I can hear is Denise telling me that the love of my life was photographed making out with that bastard! Sheldon Richards? How could you do that to me?" He was shaking with his sobs. "Did you... Did you let him fuck you the entire time you were filming together?" The words were laden with hurt and disgust.

I breathed him in, memorizing his scent, feeling him against me as I held on to him for dear life. I was dying. "No! It's not like that! I'm sorry. I shouldn't have met up with him, but it's not what you think. Pl... Please let me explain," I begged. I'd beg and plead until my knees bled if I had to. "Oh, God. Please, Cade."

His voice was soft and thick with emotion when he spoke, the back of his hand wiping at tears on his face. My heart was breaking as much as his.

"I *can't think!* All I can do is feel. And it hurts like a son-of-a-bitch! I can't even fucking breathe. I gotta get out of here. Let go of me, Brook."

I couldn't. My arms held him tighter, the fingers on both hands turning white as they clenched together.

"*Brooklyn*, let. *GO!*"

"I can't!" I screamed out my misery. I felt the earth opening up and swallowing me whole. "I'll never let go."

Cade's guitar dropped on the marble floor with a clang of strings and thud from the case, as his long fingers closed around my wrists.

"You already did!" he said through clenched teeth. "You did it when you let the motherfucker touch you! You ripped my bloody heart out!" His fingers prying mine apart seconds before he broke free, and strode quickly out the door; slamming with a loud bang behind him.

I fell to the floor in a sobbing heap, praying I would die... so the pain would stop.

*****

Cade, please let me explain. I'm begging you.

He ignored text after text. He wouldn't answer when I called. Time dragged, and I wanted to die. It was like he didn't exist; except in my mind.

You know I'd never cheat. Please.
I'll never do another movie with him again. I won't.
It's not worth it.
Cade, PLEASE CALL ME! PLEASE. I love you, so much!

This is killing me!

After a hundred and fifty unanswered text messages, I was a sobbing, inconsolable mess. I didn't even know if he'd replaced his phone. My mother and manager came over, picked me up off the floor, and hauled me into bed.

"Pick her up," someone said, and two sets of hands began grabbing at me.

"Leave me alone!" I shouted, crying. "Just… leave me alone!"

"Brooklyn, we're here to help you."

I heard my mother's muffled words as if I was underwater. My head throbbed, my eyes were swollen shut, and there was so much snot running down my throat I started gagging. I gagged until I crawled to the edge of the bed and heaved the contents of my stomach onto the floor. The vomit got in my hair and on my face on the way out. I didn't care if I lived or died. Lucky whined from somewhere behind me.

Cade was gone. He left me, and I'd lost him. I coughed and gagged on more mucus, the tears still seeping from my tightly clenched eyes. It was like a black hole sucking me in, and I was helpless to stop it.

"Oh, Jesus!" Jeanne said.

My mother was next to me pulling my shirt over my head and using it to wipe off my face.

I turned from her, and curled into a ball; the pain inside threatening to kill me. "No one can help me, except Cade!" I sobbed. "Oh, God!" My body racked and heaved as I clawed at the bed covers, still filled with the scent of us, and of him. "I hate myself!"

I'd find out later Jeanne had called my mother while I was running through the house with my heart in my throat as I searched for Cade; praying I'd get to him, to explain before anyone else called him, but I was too late. He was frozen, crying, and broken when I'd found him in our bedroom. At the sight of me he'd gotten up and immediately started throwing shit into a bag.

"What am I going to do? He won't talk to me!" I gasped for breath between sobs, finally sucking in enough air to scream. Maybe if I screamed loud enough, the pain would stop. *What had I done?* What price would I pay for five fucking minutes that meant nothing? The press, the haters, all of it had been worth it because I had Cade. This shit storm would only get worse, but it didn't matter. Only Cade mattered.

"Jeanne, can you call Denise?" my mother asked. "Maybe Cade called her."

"I've spoken with her. Cade isn't taking any calls. We don't know where he is. She said... he sobbed like a baby when she told him. I can't believe this is happening." She sighed heavily and sat on the bed opposite my mom. I barely registered any of it; the pain in my heart ate me alive. I just wanted to be alone.

I listened to them talk as my sobs lessened. I was exhausted. I didn't know how much time had passed, but I must have been crying for hours. My eyes were sore and beginning to get heavy. I'd lost him. It was unbelievable. I couldn't wrap my head around it and my heart refused to accept it.

My mother stroked back my tangled hair, despite the puke still clinging to it. "Brook, you should take a long bath in the whirlpool, and wash your hair. You'll feel better."

How could she think anything would make me feel better? My eyes slammed shut again as another wave of pain seized my chest. We made love in the tub the night we moved in. How many times had he whispered how much he adored me in the candlelight? The thought was more than I could bear. How could I have let this happen? Nothing meant more to me than him. I was so fucking stupid! I'd never wanted to die before, but I did now. Every breath felt like a red-hot knife slicing through my soul.

Jeanne's phone rang and my heart jolted; hope it was Cade making me pause.

"Hello?" she answered. "What? No! I don't think we should address it. It's best not to say anything." I sat up and watched Jeanne get up from the bed and pace around the room, agitated. "That would be like professional suicide. Can't he just handle it privately?" Jeanne ran a hand through her short hair and met my eyes. "Okay. I'll advise my client. Just keep him the hell away from her. No phone calls, nothing! If I have to, I'll have Joel slap him with a restraining order."

She hung up the phone and shot me an angry glance. "Want to tell me what the *hell* you were thinking, Brook?" she railed at me. "We're in a world of hurt right now! Sheldon Richards is threatening to give a statement, which will only makes this nightmare more real in the eyes of the public. Goddamn it!"

"I *wasn't* thinking!" I yelled back, wanting to share the pain. "He called and wanted to talk. He said it was about a movie he was producing, and he wanted to discuss it." I shook my head and ran my hand through my sticky hair. Normally, it would have grossed me out, but I fucking deserved it.

"In a park? You do that in a meeting with your agents and managers in tow!"

"I *know!*" I reached for a tissue, loudly blowing my nose. Resentment rose up inside me. I didn't want to talk about this with anyone but Cade. "It was stupid, but I seriously thought he was serious about a movie role."

"Baby, what happened?" my mother asked. Her eyes were sad, but also disapproving. I glanced between her and Jeanne, who was now standing with her arms folded across her chest.

"It doesn't matter! All that matters is that I get Cade to listen to me! I just need the two of you to trust me. Why does the whole world assume the fucking worst about me? Even you two!"

I scrambled off the bed and grabbed my phone again, furiously typing out a text, my face crumpling.

Cade, please. I can explain if you'll give me a chance. I LOVE you so fucking much! You know me. You know I'd never hurt you!

"What is Cade going to see when those pictures break, Brook?" Jeanne asked harshly.

I threw the phone down and turned furiously toward her. "He's going to see that asshole plastering me up against a tree and trying to kiss me in my fucking car!" I screamed at her and then fisted both hands in my hair, pulling hard. If only the physical pain could end the ache in my chest.

"What was he doing in your car?" she asked accusingly.

"Jeanne, is this necessary?" my mother asked

"Sorry, Diane, but yes, it's necessary. I'm the one who has to clean up this mess, so let me do my goddamned job!" She turned back to me. "*What* was he doing in your car?"

"When I got there, he didn't have a ride! He said he got in a fight with his girlfriend and she left him there."

"His girlfriend? Sheldon Richards doesn't have a girlfriend. He has a harem." Jeanne's eyebrow shot up. "How convenient."

"Yeah," I muttered, and walked to the window. "That's what Cade said."

"Then why didn't you listen?"

"I told you! Sheldon said it was about a film. He was fine on set. I had no reason to expect this."

"When did this happen?"

"Three days ago."

"Before the awards. And you didn't tell Cade? If it was so innocent, why not?"

I turned on my heel away from her. "No. I didn't tell him." It was a simple statement and I'd be damned if I was going to explain. I didn't want to hurt him over something that meant nothing. I thought I'd handled it. I'd pushed him away, kneed him in the balls and left him there. If there were pictures of the kiss, then there had to be pictures of the rest, too.

"Why?"

"Look, I'm fucking dying right now and Cade is the only person I want to talk to about this."

"It's a little late, Brook," Jeanne spat out.

"No, it isn't." My chin jutted out in defiance. We love each other to the point of pain; he'd eventually listen. I had to believe that or I'd die on the spot. I knew how badly he was hurting because of the night I'd seen Wendy in his apartment wrapped in a blanket. I grabbed my phone again, willing the blank screen to light up with his response. Its silence caused my fragile heart to shatter again.

"I hope you're right, but he just said he didn't understand cheating in a public interview. Do you really think he'll listen? If he forgives you, it will hurt him. Everyone will call him a pussy, and stupid unless he leaves you flat on your ass."

"I didn't cheat, Jeanne!"

"It won't matter! You know how it works, Brook! The paps will use anything they can to sell a picture, and the rags don't give a damn if they print the truth. All they care about is selling copies and racking up clicks online. You'll both be labeled. We're screwed. If Cade is smart, he'll lay low for a while and let the heat fall on you. Sorry, but that's the truth. If he were my client, that's what I'd advise."

I closed my eyes as more tears welled, a sob caught in my throat and I pressed the heel of my hand to my eyes. "He can stay away from me, but Jesus, God... I need him to listen."

Caden

I WASN'T SURE WHAT day it was. I wasn't sure how long I'd been here in this dump, how many of Brook's calls I'd ignored, or how much scotch I'd consumed. Somehow, Davina heard I'd taken off and called offering me her house while she was away on holiday. It seemed a good decoy; the press would never look for me there, but if I were discovered, it would only trade one scandal for another. And, it would hurt Brook.

What a joke! I'd never have peace again and I wasn't thinking about those fucking photographers. What did I care if I hurt her? She destroyed me. The thing about cheating is that it can never be undone. It would always be there, hanging between us, ripping my guts out... *as long as we both shall live.*

I laughed bitterly, through the errant tear that rolled down my cheek. I wiped at it with the back of the hand holding the glass of scotch. How quickly the meaning behind those words changed. Even drowning in alcohol, I was still miserable. I threw the glass at the wall, grabbed the bottle by the neck and stumbled to my feet. I wasn't angry anymore. I was dead inside. Now if only the pain would stop...

My phone rang for the ten-thousandth time in an hour, but I couldn't bring myself to look at the screen. It was new because my other one lay in pieces on the floor of my house. As it rang, I chastised myself. I shouldn't have gotten it. It made me sick how much I wanted to talk to her; like the sound of her voice would somehow fix everything, and I'd wake up and to find it was just a bad dream.

I couldn't show the world how broken I was; I couldn't show Brook the damage she'd done. I had no clue how I managed to make it out of the house and through the pack of press at our gate, without completely losing it.

My heart was pounding so hard it made the blood thunder in my ears, and I felt like I was drowning. I was drowning, only now, when no one could hear me, I let myself scream and pray the sickening thumping in my chest would stop.

Thank God I found this motel in the middle of nowhere where the owner didn't know who I was. He was old and out of touch with Hollywood and front-page news. I threw down a wad of cash and told him I'd take every room he had, and all the others as the guests left. I hoped I'd get it together before I had to promote my movie, but as days passed, it wasn't looking good. I'd anticipated its release for so long; now I dreaded it with everything I had. The timing couldn't be worse. I was just thankful it wasn't one of the Remembrance movies on deck to promote. I could put on a stone face and muddle it through, but not if she were close.

They say that your life passes before your eyes right before you die... well, every moment of our relationship was flashing in fast forward, then slow motion misery as I relived each precious and heartbreaking second. When I didn't think she'd ever be truly mine, when we had to sneak and hide to find time together, when we were half a world apart for months on end and the rags planted nasty rumors designed to sell copies... I never thought this would happen. I never for once considered she didn't love me. But now everything I believed about Brook, about myself, and about how nothing could touch us, lay in shambles because I'd seen it with my own eyes.

How could she do that? I thought we were solid, unbreakable: un-bloody-touchable. A broken sob rose up in my throat. I fell on the bed and curled into myself, crying harder than I'd ever cried. The bottle fell from my fingers, the liquid soaking the covers and into my jeans as it seeped out. I let it all out in a torrent of pain; my body shaking violently. I slapped at my head hard; over and over again, trying to displace the pain in my chest. I begged God for death; for my life to rewind so I could stop that bastard from touching her.

The pictures were everywhere now. In magazines, on the TV gossip shows, online. They flashed behind my closed lids in merciless torture. I wasn't strong enough not to find them online after I'd thrown the TV on the floor in a crash of broken heap when I'd heard the first mention of it. I couldn't bear to break my phone again. I wanted to. But it's like wanting to commit suicide and not being brave enough. I wasn't strong enough to destroy the connection completely. I justified it by telling myself that it was so my family or Denise could reach me. But the hell it was... it was because I needed to know Brook was trying to get me back.

The phone stopped then rang again immediately: again and again it raged at me until I couldn't take it anymore. Reluctantly, I dragged myself off the bed and over to where it lay on the carpet by the wall. The screen mocked me with Denise's name. My heart fell with a sickening thud to my stomach, but I grabbed the phone and slid down the wall until I was a crumpled heap on the floor.

"Yeah?"

"Cade?" she asked.

My voice was hoarse and thick; my throat raw. "Yes."

"Honey, are you okay?"

Tears pushed from my closed eyes. "Do you *think* I'm bloody okay?"

"A lot of people are worried about you. Your family is going crazy wondering where you are."

"I need to be alone. I can't be around anyone right now." I sucked in my breath. "Just... tell them I'm fine." Was she going to mention Brook? I hated that part of myself that still needed to know she was okay.

"I have." I could hear the hesitation in her voice and sat up in panic.

"Did Brook hurt herself?" I asked anxiously. Despite everything, I couldn't bear anything to happen to her. Even if I never saw her again, I'd accepted that I'd love her forever no matter what she'd done. I couldn't fight that part of me that she'd become.

"No, other than refusing to eat and crying until she pukes. Cade, I need to tell you something."

I relaxed to a sitting position against the wall, both of my knees drawn up. "I don't want to know anything else. I'm going through enough hell, Denise." My nose was running and I wiped it against my sleeve. I didn't fucking care.

"You need to know this. I don't want you to be blindsided. Brook said she left a message about it, but I know you haven't heard it or you would have stopped her."

"No, I haven't listened to any messages." But it was all I could do to resist.

"She had Jeanne call People Magazine and issue a statement."

"What?" I yelled, sitting up away from the wall. "Why in bloody hell would she do that now?"

"Because Sheldon was going to talk. But mostly, because you wouldn't take her calls and she's more desperate than I think I've ever seen anyone. She loves you, Cade."

I needed those words and the comfort they were capable of, but I wasn't sure I believed them. "If she loved me she wouldn't humiliate me publicly," I huffed in disgust. "Or screw that stupid fuck."

"You know she didn't screw him." Denise's voice was matter-of-fact and a little reprimanding.

"I don't know shit!" I tried to laugh, but it came out sounding more like a sob. And hating myself, I asked the question. "What'd she say?"

"That she's sorry that she hurt the person she loved more than anyone else. You. She finally said she loved you to the world, Cade."

"Now? After she fucked me over?" I asked angrily, welcoming the return of the fury. It felt better than the pain. "If Brook really loved me, none of this would be happening. It's probably just Jeanne on damage control."

"No, it isn't. Jeanne and I were both at the house telling her not to do it. It's career suicide. We told her to ignore it and it would die down eventually. But, you know Brook. She's stubborn, and she was desperate to get through to you. She knew if she made a public statement, you'd hear it at some point. And being public was what you wanted most."

I inhaled deeply and pressed the heel of my hand to my eyes.

"Bloody hell! She'll be butchered by haters. They'll eat her alive for admitting to shagging that bastard the entire time."

"Cade!" Denise hollered back. "She said it was barely a kiss he forced on her, and then she kneed him in the nuts. I believe her."

I should have laughed, but I felt defeated. "Even if that's true, she may as well have slept with him. How many times does it have to be proven? People don't give a rat's ass about the truth," I said tiredly. "They want a story and the dirtier, the better. It doesn't matter who gets hurt in the process. And besides, it's Sheldon Richard's reputation to plow through one woman after another. Jeanne shouldn't have let her do a film with him in the first place. She should be nowhere near him."

I didn't know what I believed. Why did I care how the world saw someone who cheated on me? My fingers splayed across the front of my shirt as my chest tightened again. I fucking hated my weakness.

"The only opinion Brook cares about is yours. We have to do some damage control of our own, Cade. *Now*." Why was she talking about business when all I could think about was that Brook and I were done?

I shook my head with a wry grimace. "I don't care about anything right now, Denise. Everyone and everything can go straight to hell! I don't give a shit if I never work again."

"Stop it!" she shouted. "I won't let you do something you'll regret. I think Brook should move out of the house, but we can let her know it's just for show right now."

"Maybe I don't want it to be for show."

"You mean... you'd actually leave her?" she asked incredulously.

"Look, I don't know what the fuck I'm doing! I've just been gutted from the neck down. I never thought Brook could do anything like this."

"You need to talk to her before you judge her. Jeanne and I have been hard enough on her. She's young and impressionable. People make mistakes."

I swallowed at the lump in my throat. "I saw the photos."

"Cade, *why?*"

"Because I'm a stupid asshole that's glutton for punishment! Why do you think? Because they'll be around for fucking *ever* and I'll have to deal with them at some point. I might as well get it over with, for Christ's sake!"

I ran a hand through my hair and went into the bathroom intending to splash cold water on my face. I looked like hell. My eyes were red-rimmed and the lower half of my face was covered in fur. My hair was a dirty mess.

"I gotta go," I muttered into the phone.

"Should I tell Brook to move out?"

"No, I'll tell her." I hung up the phone before giving Denise a chance to answer, set it down on the vanity, and turned back to the running water. I splashed more on my face, then turned on the shower and peeled off my dirty T-shirt. It was one Brook had been photographed in ten times. I sucked in a painful breath and hesitated as the internal struggle with what to do came to a head. I grabbed the phone and punched out a text before I could stop myself.

I need you to move out of my house. And get rid of that fucking car. I'll send someone for Lucky.

I couldn't bring myself to ease her pain when I was still dying inside. Even though I wanted to hate her, I knew I still loved her or I wouldn't want to stop breathing. I didn't know what the whole truth was and I wasn't sure I wanted to drag myself through finding out. I wasn't sure if I was strong enough to face her and I wasn't big enough to let her stop suffering when I was in such hell. Just when I stepped in the shower, my phone dinged as a new text came in. I stepped out to glance at the screen, my heart rammed into my ribs when I saw her name. Would she still plead with me, or would she finally let go?

> ***Okay, if that's what you want.***
> ***But I'll love you until I die… it will always be you.***

I turned back into the shower with clenched fists as I leaned on the wall, fresh tears forcing out from under my closed lids. Everything hurt. I hated my weakness, but I loved her. I needed to believe those words because they defined the reason for my very existence. I wanted them to be true because even though my head told me to, my heart wasn't ready to walk away from her completely.

Brooklyn

I reread Cade's messages ten times.

> *I need space, Brook. I'm a mess.*
> ***I'm sorry, Cade. Just let me explain. I'm begging you.***
> *I'm not ready to hear it & can't promise I ever will be.*
> *If I want to talk, I'll call.*

I stared in disbelief at my phone, the words starting to blur, my head aching and my eyes so tired. Two weeks. It had been two weeks since he'd sent the last text and God, it killed me but I'd left him alone.

I moved out like he'd asked and I donated the car to charity, clinging to the hope that if he wanted the car gone it meant there was a chance. I went to the gym to train for my next movie. My dad said it would help take my mind off of Cade and make me feel better to get back in the swing of things. It didn't, and I didn't.

I told the studio to put my next film on hold indefinitely. If they sued me, they sued me. I was doing everything in my power to show Cade he was the only thing that mattered. I missed him like I never had before because then I was sure he'd come back to me. This time, he might not.

I tried not to listen to the bullshit news or surf online, but I needed to find out as much as I could, even though most of it was pure speculation and lies. Cade's fans hated me more now than ever, because now they thought they were justified... Even I hated me. Jeanne said he wasn't in L. A. but that was all Denise had shared with her. I wondered if he'd gone back to London and my heart fell at the thought. How would I ever face his family again? They'd hate me now and who could blame them? I prayed they didn't think I'd been cavorting with that bastard the whole time I was working with him. I spent a lot of time with them so I prayed they'd know better.

No one knew where Cade was, or at least, they weren't talking. I did my best to breathe in and out every day, to get out of bed, to go through the motions and not cry every single second that I didn't hear from him. I tried not to scream, "Just leave me alone!" at the top of my lungs whenever anyone asked how they could help me. No one could help me, except Cade. Didn't they all know that?

The seconds felt like years; each one eating away another small piece of me that I'd never get back again. It all seemed so surreal, like a world where Cade and I weren't together just couldn't exist. I was alone and hardly coping.

The paparazzi were stalking me and camping outside my parent's house, so I had to get out of there. My brother barely spoke to me as he dumped me in the trunk of a rental car so that he could take me to Jennifer's without being followed. He was wearing a disguise and sunglasses, but in my mind I could see the disgust in his eyes when he looked at me. Nate and Cade had become fast friends; the brother neither of them had.

My lips were dry and cracked, and I tried to moisten them with my tongue. My eyes were swollen and felt bruised from rubbing and wiping away the endless tears.

So, I waited and prayed. I barely ate; my appetite vanished. I got up to turn on the Blu Ray before flopping back down on the bed. I ignored the sandwich my friend had placed on the nightstand and stared at the TV through the inky darkness. I never wanted to leave the room again.

The Future of Our Past had just come out on DVD and I watched it over and over every night until the copy I had started to skip. I was grasping at some small shred of peace... part of Cade... clinging to happier times when I hoped he loved me even though I had no right to want him. Yet, it was there; always there. We both felt it in every glance and the slightest touch. It screamed on the screen.

God, I need him. My heart seized. I loved him more than ever. He'd been so kind and helpful at the beginning of all this, so amazing, loving, and consuming.

I railed at myself. This was my own fault because I didn't tell him the night it happened. That stupid meeting was the only secret I ever kept from him, besides those days when I loved him but couldn't tell him because of David.

"Please, he has to forgive me," I cried into my pillow. My chest was hollow, yet tight. I couldn't breathe. I fought sleep because I didn't think I deserved the solace it would afford. I deserved to suffer every cutting edge of every word Cade hurled at me; of the world's scorn and my own hatred of myself. But did I deserve to lose him? I couldn't lose him or I'd lose myself.

The credits started to roll and my burning eyes began to droop; my arms empty. The sharp, stabbing pain in my heart had reverted to a dull, ever-constant ache.

The phone I'd clung to for hours rang in my hand and I startled. It was Cade's ringtone but my brain registered it as just another nightmare where I'd say hello and he wouldn't be there or his voice would be saying *"I'm through with you, Brook. I don't love you anymore."*

"Oh, God!" I rolled over onto my stomach and cried and cried. "Caaaaaaddddddeee!" I screamed into the mattress as the last notes of the Ryan Cabrera song, *I will Remember You* faded and the screen turned black. I was so tired; barely able to hold my eyes open as I lay there torturing myself.

The phone rang again, but this time I pulled it up and looked at it. Cade. Cade. Cade. His name blinked at me over and over as if it were mocking me, daring me to see if he were really there. I scrambled into a sitting position and flipped the phone on.

"Cade?" I sniffled. Breathless; I waited for his words; words that would save or destroy me.

"Yeah, it's me. Are you alright?" He sounded as exhausted as I felt. His voice was lacking his usual exuberance for life.

My face crumpled and I shoved the heel of my hand against my

mouth to stifle a sob. "No. I'm huh -horrible." I gasped. "I'm barely...
breathing."

"Me, too." Sadness saturated his voice.

I wanted to crawl through the phone and straight into his arms,
but instead, I fell onto the bed, rolled onto my side and curled into a
ball as tears dripped endlessly from my eyes. I didn't want to cry, but
the damn tears wouldn't stop. I didn't want to make him feel worse,
but I had absolutely no control. "I'm sooorrrryyy! So soorrryyy. Plea...
please don't say.... Don't say we're over."

I could hear him crying softly on the other end of the line. I wanted
to hold him, to be held by him and for this fucking ache to go away.

"I don't know which end is up. I thought we were invincible. I can't
believe any of this is real."

"It isn't."

"Isn't it? Then why is it killing me?"

I couldn't stand the hurt in his voice. "It's all lies, Cade."

"I never could have imagined how much it would hurt seeing the
goddamned pictures of his mouth and hands all over you."

I gasped out loud. "I tried to tell you; it's not like it seems. Will you
let me explain?" I needed to get him in front of me. I needed to get my
arms around him and not let go until I could make him believe me. I
didn't care how I did it or if I had to beg forever.

He sniffed again. "I've been watching Twitter. I searched our
names. Someone told me to listen with my heart... and you to make
me believe."

I wiped at a tear and silently prayed. "I can, but only if you'll hear
me. Will you?"

"I don't have a choice, Brook. I can't function like this."

No matter how much I was hurting, I knew his was the ultimate suffering because he believed I betrayed him.

"Will you come to me?" I tried to keep my voice from breaking but it did anyway, tears were streaming from my eyes as I waited for his response. "I don't want to have this conversation on the phone."

"Yes. Tomorrow. Denise said you're staying with Jennifer."

My throat was tight and fresh tears started for completely different reasons. I sucked in my breath. "Yeah."

"I thought you'd be at your parent's."

"I was for a couple of days, but the press was camping outside. I had to get away from my family. Nate hates me, and my mom keeps asking me how I am when she can easily see what a mess I am. All I do is cry.

"I know. I shut my phone off and drank a gallon of scotch."

"Did it help?"

"Not at all."

"Did you talk to your parents?" I tried to stop the trembling in my hands as I waited for his answer.

"Not much. A few texts and one call to my Mom when I wanted to kill myself."

Tears squeezed out from my closed eyes as I started to cry hard, my shoulders shaking violently. It hurt so much.

"Jesus don't say that, Cade..."

"I did. Nothing has ever hurt this much."

"I know. I miss you."

"Me, too. I lost more than my girlfriend. My best friend... the best person I ever knew... went down in flames."

"I may be on fire, but I'm still with you. Always."

"Uhhggggg." He cleared his throat but I could still hear the tears in his voice. "I gotta go. We'll talk tomorrow."

"Okay." I didn't want to hang up and lose this connection. What if he changed his mind? I closed my eyes and knew I couldn't push. I had to trust him because that's what he deserved. "Thanks for calling. I love you."

"Bye, Brook."

My throat began to ache. He didn't say he loved me back.

Caden

I WAS NERVOUS, which was stupid. This was Brook, and I was sure that if I could get beyond all of this bloody bullshit and forgive her, she'd still be with me. The problem was, I wasn't sure I could live with it or if I could take the ridicule of Denise or my friends. The world was one thing, but those in my personal circle meant a lot to me. I'd spoken to Daniel, and he told me to walk away and never look back. I shook my head. He'd always been so fiercely protective of Brook before, and now he was looking out for me and me alone. He'd traveled all the way from London to come out into the middle of the desert to check on me and drag me back to civilization

My fingers ran through my hair. It was longer and I was thinner. I shaved because I didn't want Brook to think I was totally broken or I'd lost it. I already felt weak. Even though it appeared I had all the power; I was basically a slave to my love for her.

"Are you ready?" Nate asked. He agreed to bring me. Jeanne and Denise were being tailed everywhere they went.

"Yeah. How'd you get out today without those slimy bastards following you?" I asked.

"I'm staying at my dad's. Did Brook tell you the folks are breaking up?"

"No. I guess with everything going on, she forgot. Sorry, man. That's got to be touch. The timing sucks."

Nate shrugged. "It is what it is. They both seem okay. I had this rental for the past couple of weeks so I could take Brook if she needed to go anywhere without being followed. Are you guys breaking up?"

My throat tightened at his question. "I'm not sure what's going to happen. I hardly know... what I'm capable of. Not until I see her, and..." I let the words fall off with a slight shrug.

"I'm sorry, dude. Really very sorry you're dealing with this shit." His tone was disapproving and I gathered he wasn't happy with Brook. I didn't answer and glanced through the dark windows and pulled my sunglasses from the neck of my T-shirt before shoving them on. There weren't any paparazzi visible, but then you rarely saw those bastards when they lurked about.

"Best get on with it," I murmured before quickly opening the door to the black SUV. I hopped out quickly and hurried to the door. Jennifer opened it before I had a chance to ring the doorbell and held it open for me to enter.

"Hey, Cade."

"Hi." My eyes darted past her, into the living room, scanning for blue eyes and dark hair, but it was empty.

"How are you?"

"Been better. Where's is she?"

"In the spare room. She asked that you just go in. I'm going out for a while. Tell Brook to text me when you're finished. I want to give you complete privacy."

I nodded and ran a hand over my mouth and down my jaw, my eyes anxiously fixed on the door to Brook's room.

"I appreciate it, Jen. Thanks."

She hesitated, her hand on the door. "She's taking this hard."

I nodded again and looked at the floor before returning my gaze to her face. "I know. I saw pictures of her the two times she's been out," I admitted. I couldn't help but watch every move she made.

"It's obvious you still love her as much as she loves you."

"Obviously, I'm not able to shut it off like a faucet."

"You guys can make it through this." She hugged me. "You will, Cade."

"We'll see," I answered. I waited until she left and then knocked lightly on the door with the knuckles of my right hand.

"Cade?" Brook's voice was soft and close to the door. I closed my eyes and flattened my hand against the surface of the door. I could picture her with her forehead leaning against the wood, exactly opposite where my hand lay.

"Yes, Brook. It's me."

The door opened immediately and I stood face to face with her for the first time in weeks. Her eyes were bloodshot, hollow and dark. She looked gaunt. My heart hammered a million miles an hour as we stood there staring at her and hesitating like we were awkward strangers. I didn't know what to do with all the pain hanging between us. I swallowed at the lump in my throat, but it wouldn't move.

"Come in," she murmured, standing aside.

I walked past her and the air moved. I could feel her mentally reaching out, but fighting the same internal battle that I was. I wanted it all to disappear like it never happened; to take her in my arms and tell her it would all be okay. But, I couldn't. I didn't know if it would be.

She automatically reached for me then drew her hand back, uncertainty washing over her face as her eyes filled with tears. "Um, thanks for coming."

I sat on the foot of the bed. Jen's house was small and Brook hovered a few feet away, shifting her weight from one foot to the other. I could see she was worried and didn't know what to do. I inhaled as much air as my lungs would hold and let it out. "I'm listening."

She was in sweat shorts and one of my T-shirts. When she started pacing in front of me, running a hand through her hair, I could see how scared she was.

"I don't know where to start."

"Just... start."

She nodded and faced me, wiping at the soft tears rolling down her cheeks. "Sheldon called me when I was leaving the gym and said he needed to speak to me about a new movie he was producing. He said the studio wasn't sure they would let him direct it because he'd never done it before. He fed me some song and dance about how I could help convince them since we'd just come off a film together, and they were considering me for several films. He said he needed help."

"That's rubbish, but even if it were true, you didn't have to meet him for that," I stated simply. "Especially not at some obscure park in Beverly Hills."

"I know. He said he'd gotten in a fight with his girlfriend and she kicked him out of the car. He needed a ride." She shook her head and started to pace again. "I know it's ridiculous, but I didn't think much about it. I was out in my car already. I could give him a ride. No big deal."

My jaw tightened. "You knew he wanted you, and you knew what I said about his reputation on every fucking movie he ever worked on. How could you put yourself in that position?" I demanded. The skin of my face felt hot as it flushed. I hated that bloody bastard more than

I'd ever hated anyone and she knew it. I'd always thought he was after her. I could see it in the way he looked at her, but she'd always blown me off like I was insane for even thinking it. Now, she knew I was right.

"I was stupid, Cade. I don't have another explanation. I had no reason to doubt him. He'd always been nice and respectful."

"Because he knew I'd beat the hell out of him if he touched you, and for no other reason."

She was still pacing in front of me. "Maybe."

I should have, I thought miserably. "Go on."

"When I got there, he asked me to get out of the car to talk about the movie. It didn't seem like a big deal. When he came up behind me and pushed me against a tree, then held me there with his body. I didn't expect it. I got away within seconds. The one picture that looks like I'm holding him was really me pulling his arms away so I could move. It was so uncomfortable and, to be honest, I was stunned. When you look at those fucking pictures, you can see him looking over his shoulder at the photogs. I haven't figured out why he'd want to set me up like that."

"Because his career is in the toilet and the world will forget him in a week and a half, while you are a hot commodity right now, Brook!" I spat. "He'll go down in infamy for breaking us up!"

Her head dropped and she started crying again. "Not if we don't let him."

I stared at her and sighed deeply. "What about the kiss?"

"He was sorry, he said. He asked me to drive him home. I didn't want to hear it, especially, but it made sense. On the way, things got weird. I stopped and told him to get out of the car. He came at me then, Cade..." her voice broke, "if you've looked at those pictures you see how I was pulling away from him. He came at me and I tried to back away, but that car was small. I screamed at him at the top of my lungs and slapped him, but, of course, no pictures surfaced of that part of it. I got out of the car because he wouldn't. He came around, and then I kneed him in the groin and left." She fell to her knees in front of me sobbing. "I need you to believe me. Cade, *please*. Those pictures aren't what they seem."

I wanted to. Christ did I want to. "Is that all?"

She shook her head. "By then, I knew the paps were on us. They weren't even trying to hide anymore. I couldn't just sit there and let them click away! I took off, but that's not what hit the newsstands."

Air rushed from my lungs as I looked into Brook's crying face, the tears welling magnifying the blue color of her eyes as they pleaded with me to believe her. Without makeup, she looked so young, like when we'd first met. My mind flashed to another time when she was on her knees crying in front of me; the morning after the first wrap party when she asked me to kiss her. My heart exploded inside my chest.

Still, I couldn't reconcile that she hid it all from me. "Why didn't you tell me the day it happened?" My voice was still hard and I could feel my jaw stiffening of its own accord. "You didn't trust me enough. I thought we told each other everything!" I practically shouted.

A sob broke from her chest and her hand reached for mine. "I wanted to, but I was scared you'd believe the worst, after what you'd expected of him and I didn't want to upset you. We had the MTV thing the next day. I just wanted it to go away. I know I should have told you, but that is the only thing I'm guilty of."

"Then why did you publicly humiliate me with that apology speech?" My fingers held hers back against my will. "You basically admitted an affair."

"I thought I was only admitting I love you... not that I cheated on you. I needed you to hear me and I didn't care what it cost. I didn't know how else to make sure you knew. You were all... *are* all that matters."

She wiped at her nose with the wad of Kleenex clutched in her fist. Her shoulders were trembling, her pain as tangible as my own.

"I'm so sorry! I didn't know what else to do. I just needed to talk to you." Her fingers tightened on mine, begging me to thread mine through. "I don't want to lose you."

"Now that prick is flapping his jaw. Something has to be done to quell the damage."

"I don't care what he says," Brook said, still crying hard. "I only care what you believe."

What she said made sense and I was a bastard for not listening to her the day I left. I couldn't fight it anymore. I launched forward onto my knees and pulled her tightly to me. We clung together, falling apart in each other's arms.

"Please forgive me, Cade. I need you to forgive me. I love you so much!" Her little hands clutched at the flesh of my back so hard it stung through my shirt.

"If I want to make it until tomorrow, I have no choice. I can't live without you. Even if you had shagged him."

Her arms tightened and she cried even harder into the curve of my neck. "Buh...buh... but, I didn't!"

"I know, sweetheart. It's going to be okay, Brook." My hands stroked her hair and I kissed the side of her face, the salt of her tears landing on my tongue. I knew her better than I knew myself; there was no way she'd be such a mess if she weren't telling the truth. "I'm here and I'm not going anywhere."

I knew we'd have hell to pay, but we would handle it by saying nothing, by going on with life as if that bullshit had never happened and refusing to talk about it with anyone ever again.

She pulled back and I cupped her face, wiping at her tears with both thumbs. "What will we do? What will we tell everyone, I mean?"

"Nothing." I shrugged. "We'll just be together. The world can fuck off. We don't have to justify being together to anyone other than each other. Jeanne and Denise can deal with the press. Joel can file a lawsuit against Richards if he doesn't stop the lies. "

Her fingers curled into the front of my shirt and she nodded. "I want to kiss you, but I'm full of snot."

"Me, too." It didn't matter, though. I had every intention of kissing her senseless.

We kissed long and hard, both of us starving for the other and for the first time in weeks I could feel my chest relax and that sick, empty feeling began to ebb. I was overcome with relief. My life had just been given back to me and I was never going to let go of her again.

I finally pulled her with me onto the bed and we clung together like children for what seemed like hours. Part of me wanted to make love, but I just needed to hold her close to me and know that we were fine.

"I love you," Brook sighed. On the precipice of exhausted sleep, she snuggled closer into my neck, her arm wrapped around my middle. The warmth of her breath against my skin and her body plastered up against mine reassured me that this was real.

"I love you... and I'm sorry I was an idiot and didn't let you explain before."

"I'm sorry I was stupid and didn't tell you the minute it happened."

My lips lifted in a smirk at how much misery we could have saved if we'd just talked it out. "We're ridiculous, you know that right?"

She smiled and we both laughed out loud. It was the most beautiful sound I never thought I'd hear again.

Chapter 19
Real Reel Love

Caden

"UGHHHH... MISS YOU," I said into the empty hotel room as if she could hear me. I loved this film and the cast was incredible, but I felt hollow. Things were easier now that the world knew about Brook and me, but the separations still killed us. This film was a period piece split between London and a villa in the South of France. I felt ridiculous in the period costumes.

The time in London wasn't so bad. I had my family and especially my mates to keep my mind off of how much I missed the one person I missed the most.

Brooklyn.

Her name throbbed inside my head and bounced around my chest. It hurt. Everything hurt. Her birthday was coming up and it would be the first time in three years we weren't together for it.

The love scenes for my current film were shot in London and Brook teased me about screwing the bloody minions, but I knew she was covering. I'd be a mess if it were reversed. After the Sheldon scare we were stronger, but some parts of this job never got any easier.

Brook came to London for Fashion Week and then we'd flown back to New York together for a premiere of *Only Us* and some promotional shit she needed to do for *Dystopia*. The time in New York was wonderful. My heart was so full having her with me at my premiere. She'd insisted on coming in late, without fanfare, saying that it was Davina's night and she didn't want to detract from that. It had taken all I had to convince her to show up at all, but having her there with my family had been incredible. We went to the after parties, openly together, and even though we didn't feel the need to sneak around as much, the paparazzi were still ruthless. We were seen together, we held hands, they saw her coming and going from my house more often, but we hadn't admitted we were together when asked in interviews. It was a question I was getting good at dodging.

I drew in a deep breath and looked at the clock next to the bed. Ten hours separated us. It was only 6 AM in Los Angeles, and I had some scenes to shoot later so wouldn't be available for a call in the middle of her day. I hated not hearing her voice in the morning.

I pulled out the shirt I kept under my pillow and pressed it to my nose. It was my shirt, but she'd slept in it for two nights in New York before she left to fly back to L.A while I flew back to Europe to resume filming. I inhaled deeply. The scent of Brook's perfume and the smell of her skin were getting fainter, but still I found it comforting.

I had Denise doing everything she could to get me off this damn set for a few days over Brook's birthday. Brook had a big push for *Dystopia* soon and would be busy and unable to come here. I'd seen the rushes and she was amazing in it. My heart swelled with pride. I was upset I couldn't be with her at her premiere like she had been with me mine. Her attitude was somewhat nonchalant, telling me to get over it.

My phone rang. I set the shirt aside and answered.

"Hey, Denise, did you get the schedule fixed?"

"Unfortunately, nothing can be changed, Cade. You know how this crap works. The production crews and locations are scheduled. I'm sorry, honey."

My heart fell to my stomach. "Yeah, I figured as much. Thanks for trying." Disappointment throbbed through me. "It's just... I haven't been away from her for her birthday since we met, and this is her twenty-first."

"What's Brook's schedule like? Can she come to you?"

"I've thought about it, but she has so much going on and her parents might want to celebrate it with her. Outside of her dad coming to Vancouver during *Don't Forget to Remember Me*, she hasn't spent her birthday with her family since I've known her."

Something rustled on the other end of the phone. "Cade, if Brook had her choice, where would she be?"

I smiled because I couldn't help myself. "I see where you're going, but I'd feel selfish asking her."

"Selfish, smelfish... I'll call Jeanne."

My phone beeped as another call came in. "I have to go. I'm due on set in thirty minutes, so I'll talk to you later."

"Sure. I'll let you know what I find out. Bye."

"Hello?" I clicked over to the other call.

"There's my British boy." I could hear the sleep in Brook's voice and instantly pictured her all rolled up in her bed. "Whatcha' doin'?" she asked.

"Missing you."

"Yeah, yeah. Besides that."

"Getting ready to go to set. It's awfully early for you, love."

"I knew I wouldn't get to talk to you if I didn't call early. I just wanted to tell you that I love you and miss you madly."

"Me, too. I wish I had more time to talk." I started out of the room and down to the lobby where Bill and the other bodyguards waited. It was easier outside of the United States, but it was still madness to a degree.

"It's okay. I'll get up and make Lucky breakfast."

I smiled. He was growing up fast and I adored him. He barked in the background as if he knew Brook was speaking to me. "I miss him."

"He misses you, too. He sleeps on your pillow."

"What do you want for your birthday?"

"Nothing." I could picture her chewing on her lower lip. "I have you."

"Not when I'm bloody stuck on the other side of the world."

"It's not forever, baby." She said the words, but I wasn't convinced she was as fine as she wanted me to believe. "You'll be home soon, and we have the promotional tour for *A Love Like This*. Last one."

I heard the sadness in her voice.

"Yes, but Denise sent me my itinerary and I can't go with you and Noah to Australia, Mexico, Spain... should I keep going?"

"No. I get the point. You better get your sexy ass to work. Call me later. Even if you'll wake me up. Promise?"

"Okay, sure."

"Mmmm... Will you add me to your ravished minions, Gerard?"

She called me by my new character name and I chuckled at her funny French accent. It was horrible.

"Uh... no. I could not ravish you without losing my heart. The others are only a means to an end, while you, my dear, are the end in itself," I said, my own French accent practiced and polished with a voice coach for my role.

"Bleh," she said and then fell into a soft laugh.

"Seriously, Brook. I really miss you, love." My voice was once again my own. "I wish…"

"You wish?"

"Well, I don't want to be away from you on your birthday."

She sighed on the phone. "No biggie. It's just another day, and you know that weekend *Dystopia* opens nationwide. We'll celebrate soon."

"Not soon enough. I have to go, sweetheart. Tell your family I said hello. Especially your mum."

"Love you, sexy beast. I really love you, Cade."

"Love you, too, Brook. Bye for now, love." My heart thumped as I closed my phone and shoved it back into the pocket of my pants.

Brooklyn

I WENT DOWNSTAIRS and flopped on the couch in the den. Nathan was visiting; playing Guitar Hero on Cade's PlayStation. He glanced in my direction, but didn't stop his attack on the Aerosmith song he was working.

"Hey," he said.

I picked up Lucky and wrapped my arms around him. He nuzzled my chin and licked my cheek. I kissed the top of his furry head. "Hey. Wanna do something today? I'm bored."

"Doesn't Jeanne have you busy promoting the film?" He finished the song, put the game on hold, and then sat down in the big chair opposite me.

I stretched my legs out in front of me and continued to stroke the puppy. "Not today. I'm thinking I'm gonna blow off the London premiere."

Nathan's eyes widened. "What? I thought you'd want to go and hang with Cade's Family."

I shrugged. Cade was leaving for France the next day and would just miss me. "London won't be the same without him. It's bad enough in L.A." He looked at me for a moment, studying my bland expression. I glanced up at him. "What?'

Nate shook his head. "Nothing. I never thought I'd hear you say you wanted to skip something for this film. You were so jacked to get this role."

I shrugged again. "I know. I guess my priorities have changed."

Nate got up and went toward the kitchen. "Want something to drink? I'm thirsty."

"Nah. Thanks, though." I stared at the ceiling and ran a hand through my hair when Lucky hopped off my lap and settled next to me. The wide release of my film was the same weekend as my birthday, and even though I told Cade it didn't matter, I was sad we wouldn't be together. "Nate, does Mom or Dad have anything planned for my birthday?" I called loudly, so he could hear me in the other room. The refrigerator door opened and shut with a bang before he wandered back into the room. With their separation it might be better just to skip any family gatherings for a while.

He was scratching his stomach through the dark red T-shirt he was wearing over his jeans. "Even if I knew, I couldn't tell you, sis. Mom would have my ass."

I turned and lay down on the couch when he returned to the big chair he'd been sitting in. "Please? I really need to know."

My brain was racing, remembering how much fun it had been to surprise Cade on that first Christmas in London, between shooting our first two films. My heart ached and I felt so empty without him. There couldn't be a better birthday present than seeing him.

"Why? You haven't made plans, have you? You said Cade will still be working in France, so...."

"Yeah, exactly." I looked him in the eye and his eyebrows shot up.

"Are you thinking of going to France?"

I bit my lip. "More like just *decided*. I spoke to him this morning and we're... it's been over a month since we've seen each other. I know, you think I'm sappy, and but I miss him."

"Maybe two years ago I would have considered it sappy, but not after you two got together. How's he doing over there?"

"Okay. I'm sure the film will be brilliant, but he's lonely. I can hear it in his voice. So? Do they have plans for my birthday or what?"

"Yeah. Mom and I were coming to the London premiere."

My heart fell slightly at the possibility of disappointing my mom, but I knew he'd understand if I explained.

"That's really sweet, but I'm sorry, but I have to do this. I'll pay him back for the tickets and hotels. Or why don't you still go? It's the next best thing to my being there."

"Seriously? Awesome!"

I left Nathan in the den and went into the kitchen to get my phone.

Jeanne answered on the first ring. "Hey, baby! Are you excited for this weekend?"

"I am now, Jeanne. I've decided to go to Toulon."

"Ugh. You have the release of *The Dysto-*" she began.

"I have a lonely man over there, and nothing you can say will change my mind."

"Have you considered that he's trying to get to you? Wouldn't it just be the shit if you passed each other over the Atlantic ocean? And the movie studio won't be happy if you go MIA this weekend."

"Tell them what's up and call Denise. Make sure Cade doesn't leave Toulon." My heart was beating faster in my chest.

"We knew you'd do this, Brook. It's been done," Jeanne said with a laugh.

"What?" I asked, out of breath, excitement pulsing through every cell.

"KLM is the only airline with a flight from L.A. to Toulon, but it's got one stop for fuel in Paris. It's twelve hours in flight, Brook."

My eyes widened. I wished I could hug her. "Jeanne! I love you for doing this. Did you book me?"

"Yeah. The flight leaves at 7:48 tonight and gets into Toulon around 1:30 in the afternoon their time tomorrow. The guys will pick you up at 5:30."

My heart was about to fly from my chest. I had all day to pack, but I was already pulling my bag from the closet. "I fucking love you, Jeanne!"

"Well, you owe me and Denise's big time! Cade is in a foul mood because she practically nailed him down over there."

"He hinted that on the phone this morning, but he didn't seem mad at her. He's almost finished filming, and if I were rational, I could see him in a few weeks when we're both free, but..." I laughed out loud, giddy with excitement. "I'll admit it, I'm not rational when it comes to Cade. I can't wait to get my hands on him, Jeanne! Oh my God! I'm so excited to see him."

She laughed on the other end.

"He doesn't know, right?"

"Nope. We didn't want to get his hopes up in case I couldn't get you out of your commitments."

"Let's keep it that way. I love surprising him."

"He'll be one happy Brit, Brook. It's your birthday, but he's getting a present."

"Seeing him is the best gift I could get. I need to call my parents. Maybe my mom and Nathan can come out in a few days? I want to have a couple days alone with Cade first, though."

"I'll check with Diane and try to work it out, Brook."

"Great. Thanks, Jeanne. You rock. Love you!"

Caden

CHRIST, I WAS TIRED. And I was worried. I hadn't talked to Brook all day, and she only answered one text. My driver was rushing through Toulon to the little jeweler that Denise found on the west side of downtown. Very exclusive; full of antiques, but also unique pieces. The owner was an old man who was known for his special orders.

I sighed and ran a hand through my hair, which was still caked with the gel they put in it for my character. It was longer than I normally liked it, but the producers wouldn't let me cut it. It was driving me bonkers and the only benefit to having it longer wasn't with me. Brook loved to thread her hands through it and tug on it when we made love. Now there was a thought.

I glanced at my watch. It was ten in the morning and so it would be midnight in L.A. I pulled out my phone and looked at the list of incoming calls; one from my mum, one from Daniel, and two from Denise. Not one from my girl. *What the fuck?*

I was living on our playlist and every photo I could find of her online when I wasn't on set or sleeping. I was thankful for the exhaustion because otherwise I wouldn't sleep at all. I was constantly clock-watching, trying to get in a call to Brook whenever I had a minute. I'd had months of commitments, but I was to the point that I needed some extended time off. I needed a break to see my family, write music, train my dog and be with Brook.

The shop was old and musty smelling, and had deep red carpeting and lots of glass cases with brass fittings all around. A crystal chandelier hung from the center of the white ceiling lined with antique tiles embossed with a Fleur de Lis design. I was anxious to see what he had made for me. I'd described the bracelet that I'd given Brook on her birthday last year in the hope that he could duplicate it in to a necklace. The bracelet didn't grace her wrist often, not when she was in public so much, so the necklace could nestle underneath most of her clothes and not be seen. At least she'd be able to wear it more often.

I fingered the black shoestring that was tied around my right wrist. Ever since that limo ride back from Comic Con last year, we both wore it whenever we were apart. So many of the fans noticed and made the connection, but it was something we could do without blatantly going against our contracts. Those days were over, the contracts no longer valid, but we still wore them because it kept us close.

Mr. Abel, the proprietor, must have been eighty years old, but still his frail hands were steady as a rock. He looked up from where he was working, a smile splitting across his weathered face. "Ah! Caden!" he said, his accent thick as he scooted off of his stool to move toward me. "It's finished! Just as you wanted!"

"Thank you, sir," I said politely, but bristled with impatience as he turned to retrieve the leather box from the case behind him. He opened it and set it in front of me. Nestled on the black velvet lining was a perfect replica of Brook's infinity bracelet. Platinum with one diamond and one emerald in the center, a very fine box chain ran through one of the loops.

My fingers hovered over the delicate piece. "It's perfect."

"I see how strong you love this girl, Caden. She is a lucky girl," the old man said quietly.

"Thank you for getting it finished. Her birthday is in four days, and now I have time to send it to her. It's brilliant." I smiled and closed the box, pulling out my wallet and handing him a wad of cash. Credit cards left trails and this wasn't something I wanted to share with the world. This was between Brook and me.

"Maybe you come back for wedding rings, eh?" The old man's brown eyes were alight with mischief and I smiled broadly in response. "You marry this girl, yes?"

"Yes, I'm sure I will. She already has an engagement ring, but you're the first on my list for wedding rings when the time comes."

"You bring her here? I have special present for the two of you." He put the jewelry box into a bag and shook my hand before handing it to me.

"I would if I could, sir, but Brook won't be in France at all during this trip." I silently cringed since I doubted we'd have an occasion to be back unless we made it a point to do so.

"Oh, no. That is very sad. I am sorry. Will you sign?" He pointed to a piece of paper on the counter. I glanced at it. Was he asking for an autograph? It was blank, not a photo or book, which were the normal canvases I was asked to sign on.

"Uh... of course." My brain was shooting off warning signals that I shouldn't be leaving any evidence that I was there, but the old man was so kind, I couldn't resist. I signed the paper quickly.

"Please come back. Five days?" He asked with a smile. "I will have a gift."

"That isn't necessary, Mr. Abel. I am so happy to have this finished. It's all I could ask..."

"Caden, come back. Five days." He patted my shoulder and nodded.

"Yes, sir. I will." I thanked him again, and Bill, the bodyguard, motioned that it was clear to get back in the car. I leaned my head back on the leather seat and closed my eyes, the box in my hand burned and my heart swelled as I smiled. She loved the bracelet and she would love the necklace as well. Too bad I couldn't see her face when she opened it.

"Back to set, right, Cade?" Bill asked from the front seat. I still had one more scene to shoot before sundown; an outside scene in the streets. I found it funny the studio used the South of France to find a set akin to 18th century Paris. Paris would have worked, but it was expensive and crowded. I glanced at my phone again; still no call from Brook.

"Yes," I answered tiredly.

"It's almost over," Bill said quietly.

"One more week." I was supposed to go to London when I was finished, but if I couldn't convince Brook to meet me there, I knew I'd be headed back to Los Angeles. Either way, in a week, she'd be in my arms no matter what.

Brooklyn

I WAS SLEEPY. It was 1:45 in the afternoon, but to me it was just before 4 AM. I hated jet lag. As the bodyguards rushed me through customs, I was thankful that there weren't any press shoving cameras in my face. Europe wasn't nearly as horrific as the United States and it was one of the things I always enjoyed about visiting. This smaller town was even less invasive.

Cade would be working, so I had time to go back and clean up. Denise made arrangements to get a key to Cade's room for me and I was strangely excited just to walk through those doors. He wouldn't be there, but his stuff would be, his scent... and it would ease the constant ache.

My stomach fluttered as I passed the key in the lock and the door clicked. I pushed it open, and one of the guards followed me in with my bag. I pointed to the couch and he set it down.

"Will there be anything else, Ms. Halloway?" the man asked. I didn't know him well; he was someone that Jeanne had the agency send last minute specifically for this trip. His name was Steve or Sam or something. I couldn't remember.

"Um, not for an hour or two. I'm going to shower and then I'd like to surprise Cade on set. Do you have access?"

"I can make some calls. Denise can make it happen."

"Thank you... uh..."

"Steven." He smiled shyly at me. He was huge, as they normally were, towering over me, with dark brown eyes and closely cut hair.

"Thank you, Steven." I smiled, silently praying he would leave quickly.

When he did and the door closed loudly behind him, I turned into the room and looked around. Cade's clothes were strewn everywhere, over the couch, the floor, in a pile at the bottom of the closet. A pair of Adidas dropped on the floor in a haphazard manner near the coffee table and there were beer bottles, remnants of a sandwich, and an empty water bottle on top of it.

"Hmmmph!" I huffed. He probably didn't let the maid in for fear she'd steal his underwear and sell it on Ebay. I smiled, kicking off my shoes and letting them land next to his. I went into the bedroom and glanced over the bed. His guitar was lying on the un-slept-in side, inside its open case, while the covers were pushed back on the other. An impression of his head was clear on the pillow and I fell into it, face down and inhaled his scent, clutching at the sheet at the same time. My heart was racing, his essence emanating from everything around me. I was really *here*. I was going to see my man in a matter of an hour or two and I couldn't freaking wait.

"Cade."

I had to stay awake for at least seven more hours so I could lose the jet lag, but I didn't want to be dragging when I finally got to Cade. I pushed off of the bed and walked to my purse, pulling out some Excedrin, picked up the phone and ordered coffee from room service. Caffeine. I needed caffeine. I didn't know much French, but *cafe'* was a must know.

Twenty minutes, two cups of coffee and a shower later, I applied a light layer of makeup, a little blush, and some gloss to my lips. I couldn't stand waiting one more minute. Dressed in jeans, a T-shirt, and black hoodie, I pushed my feet back into my Chucks and texted Steven.

Within five minutes, there was a knock at the door and he and one other dude were there to take me to the movie set. In the car, my knee bounced up and down and I found myself biting my nails. Ugh. I pulled my fingers from my lips and shoved both hands under my thighs. It was only a ten-minute ride, but somehow it felt like ten hours.

"Brook, Cade has just finished and has gone to his trailer. Should we let him know you're here?" Steven asked casually, leaning one arm over the front seat so he could look at me.

"I'd rather surprise him. Is that possible?"

He smiled. "Sure, but I have to coordinate with Bill, Cade's bodyguard. I'll tell him to keep it quiet."

My hands were shaking by the time the car pulled up into an array of white trailers, scattered closely together over a small lot. I wondered how they knew which was Cade's, but they pulled up next to one near the center and stopped.

"This is his trailer, and he's in there now. You should knock. He might be naked or something," Steve teased with a grin.

I smiled brightly, my hand going for the door handle.

"Keep your hood up and crouch down. Never know where there are photographers. We think it's clean, but it wouldn't hurt to be careful," he warned.

"Okay. Thanks, Steven. I'll go back to the hotel with Cade and Bill. You can take the night off."

He smiled. "Okay, but call me if you need me. I should be with you if you decide to go out."

"Sure. I promise." I was already scrambling out of the back of the big SUV and hurrying toward the trailer door. My hand grabbed the silver knob and pulled it open. There was music playing, but I didn't see Cade when I poked my head inside. I quickly closed the door behind me with a loud bang, hoping to get him out in the open.

"What the hell?" he mumbled in his delicious accent. "Don't you bloody knock?"

I could barely contain the happiness bubbling up inside me as he walked out of what must have been the bathroom. He was still dressed in his costume, his hair gelled and pulling at the old fashioned tie around his neck, his long vest unbuttoned.

"Uh, no, I didn't think I needed to knock," I said, tongue in cheek as his eyes fell upon me for the first time.

Cade's face lit up and he rushed toward me and I was instantly swallowed up in his arms, my feet dangling off of the floor as we held each other as if we'd never let go. "Oh my God!" Cade breathed into the hair at the side of my neck. "I'm gonna kill Denise. Then I'm gonna kiss her!"

My hands stroked at the back of his head as we stood there, wrapped up tight. "I know. It never gets any easier, does it? Happy birthday *to me*." I whispered, just before his mouth closed hungrily over mine.

Cade laughed softly before swooping down to claim my lips with his.

We kissed again and again, not able to get enough of each other, sucking and feasting on each other as if we were starving. We were. My hands wound in his hair and pulled him back after he managed to sit down on the couch and wrap me in his arms. Finally, his mouth lifted and he rested his forehead against mine. "You smell so bloody good. Just like my baby."

Tears welled in my eyes at the overwhelming emotions. I would never get used to how much I loved this man. "I love you." I pushed his hair back and he chuckled when the gel made a crinkling sound in my fingers. I smiled against his cheek and kissed it softly. "I didn't know they had hair gel in seventeenth century France," I giggled against him and he joined in.

"Probably something equally enchanting like afterbirth or lard," he laughed happily and kissed me softly again. I turned into his arms and wound mine around his shoulders again. "I can't believe you're here. I'd resigned myself to not seeing you for your birthday. Do you have to leave? *Dystopia*...?"

"Will premiere without me." I looked into his beautiful blue eyes. "I'm where I want to be and I'm not budging."

I turned so that I could face him, my knees beside his hips on the leather; I wiggled in his lap and grinned at him. My eyes locked on his, I pulled the tie completely free and threw it over his shoulder. "You don't need this..." I said softly, making short work of the buttons on the shirt. I pushed it open and splayed my hands on his chest and it expanded as he sucked in his breath. "Or this..." I murmured.

Cade's hands closed around my hips and he pulled me tighter against him. "I find I have an affinity for this position," he said softly, his hands moving from my hips to my thighs.

I couldn't help it; I moaned as my mouth settled back on his and my hips surged forward. It launched Cade into action and he stood up, holding me and turning to lay me down on my back. He followed me down, coming into the cradle of my body in one smooth motion. I welcomed him with open arms, my legs wrapping snuggly around his hips, as he pushed his hardness into my heat as we kissed hungrily. "God, Brook. I need you. I want you so much. I've been starving for you."

We'd made love hundreds of times by now but he still made my heart race, his hands pushing up the front of my shirt so that the bare skin of his stomach was now infused with mine, and then cupping my breast, his thumbs teasing my nipples. He knew how to bring heat and wetness to throb at my center. Soon my hands were clawing at his clothes like his were clawing at mine, our mouths sucking and worshiping, dragging across each other's skin and back, hunger for the other a nagging ache that couldn't be sated.

The couch was too small, confining as he pushed my shirt up and away, his hands then moving to the button and zipper of my jeans. We tumbled to the floor, Cade landing beneath me with a thud, but completely shielding me from the hard floor. It was covered in carpet, but it offered little cushion.

"Baby, are you okay?" I groaned, trying to look in his face for traces of pain. There was only passion and desire. His eyes were hooded, and glowing, his full lips slightly open as his breath rushed in between them in rapid succession. He pulled my shoes off and then my jeans followed, soon I was lying naked beneath his heated gaze. I couldn't take my eyes off of him. He was so fucking beautiful as he shrugged out of his shirt and vest in one motion then he made short work of the opening of his pants.

"Brilliant. I'm about to make love to my wife," it was a guttural groan as he raked his hands over my body, starting at my breasts, down over my ribs and hips until both thumbs worked in gentle prodding at my clit.

I arched into him and sighed. "Uhhh...."

"You *are* my wife, Brook. In my heart. There will never be anyone else but you. I love you more than anything on this earth. I wish the wedding on the set of *Don't Forget to Remember Me* had been real." Cade's eyes darkened a deeper shade of blue as he looked at me. The sun was going down, and only a small light from the bathroom shone over us, casting shadows over the sharp planes of his face.

I closed my eyes against the pain of what his words did to my heart. I felt like I would burst and my eyes burned with tears. He was so perfect. "Cade..." my voice cracked on the word but it felt like a prayer. If I could only say one word for the rest of my life, it had to be his name. "I love you that much, too. No one else exists for me."

He made love to me like it was the first time... and the last. His body pushed into mine over and over a mixture of urgency and tenderness until we were both breathless. Our hands worshiped with every touch, our lips tasting and savoring. We forgot about the bodyguards waiting for us on the other side of the thin walls, not caring if they heard the breathless sounds we elicited from each other as we made love.

Cade was my reality; on screen or off. In all the world; there was only us.

Epilogue

Caden

MY HAND STROKED the bare skin of Brook's back, my lips pressed to her forehead as we clung together, our breathing still labored. My heart ached with the ecstasy of her presence. She was here in my arms; real, loving me, right here and now.

"Do you have any idea how much I love you, Brook? I mean, really?"

"Mmm..." she moaned and turned her head to press a series of butterfly kisses to my chest. It felt like heaven. As much as I wanted her and how our passion consumed us, moments like this, when we were close, talking meant just as much. "I think so, yes. But it still amazes me."

I pulled her up a little more on my body, so my arms could wrap more fully around her small form. "Have you lost weight? You seem thinner."

"I wasn't trying to, but maybe a little. Should we go? The guys are waiting to take us to dinner."

I shook my head and tightened my arms. "Not yet. I'm not ready to let go of you. They know we're shagging each other senseless, so why do we need to rush?"

Brook giggled, her shoulders shaking. "Cade, you have such a way of putting things. God," she admonished.

"It's the bloody truth. So what?" We both laughed together. "How long are you here for, love? Does Jeanne have you back in the States on a junket this weekend? I thought that was the plan?" The London premiere of her film was supposed to be Wednesday then the American premieres in New York and L.A. were slated for Friday and Saturday nights. The traveling for these things was horrendous.

"Well, I changed the plan," she said casually and shrugged. "After our phone conversation, I just didn't want to be away from you for my birthday. It felt wrong." Her head tilted up, and her mouth brushed against mine.

"I know. This isn't the life I want for us; we're always on opposite sides of the world. I bloody hate it. I hate that sometimes nameless people know as much about what's going on with you as I do."

"The world isn't dialed in like you. You can get to me anytime, babe."

"No, I can't. Today I couldn't reach you and it drove me crazy."

"Because I was flying here, duh."

"I get that now, but at the time I was worried."

Brook sat up and started gathering her clothes. I watched her as she dressed slowly, enjoying her movements and her nakedness. She pulled on her black bikini panties and a T-shirt, glaring at me as she went. Reluctantly, I started throwing on my clothes.

"You worry too much."

She hadn't answered my question about when she had to leave, and I was uneasy. The last thing I wanted to hear was that she had to turn right around.

I pulled on my jeans but hadn't done them up. "How long can you stay?" I asked quietly, my fingers closing around hers and pulling her hand to my mouth. I met her eyes and her other hand reached out to brush along my jaw.

"Oh… should we negotiate that? What's it worth to ya?" she grinned.

My arms closed around her and hauled her up against my body. Brook laughed "Everything," I answered, kissing her neck and the side of her face. "Anything."

"Let's start with food. I'm starving. My man is demanding. I'm sure he's gonna want more lovin' later and I need to power up." She was teasing me and her voice was amused, but her eyes were serious as she looked into mine.

I nodded and kissed her fully on the mouth and then placed a few kisses at the corners. "Thank you for being here, Brook. It means everything."

She pushed my hair back and kissed my chin. "If you feed me, I have a surprise. Do you think room service has fresh strawberries?"

"Bloody hell, did you smuggle in some Twinkies?"

"Maybe. Would it make you happy?"

"Delirious!"

When we opened the door to the trailer, Bill was waiting, leaning against the side. He quickly straightened and opened the back door so Brook and I could dive in. The fans in Toulon weren't as rampant as they were in the U.S. or even London, but it would be easier if we stayed off the radar.

I, for one, was bloody sick of all the bullshit. Telling them straight on wasn't enough to get the press to back off. Nothing ever satisfied those bastards. It was particularly hard on Brook. We could barely tolerate them.

Tonight I breathed a sigh of relief when we made it in the car and off toward the hotel without incident. My hand entwined with Brook's and her head was leaning on my shoulder. She had to be exhausted with the time difference. I rubbed my thumb over the top of her hand. My lungs expanded as I breathed in deeply, a sense of contentment like I hadn't felt in a month settled over me.

"Hey, Bill, can we stop and grab some food before we get to the hotel?"

"Yes. Any requests?"

"Just fast. Burgers, okay?" Amazing how many Burger Kings and McDonald's were scattered around France. No In-N-Out Burgers, though. The one thing I missed about L.A., besides the woman sleeping on my shoulder.

"Of course."

When we arrived at the hotel, it was standard procedure to enter through the underground garage and take the stairs up to my room. Brook was wiped.

"We're here, love." I nudged her softly, and then kissed her forehead.

Bill opened the door as I lifted her in my arms, grabbing the burger bag from him before starting up the stairs.

Brook snuggled into my neck. "What did you get me for my birthday?"

I smiled as I climbed the twelve flights of stairs. "It's in my pants, baby," I teased.

"Pfft," she scoffed. "You can't give me something that's already mine." Her words were slurred. I wasn't even sure she was aware of what she was saying, but I was grinning my bloody ass off. "You spend an awful lot of time trying to get what's in your pants... into *my* pants."

I laughed out loud, the sound bursting from me and echoing through the stairwell. Happiness was a precious thing. Brook was a precious thing.

Brooklyn

IT WAS DARK AND I opened my eyes, running my hand over my face. The room smelled like Cade; musky and salty with just a hint of his cologne. I stretched languidly, my back arching and my arms reaching for him in the bed. He wasn't there. The clock by the bed said 1:46 in the morning, the red digital numbers blaring in the darkness.

"Cade?" I called softly. "Hon?"

He suddenly appeared in the doorway between the sitting room of the suite and the bedroom. He was naked, which made me smile.

"Yeah, love." His eyes glowed in the dark as he moved toward me. I scooted over and lifted the covers for him. I didn't remember how I got that way, but I was naked, too. His strong arms slid warmly around me, pulling me to him in one smooth motion, pressing his body to mine and tangling our limbs together. "I thought you were sleeping."

I snuggled into him further, my forehead resting against the side of his jaw. "Why are you up? Are you sick?"

"Nope. My stomach was growling."

His words made me laugh softly. "Twinkie diving are you?"

"Mmm... but epic fail. I didn't find them. Were you teasing me, sweets?”

“Nope.” My hand traced over the soft hair that covered his strong forearm. My body quickened. He had to be the sexiest man on the planet. Happiness rushed through me. He was all mine. “But I need strawberries before I’ll break ‘em out.”

“It’s ridiculous how in sync we are, Brook. I ordered them from room service. They’ll be here soon.”

“I knew there was a reason I loved your sexy ass.”

“You never said how long you’ll stay.” He nuzzled into my neck and pulled me closer. My hands found their usual place threading through the soft hair at his nape as I tilted my face up, my nose brushing along the side of his jaw.

“I thought I’d hitch a ride to London.”

“Seriously?” I felt, rather than saw a big smile spread across his face. “That would be brilliant!”

“If you give me my present, now.” I was feeling mischievous.

He laughed and rolled me over roughly, settling between my legs and pushing my hair back. “I’ll give you a present, all right.”

“Pfft!” I pushed playfully at his shoulders. “We’ve already had this conversation. I own that already.” I grinned and then reached between us to close my fingers around his full erection. “It’s becoming a problem, isn’t it?” Cade grunted and kissed me a couple of times on the mouth, surging his hips to thrust into my hand.

“Not when you’re with me, love, but I have a bloody awful time with it when you’re not.” He began to tickle me by poking me in the ribs.

We were rolling around on the bed laughing when room service knocked on the door.

Cade looked at me horrified as I lounged under the covers, making no effort to get up and go to the door. "I'm not getting it. I have a boner, Brook!"

I fell over laughing. "And...?" I giggled. "Uh....okay, I'll go." I pushed off the bed and tugged the sheet with me. Cade grabbed it and tried to pull it from me.

"Uh, unless you want this dude to have a bird's eye view of my vajayjay, you'll let go of the sheet, Cade." We both laughed. "I need some cash to give him."

Cade got up in all his naked glory, pulled some bills from his jeans and handed them to me before I went and got the strawberries he'd ordered. There was also some champagne and bottled water.

I went to my suitcase and threw three packages of Twinkies on the tray. Cade was sitting on the bed, now in his boxers and a T-shirt and holding a black leather box. He wagged his eyebrows at me.

I smiled and set the tray down, reaching for the box at the same time. He pulled it back out of my reach. "It's not your birthday until Saturday, so..."

Lunging at him and ripping the box out of his hands in the same motion, I somehow ended up on his lap, his arms wrapped around me, and the sheet precariously close to falling away.

"So? Can I open it?" I asked hopefully. "Please?"

Cade nuzzled into the hair at the side of my head. "Mmm, hmm."

I flipped open the box and immediately saw a duplicate of the bracelet he'd given me the year before only as a pendant. "It's gorgeous," I said simply, turning my head to kiss him on the mouth. " It's perfect." I thought about the gorgeous diamond R & J bracelet he'd given me before we were together, at the end of our first film, the one that matched this necklace, and the engagement ring that I could still only wear in private. My heart tightened. "You're so thoughtful, baby.

I love it. If I could, I'd wear them all and never take even one off."

"I know," he whispered against my skin. "As long as you know how much I love you. It's just at times when we can't be together; I want you to have something of me that you can keep close."

I closed my eyes and rested my head against his, love threatening to burst my chest wide open. "Cade," my voice throbbed. He touched me so deeply that if there were nothing but his words between us, it would somehow be enough. "You're always close to me. You're part of me. Always."

His arms tightened and we held each other for a minute or two without words, his hand rubbed my thigh over the sheet and I snuggled into his neck, holding the box in my hand.

"I never want to be apart from you, Brook. Maybe we should just chuck it? We have more money than God."

I let out a soft chuckle. "You know you'd never be happy not working. I know you talk about it, but I know you'd miss it. So would I."

"Sure, but I also want to do music. Daniel has a new record out. I'm annoyed that I don't have time to do any myself. Besides, it turns my girl on." He flashed the crooked grin I loved.

I moved off of his lap and removed the necklace from the box. The chain was long, so I could just loop it over my head. The pendant settled between my breasts and Cade bent to kiss it.

"Aren't you hungry?

"Starving," he mumbled against my skin, his gentle hands pushing my back on the bed.

"What about...."

His eyes danced as he peeled the sheet from my body. "Remember the first time we had Twinkies and strawberries, Brook?" His hand took a strawberry from the tray and he started to squeeze it, the juice running over my breasts and down my stomach. I fell back on the pillows as his tongue began to run a hot path echoing the juice trails.

I remembered. We were still getting over that shit with Wendy and were traveling to promote one of the films. We were so close, the emotions and love spilling out of us unabashed.

"Yes. That weekend was so beautiful."

He squeezed more juice over my breasts and his tongue circled a nipple, using suction, he pulled it into his mouth to suckle softly, causing me to gasp and throb deep in the pit of my stomach. "Cade... ugh..." I breathed in as he worked his way lower over my navel, kissing my stomach and hipbones. I wound my fingers through his thick hair.

"You taste delicious. It's bloody ridiculous."

"Cade." His name broke from my mouth as tears welled in my eyes. "I love you. I'm so thankful for you."

He lifted his head and kissed me softly. "I love you, so, so much. I could die right now, and not regret it."

The tears finally squeezed from my eyes and I nodded. "Me, too," I choked out.

"Love, why the tears?" He asked, pushing back my hair and the salty tears leaking from the corners of my eyes.

"I told you on the first strawberry night... it's the love. There's too much to fit inside me and so it has to come out. It never goes away. It's always so much more." A small sob escaped me as Cade buried his face in the side of my neck, his warm breath washing over my skin.

"Yeah, I know."

Caden

FILMING WAS DONE, and Brook's family had come in for her birthday yesterday. It was a nice surprise for her and I'd invited them to come back to London for a few days, but they declined.

Brook and I had discussed it at length and decided to say *fuck it*. Fuck it to hiding, fuck it to the paps... we still weren't going to talk openly about it, but the prospect of traveling back to London separately when we were both going there had just really pissed me off. I'd finally convinced her. *Fuck it.*

Brook was tired. She'd been on set quite a bit, and in order to do it without being seen, she went apart from me very early in the morning. Denise leaked my call time so the fans and press wouldn't hang out too early and Brook was able to get in unknown to any of them. It was cool having her on set, but weird to have her watch me marry someone else. She smirked when I'd mentioned as much to her.

"It's fine," she teased. "Marry them all as long as you're in bed with me." Some of the other cast heard her and raised their eyebrows. When I looked at Brook for her reaction, she simply said, "Fuck it, right?"

I laughed and the tension was over. "Right."

Now she was curled up against my shoulder as we made our way to the airport. I had Bill and three other guards with us, because it would be madness and I wanted Brook protected at all costs. The plan was that I would walk through with Steve and Bill and Peter would walk on either side of Brook behind me. Closely behind. I wanted this over with as quickly as possible. We were taking the guards on the plane, because there would be bloody more of the same in London when we landed; likely more since the world would then know that Brook had been with me in France.

Fuck it. The words reverberated through my brain and I laughed out loud.

Bill looked over the back of the front seat. "What?" he asked.

"Nothing. I'm just really bloody happy." Brook's small hand curled into the front of my shirt and I put mine over it.

As we headed through town, I remembered Mr. Abel and my promise to stop by again. Plus, Brook was here now and she could meet the old man.

"Bill, I need to stop at Abel's, please"

He glanced at his watch. "We'll be cutting it close, but we can spare a few minutes."

"Thank you." I leaned my head down to the sleeping head on my shoulder. "Brook, babe, wake up, can you?"

She moaned and shook her head. "No. Why?"

"We have to make a quick stop. I promised to stop and see the old man who made your pendant one more time."

She sat up then and pushed her hand through her hair. "Okay. That would be nice." A smile tugged gently at her luscious lips and I couldn't help it, I bent down to capture them with my own in a brief kiss. "Love you," she whispered, and I squeezed her hand.

Mr. Abel's eyes glowed with excitement as I ushered Brook into the little shop. "Mr. Caden! You came back! Is this beautiful girl your young lady?"

"Yes, sir. This is Brook."

Brook was beaming at the old man who placed his hands on both sides of her face. "Okay to kiss you?" he asked. His English was good but broken with a heavy accent.

She nodded and he kissed first one of her flushed cheeks and then the other.

"Very nice to meet you, Mr. Abel," Brook murmured. "Thank you for making the beautiful necklace. It's really pretty. I love it."

"Oh! Pleasure!" We watched the hunched old man walk back to his workbench and then return. He held out a hand to Brook, indicating that he wanted her to give him her left hand. "I apologize for the size. You are smaller than I expected."

My face ached from smiling. Brook was glowing as the old man slid a gold ring on the middle finger of her left hand. "My gift to you. Your young man loves you. You keep him."

She blushed and smiled widely. "I'm planning on it, for sure." She glanced down at the ring and gasped. "It's amazing." Her eyes filled with tears and she reached out to hug Mr. Abel. "Amazing. I'll treasure it. Thank you."

Her thumb ran over the ring and I asked to see it. "Look," she said softly, wiping away the one errant tear that managed to fall from her eye.

I glanced down at it. It was simple. Solid gold and plain save for some embossing on one side. C A D E.

"It's in your handwriting. How?" she shook her head in disbelief.

I only had gratitude and love for the old man whose gesture was so incredibly touching. "Mr. Abel. That's... just brilliant. Beautiful. Thank you."

"Oh, my pleasure, my boy." He patted my shoulder then shoved a piece of paper in front of Brook. "You sign. I make one for Caden. I can ship to your home."

Brook and I both stood there stunned. "Really? Oh, my God, that would be amazing."

She signed her name and he measured my ring finger. It was the one I thought would be less obvious for everyone to notice. "I'll cherish it always. Thank you for everything."

We both hugged him goodbye and promised to stop in again if we ever returned to Toulon. It was a reminder that although we were surrounded with madness, we could have these rare moments of radiance when someone saw us as just a man and a woman. Real people who happen to love each other desperately. My heart pounded in my chest as I watched Brook shove on her sunglasses to hide her teary eyes. I reached down and threaded my hand through hers.

We were on our way to the airport and soon we'd be dealing with the river of madness. I knew these rings would become our wedding bands.

"Now I really feel like *fucking it*, yeah?" I tried to make her laugh, although my throat was aching with the remnants of the moment. The thumb of my right hand brushed over the top of the ring, feeling the letters of my name.

She laughed through her tears. "Yeah. Totally." Brook's other hand closed around my bicep and squeezed gently as she nodded. "That was just amazing, wasn't it?"

"Yeah. I can't wait until I get mine, Brook. It's perfect."

"The whole thing is pretty perfect." Her hand reached out to brush along my jaw and I bent to kiss her. Our lips clung together for a brief moment.

"Mmm...I wouldn't change one second of the last three years. Chaos and all, Brook, it's the reason I have you. I wouldn't change a bloody thing."

The End

About the Author

Kahlen Aymes is a USA Today best selling author who writes steamy romance novels that cross genre lines between New Adult, Adult Contemporary and Erotica.

Kahlen has been on several bestseller lists including Barnes & Noble, Amazon, Smashwords, Publisher's Weekly, iBooks and USA Today! She began her writing career writing Twilight Fan Fiction and won multiple awards in the genre, including BEST Author, BEST Robsten, Best All-Human that Knocks You Off Your Feet and several others!

Her interests include reading, as well as writing, theater arts, cooking, roller skating and going for long walks. She is the proud mom to one teenage daughter and two golden retrievers.

She LOVES writing more than most anything else, and you can count on her to deliver strong, relatable characters, deep and detailed plots, and emotion overflow!

Connect

Facebook: https://www.facebook.com/kahlen.aymes.author?fref=ts
Goodreads: https://www.goodreads.com/
search?utf8=✓&query=Kahlen+Aymes
Twitter: @Kahlen_Aymes
Pinterest: https://www.pinterest.com/kahlenaymes/
Booktropolis Social: https://booktropoloussocial.com/index.
php?do=/

Visit Kahlen's website for merchandise, signed books, Julia's recipes, missing scenes, events, Kahlen's Blog, and series playlists: KahlenAymes.com

News/Giveaways & Exclusive Excerpts/Book Discussion:

Sign up: Kahlen's Newsletter: http://eepurl.com/RuW4X
Join: Kahlen's Book Babes on
FB: https://www.facebook.com/groups/252301134873105/

Request an eBook autograph at: http://www.authorgraph.com/authors/
Kahlen_Aymes

Literary representation and rights information: McIntosh & Otis Literary, Inc.
353 Lexington Avenue • New York, NY 10016
Tel: 1-212-687-7400 • Fax: 1-212-687-6894 • Email: info@mcintoshandotis.
com

Other Books By Kahlen Aymes

The Remembrance Trilogy & Prequel

Prequel: Before Ryan Was Mine
1. The Future of Our Past
2. Don't Forget to Remember Me
3. A Love Like This

The After Dark Series

1. Angel After Dark
2. Confessions After Dark
3. Promises After Dark

The FAMOUS Novels
1. FAMOUS
2. More Than FAMOUS
3. Beyond FAMOUS

Coming in 2016-18
One Step Closer
Covered in Raine
Soulmate
Unfinished Business
So Damn Beautiful
Stripped
Rockin' After Dark
Flesh and Blood
(And maybe a Famous Novella and an outtake from The Remembrance
Trilogy)